SHADOWS
of the
STONE
BENDERS

K. PATRICK DONOGHUE

Leaping Leopard En~~terprises, LLC~~

SHADOWS *of the* STONE BENDERS
Copyright © 2016 Kevin Patrick Donoghue
ISBN: 978-0-9973164-0-7 (paperback)
ISBN: 978-09973164-5-2 (hardcover)
eISBN: 978-09973164-1-4

Published by Leaping Leopard Enterprises, LLC
www.leapingleopard.com

First edition: May 2016

Printed in the United States of America

Book interior design by Sekayi Stephens
Cover art and design by Asha Hossain
Photograph of the author by Donna Owens

DEDICATION

To my wife and best friend, Bryson

Sparkle in your eyes,
Open arms and soothing soul;
Your love ever bright.

ACKNOWLEDGEMENTS

As the main character in this novel, Anlon Cully, knows all too well, great feats are best accomplished with excellent teamwork. The process to create *Shadows of the Stone Benders* was no exception. While the story may have originated in my own imagination, it certainly didn't arrive in your hands without the assistance of some special people I would like to acknowledge here.

First, I'd like to thank my wife, Bryson, and my two sons, Michael and Stephen, for their encouragement and support throughout the process to write, edit and publish my first novel. You guys were amazing sources of inspiration, even though it may not have seemed like it while I was sequestered writing!

Second, I'd like to offer my gratitude to the team of people who helped turn my original manuscript into the finished work before your eyes. To Kimberly Day and Cheryl Hollenbeck: thank you for your insightful and meticulous editing skills. Your contributions helped make *Shadows of the Stone Benders* a better story. To Asha Hossain: thank you for investing your creativity to translate the essence of my story into an excellent cover design. To Amber Colleran: thank you for your contributions to the design concepts that influenced the ultimate cover and web site designs. To Sekayi Stephens: thank you for your prowess in designing an easy-to-read interior layout of the book. To James Lee and Kevin Maines: thank you for your elegant and streamlined design of my author website. To Donna Owens: thank you for capturing an author photo that makes me look better than I really do.

CONTENTS

INTO THE SHADOWS

Halting to rest, Devlin Wilson, PhD, leaned back against the cold boulder and drew in several extended gulps of air. He was struggling with the change in altitude, combined with the exertion required to scramble over and between the sharp-edged slabs along the trail.

Wiping perspiration from his brow, Devlin squinted into the bright rays of sunrise beginning to shine over the ridgeline and fished for the water bottle holstered to his belt. He swallowed greedily before dragging the fleecy sleeve of his jacket across his mouth and restoring the bottle.

Focusing attention on the GPS tracking device he now held in his left hand, Devlin peered at the screen to judge how much farther he needed to climb. The flashing red ping of his target destination was roughly a mile ahead and another 600 feet higher in elevation.

Gathering his energy, Devlin stepped forward to resume his ascent, disappearing into the shadow of the mountain's jagged profile. As he trudged on, his anger grew more pronounced.

"Why bring it here?" Devlin fumed.

From the tree line below, a hooded figure mirrored Devlin's climb, careful to avoid the trail as much as possible. Far enough away to remain hidden from Devlin's view but close enough to stay in range, the figure followed the wizened archaeologist with intense focus.

Spying the terrain ahead, the figure searched for an opening in the trees from which to attack Devlin. With cat-like quickness, the dark-clothed shape bounded over rocks to reach the gap between the thick pine trees.

Devlin paused again and placed both hands on his hips, bending forward to assist his breathing. He exclaimed, "I'm getting too old for this nonsense."

He checked the GPS device again in exasperation as he craned his neck up at the near-vertical section of stone he was meant to climb next. Grasping the device in one hand, he used his free hand to steady himself as he mounted the stair-like gap cut between the rocks. Panting heavily, he urged himself upward, "Only 20 feet more until the next plateau. Come on you slacker!"

He was within five feet when he felt the sickeningly familiar tickling sensation rumble in his midsection. Within seconds, the vibration shuddered throughout his entire body, causing nearby smaller rocks to tremble. Devlin's eyes widened as he shot wild disbelieving looks in every direction. But it was too late.

Devlin was lifted 100 feet up in the air, twisting and writhing his arms and legs in panic. He tried to cry out but no words would form in his quivering throat. Suddenly his catapulting rise stopped as he passed briefly into the sunlight. He dangled, suspended in the crisp mountain air for only a second or two, before his body shot down in a violent arc back into the shadows.

Devlin crashed into a pine tree with bone-crushing force, tearing his aorta. He bounced off rocks and tree limbs as his fall continued, snapping his leg bones and shattering his skull. By the time he tumbled onto the sanctity of a pine needle-covered outcrop close to the blazed trail, Devlin was already dead.

The hooded figure watched Devlin's plunge with fascination before thrusting the weapon deep into a backpack and heading back down the path. The plan they discussed had been clear: "Make sure he's dead, but don't get close enough to the body to leave tracks. Make sure it looks like an accident, and above all else, make sure no one sees you."

The dark shape clambered down the ledges of stone and settled in the underbrush 100 yards below where Devlin's crushed and bleeding body lay motionless. Other hikers would be scaling the trail soon, the figure knew, and Devlin's body was close enough to the trail that they would surely see it.

A half hour later, the wait paid off. A single hiker emerged on the trail astride the outcrop and immediately spotted Devlin. Shortly afterward, another two hikers joined him. They briefly looked Devlin over and realized he was dead. One of them pulled out a cell phone and made a call while the other two stood with hands on their heads, stunned by the unexpected discovery.

Removing the hooded jacket and stuffing it also into the backpack, the killer silently resumed a clandestine descent. Mission accomplished.

I
A SIMPLE LIFE

With a faint hiss and then a sudden rush, the fire pit sprang to life. Anlon Cully sat back and absorbed the chill of dusk while awaiting the halo of the fire's warmth to reach him. Glancing at his watch, he closed his eyes and listened for the sound of Pebbles' scooter approaching from the village.

At this time of year, it was easy for Anlon to detect the whining putter of the moped as it wound down the mountainside streets of Incline Village, a sleepy enclave ringing the north shore of Lake Tahoe. The deluge of summer visitors and their attendant clamor would not overtake the otherwise tranquil community for another month or so, and Anlon reveled in the relative peace of this early May evening.

Opening his eyes again, he scanned the horizon beyond the stone patio of his lakefront lodge. Between towering pine trees to his right, he could still see the trailing edge of the sun dipping below the western ridge of the mountains cupping the lake. In front of him, the lake itself was placid with the purple-blue reflection of the mountains waxing as the golden shimmer of sunset waned. And to Anlon's left, a wooden pier extended its lonely reach into the frigid waters, his boat ebbing against its mooring.

Anlon sipped on chilled tequila and sighed in relaxation. His simple life these days was much different than it used to be and that suited him just fine. In the span of 15 years, he'd gone from obscure academic to celebrated inventor to wealthy recluse.

At 42, Anlon was active and in decent shape. He was of average height and build and maintained a summer tan through winter — not from a salon or bottle, but from frequent sojourns to his Los Cabos casita to escape the winter blues. With tiger-like green eyes and short cropped greying, sandy hair, he carried himself with an aura of understated, carefree confidence.

Tonight, he was eager to see Pebbles for their standing Friday starlight cocktails and takeout food. Since their inaugural lakeside happy hour a little less than a year ago, the weekly gathering had become a satisfying ritual for Anlon. And given the stunning call he received earlier from Matthew Dobson, he yearned for tonight's get-together more than usual.

It was Pebbles' turn to bring their meal this evening. She most often chose an assortment of appetizers, chips and dips from the village Mexican restaurant, partially because the restaurant was in the same shopping strip as the bistro where she tended bar on occasion, and partially because Mexican food fit easily in the saddle bags straddling the seat of her aging, pale pink scooter. She was, after all, a very practical young woman.

They were an odd pair when you got right down to it, Anlon considered, but the chemistry of friendship between them worked and that was all he cared about. Yes, they attracted a lot of curious attention when together in public given the gap in their ages and their decidedly different styles, but it was obvious to even the most casual of observers that they shared a warm camaraderie.

Everyone noticed Pebbles first. Partly because she was stunningly attractive but more so because she was extraordinarily eclectic. Tall and lithe with porcelain skin, penetrating ice-blue eyes and aquiline facial features, she could command the focus of any room she strutted through.

But combine that with her black lip ring, a diamond stud adorning her right nostril, shaggy purple hair (at present), dangling silver bracelets and necklaces, black nails, tattoos and a leather buckle-and-zipper dominated wardrobe, the 27-year-old Pebbles McCarver brought new meaning to the phrase "jaw dropping" no matter where she went.

It was a stark contrast to Anlon's simple, laid-back appearance. During the peak of summer, he usually donned shorts, t-shirts and sandals. The rest of the year he was most often arrayed as he was tonight — jeans, sweatshirt and hiking boots. A typical Tahoe wardrobe that blended in with tourists and residents alike.

Just then Anlon's ears picked up the faint whir of Pebbles' scooter and he uttered, "Finally!"

As he sat anxiously awaiting for Pebbles to appear along the slate path leading from the driveway, he still found it hard to imagine she'd ever been anything but the clash of beauty and personality she was today.

She had been born Eleanor Marie McCarver outside Atlanta, Georgia, and raised in the bosom of a prominent Deep South political family.

A family with four older brothers whom she fought, kicked and fiercely competed with in every way imaginable. The same brothers who indelibly branded her with the nickname "Pebbles" at the tender age of 10 — an homage to her failed attempt to body surf on a dare during a family beach vacation that resulted in a vicious tumbling through the Daytona Beach breakers.

The brothers callously howled with laughter when she staggered up out of the chilly surf with a bikini bottom full of sand and pebbles, and a missing bikini top.

Many girls would have trembled with shock and cried in embarrassment, but not Eleanor. Instead, with a scowl of determination, she slicked back the matted jet black hair splattered across her face, fished her bikini top out of the surf and dove back into the water. Wading out beyond the breakers, she glared at her older brothers as they continued to tease her. Beneath the comparative privacy of greyish-blue water, she reattached her top, slung off her bikini bottom temporarily to unload the deposit of sand and pebbles from her bum and then swam to position herself for the next good wave to ride in.

When she chose her wave, she glided across the surface somewhat awkwardly but came all the way into the beach without a repeat tumble. Stepping triumphantly from the ocean, she briefly adjusted her top, placed both hands on her hips and stuck her tongue out at each of her brothers in succession. They applauded uproariously and one of them (the brothers still fought over who should receive the credit for it) shouted out, mocking her failure while praising her toughness, "Way to go, Pebbles!"

The nickname stuck within the family and Eleanor, aka Pebbles, grew to like it, adopting its use informally among her close friends as she passed through high school, college and law school.

As a first-year associate in the Manhattan office of a global law firm though, "Eleanor" had dropped the nickname and been as buttoned down and prim as all the other freshly minted attorneys beginning the partner climb. Her path seemed clear, her future bright…and in a heartbeat it all fell apart.

Anlon had not yet made an effort to coax from Pebbles the story behind her transformation, but he knew for certain something traumatic had happened that caused her to pitch it all, including burying the use of the name Eleanor, and go on walkabout.

Rising now to meet her, Anlon reached to relieve her of one of the two large bags stuffed with their dinner. Pebbles' smile cut through the grey veil of nightfall and she blurted, "Pour me a margarita, A.C. I need a drink bad!"

She was the only one who called him A.C. and he chuckled in response, "Amen to that! But you'll have to settle for straight tequila for the moment. The margarita pitcher is still inside."

Pebbles placed the remaining bag down on the patio next to the fire pit and plunked down onto one of the wide, thick cushioned wood chairs next to Anlon. Propping her black, knee-high-length, buckle-laden boots on the stone ledge encircling the fire pit, she tossed back her head and peered upward through the pine trees at the darkening sky.

"I can work with that," she answered.

Without further prompting, Anlon withdrew the bottle from its chiller and poured Pebbles a shot. She whisked it from his hand and threw back the curious mix of cold liquor that burned hot as she swallowed. "Ah," she sighed, "that will do nicely. Another, please."

"Now, now, young lady, pace yourself," Anlon playfully admonished as he refilled her shot glass. "I'm going to need your full attention while we're eating to tell you about the strange call I received today."

Pebbles smiled at his use of "young lady," demurely winked at him and dramatically placed the full tumbler on the table between their chairs in a gesture of feigned obedience. In silence, they both absently stared at the flames licking the air before them.

Aroused from her reverie by the sound of Anlon unwrapping a burrito, Pebbles softly laughed.

"What?" Anlon asked as he handed her the partially unwrapped burrito and then reached in the bag for another one for himself, "What's so funny? You looked like you were a million miles away."

She blushed ever so lightly and said, "I love when you call me 'young lady' like you just did. It reminded me of the first time we met. I was so crushed when you left without saying goodbye! I don't know why I just thought of it, but it was a fun memory."

"I see," Anlon nodded. "Believe me, I would have loved to talk with you until closing time that night. I was very taken by you, even though we barely got a chance to chat. But you were very busy as I recall and I knew I'd be back again."

"Well, I'm glad you did come back! If you hadn't, what would I do on Friday nights? And where in the world would I be living now?" Pebbles said as she bit heartily into her burrito.

As her friendship, bordering on relationship, with Anlon blossomed, she had discarded her plan to move on at the end of last summer. It wasn't about strings she assured herself, she just enjoyed being around him and wasn't ready to pack up just yet.

"So what about this phone call you mentioned? Sounded kind of spooky."

"Do you remember meeting my Uncle Devlin around Christmas when he visited on his way back from Pakistan?" he asked in reply.

"Yes, of course. He's the archaeologist, right?" she responded, already halfway through her burrito. She ate remarkably fast (when you're the youngest child in the family with four older brothers you learn to eat quickly or not at all).

"That's right. Well, it's sad news. His research partner, Matthew Dobson, called to say Devlin died a few days ago. Apparently he fell off a cliff in New Hampshire. Dobson was so upset during the call he could barely talk," Anlon shared.

Wiping her lips after swallowing the last bite of her first burrito, Pebbles said, "Oh my God, I'm so sorry."

"Me, too. He led such a fascinating life. Every time I was around him it felt like disappearing into an adventure," he mulled, placing his barely touched burrito back on the table.

"Hold that thought," Pebbles replied. "We need the margaritas before you go any further."

Vaulting up, she dashed up the stone stairs to the back door of Anlon's stone and beam home. Less than a minute later she returned down the stairs, her tall boots clip clopping on the slate as she descended, with two glasses and the pitcher in hand. She poured them each a drink, rooted in the takeout bag for another burrito, flopped back down on her chair and announced, "Okay, continue, A.C."

For the next several minutes Anlon recounted various stories about Devlin Wilson, explorer, raconteur, historian and curmudgeon. Pebbles watched Anlon closely as he talked, his eyes transfixed on the leaping flames. There was a tremble in his voice that revealed a deep sense of loss, she thought, knowing the signs herself all too well. When he finished talking, Anlon reached a hand to cover hers and said, "Thank you for letting me go on."

"Don't be silly," she admonished, "A small repayment for your many kindnesses to me. Let's toast to the memory of Devlin Wilson."

"Here, here," Anlon softly echoed, "to Devlin, a great man who made history come to life. I will miss you. Cheers."

Pebbles clinked glasses with him and sipped on the margarita. For several more minutes, she sipped in silence waiting for Anlon to emerge from his thoughts.

"Sorry," he finally said, "lost in memories. Anyway, that wasn't all Dobson said when he called."

"Oh really? There's more?" Pebbles exclaimed as she dove into her second burrito, feeling as if it was now kosher to continue eating.

Watching her chew furiously while awaiting his answer, Anlon offered a muted laugh. Pebbles knew how to lighten a mood, even when she didn't speak. He continued, "Yes, it appears Devlin made me the executor of his will and left me a chunk of his estate. Dobson said I could do most of the estate work by phone and mail through Devlin's attorney, but he practically begged me to fly back east to meet with him this weekend. Tomorrow, in fact."

"What? Why so urgent? I assume you want to go to the funeral for sure, but that wouldn't be so fast, would it?" she questioned.

"No, you're right. The funeral is not until this coming Wednesday. Dobson was insistent that I come tomorrow though. He was very evasive when I asked him why. All he said was that he had something very sensitive to discuss with me regarding Devlin's research. It would appear I've inherited his artifact collection and research papers as part of the estate. But I agree with you, the urgency struck me as odd."

"Are you going?" she inquired while refilling both their margarita glasses. Unconscious bartender habit, she rationalized after pouring the drinks.

Anlon took a long gulp from his glass and responded, "Yes. As soon as I got off the phone with Dobson, I booked the first available flight out tomorrow. It's a connecting flight through Chicago so I won't get into Albany until late and then I have to drive to Stockbridge. I'm set to meet with him at 10:00 tomorrow night at Devlin's house."

"Oh, okay. Do you want me to come with you? I'm sure I can get someone to pick up my shifts the next few days without a problem," a visibly eager Pebbles offered with sincerity.

"No, that's okay," he smiled, "but it's sweet of you to offer. I'm sure I'll be back by next Friday's happy hour at the latest."

II
FIRESIDE TALE

While the fireplace crackled beside him, Anlon waited for Matthew Dobson to speak. The old man sat facing Anlon in the dimly lit room, but did not look at him directly. The earlier part of their conversation had been spent catching up on each other's lives and reminiscing about Devlin Wilson. But now it was time to discuss heavier matters.

The flicker of the flames washed over the walls behind Dobson in swells each time blasts of the howling wind outside forced their way down the chimney. Draining the last of his scotch with satisfaction, Dobson cleared his throat and leaned forward, saying, "It's a hard story to tell because, frankly, it's hard to believe."

Anlon smiled softly and replied, "Please, Dobson, I always knew Uncle Devlin to be eccentric, but I also always knew him to be brilliant, so nothing you say will surprise me."

"Yes, yes, quite true on both counts," Dobson nodded in agreement, his thin, wrinkled hands wringing together before him, slightly shaking.

The two sat on opposing well-worn mahogany leather sofas in the study of Devlin Wilson's house which, along with most of Devlin's other physical possessions, had been willed to Anlon. Rich cherry paneled walls lined with built-in shelves sat on either side of the central stone hearth. Filled with an assortment of reference works and artifacts from Devlin's travels, the shelves offered an accurate snapshot of the man, Anlon thought. The seriousness of thick academic tomes mixed with the beauty of simple ancient objects captured Devlin's personality perfectly. He was a man of intense, unrelenting intellectual curiosity on a quest to discover the secrets of ancient man, both great and small.

"He obviously left me his collection and research papers instead of donating them for a reason, but your call was very cryptic. Curiosity is eating away at me," Anlon responded.

With a smile and a nod Dobson replied, "I think the Professor counted on that!"

Gathering up his glass and pouring another splash of scotch, Dobson continued, "As you know, the Professor was forever curious and refused to accept conventional thinking about anything and everything. It's what made him special and opened his mind to possibilities others were unwilling to consider.

"Yet, to move along, he had to get along, and that meant suppressing some of his instincts and beliefs in order to further his career to the point where he had enough freedom and money to explore questions his peers accepted blindly, questions that just didn't add up to him."

Anlon sat back and stared at the reflection of the roaring fire in the beveled surfaces of Dobson's scotch glass. The way Dobson described Devlin was exactly how he'd remembered him over the years, but Dobson was waxing romantic about Devlin's ability to suppress his views.

He was no stranger to controversy and had a well-known reputation for challenging conventional thinking. His published research was, for the most part, contrarian and hence he was somewhat shunned by colleagues in the fields he studied and worked.

"In any event, the path he embarked on that led you here had a simple beginning in four questions the Professor couldn't satisfactorily answer. He was puzzled how, in the 1400s, maps were published with accurate, detailed topography of the Antarctic continent land mass when the continent had been buried beneath a massive ice cap for at least 10,000 years at that time.

"He was frustrated there was no logical explanation for the sudden rise of the full and rich Egyptian dynastic culture and architecture without an apparent transfer of knowledge and culture from other societies that predated dynastic Egypt.

"He was stumped at how the massive central monument of the ancient Andean Tiahuanaco complex could possibly have been shaped, moved and placed — a feat viewed as nearly impossible to accomplish even today.

"He was staggered at the unearthing of Harappa in what is now Pakistan, a fully developed and planned city by our modern standards, but dated conservatively to be over 5,000 years old with, again, no apparent precursor culture. It was as if someone out of the blue dropped down a full, modern city.

"Conventional wisdom said civilized societies emerged from cavemen-like beginnings between 10,000 and 5,000 B.C.E. Yet these pieces of evidence seemed to contradict that view. How were these technological accomplishments achieved when presumably man walked around with stone flints and spears?

"Many of Devlin's colleagues considered these inconvenient and unexplainable facts as scant evidence to challenge their theories of societal development, let alone overturn them.

"But your uncle was not convinced. And so he began picking at the threads of these baffling facts. For more than 10 years, he hunted and pecked in every major research library, at every major archaeological site he could gain access to and with every renowned expert who would talk with him. He tried to do so quietly and discreetly so as not to attract the ire of his peers, but without much success.

"Upon learning of his investigations, many of his peers shunned him and turned their eyes away from his work and whereabouts. Though he didn't intend it, the blind eye his colleagues cast in his direction actually helped your uncle make the first in a series of major discoveries about three years ago. Those discoveries shed light on the unexplained questions and may very well one day change our understanding of the entire history of man on Earth."

If the look on Dobson's face had not been deadly serious, Anlon would have laughed at this last remark, but instead he challenged, "Come on, Dobson, that's a pretty bold statement. If he made such discoveries, why didn't he triumphantly publish his findings and take a decade-long victory lap? I know my uncle, and if he knew he was right about something, anything, he would crow from the highest spot he could find."

"Wouldn't he though," chuckled Dobson in agreement. Dobson swished around the scotch in his glass and then dashed it down inhaling deeply afterward to absorb the alcohol's hot sting.

Leaning forward and lacing his fingers together over the knees of his threadbare corduroys, he paused for a moment, peering deeply into Anlon's eyes before replying firmly, "He said nothing because he was on the trail of something bigger and he didn't want anyone else to get there before him.

"You see, it's not that his peers are stupid, they are just brainwashed. Presented with irrefutable, powerful evidence, his colleagues would eventually turn their profound intellects to swarm the globe seeking the final pieces to the puzzle your uncle began to unlock before his untimely death. And the Professor recently had reason to believe he was not the only person quietly seeking these answers."

Anlon absently ran his hands through his hair while shaking his head. This doesn't add up, he thought. Standing, he turned to the fireplace and warmed his hands while trying to absorb Dobson's words. Turning again, he said, "So what you're trying to tell me is my Uncle Devlin found evidence that proves that civilized human society predates consensus views? While I can see that would rock the scientific community, it hardly seems worth suppressing for fear others would take partial credit for it."

Dobson sneered, "Oh, it is well beyond such pettiness. No, no, young man. Your uncle was on the trail of a story so amazing and potentially dangerous that if he shared what he found with the world before having all the answers, people with a thirst for power and wealth would swoop in to capture the final pieces of the puzzle and not only have the ability to suppress forever the evidence your uncle found but potentially use the evidence with great harm and effect."

Eyebrows arching, Anlon backed up a step, his legs sensing the heightened intensity of the fireplace behind him as the wind blasted down the chimney again. "Okay, now you're spooking me. What could he have found that was so ominous?"

Dobson didn't say anything at first. He just sat watching Anlon while he contemplated his next words carefully. Rising, he paced across the room to a bookcase adjacent to the stone fireplace. Removing a dozen books and a few trinkets, a hidden safe was revealed.

Pressing his finger against an optical reader, a flash of blue filled the room when the device recognized Dobson's fingerprint, and the hidden door opened. From within, he drew out a black container about the size of a cake box. Pacing back across the room, he placed the box on the table between the two men. Lifting the lid, Dobson gingerly displayed two objects on the table in front of Anlon.

The first was a smooth, oval stone that was tan in color and slightly larger than an average man's hand in circumference. The second was a thin, flat, square stone of a more reddish color about the size of a salad plate, but with decorative markings etched upon it.

Sitting back on the sofa opposing Anlon, Dobson motioned to the two objects and said, "These are the first two objects your uncle discovered. Well, that's not entirely accurate. These objects were discovered initially by other archaeologists many years ago and were in storage at two different internationally renowned museums. But the archaeologists and museum curators had no idea what they had in their possession.

"To them, these two pieces were simply pottery used for dining or for ceremonial purposes and their lineage had been forgotten. It was your uncle who invested the time to rediscover where the objects originated and where in the specific dig sites they were found. Then he examined ancient texts and drawings from the Egyptians, Mayans, Olmecs and others. He came to the conclusion after much consideration that these were not ceremonial pieces or dining surfaces."

Anlon gazed at the oval and square artifacts while listening to Dobson wax on. They appeared incredibly ordinary, of no significance at all. Anlon was not an archaeologist or anthropologist, but if an expert of either branch of study had declared the objects ceremonial pieces or dining surfaces, he would have shrugged and accepted their judgment. He asked, "So what's so special about them? They don't look significant to me."

"I'm going to need another scotch before I answer," Dobson announced as he again reached for the decanter and drew another three-finger shot into the lead crystal glass. Anlon observed the older man with a mixture of curiosity and concern. On one hand, he was anxious to hear more, yet on the other hand, he was unnerved by Dobson's wariness.

"May I touch the stones?" Anlon asked, as Dobson sipped away.

Dobson nodded in assent and mumbled, "Please be careful. They are both priceless beyond measure."

Anlon first picked up the oval stone. It was lighter than he expected. Turning it over, he noticed the stone had been worked into a modestly concave surface, thicker at the edges and progressively thinner towards the center, which had a slight oval bulge. He could understand why someone might consider it a bowl of sorts, even though it was far shallower than a bowl typically would be.

He returned the oval to the table and lifted the square stone by its edges. This one was much heavier than the oval and coarser along its surface. The etchings upon it did not appear to be letters or glyphs. They looked more like a fanciful design. Anlon wasn't sure which side was supposed to be top, bottom, left or right, but the image seemed to make the most sense in the direction Dobson had placed it on the table in front of him.

In the upper right-hand corner of the square stone, there were two closely placed circles. Towards the bottom a horizontal line ran across about midway before arcing up in a sharp curve that ended beneath the two circles. Flipping the stone over, Anlon saw no markings but there did appear to be a smoothed circle in the center.

Anlon placed the square back on the table and cast his eyes back at Dobson. "Okay," he uttered, "What gives? What are these objects?"

Dobson paused again before leaning forward and pointing at each object. "Anlon, my boy, these are two pieces of ancient technology that were almost assuredly created at least 10,000 years before Christ walked upon the Earth."

Dobson let that soak in for a moment before continuing on. "Technology that was lost to us in cataclysmic events that occurred in that same time range.

"These objects give us the beginning of an understanding of how man lived, built, moved and thrived in at least one highly advanced society for thousands of years before any archaeologist would ever admit."

"These two pieces of rock? Come on, how's that possible?" Anlon scoffed while reaching for the scotch bottle sitting next to the two objects on the table. It was time he had a drink.

"It's very possible if you are willing to open your mind and consider what the possibilities might be. Let's take a step back, shall we? What's the constant refrain from scientists who recoil when some colleague or even novice dares to suggest that man thrived on the planet longer than we give credit for? When someone questions whether a high-functioning society existed before dynastic Egypt sprung out of the desert seemingly out of nowhere fully formed?" rebutted Dobson.

Poking his finger in the air as if arguing the point with an invisible debater, Dobson, with voice raised, spat, "I'll tell you what they say. Show us the proof? Where are the buildings? Where is the language? Where is the art? Where are the physical signs of culture?

"The basic supposition being that a high-functioning society could not have possibly existed without these things because that's what we view in our world today as the measures of society — man creating objects and structures, recording thoughts and historical events and other telltale signs of applied intelligence and the conquer of nature."

Anlon wasn't sure whether it was the first swallow of scotch or Dobson's rising indignation, but he was definitely paying attention now. Dobson railed on after taking a deep breath, "And therein lies the problem Anlon. We always look at the world through our own lens. We are too arrogant! Except, God bless, your uncle and heretics like him.

"You ask me what these objects are? I tell you they reveal two fundamental technologies that at least one advanced culture used for millennia before our recorded history begins. Technologies lost to us for the most part that we are only now starting to consider again. Technology that didn't seek to conquer nature as almost all technology we utilize today seems to attempt. No, these technologies took advantage of the simple aspects of nature we tend to overlook to build, communicate, move, record, fight and heal!" Dobson roared, stabbing the air yet again in a volley of triumph.

"Okay, okay, calm down," Anlon said. "What technologies?"

Dobson sank back on the sofa, exhausted from his rant, and in between gasps for air, he said in a barely audible tone, "Sound and magnetism."

Peering back down at the objects, Anlon reconsidered their appearance. Sound and magnetism Dobson had said. Lifting the oval stone again, he could visualize its shape as similar to that of a speaker system woofer. Placing it back down again, he turned his gaze to the square red stone and assumed it must be a magnet of some sort. With these conclusions fresh in his mind, he said, "So, one is a speaker and the other a magnet?"

"No, no, no," Dobson responded, waving his arms as if signaling a missed field goal attempt. "Not a speaker, a projector. Not a magnet, but a storage device.

"You see, the ancient culture that fashioned the projector lying by your hand discovered a way to naturally emit sound waves through stone. With this technology, they could cut and move other objects, communicate over long distances, heal injuries and create power for irrigation. It was so simple yet so profound in its use."

Anlon wrinkled his brow and nose in a gesture of disbelief. "How did Devlin know all of this? I mean how did he figure out it was used for these purposes?"

"Excellent question!" Dobson answered with a proud smile etched upon his face. "They told us all we needed to know on the storage device next to the projector."

"Huh? You're saying that this square piece of rock is like a flash drive? And who is 'they' exactly? And how did Devlin figure out how to access the drive?" Anlon challenged, his arms folded across his chest.

"Yes, yes, all good questions. 'They' refers to the culture that created the technology, or at least used it, to record on the stone. Your uncle called them the Stone Benders," Dobson clarified. "And Devlin's research assistant, Pacal, is the one who stumbled on the clue that helped Devlin figure it out.

"Pacal was in Devlin's office in the barn just up the driveway from here unpacking from an excursion we'd all gone on in Peru. He happened to remove a compass from one of the backpacks and when he put on the counter, it went haywire. Curious, the little fellow picked up the compass and jiggled it. He turned in a circle to see if he could reorient the compass and noticed that when he held it in certain directions, the compass returned to normal. So he concluded there must be something in the shop that was disrupting the magnet in the compass.

"So he walked around the shop holding the compass before him and slowly narrowed down the source of the disruption to the red stone sitting in a tray on Devlin's artifact shelves. Excited, he ran out of the shop and down the hill to the house to tell Devlin of his discovery. I was sitting in this very room when he burst through the door chattering in half Portuguese, half English. He told Devlin his story and Devlin raced up to the shop. He stayed there all night puzzling over it, and then he had one of those 'aha' moments. Simple as that!"

"Simple? I'd say extraordinary!" Anlon exclaimed as he drained his scotch. "If it's not data, then what's on the stone?"

"This will be the hardest to believe, I'm afraid. It is more of a narrated video of a slice of time before the cataclysmic event occurred that wiped it all away, accumulated by one of the survivors of the event," explained the old man.

His words hung in the air as Anlon's head swooned further. Without a word, he shot a sharp glance at Dobson and then the scotch bottle, back at Dobson, and then grabbed the bottle and refilled his glass.

Gulping down half the glass in a single swallow, Anlon fell back on the couch, crossed his arms and closed his eyes. This was too much to take, he thought. Uncle Devlin had always been a little off in his interests, but he was a solid scientist and researcher. If what Dobson said was all true, he began to understand why Devlin wanted to keep it quiet. This was beyond controversial — it was downright heretical, as Dobson had said earlier.

But it was also amazing. The more Anlon contemplated what Dobson told him the more curious and excited he became. Goosebumps ran up the back of his neck considering the implications. Hell, if they hadn't discovered anything else beyond a recording of historical events from 10,000 years ago that showed advanced societies, it would still be the greatest discovery of all time.

"Wow," Anlon finally exhaled unfolding his arms and pushing his hands through his hair. "I don't know what to say."

"Perfectly understandable, young man. It is stunning to say the least. And hold onto your hat, I've only told you a little of what Devlin uncovered. His research went much deeper and his discoveries go far beyond these two simple objects. And as I said at the outset, his work is unfinished. He was on the trail of four new lines of inquiry when he fell from that cliff. Mind you, I don't really think he fell."

"Whoa, say what?" Anlon responded. "You don't think Devlin's fall was an accident?"

With pursed lips Dobson paused and slowly wagged his head back and forth before declaring, "No, sir, I do not."

Jesus, what else was Dobson going to reveal, Anlon thought. The old man's face twisted into a resolute snarl to emphasize his conviction.

"What about Devlin's death makes you think it wasn't an accident? I thought you said he fell off a cliff. Do you think he was pushed?"

Dobson winced and said, "Yes...and no."

"And what's that supposed to mean?"

"It means, my boy, that I think he was lured to the mountain by someone and that someone sent him over the edge to his death," Dobson posited.

"So he *was* pushed?" Anlon countered.

"Not in the traditional sense. There was no trail along the ridge above where his body was found. I know, I went and snooped myself. And there were no defensive injuries on his body to indicate a struggle. At least, that's what the police said when I asked them whether it was possible he might have been pushed," said Dobson.

"So you talked to the police about your suspicions? Did they take them seriously?"

Dobson lowered his head and stared at the floor, "Yes. I had to go identify the body. I didn't want to believe he fell. It seemed inconceivable to me that he would take such a risk to climb to where he supposedly fell from. And why the White Mountains? Devlin had never mentioned them in all our conversations of potential sites to explore. And why did he go off on the excursion in the first place? It was very unusual of him to go to a site without me or Pacal, or both of us!"

Anlon listened to Dobson intently. Though he had been a stalwart friend and colleague to Devlin for over 30 years, he also had been a wise and level headed counselor that had served as a balance to Devlin's crazy notions on numerous occasions. At least, that's how it seemed from the stories they'd shared with him over the years. So Anlon gave Dobson's misgivings the benefit of the doubt. Instead of challenging Dobson, he asked, "Okay, if we accept all of that, what do you think happened?"

Dobson fidgeted nervously and continued to stare down at his weather-beaten boots. To Anlon, he was obviously very conflicted. It didn't seem right to push him any further on the subject.

At last Dobson raised his head and shrugged his shoulders, saying "Ah, I'm probably imagining things. Look, I'm pretty beat and think I've already given you plenty to chew on. Let's call it a night and we can reconvene here again tomorrow and pick it up from there. And besides, Pacal should be here tomorrow, too, and he can help fill in some blanks."

Anlon reluctantly agreed. He was beat, too, and there was no way he could absorb any more without the chance to clear his head and go over their conversation in peace and quiet. He polished off his scotch and said, "Sounds like a plan. I'm really glad you asked to meet with me and share all of this. I know it must have been hard to keep these discoveries a secret."

"Not at all," Dobson replied as they both stood to leave. He stepped over to the fireplace, closed the glass doors and shut off the gas feed with a flick of the remote control resting on the mantle, quickly extinguishing the fire as the wind rattled the glass doors. "Are you planning to stay in the Professor's home while you sort out his affairs? I understand he bequeathed it to you."

"I'm not sure. Honestly, the last 24 hours have been such a whirlwind, I don't know what I'm going to do about any of his estate. I don't feel comfortable yet staying in his house. For the time being, I think I'll just stick with the Two Lanterns Inn in Stockbridge," answered Anlon.

Nodding with understanding, Dobson carefully placed the two objects back in the black box and returned them to the safe. Motioning Anlon over, he said, "Come over here and let's get your fingerprint registered with the safe lock so you can open the safe yourself. These artifacts are too precious to just leave out on the table."

After recording the fingerprints of Anlon's right index and middle fingers two separate times each, Dobson handed him a slip of paper with the security codes for the safe, the office barn alarm and the house alarm. He then provided Anlon with a tutorial on setting and disabling the house and barn security systems.

Outside, shivering in the late night chill, they stepped towards their respective cars and shouted farewells over the competing howls of the cold front moving through. Tired as they were, they didn't notice the black-clad figure hiding at the edge of the woods observing their farewell through swaying leaf-covered branches.

It was the last time Anlon saw Dobson alive.

III

RUDE AWAKENING

The pounding was faint at first, a part of Anlon's dream. It sounded like a drum beat to his scotch-bleared, semi-conscious mind. He found himself amidst a tribunal of sorts with natives banging on drums as he stood before a blazing fire and the watchful eyes of a menacing inquisitor. The pounding rose louder and more urgent and the natives in his dream circled him closer and closer. He began to panic, unsure what to do or where to run. His head writhed back and forth against the pillow as if trying to escape the natives and the dream.

His eyes fluttered open in the brightly lit room and he cringed. Too much scotch, he thought. Only then did he notice that the pounding was real. Someone was at his hotel room door knocking with gusto. A raspy female voice called, "Anlon Cully? Are you in there?"

"Hold on, hold on, I was asleep," he called back, sitting up gingerly in bed, tossing aside the sheets and kneading his throbbing forehead with both hands. Padding over to the hotel door in a t-shirt and boxers, he darted a look at the alarm clock, 7:13 a.m. it read. He continued, "Who is this and what do you want?"

"Detective Lieutenant Jennifer Stevens from the Massachusetts State Police. I need to speak to you about Matthew Dobson," she bellowed through the door.

Anlon took a step back from the door with a quizzical look on his face and said, "Dobson? Can't this wait for a more reasonable hour? It's Sunday after all."

"It's early for us all, Mr. Cully. I'm sorry, but it can't wait I'm afraid," she replied.

On her side of the door, Det. Lt. Stevens was already annoyed. First, her morning run had been interrupted by the unexpected call from her boss, Detective Captain Bruno Gambelli. He'd given her a quick run-down of the details of a suspicious death on the outskirts of Stockbridge and tasked her to find, detain and question a Mr. Anlon Cully immediately.

Stevens had dashed home, taken a lightning quick shower, tossed on clothes and raced to the Two Lanterns Inn, where she'd met up with two uniformed officers from the local Stockbridge Police Department.

Next, Stevens had contended with the calcitrant inn manager, Mrs. Katherine Neally, whom she'd inconveniently rousted from her morning coffee and pastry to acquire Mr. Cully's room number. Mrs. Neally was protective of her guests and expressed distaste over Steven's brusque response when she inquired as to the nature of the room number request.

After Stevens blurted a few threats that drew hidden snickers from the local officers, Mrs. Neally begrudgingly searched the computer room registry and led the police trio up the creaking wood stairs of the historic inn's central staircase to Anlon's door.

With the harried hotel manager standing beside her imploring her to lower her voice, Stevens pounded on the door again. Other guests, disturbed from their sleep, peeked out into the hallway to ascertain the cause of the commotion. Mrs. Neally whispered an apology and reassured them that all was well.

"All right, all right. Hold on a second," Anlon called. He turned and fished the jeans and black sweatshirt he wore the night before from the chair beside his suitcase and tossed them on. Moving towards the door he made a perfunctory effort to arrange his wildly disheveled hair before reaching for the doorknob.

Tapping her foot restlessly against the hardwood floor outside the room, Detective Lt. Stevens' hoarse voice replied, "Please, just open the door, Mr. Cully."

Anlon's cloudy mind had not expected what met his eyes on the other side of the door when he finally cracked it open. Det. Lt. Stevens was not alone. By her side stood two large, intimidating uniformed officers with stern faces and holstered weapons. But Anlon's eyes were transfixed on her.

Intense, blonde and athletic, she appeared nothing like what Anlon expected, given her gravelly tone. Thirty-something, clad in a charcoal grey pant suit that was clearly tailored to accent her curves, she stood with badge extended for Anlon's inspection. Her golden hair was tugged into a tight bun and her forehead glistened with perspiration, as she had yet to fully cool down from her run and quick shower.

He nodded in recognition as he offered a polite smile. She returned the badge to her belt and pressed into the room. As she did, her suit jacket lifted to reveal a cranberry blouse dampened in spots and a holstered Glock.

He started to protest but was cut off by the diminutive and obviously flustered Mrs. Neally, who also nudged into the room behind the two uniformed officers. "Is everything all right, Mr. Cully?"

"I don't know, you tell me!" he exclaimed, throwing his exasperated arms to the heavens.

"Well, I'd appreciate it if the four of you conduct your conversation with discretion so as not to bother the other guests," she scolded as she straightened her jacket and smoothed her frazzled fiery red hair.

"Thank you, Mrs. Neally," interjected Stevens as she waved an impatient goodbye with her hand. "We'll do our best. Now if we could have some privacy, please."

With a harrumph, Mrs. Neally spun on her heels and stomped away. Stevens motioned to one of the uniformed officers to close the room door.

Awaking from the slow motion trance that ensnared him as the surreal scene unfolded, Anlon was reminded of his throbbing head and realized that he likely looked as terrible as he felt. He replied, "Okay, what's this all about?"

"Do you know a Mr. Matthew Dobson?" Stevens inquired, ignoring Anlon's question. She stood now with notepad in hand peering at Anlon's face. Though she was putting on the "one tough bitch" routine to unsettle Anlon, it came across with extra relish given her irritation dealing with the snooty Mrs. Neally.

"Yes, of course I know Dobson. He's a long-time family friend. Is he in some kind of trouble?" Anlon asked, wondering if Dobson had maybe had one too many scotches last night and been pulled over for driving under the influence.

"Mr. Dobson was found dead this morning," she shot back, "and from evidence recovered at the scene, you seem to be the last person to see him alive."

She studied his face for a reaction. His eyes widened, a puzzled look emerged across his face and he staggered backwards a step. He shook his head in denial. "What? Dobson is dead? I don't believe it. How?"

Anlon's mind was swimming. He barely was awake, still trying to absorb last night's revelations from Dobson, and now through a hangover, he was confronted by the news Dobson was dead. He needed some time to gather his senses, and all of a sudden he felt oddly self-conscious about his rumpled appearance with the trio hulking around him.

Stevens replied, "I'm not at liberty to say at the moment. May we conduct a quick search of your room?"

"Um, okay," he said as she brushed past him, nudging his shoulder. Her delicate floral perfume wafted over him in sharp contrast to her hardened manner as she motioned to the two uniformed officers.

"Can we hold up a minute, Detective? I have no idea what's going on here. Why do you need to search my room? What happened to Dobson and why are you here?"

Stevens didn't bother looking over her shoulder while she continued to paw through his belongings and replied, "It's Detective Lieutenant. And I guess you'll find out soon enough. He was found by a neighbor out walking her dog this morning. He was dead, sitting in his car in his driveway. And next to him on the seat was his iPad with your name and hotel information listed in his calendar, alongside an appointment with you for last night at 10:00 p.m."

Soaking in that information, Anlon began to connect the dots and incredulously inquired, "And so you think what? That I killed him? And you're here searching for evidence? How stupid would I be to kill a man, leave evidence of my meeting with him and then return back to my hotel and go to sleep?"

"Murderers do stupid things all the time, Mr. Cully. Not of course implying you are either stupid or a murderer. But we have to chase leads as fast as we find them when there is a suspicious death. And the circumstances of Mr. Dobson's death are definitely suspicious. Find anything?" she asked the two officers.

"No, nothing so far. His car keys are on the table over there. We should give it a look. Where is it parked, sir?" asked one of the officers.

"Look," Anlon countered, "this is crazy, but you can search the car all you want. It's a rental car, small blue Chevy SUV. I don't know what kind of Chevy it is. There's nothing in it but the rental car ticket, but you are welcome to look. But can we just slow down a minute. Christ, I haven't fully woken up yet."

He flopped down on the edge of the bed and threw his hands up in the air again. Stevens strutted to where he sat and peered down at him with arms crossed. "I know it's a shock, Mr. Cully and I know it's an intrusion, but it's necessary. While they go check the car, let's talk."

Stevens stood back and leaned against the bureau opposing the bed. Looking over Anlon from head to toe, it seemed to her he had been genuinely caught off guard. He smelled of alcohol and his short, wavy grey/blonde hair lay in a modern art-like pattern pushed to one side of his head, presumably by the pillow he'd laid against. His black sweatshirt was wrinkled, his face was stubbled and he wore no socks or shoes. Cautious to keep an open mind while at the same time rabidly intent on following the lead the Captain assigned her, Stevens softened her tone and bearing ever so slightly.

"Actually, why don't you take 10 minutes to get yourself together and when you are ready, we'll go down to the lobby for coffee and a talk," she offered while uncrossing her arms and reclining in the armchair by the bureau.

Anlon gave a mock gesture of hallelujah to the ceiling and disappeared into the bathroom, grabbing fresh clothes from his suitcase on the way. He showered and shaved quickly, brushed his teeth and hair and donned fresh jeans and a slightly wrinkled, untucked white button-down shirt. All the while his mind raced.

Dobson dead? Anlon had thought Dobson was a little on the spooky side when he suggested that Devlin had died of unnatural causes. And the fingerprint scan for the safe in the library and the alarm system tutorial seemed a little over-protective to Anlon when Dobson first suggested the security measures. But now?

He recalled Dobson's comments the previous night about people with a thirst for power and wealth. At the time, Anlon was sure it was just hyperbole spoken by someone charged with keeping a valuable secret. Now he wasn't so sure.

Anlon emerged from the bathroom feeling somewhat more human to find Stevens wedged against the side of the sofa in the room frantically tapping on her cell phone with legs crossed, one bobbing atop the other. Maintaining a staccato of fingers and thumbs upon her phone, she darted a look up at Anlon and blurted, "Good news. The SUV came up clean on first inspection."

"No surprise to me," he responded with an I-told-you-so quality to his tone.

Together they walked in silence back to the central staircase of the inn and descended to the cozy lobby, the aroma of burning wood and simmering apple cider filling the room. Whisking into the small lounge area near the front desk under the watchful, suspicious eyes of Mrs. Neally, Stevens chose a table away from the other early Sunday risers munching away on the breakfast buffet. Their first swigs of coffee seemed to relax them both.

Stevens sat back in her chair and resumed her "one tough bitch" mode, though her voice was less coarse now that hot coffee had coated her throat. "As I was saying, the circumstances of Mr. Dobson's death are dubious and when that happens, it's imperative to follow leads quickly."

Anlon, feeling a bit more human from the combination of coffee, shower, fresh clothes and change in venue, said, "Look, I'm not trying to be uncooperative, it's just hard to grasp the news and make sense of it."

"That's why we want to talk with you, especially because it seems you were the last person to see him alive. Did you meet with him as planned last night?" Stevens asked as she sipped her steaming coffee, the imprint of her lip gloss coating the rim of the cup.

"Yes, we did meet at my Uncle Devlin's house," he answered, watching her scribble in the small note pad she retrieved again from her inside jacket pocket.

"Did you meet with Mr. Dobson alone or was your uncle there as well?" she followed up quickly.

"Alone. My uncle passed away at the beginning of the week," Anlon replied.

"Oh, I see. What was your uncle's full name and address?" she inquired without raising her eyes from the pad she wrote upon.

Nice display of sympathy, Anlon drolly thought. He sincerely hoped she wasn't the Massachusetts State Police's ambassador for extending condolences to grieving family members. While providing his uncle's information, he massaged his temples and closed his eyes. This was too much. First Devlin and now Dobson. In the span of a few days. What in heaven's name was going on?

"Your driver's license shows your home address is in Nevada, Incline Village, right?" Stevens asked, consulting an earlier page in the notebook.

"Yes, it's on Lake Tahoe," Anlon replied.

"Forty-two years old, no prior arrests, but a few speeding tickets on your driving record. Graduate of the University of California at Berkeley, PhD from USC in biomechanics. You sound pretty respectable, Mister, excuse me, I should say *Doctor* Cully," the detective finished, relishing the effect her recitation seemed to have on him. She'd assembled Anlon's brief bio from a combination of a national law enforcement database and a quick Internet search while he was taking a shower.

"I see you've been busy. What else have you found out about me?" Anlon asked, feeling a little uneasy of the speed at which she'd been able to Google him.

She ignored his jibe and continued on. "Why did you meet Mr. Dobson?"

"Dobson worked for my Uncle Devlin for many years. After my uncle died, Dobson called to break the news and requested that I come for a visit. Question for you — what makes you think Dobson's death is suspicious?"

"I'm not at liberty to discuss details of the investigation but let's just say some of the evidence at the scene didn't add up. What did you talk about with Mr. Dobson?" the detective asked, casually brushing aside Anlon's question.

Stevens didn't describe the crime scene to him mostly because she hadn't been there yet. According to Det. Capt. Gambelli who *was* at the scene, a man was found in his driveway in a locked car by a passing neighbor, a Mrs. Doris Minden, walking her dog. He might have been asleep to the average passerby, but the neighbor thought it looked out of character for Dobson.

She walked her Labrador every morning through the same Stockbridge neighborhood and not once had she seen Matthew Dobson's car parked in the spot it now occupied in his driveway in the seven years she'd lived there. The well-maintained black Mercedes E Class was always parked underneath the cover of his carport.

But this morning it sat halfway up his driveway, the dawn dew coating the windows. As she approached the car, she noticed him sitting inside, hunched over the steering wheel. Knocking on the window, she received no response. No movement. She tried to open the car door, but it was locked. Concerned, she knocked more forcefully on the window and called out his name, but there still was no response. Finally, she pulled out her cell phone and reluctantly called 911.

When the fire truck and ambulance arrived, they carefully jimmied open the front passenger door and the EMT felt for a pulse. Her fingers had barely touched his flesh when she knew he was dead. Cold as ice, she realized immediately even through the latex gloves she'd donned. Then the police arrived, followed shortly by the coroner.

By then, other neighbors had gathered beyond the yellow police tape. Tongues wagging, the frightened but curious neighbors gawked as the police questioned Mrs. Minden about her discovery.

Shortly afterward, Gambelli arrived at the scene and immediately conferred with the coroner. No apparent wounds but the body showed signs of carbon monoxide poisoning, which was strange to the coroner because the tailpipe was not blocked in any way.

Further, he'd said, his crime scene technicians had inspected the undercarriage of the car and the exhaust system appeared intact. So there was a dilemma. How did Mr. Dobson die from carbon monoxide poisoning given the visible facts?

To Gambelli, stalking the car from every angle, there were only two possible solutions to this dilemma. Either Dobson died somewhere else and someone placed him in the car afterward, or someone stopped up the tailpipe of his car long enough to kill him before removing whatever plugged the exhaust system. Regardless, it looked more like murder than suicide.

After the iPad found on the front seat next to Dobson had been searched by the crime scene technicians and the appointment with Anlon discovered, Gambelli called Stevens and sent her to find Cully.

Leaning forward, Anlon played with the residue floating at the bottom of his coffee cup as he answered Stevens' last question. "Uh, I don't think you'd believe me if I told you. Let's just say he filled in some blanks about my uncle's research. He was an archaeologist and Dobson was familiar with his work."

Stevens was not about to let Anlon off the hook. "Let's try that again. What did you and Mr. Dobson discuss?"

Though the caffeine had eased Anlon's demeanor, Stevens' snooping into his bona fides and her persistent questioning rankled him. He answered meekly, "Okay, okay. We discussed some controversial research my uncle was conducting when he died. Dull and esoteric I assure you. I think my uncle was hoping I'd pick up the ball where he left off and Dobson was supposed to convince me."

He cringed inside at the little lie he just uttered. While the subject matter had been esoteric, it was far from dull, and the more he thought about it alongside Dobson's mysterious death, the more intriguing it became. She hadn't bought the lie though, her nose wrinkling with a corresponding look of disbelief. But for the moment, she let it go.

"Did you both leave at the same time, and what time did you leave?" she queried.

Thinking back, Anlon wasn't sure when they parted outside Devlin's house. He knew it was late, but didn't recall the precise time. He replied, "Hmmm, I don't remember the time but it must have been after midnight. We both said goodnight outside my uncle's house, got in our cars and left. The wind was pretty wild last night and we both wanted to get out of the cold."

Tapping the table with her pen, she asked, "And you drove straight here? Anyone see you enter the hotel? Valet parking attendant perhaps?"

"Yes, I drove straight here. And the inn doesn't have valet parking, at least not at the time I arrived," Anlon answered with a sarcastic smile.

She recounted, "So you drove to your uncle's house to meet with Mr. Dobson at 10:00 p.m. You met for two to three hours discussing esoteric and dull research. You left together sometime after midnight, and you drove straight back to the hotel?"

"Yes, that's right," he nodded.

"Did Mr. Dobson seem nervous or uptight when you met with him? Did he say anything that struck you as unusual or out of place?" Stevens probed.

Hell yes, he seemed uptight, Anlon thought. And the whole conversation had been odd and out of place but he didn't want to go there — not now and not with her. At the time, Anlon discounted Dobson's tense appearance as being afraid to share Devlin's controversial finds. The more Stevens dug, however, the more Anlon realized he'd misread Dobson. There was fear in his eyes and in his trembling hands while he talked about the two stones. Perhaps he was genuinely afraid of something or someone. He seemed pretty convinced Devlin's death was not an accident.

Anlon's own eyes must have given him away as Stevens leaned forward waiting for his answer with pen poised. Damn, he said to himself, she doesn't miss much. Anlon acknowledged, "He did seem tense, now that you mention it."

"Did he seem depressed in any way?"

He gazed nonchalantly out the hotel's glazed glass windows at the town's quiet main street and exhaled a sigh of internal relief. Whew, she didn't press the matter. "No, definitely not," he replied.

"So your uncle dies and Mr. Dobson calls you and asks you to fly across the country to meet with him. You arrange a meeting with him, in which he seems nervous or tense, but not depressed. Sometime around midnight you both leave your uncle's home. You go back to your hotel and Mr. Dobson presumably goes home, only he doesn't quite make it there, at least not alive," the detective summarized, again tapping her pen on the edge of the pine table.

Stevens was convinced Anlon wasn't being totally upfront, but didn't think any further thrust and parry at this moment would be productive...for now.

Anlon remained quiet, sensing she spoke the summary aloud to cement what she'd heard so far. He lowered his head and thought of Dobson. A good guy, a loyal man. His uncle had trusted him with his most precious possessions and secrets and Dobson had guarded both as if they were his own.

It was then that Anlon suddenly recalled that Dobson had never shared with him how the two stones worked. He also remembered now that Dobson had said these were only the first two discoveries Devlin had made and that he'd been on the trail of four new discoveries when he fell from the White Mountains cliff in New Hampshire.

A sickening feeling came over Anlon as he realized that, with Dobson's death, Devlin's secrets might now remain hidden forever. And if he was right about Devlin's death not being an accident, Dobson's own suspicious death meant that Anlon unwittingly was caught in the middle of one, possibly two, murder investigations.

IV
REACHING OUT

After Det. Lt. Stevens concluded her questioning, Anlon had been fingerprinted, provided hair samples and been swabbed for DNA. Released on his own recognizance with a warning not to leave town for at least the next few days, he went back to his hotel room and crashed for another two hours of fitful sleep, feeling violated on multiple levels.

When he awoke, he laid on the hotel bed and tried again to make sense of it all. The stones, Devlin's death, Dobson's death and the ominously vague unfinished research. The longer he grappled with unanswered questions in his mind, the more determined he became to find the solutions. Yet, at the same time, he was certain he would not be able to unearth all the answers on his own. The range of possibilities was too vast for Anlon to comprehend alone. And so, as he'd done throughout his career, he realized he would need help to solve the labyrinth of riddles before him.

His initial text to Pebbles read, "Holy crap! You can't believe what I walked into. Need your help! When can you talk???"

Pebbles reply followed a few hours later. She would claim the time zone difference was a factor, but in fact she had slept until noon. Her reply, "K, on it. Will call u in 1 hr."

When Anlon read her text, his tensed muscles relaxed. It was hard to explain, but Pebbles' edgy can-do attitude always made him feel like he had an angel on his shoulder. It didn't matter if it was something as mundane as her hustling to draw his IPA on a crowded night at Sydney's, Anlon sensed her protective spirit coming to his rescue. Not that he needed rescue, he assured himself. Still, it was a comfort to know he was not alone.

By the time Anlon returned to Devlin's house for the phone call with Pebbles, it was approaching sunset. Motoring up the driveway, Anlon took in his first real look at the home in the fading daylight.

Custom built by Devlin, the outer shell looked like a classic farmhouse; white wood siding, black shutters and a crimson painted front door. The main level of the five-bedroom, four-bathroom house sat one story up from the ground level garage and basement. A wide-covered porch wrapped around the entire main level and was adorned by a variety of comfy outdoor furniture nestled in its four corners. Extra-wide staircases extended from the front door and back porch along separate, dedicated walkways abutting the macadam driveway. Inside, Devlin had spared no expense in the home's fittings and furnishings. Each room reflected the elegant and exotic tastes of the renaissance man.

Anlon was swaying in an oversized rocking chair on the porch when Pebbles' call came through. Before they even exchanged pleasantries, she dove in, "What's happened? Are you okay?"

"Yes, yes," Anlon shrugged, "I'm fine."

Pausing to consider his answer, Anlon dropped the faux bravado and revised his statement, "Well...I'm fine in the sense that I'm alive and uninjured. But some crazy things have happened and I need your help. Short summary...I met Dobson, he told me a nearly unbelievable story, a story I'm having trouble grasping, a story he left unfinished before we parted. We said goodnight and somewhere between then and now he was murdered! And the police suspect me!"

On the other end of the phone, Pebbles sat on a battered, rickety Ikea sofa in the spartan confines of her studio apartment clad in daisy dukes, a lime green tank top and flip flops. On the equally unstable used coffee table before her rested evidence of the previous night's meal…a pizza box and empty beer bottles. As Anlon talked, Pebbles quietly nibbled on a rare leftover pizza slice while she cleared and wiped down the table. Bartender habit again.

"Whoa," said Pebbles, "slow down, A.C. Of course I'm happy to help, you know that. But let's go back to the beginning and go step by step."

Anlon smiled and welcomed Pebbles' methodical and rational approach. Taking a deep breath, he ran through his tale from the start. He told her about the stones and Devlin's research. He conveyed Dobson's skepticism about Devlin's death. He shared the little he knew from his conversation with Det. Lt. Stevens about Dobson's death. The more he talked, the more questions Pebbles asked. The more she asked, the more intrigued she grew. Twenty minutes into the conversation she announced, "I'll try to get a flight out tonight. If not, I'll be there by this time tomorrow at the latest."

"That's great! Look at flights and when you find one that's good, email me the itinerary you want and I'll book your flights. Don't worry about how much it costs, just look for flights to get here as soon as possible. Oh, and can you do me a favor and stop by my house and pack some extra clothes for me? I think I'm going to be here more than a few days," Anlon requested.

"Okay, will do!" she replied forcefully, feeling energized. Finally, here was a chance to repay Anlon for his unconditional generosity and friendship.

Pebbles and Anlon had first met the prior June during her first week on the job at Sydney's, the bistro in the village where she still filled in as bartender now and then. She'd rolled into Tahoe seeking a summer job that would provide her freedom to hike, water ski, rock climb and mountain bike during the day. A job that would allow her to be somewhat anonymous if she chose, but also one where she could meet people and make new friends when the mood suited her, knowing full well she intended to move on at summer's end with no strings attached, romantic or otherwise.

Though the bistro's namesake owner, Sydney Armstrong, had been reluctant to hire Pebbles given she possessed little experience tending bar, she'd used her considerable feistiness to overcome his objections. She'd told him she would come in early, stay late. She'd work the crappy shifts no one else wanted. She'd bus tables when the bar was slow. Still Sydney had wavered, that is until Pebbles offered to work for tips only. He gave her a week to prove herself. Nowadays he begged her to take extra shifts and paid her more than anyone else that worked for him.

Anlon had come in for a late afternoon drink after spending the day out on his boat. It was a quiet time in the bistro, wedged between the lunch and dinner rush. Pebbles was washing out glasses when she heard the sound of a stool scraping against the bar's slate floor behind her.

"Be with you in a sec," she called over her shoulder as she placed cleaned pint glasses in the bar's cooler.

Anlon, appraising her shapely, miniskirt-covered backside as she leaned over the cooler, called back, "No rush, I'm not in a hurry."

It wasn't until she fully stood that Anlon realized how tall Pebbles was and that her shoulder-length raven hair was streaked with pink highlights. When she spun on the heels of her black sneakers to greet him, he was caught off guard by her edgy yet captivating looks and unintentionally flinched.

Pebbles wore a tight white crop top to go with the equally snug black miniskirt. Together they worked to accentuate her body's curves, long legs and toned abdomen. On her forearms, she wore silver bangles that partially obscured tattoos on the underside of each wrist. Another tattoo on her neck was somewhat hidden by the aforementioned black and pink hair. Nose ring, eyebrow rings, tongue stud and the hint of an another tattoo on her shoulder peeking out from beneath the crop top completed the ensemble.

Her lips widened into a thin smirk and she asked for his drink order. Though Pebbles had only been on the job for a few days at that point, she was quickly getting used to the reactions caused by her offbeat appearance compared to the typical beach-blonde California girls that worked up on the lake during the summer. Some reactions were funny, others rude, but most were just plain shock.

Anlon's reaction was different, she thought. Yes, there had been the extra eye blink that signaled mild surprise, but there had also followed a subtle raise of one eyebrow and a slight purse of his lips that came across to her like admiration more than derision.

She walked away to draw his ale request while trying to size him up further. It was one of the things she already liked about being a bartender — the chance to use her wits to create a caricature of the people she served. It made the job more fun and interesting and helped her engross customers in conversation that, in turn, led them to stay longer, eat and drink more and tip with greater generosity.

She took note of his somewhat disheveled appearance. His powder blue golf shirt was untucked and a bit rumpled. His clean shaven face and arms glistened with perspiration and she detected the unmistakable scent of sunblock. His sandy grey hair was damp and had the look of someone who had used his hands to absently guide it into place on his way into the bar. Yet, he was attractive and he emitted the vibe of someone relaxed and untroubled.

"Thank you," Anlon said when she brought him a pint of his favorite San Diego brewery IPA. "You're new here, aren't you? My name is Anlon, by the way."

What an unusual name, she thought. Wait until he hears my name! She took note that he was seated alone, away from the few other customers surrounding the horseshoe bar, and he wore no wedding ring. She also noticed that, unlike most other bar patrons who came in alone, he wasn't already glued to his cell phone.

Nodding, she extended her hand, bangles jangling, and replied, "Yes, I just started this week. Pebbles is my name. Nice to meet you, Anlon."

With these clues in mind, she started to develop a picture. She figured he was a regular given that he had noticed she was new. This meant he came here often, which in turn meant he must have a place in Tahoe or visited the area frequently. She reckoned he must have just finished golfing at the nearby mountain resort course. Golfers often stopped in Sydney's after their round.

"Pebbles?" a curious Anlon queried while returning her handshake, "a pleasure to meet you as well."

He spoke with the formality of someone well educated. Given his age and country club casual attire, she surmised that he must be on vacation or at least had taken the day off from work. This conclusion, Pebbles thought, was further supported by the fact that it was four in the afternoon on a Thursday and he was in a bar instead of working. He was too young to be retired and too old to be a student. Probably just took advantage of the nice day to sneak in an early summer round of golf, she thought.

"Yep, Pebbles," she answered as she watched his bewildered expression with a thin smile. Most people went straight to quips like "Is that your real name?" or "Where's Bam Bam?" or other inane comments. But Anlon didn't take the bait. He nodded his head with unquestioned acceptance, raised his glass in a salute of sorts and took a deep sip of the IPA.

Pebbles became distracted by the entrance of a loud quartet of 20-something beach-goers who'd stumbled into the bar already half-lit after a day of jet skiing on the lake. She excused herself to tend to the new guests. However, she found herself every so often peering over at Anlon, still crafting a picture of the man.

He had now been there half an hour and just ordered a second IPA. She hadn't noticed him check his watch or pull out a cell phone to text or email, so it seemed to her he wasn't waiting on anyone. For the most part, he idly watched a Giants baseball game on the TV hanging above the bar. He kind of came across as someone who was bored and killing time. Traveling businessman maybe?

Every now and then she caught him gazing at her. But it wasn't a leer; the drunk beach-goers were doing plenty of that every time she leaned forward or bent over. His gaze was more a look of thoughtful study. His striking green eyes followed her movements not her body parts, she noticed. She speculated he was attempting to size her up as well. Suddenly self-conscious, she smoothed down some loose strands of hair.

What a beautifully disruptive young lady, Anlon thought, observing her glide around behind the bar. The way she dressed, her piercings and tattoos and even her name all reinforced to him the image of someone who liked to shake things up.

And while her alluring appearance and unusual attire demanded attention, it didn't feel to him as if Pebbles was the sort of woman who sought attention for attention's sake. If she was that shallow, he would have expected her to be loud, more openly flirtatious and overly demonstrative. But as he observed her filling orders and bantering with customers, her manner was warm, reserved and cleverly engaging. There was a genuine quality about her and so he perceived her disruptive appearance as more a statement of independence rather than a cry for attention.

Anlon assumed she was one of the bistro's seasonal fill-ins given that the previous week Sydney had chatted with him in the bar and mentioned with a wink that his expanded staff would be starting soon.

Sydney, knowing Anlon was a confirmed bachelor, was forever trying to match him up with women when he dined or had a drink at the bistro. However, given the steady parade of classic California blondes Sydney had introduced over the years, Anlon doubted seriously if Sydney had Pebbles in mind when mentioning his incoming summer crew.

When Pebbles delivered his refill, curiosity got the better of her and she abandoned her silent study of Anlon. Now she wanted data to analyze. "Waiting on someone?"

Anlon nodded thanks for the beer and said, "No, just taking the edge off the day before I head home."

Ah, Pebbles recorded mentally, so he's not a vacationer or traveling businessman. He lives in Tahoe.

"Long day at work?" she followed up, looking away to wipe down the bar counter on each side of Anlon so as to avoid seeming overly interested in his answer.

"No, no work today. I was out boating on the lake this afternoon. It was hotter than I expected and I developed a thirst for an ice cold beer or two."

Okay, she catalogued, strike that...he wasn't golfing. So far she wasn't doing very well measuring Anlon. She pondered further. He must be a banker, tech executive or an attorney. Most of the people who she'd met so far that lived on the lake were from Silicon Valley or San Francisco and resided on the Nevada side of Lake Tahoe to escape high California taxes. Invariably they were technology titans, investment bankers or lawyers.

"Ah. It must have been beautiful out there. I went hiking around Mt. Rose this morning and the lake was so blue from the summit. Do you go out on the lake often?" she queried in response.

Cleverly engaging as he'd imagined, Anlon smiled to himself. He could tell she was curious about him but rather than interrogate him outright, Pebbles was making an effort to connect with him while she elicited the information she sought. Okay, he thought, I'll play along and see where this goes.

"Some weeks I go out almost every day, but most weeks I've got other things going on. How about you? Do you like getting out on the water?"

Pebbles shook her head and said, "Haven't had the chance. I've only been up here about two weeks. I'm not a local, just working here for the summer. But I will before I leave in August, I'm sure."

So he has a lot of free time but in spurts. Ruminating on this new information, she mused...maybe he's an airline pilot. She could imagine him all dressed up in a uniform looking very distinguished.

"Where do you hail from?" Anlon asked, pleased he'd pegged her status as a summer worker. He was careful not to offer her an outing on his boat, at least not yet. Anlon was cautious when it came to women. Most he met nowadays were more interested in his money than in him. It was one of the downsides of sudden notoriety and instant wealth that he'd learned the hard way. And it was one of the reasons he now led a fairly solitary lifestyle.

"I've been kind of a vagabond for the last year, but I'm originally from the South," Pebbles answered. "Have you lived up here long?"

Anlon replied, "About three years. I'm originally from the East coast but I lived most of my life in Cali."

As they talked, the early dinner crowd started filing in and there was a sudden surge in new bar customers. Pebbles noticed Sydney giving her the evil eye and said, "Oops, better get busy or I'll be in trouble. Are you hungry? Need a dinner menu before I scoot?"

"No, thank you," he politely replied. "I'll order in pizza when I get home. I can't risk missing *The Hunted* tonight."

The Hunted was a wildly popular suspense serial with breathtaking, unexpected twists. It was nearing the end of its third season and the promotions for the final two episodes of the current season hinted at major plot reveals and a turn of events that devoted fans were warned not to miss.

It just so happened that Pebbles was a rabid fan of the show, too, and she thrust her palm towards him in an urgent "stop" motion as she walked away. "Don't say anything. I'm an episode behind."

Anlon laughed and raised his hands in surrender, "I promise, I promise. I won't spoil anything. Go take care of your customers, young lady."

Later, when she finally managed a free moment again, she turned to where Anlon had been positioned and saw that he was gone. At first, she was miffed because she overlooked the $50 bill he left underneath his empty glass in payment of his unpresented $12 tab. Then she found herself inexplicably disappointed that their conversation had been truncated. And Pebbles was intrigued to boot. Despite leaving her a sizeable tip, Anlon hadn't said or waved goodbye. "Who is this guy?" she wondered aloud.

It hadn't taken long for them to bond after that first afternoon exchange at Sydney's. A week later, Anlon invited her out on his boat. Unsure of his intentions, she hesitated another full week before accepting his offer, even though Sydney cajoled her constantly in between to leap at the opportunity.

"If you don't take him up on his offer, you're nuts! Do you know how many women I've tried to get him to take out on his boat or have dinner with him? He meets you once and you get invited? You have no idea who he is, do you?" an apoplectic Sydney rambled when she first told him of Anlon's invitation.

"No, why should I? And why should that matter? Don't get me wrong, he was nice and I liked talking to him, but I don't want to give him the wrong idea." she responded while reloading beer bottles in the refrigerator beneath the bar.

"Anlon, or should I say Doctor Anlon Cully, is a brilliant scientist — or was. He tells me all the time he is 'mostly retired' now. Anyway, he was a scientist on a team that patented a way to get better fuel mileage out of our cars while at the same time drastically cutting emissions. That patent made him crazy rich. He's as eligible as they come missy... even if he is a bit older than you," Sydney explained.

"Hey, look, I'm just here for the summer. I'm not looking for a hookup. And I'm definitely not looking for a soulmate. If that's why he invited me, I don't want any part of it. And just because he's rich doesn't mean I should fall at his feet. God, Sydney, are all the girls up here so shallow?" Pebbles ranted, now standing with clenched fists pressed against her hips.

Sydney shook his head in disbelief and started to walk away from the obstinate barmaid. He turned briefly and wagged a finger in her direction, "I saw you watching him the other night and it wasn't casual indifference I saw in either of your eyes. I damn near had to pry you two apart to avoid a revolt from other thirsty customers. And if you think Anlon's interested in shallow girls, you don't know what you're talking about."

Though she adopted a stubborn attitude on the subject for a few days, the combined effect of two more relaxed and playful bar conversations with Anlon and Sydney's unrelenting badgering finally led Pebbles to lower her guard.

That day on the boat had been close to magical. The weather had been surreally beautiful, their conversation light and wandering, his manners thoughtful and respectful. In fact, he never made a single, romantic overture verbally or otherwise. By the time the sun had set and they were strolling down the dock back to his house, she felt a little disappointed he hadn't made a move on her.

Even as he stood in his driveway holding her helmet while she boarded her scooter to leave, he had simply said in parting, "Today was so much fun, Pebbles. Thank you for hanging out. Maybe we can do it again before summer's over."

No kiss, no hug, no handshake, not even a fist bump. Given her earlier skepticism about even going on the pseudo-date, it surprised Pebbles she was somewhat crestfallen by his polite, gentlemanly farewell. She replied, "It was an amazing day, Anlon, thank you. I'd love to see you again."

As the words came out of her mouth, she blushed. She hadn't meant it that way, but she was too flustered to correct herself. She started the scooter and fled down Lakeshore Boulevard. She was halfway to her apartment when it dawned on her that she never retrieved the helmet from him before driving off. Ugh, she thought, how embarrassing.

It was a representative example of the unconventional relationship that developed between them over the summer. While romantic tension hovered unexplored at the periphery, their relationship remained one of friendship. Neither of them totally opened up to the other but they took enjoyment from being around each other nonetheless. And even though they only saw each other once or twice a week, as summer neared an end, both grew melancholy about her impending departure.

It was Anlon who first broached the subject aloud as they sat around his fire pit drinking Cabernet one mid-August Friday happy hour. "So you're moving on at the end of the month?"

The buzz from the red wine swirling through her brain brought an honesty to the surface she'd not displayed to Anlon previously, "I don't know, A.C. I'm not so sure I want to go just yet."

His eyebrows rose in surprise while staring down at the reflection of the flames dancing along the bowl of his wine glass. He uttered with equal candidness, "Oh? In that case, I wish you'd stay a little longer. This summer has been the most fun I've had in a long time, and it's because of you."

As his sincere words filled her ears, she felt a warm sensation flow through her body, spurred on by the wine and fire pit's glow. She turned and smiled at him, "I want to stay, because of you...but, I want to go, because of you, too. It's hard to explain."

Anlon nodded his head, believing he had an inkling about her inner conflict. He knew she was fiercely independent, kept her distance and never had intended to stay beyond summer, but he also sensed she didn't want to let go of their friendship.

Secretly, however, he was thrilled with the news she was considering staying because he didn't want to let go either. Anlon had not been very open about his feelings towards her, mostly because he wasn't sure he wanted to step beyond friendship. He liked his uncomplicated life and worried a full-on relationship would disrupt it, but he knew with absolute certainty he wanted her in his life someway, somehow.

He didn't know how to straddle the line between the two "wants" but, with defenses lowered by the wine, he felt it was time to be more transparent. He leaned towards her, his eyes locked with hers, and asked, "Is there anything I can say or do to sway you to stay? It would be devastating to lose you in my life."

Pebbles flushed redder than her wine as a heart-stirring smile flashed across her face.

Her mind wandered back to the previous day when she climbed up a rocky slope near Sand Harbor and sat soaking in the sun. Sydney had once teased her that Tahoe has a way of invading one's soul and to not be surprised if she found it tough to leave at the end of summer.

As she surveyed the lake's postcard worthy vistas, she silently cursed Sydney for his prescient warning. And yet the ache she felt when she thought about leaving seemed interwoven with memories of Anlon as much as Tahoe's silent calling.

Anlon's sweet entreaty was the final catalyst that melted her resolve. Pebbles affirmatively nodded, stood and reached for his hand, tugging him to stand as well. She wrapped both arms around him and held him tightly, nuzzling her face against his shoulder. They rocked gently and she raised her lips to kiss his cheek. Decision made.

And so she stayed. Pebbles continued to work part-time at Sydney's and took a second job working at Heavenly ski resort over the winter, learning to ski and snowboard in her free time. She even traveled with Anlon to his Los Cabos home once during the winter and fell in love with his cliff-side view of the Sea of Cortez.

Upon returning from the Cabo trip, Pebbles discovered her clunky, noisy scooter had been stolen from the apartment parking lot. Anlon had it replaced within 24 hours with a brand new hot pink upgrade.

Though it killed her to do it, she rejected his gesture, saying, "Look, A.C., I love it, and you are incredibly thoughtful for doing this, but I can't accept it. I need to fend for myself. I don't want to depend on anyone but me. I'll buy another used one with the insurance money. I'll be fine."

Anlon was dumbfounded but respected her decision. She was, after all, adamant about her independence. As protective, he realized, as he was about his own. Maybe that's the glue that somehow weirdly binds us, Anlon thought. He decided it wasn't advisable to mess with the glue.

But Anlon could be stubborn, too, and so he kept the shiny scooter instead of returning it and left it parked in the garage next to his Jeep just in case she ever changed her mind.

As Pebbles now searched for flights on the laptop in her austere apartment, she thought of the shiny pink scooter in his garage. "Finally, I have a chance to *earn* that scooter!" she excitedly exclaimed.

V

BACK PORCH DETENTE

When they hung up, Anlon felt as if a huge weight had been lifted from his shoulders. He was soothed knowing he could count on Pebbles when the chips were down.

Clad in a heather-hued sweatshirt, jeans and scuffed up brown hiking boots, he strolled to the kitchen of Devlin's house and gave a small victory shout when he discovered a six pack of Great Barrington's finest microbrewed IPA front and center in the refrigerator. He layered three of the beers amid ice cubes into one of the copper pots dangling above the center island stovetop and headed for the back porch.

Seated now on the steps leading from the house's covered porch to the backyard, Anlon uncapped the first bottle and stared down at the mysterious oval and square stones he'd removed from the safe and placed on the step beside him. He ruminated on the last two days' events and shook his head. It was all too fantastic. No way these were anything more than run-of-the-mill artistic pieces from some ancient temple. Yet Dobson had been so passionate, so sure they were anything but.

Raising the sweaty IPA bottle towards the sky, he toasted to Devlin and Dobson with a silent promise to continue their work and catch the bastard who killed them.

Lowering his gaze, he peered at his uncle's office perched on the small rise 50 yards in the distance. It was actually an old barn that Devlin had gutted and remodeled to his specifications. From the outside, it still looked like a classic red and white New England barn, complete with a steeple and black rooster weather vane.

The barn was surrounded by a lush rolling green field that, in turn, was bordered along the edges by a knee-high, stone wall. Just beyond the wall surrounding the field was a line of trees that marked the boundaries of Devlin's five acres. From that tree line, for a second time in as many days, a dark, solitary figure watched in unnoticed silence. As Anlon sipped on his beer, the figure trained binoculars on the two stones resting on the steps beside Anlon.

Anlon debated internally whether he should tackle the office tonight or wait for Pebbles to arrive tomorrow. Still exhausted and unsure of what else he might discover, Anlon opted to remain planted on the steps and watch the sun dip below the Berkshires in the distance. He thought of his own home's sunset view and wished he was there now. But given what had transpired over the last 48 hours, Anlon didn't think he'd see his home for at least a couple of weeks.

Setting aside the mystery surrounding the stones, there was Devlin's funeral to attend (and now Dobson's as well). He also needed to meet with Devlin's attorney to go through the will and learn his responsibilities as executor of his uncle's estate. And then he had to figure out what to do with Devlin's house and the belongings willed to him.

Just then, Anlon's reflections were interrupted by the sound of a car idling slowly towards him. He craned his neck to peer around the wide back staircase to the winding driveway leading to the house. A small white compact came to a halt by the garage, its headlights blinding him from espying the occupant.

He turned his head away from the lights and drew another swallow of the rich citrus ale. When the car's engine silenced, Anlon heard the tell-tale sound of its door swinging open. He shouted, "I'm out back. If you're selling something, you've picked the wrong house on the wrong day!"

The car door shut with a light thud and a voice called from the driveway, "Dr. Cully? Det. Lt. Stevens. I've been looking for you."

He rolled his eyes and called back without looking, "Ugh, no more interrogation, please. I've had enough for one day!"

Jennifer Stevens softly laughed. She deserved that, she thought. She'd been pretty rough on him earlier that morning and now that they were fairly certain he wasn't involved in Matthew Dobson's death, she felt badly for her prior aggressive questioning. That's partially why she had sought him after meeting with the coroner and Capt. Gambelli.

"Good news," she said as she stepped towards his seated figure on the stairs, "you've been reduced from a suspect to a person of interest."

"What?" Anlon queried, turning his attention to her as she approached, clearly surprised by her comment. "So you're saying it wasn't murder?"

"Oh no, it was definitely murder. At least, that's what my boss and the coroner think. But there was no trace of you — fingerprints or hair fibers — anywhere on Dobson or his car. If the DNA results come back and there's no trace of you at the crime scene, then you're closer to being in the clear." Stevens halted at the bottom of the stairs and glanced up at Anlon.

Before she had left the office, she'd ditched the grey suit and now stood in tight-fitting jeans, an ivory cable knit sweater and pink and green running shoes. Her hair, bun-tight earlier in the day, was now drawn back in a silky golden ponytail. Again, the muted scent of her perfume found its way to his nostrils. He casually took another sip of his beer and said, "Well, I guess I should be glad to hear it, but I'll be honest with you, it doesn't provide me much comfort. Dobson's still dead and someone still killed him."

She dug her hands into the back pockets of her jeans and nodded in agreement, "I understand. It doesn't take the sting away, but I thought you'd like to know."

She turned to head back to her car, a move that surprised Anlon. He called out, "Hold up! That's it? You came all the way out here just to say that?"

She wheeled and smiled at him for the first time. A beautiful, inviting smile. "Well, I know it's been a tough day for you. I do have some other questions but they can wait until tomorrow. Just didn't want you going to sleep tonight thinking you were still our prime suspect. And I wanted to apologize for being so combative this morning."

Anlon was touched by the unexpected gesture of kindness from the previously stone-cold Stevens and playfully cracked, "Thank you, Detective, apology accepted. I will sleep a little better knowing I won't wake to you cuffing me in bed."

At that she giggled. A sweet, carefree giggle. She bowed slightly, her ponytail sliding over her right shoulder, and replied, "You're welcome, Dr. Cully. And you can call me Jennifer."

She turned again and slowly paced across the grass to the driveway. Anlon, uncomfortably aware he was staring at her butt as she walked away, called, "Only if you call me Anlon. And if you'll come have a beer with me, I'll answer any other questions you have."

Jennifer halted by her car door with a hidden sly grin. She was technically off-duty and so drinking a beer was copacetic. However, he was still a person of interest to the investigation, hence a semi-conflict of interest when all was laid bare.

On the other hand, she'd spent much of the afternoon conducting further research into Dr. Anlon Cully's background before the coroner's tests had largely ruled him out. The more she discovered, the more mortified she felt about her treatment of him that morning. And the more intrigued Jennifer grew to learn more about him.

Professionally, of course. He might have valuable insights for the investigation, she reasoned, and despite his apparent innocence, she was absolutely sure Anlon hadn't been fully open with her during her earlier questioning. She shared as much with Gambelli, and he, in turn, tasked her to unpeel more of the onion...his words. So while she'd altruistically sought him out to assuage his apprehension about his status as a potential suspect, she did possess an underlying motive for stopping by.

Well, possibly two ulterior motives, Jennifer allowed. She had been very impressed by what she'd learned about Anlon in the course of a couple hours of additional Internet search, and if nothing else the idea of sharing a beer with a bright, attractive, wealthy man wasn't the worst way to spend a Sunday.

Jennifer had no trouble attracting men, but all too often they were too needy and lacked the kind of ambition she found appealing. Plus, being honest with herself, it was tough for guys to date a detective. Her hours were long and sporadic and when duty called, she had to respond, regardless of what she might be doing.

Most of the guys she'd dated since leaving the Army and joining the police force had trouble dealing with her moving-target schedule. But it didn't bother Jennifer too much. She loved to be outdoors and she could run, hike, mountain climb, cross-country ski, fish and hunt on her own quite happily. Still, it would be nice to play with someone when off-duty.

She realized the likelihood of Anlon as that someone was a long shot, but her research into his background intrigued her enough to dream of the possibility.

The first thing Jennifer discovered about Anlon was his involvement several years prior in a globally renowned invention of an alternative form of propulsion — an invention that might cut combustion engine pollution in half when commercially available. She'd been floored to learn that the four-person research group he'd been part of had received a billion dollars for their patent from an upstart technology multi-billionaire itching to take on the glacial pace of the world's oil companies and auto producers to bring to market breakthrough technologies.

One article Jennifer read highlighted Anlon's contribution to the team. As an expert in biomechanics, he was fascinated by the biological systems used by certain animals and birds to generate movement over long distances, particularly those that had limited access to food in their journeys and were more efficient in consuming energy to produce movement. In studying their body chemistry and systems, he was captivated by two underlying commonalities. They seemed to burn energy in pulses or waves, not in a constant churn, and they were capable of storing more excess energy than other animals and birds. Most store excess energy primarily for fight or flight situations, but long-haul animals seemed to be capable of tapping their excess energy at will.

In the article, Anlon likened how most animals and birds generate movement via a comparison to the way combustion engines operate. Fuel is introduced, it's ignited and movement is created from the mini-explosion. But this form of movement requires constant, violent, energy-consuming and waste-generating bursts.

Anlon wondered if it were possible to either change the fuel or change the mechanics of a traditional combustion engine, or both, to create longer-lasting, less frequent bursts — more like pulses or waves observed in long-haul animals and birds. If there was a way to store the excess energy generated with each pulse or wave, then the same degree of movement could be generated as found in a common combustion engine, but with less energy required and less waste produced.

A pulse engine was not a new concept, yet the way previous pulse engines were designed was very different. Traditional pulse engines were used mostly on rockets to achieve extremely fast bursts of energy that burned quick and required few or no moving parts. Ultimately they proved too wasteful and too expensive to operate and maintain.

Anlon's idea was the opposite. Was it possible to learn from nature how to apply biomechanics and biochemistry to achieve a different kind of pulse engine, one that burned slower, consumed less and produced less by-product waste?

He shared his research and ideas with his engineering and chemist colleagues on the team who took the ball from there and ultimately created an additive to traditional fossil fuel that was combined with their redesigned vision of a combustion engine. The two concepts married together produced astounding efficiency gains in their laboratory prototype. The leader of the research team, a debonair African-American named Antonio Wallace, anointed the prototype as the Whave engine.

From the laid-back manner in which Anlon carried himself, Jennifer never would have guessed he was brilliant or wealthy. Most self-proclaimed brilliant and wealthy people she ran into in the course of her job threw their weight around and let you know at every turn how important and rich they were, invoking often the tried and true, "Don't you know who I am?" when they were caught stepping over the lines set by laws.

She'd also read some of his gracious quotes in articles published about the invention, and others about the charitable foundation he established with a chunk of his cut from the patent. In fact, she didn't find a single reference to him online that was negative, except the predictable, loathsome comments and social media posts about him and his research colleagues selling out to corporate interests. There were also dozens of articles and hundreds of photos of him reveling in his new-found celebrity and wealth.

But what was most interesting to Jennifer was the fact that the "celebrity" articles about him seemed to suddenly cease about three years ago. Since that time, it was almost as if Dr. Anlon Cully had disappeared from existence. Yes, there was the odd mention here or there of his investment in one new idea or another and the occasional tidbit about a donation his foundation made, but outside of that, he'd simply faded back into the obscurity he'd known before the invention.

No more red carpet photos with statuesque starlets, no innuendo laden articles about who was seen hopping into his Ferrari at some L.A. nightclub in the wee hours of the morning and no more videos of scotch and cigar "bro" fishing trips off the coast of the Sea of Cortez. Little did she know that obscurity was exactly what Anlon desired.

With this background in mind, Jennifer turned back around and demurely asked, "Are you sure?"

"Yes, come on. I know you didn't come all the way out here solely to make sure I get a good night's sleep. But if we're going to do this can we drop the surreptitious tactics, please? I'm okay helping you but I'd like us to be straight with one another because, frankly, I'm pretty sure I'm going to need your help, too," Anlon implored.

Beyond the reach of Anlon's gaze, Jennifer's face reddened in embarrassment at his ability to see through to her core motive so easily. He's clearly observant, she thought, as she arrived back at the staircase. Chagrined, she agreed, "Fair enough. Now where's that beer? I'm thirsty."

"Help yourself," Anlon replied, nodding his head towards the copper pot resting on the step below where he sat. "While you get settled, you can answer a question for me. You mentioned Dobson's car. Is that where he was killed?"

She tip-toed up four steps, reached forward for one of the ice-cold beers, uncapped it with a corner of her sweater and leaned back against the wooden stairway railing. As she took a sip, she gave Anlon a clipped summary of the crime scene. Gazing past him, she then spied the two stones sitting by Anlon. "What are those?" she asked.

"Good question," he said as he assimilated the information she shared. "I'm not entirely sure is the honest answer. They are artifacts my Uncle Devlin found in storage in a couple museums. He seemed to think they might be more than ceremonial trinkets, but I don't know. So how do you think Dobson was killed?"

"Best we can figure from the evidence so far it appears that Mr. Dobson was confronted by someone as he pulled into his driveway. We think he stepped out of the car to speak with the person who, at some point, knocked him unconscious in the driveway. We found blood on the edge of the driver door that seems to match up with a small gash the coroner found on the back of his head. Then it appears the unknown assailant placed him back in the car, plugged up the tailpipe, turned the engine on and let it idle until he died of carbon monoxide poisoning. After he was dead, we think the killer removed whatever plugged the tailpipe before leaving the scene," she detailed before taking another sip of her IPA.

"Did you know your uncle well?" Jennifer queried.

"So-so. I knew him all my life but only saw him every few years. He was always on the go to some new site or barricaded in his office up there on that hill, and I moved to the west coast, so our paths didn't cross that often. But I liked him and he apparently liked me, too. He willed me this property and his research, God knows why," Anlon replied while shaking his head and taking another swig himself.

"This morning you said something about him wanting you to pick up where his research left off," Jennifer commented, sliding down to sit on the step beside him.

"Yes, that seems to be the case all right, but I'm not an archaeologist. And I don't think he counted on Dobson dying. Without him, 'I'm lost in the dig' as my uncle used to say about his reliance on Dobson himself," Anlon explained, his voice trailing off as he finished speaking. He was still contemplating her description of the crime scene. Based on what she said he was having trouble seeing how he could be ruled out as a suspect.

"You said my fingerprints weren't found at the scene. Did you find someone else's?" he ventured.

Jennifer looked at him with admiration. Not a bad deduction, she thought, before responding, "Yes, there were fingerprints and hair fibers from multiple people on and inside the car, but none were yours. But there were no foreign fingerprints of any kind on Mr. Dobson's skin or clothes. That's the odd part."

"I'm sorry, but couldn't the killer have worn gloves?" Anlon shot back with an obvious solution.

"Certainly possible," Jennifer allowed, "but then we would have expected to find smudges overlaying fingerprints or signs of someone wiping away their trail. But all of the fingerprints we found showed no sign of tampering and other than prints from the woman who discovered his body none appeared fresh. There may be innocent explanations for all of the prints. People who've ridden in his car, people who've leaned against his car. Without physical traces left on his body or clothes, it will be tough to connect any of the prints with his murder."

Anlon quietly considered her analysis. Though it was genuinely puzzling, he now understood why they had lowered their scrutiny of him as a suspect.

Looking past Anlon to the two stones on the other side of him, she had to agree…they didn't look special. Shifting the focus back to her own questions, she asked, "So you're going to continue your uncle's dull and esoteric research?"

He smiled without looking at her, "Nice memory Detective, er, Jennifer. Yes, I think I'll at least take a deeper look to satisfy my curiosity, if nothing else. In fact, I've invited a friend of mine to join me in the hunt. She'll be here tomorrow."

"Thank you," she grinned as she nudged his shoulder with hers. "A good memory is kinda a requirement of my job."

She noted the "female friend" comment, but decided to not pull that thread for now. Turning back to her line of questioning, she asked, "So do you think the research might be somehow connected to Mr. Dobson's death?"

Anlon paused before answering. He wanted to blurt out, "Of course it is!" However, he didn't want to get his own investigation tangled up with that of the police. He pondered how to answer her question honestly without piquing her interest too much. He said, "You know, it's hard for me to say, but it's possible."

Jennifer noted the pause and the carefully phrased answer. Got it, she thought. He definitely thinks the two are connected. She followed up by querying, "You also said this morning that Mr. Dobson seemed tense. Is that why you think it's possible the research is connected with his death?"

Anlon hid his reaction to her question by taking the final gulp of his first beer. Reaching for the last one remaining in the pot, he cupped the icy wet bottle and removed the cap. Before taking another drink, he answered, "I see I'm not going to be able to dance around your questions, am I?"

"Hey, you were the one who wanted to drop the surreptitious tactics! And I think I've answered your questions without hedging like you are right now," she remarked, jabbing his arm with her elbow.

"Okay, okay. You're right," he replied as he smiled and rubbed his bicep where she jabbed him.

She sipped her beer and grinned without saying a word. She peered off in the distance at the now darkened horizon and waited for him to continue speaking. Though she was not a grizzled veteran detective yet, she'd watched Gambelli long enough to know that sometimes you just have to give people the space to come clean on their own.

While she waited, a small gust of wind shot past causing her to shiver audibly. Anlon felt the breeze, too, and said, "It's getting chilly. You want to head inside and sit by the fireplace?"

"Sure, why not," she winked. "It will give you more time to stall."

He stood and smiled. "Can you take my beer inside? I'll get the pot later. I need both hands to carry the stones. Dobson scolded me to handle them with care."

Once inside, he triggered the gas fire and they settled onto the leather sofa side-by-side with the two stones placed on the coffee table in front of them. Anlon picked at the loose end of the IPA label and finally spoke. "Have you ever heard a story that seems too strange to be true?"

She quipped, "Are you kidding me? I'm a cop. I get daily doses of unbelievable tales."

"Ha ha," Anlon replied, "I'm sure you do. But I mean more than the 'dog ate my homework' kind of story. For example, Dobson told me that these two stones are not just trinkets. He told me they are two priceless pieces of ancient technology that were lost over millennia. He said they actually are over 10,000 years old. If he was right, it means there was an advanced culture well before any scholar today would acknowledge."

She shrugged and said, "Okay? Not sure why that's a big deal, but I'll take your word for it."

"See," he said, returning her earlier elbow jab with one of his own, "I told you it was esoteric. Actually, it would be a very big deal if it's true. It would rewrite history. But I'm afraid we'll never know. Dobson died before he could tell me how the stones work. And with my Uncle Devlin dead, too, I'm not sure it will be possible to figure out how they work.

"Anyway, you asked about why Dobson was tense. He believed my uncle didn't fall on his own. He believed he was somehow sent off the cliff against his will. I say it that way because when I asked whether he was pushed, he said yes and no but didn't clarify what he meant. So putting two and two together, I think Dobson was convinced someone killed my uncle and that the killer was after my uncle's research or these stones or both. And now that they've both died mysteriously, I'm inclined to believe he might have been onto something."

Jennifer listened intently. He was finally opening up and she didn't want to interrupt him.

Staring absently at the leaping flames, Anlon continued. "Dobson had the stones locked up in an elaborate safe. He handled them so cautiously. I was skeptical about the story, but now I'm not so sure. I wish he'd shown me how they work before we finished talking the other night!"

Jennifer considered his story. It seemed plausible that the stones were valuable. If so, that might make a powerful motive for someone to steal them, maybe even murder for them. But the stones had not been stolen...yet. Maybe the killer thought that with Dobson and Devlin out of the way the stones would be easier to steal. She asked, "Did anyone else know about the stones besides your uncle and Mr. Dobson?"

"Hmmm...I know at least one person who did. His name is Pacal and he was a research assistant for my uncle. I've not met him before. Dobson said he would be by the office today, but if he came I missed him due to my detention this morning," Anlon smirked.

"Do you know his last name and where he lives? I think I should talk to him," she replied.

"No, I don't. I'm hoping that he'll show up tomorrow. I'm planning on staying here tonight so I don't miss him," answered Anlon.

"Anyone else?" Jennifer prodded.

"I don't know. It's possible. Dobson said that my uncle kept his discovery of how the stones work a secret, but he also said that Devlin was concerned that others were on the scent of the same discoveries. I don't know, it may not be about the stones at all. It could be something else in his research. Dobson said Devlin was on the hunt of four new discoveries when he fell. And then again, their deaths may have nothing to do with either the stones or Devlin's research," mused Anlon, rubbing the re-emergence of stubble on his chin as he considered the possibilities.

Jennifer jeered internally. If it walks like a duck and quacks like one, it usually isn't a chicken, she thought. Both of their deaths were almost undoubtedly connected to the stones and Devlin Wilson's research. But she reminded herself to keep an open mind. She also made a mental note to tell Gambelli about Dobson's suspicions about Devlin's death and to get a copy of the New Hampshire police department report and autopsy report, presuming the latter was performed.

All in all, she'd received a good cache of new information in return for her casual drive-by. She now had a lead on a suspect, a possible motive, and another potential set of clues to follow rekated to Devlin's death. Yawning, she looked at her watch and realized it was time she headed home. She took a final sip of beer and said, "Well, Anlon, for your sake I hope it has nothing to do with the research or the stones."

"Why," he asked with a quizzical look stamped on his face. "Am I about to become a suspect again?"

"No, but if their deaths are connected to the research or stones, you might be next on the killer's hit list."

VI

BEES TO THE HONEY

Huddled in a corner booth along the front window of the Main Street Diner sat a burly man with his bald head covered by a grey hood. He opened the disposable text app on his cell phone and tapped out a message: "AC definitely has the stones. I saw them."

The text recipient, username Quechua212, replied a few minutes later. "The map? What about the map? Does he know about it yet? Did you see it?"

Stirring cream into his steaming mug of coffee, the hooded figure frowned as he reflected on his frustrating vigil the prior night. He had crept to the tree line expecting to find the house dark and a golden opportunity to rummage through the barn office in search of the map. He cursed when he peered through binoculars and spotted Anlon lazily sipping beer on the back steps of the main house, handling the stones with curious wonder. For a brief moment, the hooded figure thought of sneaking up on Anlon, disabling him and stealing the stones. But as Quechua212 had reminded him prior to casing Wilson's office, "Be smart, be methodical, be patient. You already made one huge mistake. We can't afford another one."

"No. Didn't get in barn. AC was there with woman. Too risky. Wouldn't have been methodical," AucuChan1 mockingly replied, "Going back 2nite. But don't think AC has map."

"Why so sure?" responded Quechua212, ignoring his jibe.

As his all-American breakfast was delivered by the diner waitress, AucuChan1 recalled the way Anlon kept looking at the stones. He picked them up repeatedly, holding them at different angles, scratching his head frequently. He thought, if he doesn't know about the stones, there is no way he knows about the map.

His typed reply, "AC clueless about stones. No way he has map."

Quechua212 cautioned, "Or...he might have map but not know it."

There was a pause while AucuChan1 dug into his eggs in frustration. He resented being reminded of his mistake. He was sure the police wouldn't make the connection to him until long after they were gone, if they ever did at all.

Another message from Quechua212 appeared. "We are very lucky then...for now. AC is no fool. He will figure it out if he finds it before we do."

"What about the stones?" replied the man, pushing back his hood to avoid dipping the hood strings into his coffee while he hovered over his plate.

"Sound Stone not needed; I have one...as you know," came the reply.

"Master Stone???" AucuChan1 asked after he dug his fork under a heap of hash-browned potatoes.

The hooded man knew that the Master Stone, as Devlin had labeled it, was a different matter. If Anlon figured out how to access it before they found the map, it would complicate matters. There was no way to know for certain whether the Story Stone in Anlon's possession was the Master Stone, AucuChan1 realized. Neither he nor Quechua212 had viewed the stone yet, though they knew from another source that the existence of the map was first found on the Master Stone.

Quechua212, as if reading his mind, answered, "Need it bad!"

Crunching rhythmically on bacon, the burly man peered out through a crack in the diner's red checked curtains and then craned his neck to make sure no one was within viewing distance of his next text. "I can take care of AC."

"No!" Quechua212 answered with lightning speed. "Need to know if AC has the map before then. We don't want a repeat of MD. Keep your mind on prize we seek."

"K. Relax. Will go back to barn 2nite."

"Good. Further delays mean higher risk AC gets it first…and you know what that means," admonished Quechua212.

With a good night's sleep, Anlon felt refreshed and focused. He intended on making the most of the day while he awaited Pebbles' arrival. At present, he was seated in the Pittsfield, Massachusetts, waiting room of Devlin's attorney, Mr. George Grant, Esq., gazing out the window at Onota Lake in the distance.

Tiny in comparison to Lake Tahoe, Pittsfield's centerpiece lake appeared, however, to be the same sort of summer attraction for residents and vacationers traveling up the Route 7 corridor into Vermont, or so it struck Anlon on this sunny May morning.

From behind the reception desk, Mr. Grant's assistant announced that the attorney was ready to meet and ushered Anlon into a conference room.

In the center of the room was a sturdy, oval cherrywood conference table surrounded by half a dozen hunter-green, leather rolling chairs atop a thick, goldenrod carpet. On the four cherry wood paneled walls were sconces illuminating gilt-edged frames with paintings of mallard ducks cavorting in each of the four seasons.

At the far end of the oval table, the impeccably attired Mr. Grant, a rotund, balding man with horn-rimmed glasses and a warm, congenial manner, rose to greet Anlon. "Such a pleasure to meet you, Dr. Cully. I'm so sorry it is under these circumstances, but you should know your uncle was quite proud of you. He boasted of you often."

"Thank you, Mr. Grant. Please call me Anlon. I'm touched Devlin thought so highly of me. He was like an adventure movie star come to life on the occasions we spent time together. Such gusto for life and its mysteries. We are worse off for his loss."

"Quite so, quite so. A man larger than life, that's undeniable. Well, let's get to it, shall we?" suggested Mr. Grant.

For the next half an hour, Mr. Grant read through the details of the last will and testament of Devlin Allen Wilson, PhD. Anlon made notes on the copy of the will Grant provided at the outset of his recitation and listened attentively, waiting until the solicitor finished before speaking.

"That pretty much sums it up," Mr. Grant concluded as he took a healthy swig of bottled water.

Anlon waited until Mr. Grant finished drinking and said, "It seems pretty straightforward. I'm surprised by the extent of Devlin's assets, but I think he was very generous in his bequests. I just wish Dobson had lived long enough to know Devlin intended him to be independently wealthy."

Mr. Grant nodded furiously and echoed, "Too true, too true. He cared deeply for Matthew. He knew the sacrifices Mr. Dobson made on his behalf, even if he didn't acknowledge them outright, or so Devlin shared with me."

"So, with Dobson dead, will that complicate matters?" Anlon asked.

"Hard to say. Since Mr. Dobson died after Devlin, the bequest stands. It's really a matter of whether Mr. Dobson had a will of his own. I can certainly make inquiries if you'd like."

"Please, do, I wouldn't know where to start. So beyond the legacy he left Dobson, it seems there are only three other bequests besides the home and its contents he left to me, right?" Anlon inquired, trying to make sure he understood the contents of the will.

"Exactly," responded Mr. Grant. "He made additional provisions for a Mr. Pacal Flores, his research assistant; Mr. Richard Ryan, his departed sister's son and a Miss Anabel Simpson, whom I know nothing about other than an address Devlin provided. I haven't shared a copy with any of the beneficiaries yet awaiting your authorization as executor to do so.

"I will tell you that Mr. Ryan has called at least a dozen times since Devlin's untimely death inquiring about the will. It would not surprise me if he starts badgering you. Per the law, as a beneficiary, he is entitled to receive a full copy of the will and contest it if he has valid grounds. From his increasingly antagonistic calls, I think you can count on him challenging whether he has grounds or not."

Anlon reflected on the list. Devlin's cash bequests totaled six million dollars, a tidy sum for an archaeologist. Half of it was intended for Dobson, poor soul. The remaining three million was ordered to be divided equally between the nephew Richard, the unknown Ms. Simpson and Pacal. During his recitation, Mr. Grant made it clear that Devlin had already set aside these assets in a trust account, meaning that all parties would have access to their bequests very quickly, so at least Anlon wouldn't have to plow through a year's worth of probate to disperse the bequests.

He considered Mr. Grant's comments about Richard and it didn't surprise Anlon that his cousin was anxious to learn of his inheritance and that he might contest the will. He'd always seemed to be on the edge of disaster from the family stories he'd heard over the years.

"Any chance I can rely on you to run interference for me managing the bequests or if Richard does challenge?" Anlon sheepishly asked.

"Of course, of course," answered the confident Mr. Grant. "There are really no grounds to contest. The monetary amount is specific. The only question will be whether Mr. Dobson's bequest goes to heirs of his choosing, presuming he has a will, or whether Mr. Ryan or the others will seek to fight the state for a portion of the unclaimed bequest. There truly is no reason for you to get involved in the matter if you want to delegate it to us."

"I so delegate," answered Anlon. "Just let me know what to sign."

He desired no part of getting in the middle of a money squabble. Anlon understood the silent motives behind Devlin's bequests to Pacal, Richard and Dobson, although he was curious to learn more about Anabel Simpson.

For his own part, he now understood the reason why Devlin willed him his home and contents. It wasn't about money; it was about preserving his life works. And the contents of Devlin's home, including his research and hard earned artifacts, were very precious to Devlin. Knowing that Anlon was already wealthy beyond need, Devlin counted that Anlon would honor and preserve the value of his life works instead of auctioning them off for cash. Indeed, as Dobson intimated, Devlin hoped Anlon would pick up the baton and extend the life of his explorations.

"As you wish," the affable Mr. Grant acknowledged. "We will get started on the paperwork immediately."

"Thank you," a relieved Anlon responded. "Just send anything I need to sign to Devlin's address for now. I'll be staying there for the next couple of weeks. I assume from your earlier comments about his trust that his home and contents are essentially mine now? No long, drawn out process?"

"Yes, that's mostly right," replied Mr. Grant. "There are some tax consequences that will need ultimately to be addressed and the formal process of transferring the deed must be completed, but ownership for all intents and purposes transferred to you as a beneficiary of the irrevocable trust Devlin established. Of course, you can't dispose of any assets until the official documents are approved."

"Okay, thank you. As you might have guessed, I have my own battery of attorneys. I will make sure they contact you today to start the ball rolling on the documents, tax issues and any expenses your firm incurs on my behalf," Anlon said as he rose to shake Mr. Grant's hand.

"Absolutely, we'll do our best for all parties concerned. There are two matters, however, we should discuss before you depart," hesitated Mr. Grant as he stood to return Anlon's parting salutation.

"Oh?" Anlon replied with a slight air of surprise.

"Yes, I have something here in my possession that Devlin specifically, dare I say adamantly, demanded we hold in our office safe for you. Also, he demanded with equal fervor that you discuss Ms. Simpson's bequest with her directly," stated Mr. Grant.

Jennifer pressed the end-call icon on her cell phone and frowned. Strange, she thought, that Matthew Dobson was so convinced that Devlin Wilson's death was not accidental. She had just spoken with the Meredith Police Department officer who was first on the scene where Devlin fell. He filed the original police report and, she learned from her conversation with him, was the officer Dobson approached to ask if his fall might not be an accident.

The officer, Sam Keller, recited the police report to her over the phone, adding in a few additional tidbits from the autopsy report and agreed to send Jennifer copies of both. Devlin Wilson had been found lying on his side some 200 feet below a steep rocky section of the Blueberry Ledge Trail on Mt. Whiteface in the White Mountain range in New Hampshire. It appeared he had slipped and fallen backwards, hitting at least one tree and multiple sharp rock edges on his way down before rolling to a stop on a small flat area covered with pine needles.

He had died from internal injuries sustained in the fall. His body was battered with bruises, cuts and abrasions that were consistent with those expected from a fall. In other words, Officer Keller clarified, none of the injuries appeared to be defensive wounds associated with fending off an attacker.

He was found by a group of hikers making the ascent on Mt. Whiteface at around 9:00 a.m. They did not hear or see Devlin during their hike, nor did they see anyone else coming down the trail, though they passed a few hikers going in the same direction. The coroner estimated the time of death between 8:00 a.m. and 9:00 a.m.

His wallet, car keys and cell phone were found among the other items in his backpack, so there was no suspicion of robbery. Officer Keller also inspected Devlin's Land Rover in the parking area near the trailhead and found the vehicle locked and the contents undisturbed as best as he could tell.

Officer Keller stressed that the Blueberry Ledge Trail itself was considered a strenuous hiking trail and it wasn't uncommon for hikers to sustain sprains and broken bones on the trail. He did allow, however, that it was unusual for someone to outright fall to their death. In his recollection, Devlin was the only one to have died from a fall.

The coroner, he said, had wondered if Devlin experienced a heart attack or some other medical emergency that caused him to fall but she found nothing in the blood work, toxicology report or in her physical examination that indicated a medical emergency prior to the fall. The only odd thing to her was that the extent of the internal injuries seemed excessive for a 200 foot fall. The condition of the body was more consistent with a much longer fall, but the section he fell from did not wind back above the same area as it ascended. With no other explanation available from the physical evidence, the coroner noted her finding, but affirmed injuries sustained in an accidental fall as the cause of death.

Stevens only asked Officer Keller a few questions while she intently scribbled notes, mostly about Matthew Dobson and his visit with Keller the day after the accident. She explained first that Mr. Dobson died a few days after Dr. Wilson and that the circumstances of his death were suspicious. Elaborating further, she said that Mr. Dobson had expressed misgivings about the accidental nature of Dr. Wilson's death the night before he died himself. Though there was no overt connection between the two deaths, she was delegated to follow up to make sure.

"Ask anything you like," Keller said.

"It might be hard to remember," she acknowledged, "but can you recall the precise words Mr. Dobson used when he asked about Dr. Wilson's death?"

"Hmm, I don't remember the specific words he used, but it was along the lines of, 'are you absolutely certain he wasn't pushed?'. I told him there was no evidence indicating he'd been pushed but I also told him there was no way to rule it out as a possibility either. I asked him why he thought someone might have pushed the Professor, as Mr. Dobson called him. He said it wasn't like the Professor to hike on his own and especially so, given the rugged terrain of the trail where he fell. And he said was certain Dr. Wilson had never mentioned the White Mountains before and was baffled why he came there in the first place," Officer Keller recounted.

"Were those the only reasons he gave you for his suspicions? Did he mention a possible motive?" Stevens queried in response to Keller's commentary.

"Not that I remember. I did ask him if he had reason to believe Dr. Wilson was in danger. Or if someone recently threatened him, or if he thought he was in some kind of trouble. He said no to all three questions, but between you and me, he did hesitate before answering. I told him that without something more tangible to go on, it was tough to look at the evidence and conclude there was something sinister behind his fall."

Stevens agreed with Keller's assessment, but she noted his comment about Dobson's hesitation. She thanked Officer Keller for his time and insights and asked one final question. "Oh, one last thing. Did Mr. Dobson say anything that struck you as out of place?"

"Hmmm, let me think. You know, now that you mention it, he did ask a question that was a little odd. He wanted to know if we found any unusual-looking stones or artifacts near the body or in his backpack. I assured him that we hadn't found anything of the kind and I asked him why. He said the Professor was an archaeologist and wondered if he'd gone on the hike to search for relics."

Exiting her car at the Mt. Whiteface trailhead parking area, Stevens adjusted her backpack and ropes while mentally replaying the conversation she just finished with Keller. Looking up at the sheer cliffs of the summit, she muttered, "Stones again."

Anlon glanced down at his watch as he waited for the funeral home director to re-emerge with the estimates for Devlin's and Dobson's burials. It was now 2:00 p.m. and Pebbles' flight would arrive in Albany in two hours.

When wrapping up his conversation that morning with Mr. Grant, the attorney mentioned that neither Devlin nor Dobson had family in the area. Given this, Anlon decided to take charge of making their final arrangements while Mr. Grant sought to find and alert their relatives.

After leaving Mr. Grant's office, Anlon returned to Stockbridge to meet with the parish priest of the town's quaint stone Catholic church to discuss service arrangements for both men before driving to nearby Lenox to speak with the funeral home director.

Driving to and from these important errands gave Anlon the time to absorb and process the discussion with Grant and to ponder the new artifact Devlin left with Grant for safekeeping. It was another square stone like the one in the safe back at the house, but it was black instead of reddish, and this one had different markings on the face of the stone.

At the center was a sun-like etching with six "rays" extending from the center-circle. At the outer terminus of each ray were distinct etched figures, though the figures didn't make much sense to Anlon when he first studied it. Most confounding, Devlin left no note for him explaining the stone and he still didn't know how to access its contents…assuming this stone was similar to the one Dobson described.

Interrupted from his train of thought by the appearance of the undertaker from behind a curtained doorway with the estimates, Anlon wondered if he would have enough time to stop back at Devlin's house to place the new stone in the safe before driving to Albany to pick up Pebbles at the airport.

He felt a nagging sense of unease with the stone just sitting in its cushioned case inside the rental car, considering the length to which Devlin resorted to protect it. It obviously was very precious to Devlin and Anlon needed to figure out what it contained and why it was so important to him.

After all, why would Devlin have taken the stone to Grant's office only four days before his death? He had his own elaborate safe at home, why not just put it in there with the other stones? It seemed to indicate, Anlon mused, that Devlin believed he or the stone or both were in danger shortly before his freak accident. Maybe Dobson's suspicions were justified.

As he exited the funeral home, he gasped. In the parking lot, a hooded figure stood at his rental car with the driver door open peering inside the SUV. Anlon started to run towards the man shouting, "Hey! What are you doing? Get away from there."

The figure froze in place for a second and then took off into the woods behind the parking lot without ever looking back. Anlon gave a brief chase, still shouting loudly at the scurrying shape before his mind leapt to the stone, exclaiming "Oh my God, did he take it?"

He altered the direction of his dash back to the open car door. Scanning quickly, he uttered an audible sigh of relief upon spotting the case still on the floor behind the front passenger seat where he'd placed it. Lifting the case, he noticed the lock was untouched. Fishing in his pocket quickly, he withdrew the key and opened the case. The stone was still there. Whew, he thought.

It wasn't until he had calmed down for a few moments that he realized that something else was missing. The thief had taken Anlon's copy of the will, along with his notes, and more importantly the contact information for Miss Anabel Simpson. As he dialed Jennifer, Anlon blurted out, "What in the devil's name is going on!"

When the call connected, Anlon gave Stevens a breathless summary of the incident. The detective told him she would send an officer to meet him at the funeral home to take his statement and to do a forensic examination of the car. She explained that she herself was driving back from the White Mountains and wouldn't be back for a couple hours, but that she would stop by Devlin's house to check in on him later.

"White Mountains?" a surprised Anlon queried. "That's where Devlin died. Any connection to your trip?"

"Yes, as a matter of fact. I spoke with the policeman who was on scene and I went to look at the scene myself," she responded.

"Wow, you don't let moss grow under your feet do you? So you think there's something behind Dobson's hunch? Did you find out anything new?" Anlon blurted in staccato fashion.

He could hear her snicker softly through the phone before retorting, "Hold on, Doc, I'm the cop here! The answer is...maybe. Given your break-in, I'm leaning towards a strong maybe. But I need to go over my notes from the trip with my Captain when I get back and get his input. He's shrewd. If there's something fishy, he'll zero in on it. Like I said, I'll stop over later tonight and we can talk more then."

Anlon slumped down on the curb next to the rental car, suddenly exhausted, and said, "Okay, I understand. Makes sense. Do you think it will take long for your officer to get here? I need to go pick up my colleague at the airport in Albany."

"No, I'll get someone there pronto. Probably will be an officer from the Lenox Police Department. They can get there quicker than someone from my barracks. By the way, did you meet up with Pacal?"

"No," Anlon answered, "unfortunately not yet. I had too much to do this morning, but I did leave a note for him on the barn door asking that he not enter the shop until we spoke. In the note, I asked him to come by the house tonight at seven o'clock. Oh, and I also found out his last name and address from Devlin's attorney. His last name is Flores, but I don't have the address. It was written on the copy of the will that was stolen from the rental. If I recall correctly, it was in Great Barrington."

"Got it, thanks. I'll find out his address, but if it's Great Barrington, it's pretty close to Stockbridge. How about I plan to be at your place at seven in case he shows up. That way we can kill two birds with one stone," she winced, her voice trailing off as she realized the unintended lame pun.

Anlon said, "Ha ha, Jennifer. Sounds good. If he's somehow involved, it would be good to have you there. See you at seven."

An hour later, Anlon was on his way to Albany in Devlin's Land Rover. After the Lenox police went over the rental SUV for fingerprints and other clues, he drove it back to Devlin's house and switched vehicles. He reasoned that the thief must have followed him to the funeral home and so knew the kind of automobile he was driving. He hoped by switching up vehicles there was less chance of being followed. Plus, at the moment, he felt the rental had some bad mojo hanging over it, having now been the subject of police searches twice in as many days!

VII
WAITING ON PACAL

Anlon and Pebbles warmly embraced in baggage claim and awaited her oversized zebra-patterned duffle bag and his titanium shell rolling suitcase to emerge.

He was taken aback by her subdued appearance, but managed to hide his surprise. She'd dyed her hair jet black and had it pulled into a bun atop her head. She wore no lip ring, nose stud or eyebrow rings. She stood in a plain white t-shirt, faded tight-fitting blue jeans and simple red flats. No bangles, just a thin wristwatch. If one discounted the tattoo on her neck and the other two on her wrists, one might have thought she was a fashion model returning from a weekend getaway.

"It's so great to see you, thank you so much for coming," Anlon said. He didn't mention her changed appearance, even though he was curious about the transformation.

"You needed me, I came. That's what friends are for, right? Oh, and thank you for the first class seats. You didn't have to do that," she answered, wrapping her hand in his with a squeeze.

"Hey, I needed you, you came. It's the very least I could do by way of thanks," he replied.

When the bags finally arrived, they loaded them in the Land Rover and started the drive back to Stockbridge. Along the way, Anlon filled Pebbles in about the visit to Devlin's attorney, the theft, the mysterious new stone and a snippet from his call with Jennifer.

When he finished his monologue, Pebbles said, "Wow! Who knew so much could happen during six hours and two plane flights. So you think Pacal and the detective will show up at seven? That's like in 45 minutes."

"Yes to both. You're going to jump right into the cauldron with me. So, I've given you a bunch of random threads. What do you think?"

Pebbles took no time to answer. She burst out with, "Oh, they definitely were killed because of those stones, A.C. How are we going to figure out how to use them? I can't wait to see what they look like!"

Unvarnished, no hesitation, straight to the heart of the matter. It was exactly the kind of feedback Anlon needed. Even if her conclusions didn't jibe with his own, at least he'd have someone he trusted to debate their findings. And he had to admit, he found her enthusiasm for the mystery inspiring. Anlon wasn't sure that she appreciated the potential danger of the situation, but he didn't raise it for fear of dampening her enthusiasm.

When they finally arrived at Devlin's house, they had enough time to stow Pebbles' duffle bag in one of the upstairs bedrooms and settle on the leather sofa in the study with glasses of Cabernet in their hands and the ancient stones on the table before them.

Pebbles, with fascination glittering in her eyes, stared down at the three stones. Sipping on her wine, she asked, "So the square ones are the ones with the recordings on them?"

"Yes, that's what Dobson said. He said they were very magnetic, so I think somehow they must need some kind of player that can interpret embedded magnetic data. If you flip the stones over...carefully... you can see a round depression in the middle and two semi-circular depressions on two opposing sides. If I had to guess, I think those depressions are notches that must align with prongs on whatever device is used to play them. Sort of like how a cassette tape fits into a tape recorder...though you may be too young to remember what a cassette player is," Anlon smirked as he nudged Pebbles' thigh.

"Ha ha," she retorted sarcastically. "I've seen them in museums. I can see what you mean. They do look like they should fit into something. So, if you're right, we need to find the player, right?"

Anlon nodded in agreement, "Yes, but before we look for anything I'm hoping Pacal will be able to tell us what we're looking for. I'm actually hoping he knows where the player is, and I'm betting it's in the barn I pointed out to you when we parked."

"You've given this a lot of thought already, haven't you, Dr. Cully?" she winked, admiring Anlon's ability to visualize how the square stones were accessed. Guess he really is a scientist, she thought.

Peering back down at the two square stones, she noticed the two distinctly different etchings on the front of each artifact. She ventured, "What do you think the different etchings signify? Maybe they hint at what's on each stone, kinda like a label on those bygone cassette tapes you talked about."

Anlon smiled admiringly at her, impressed with her deduction, "Not bad, Pebbles. I hadn't really given that as much thought yet, but I think you might be right. If there are bunches of these and someone wanted to find the right one, it would make sense for them to be labeled or somehow coded. Otherwise you'd have to look at each one individually to find the recording you wanted to view."

"Oh, and maybe the different colors are part of the coding. Like in some card games, different color cards have specific purposes," she excitedly suggested.

"Again," Anlon answered, "you blow me away. At the rate we're working through this, we should have the whole mystery solved before we finish the first bottle of Cabernet!"

Pebbles beamed with sheepish pride and flexed a bicep. She was getting into this and his unsolicited encouragement was motivating. She really wanted to prove her worth to Anlon, wanted him to know she was more than a washed out first-year lawyer, now bartender. She suspected Anlon knew she was much more than that, and he always treated her like a peer of equal standing, but the competitive spirit in her wanted him to see her intellect on display.

They were so wrapped up in their hypothesizing that they didn't hear Jennifer's car pull into the driveway nor her approach to the front door. When the doorbell suddenly rang, they darted startled looks at one another.

"Showtime," Anlon whispered, as he rose to answer the door.

"Hello, Jennifer, come on in," Anlon casually announced. "I'd like to introduce my friend Pebbles."

The initial glances between the two women were akin to prize fighters facing off before a bout, though of course in a friendly, smiling, dagger-type way.

Pebbles interrupted Anlon as she extended a hand to greet Jennifer, "Actually, Pebbles is a pet name Anlon calls me. My name is actually Eleanor McCarver. It's nice to meet you, Jennifer."

Inside Pebbles glowered...Jennifer, he called her? Since when did police detectives and suspects refer to each other on a first name basis? She felt a little insecure as she observed the self-assured stride and mannerisms of the athletic-looking detective. She was very cute in her sweatshirt and yoga pants and her long, honey tresses were eye-catching. She was also closer in age to Anlon and had an air of quiet, tough-bitch confidence that was slightly intimidating to Pebbles.

Jennifer, unbeknown to Pebbles, felt uncharacteristically intimidated in return. Pebbles? Really? A pet name? Okay, that means they are "close," maybe she'd misread the playful nudging she and Anlon engaged in the prior night. And God, she's tall and gorgeous — and young! Pushing these irrational insecurities aside for now, however, Jennifer refocused on the matter at hand. "Eleanor, it's nice to meet you, too. Well, Anlon, should we compare notes?"

Anlon stood watching the two women with a degree of unexpected alarm. Uh oh, he thought, a little icy. And where did Eleanor come from? What was up with Pebbles, he wondered. First the change to a mainstream look and now the name change. He would have to probe that later.

As a man who didn't spend a great deal of energy courting women these days, he realized he might have missed something and unintentionally created the tension between them. He wasn't sure at the moment how he could ease the tension, so he ignored it in favor of getting back to the mystery. He said, "Yes, let's do that. I'm not sure if or when Pacal will come, but it would be best to make sure we're all up to speed before he arrives, if he arrives."

"Right," Jennifer said, "So fill me in on what happened at the funeral home again. I did get a chance to hear it from the Lenox officer who came to take your statement, but I'd like to hear it from you in more detail."

Anlon went through the story again. Pebbles listened intently as he added new details he hadn't included in the car ride from the airport. Jennifer, in return, gave a synopsis of the police report. When she finished, Pebbles was about to ask whether Anlon saw the thief's face when Jennifer asked, "So you never saw the thief's face? He never turned in your direction? You told the officer he was wearing dark clothes and a hood. Can you remember what color clothes and hood?"

Notch one for the detective, Pebbles thought. She's sharp!

Flustered, Anlon threw his hands up and said, "No, I didn't see his face. He never turned to look back, which seems weird, doesn't it? His clothes? To tell you the truth, I was so shocked when I saw him leaning into the Chevy, I wasn't very observant. My first thought was to stop him. It could have been dark blue or black, but I don't think it was brown."

"Don't sweat it, Anlon," Jennifer said as she adopted a more casual posture on the sofa hoping to relax him. It was something she knew she had to work on. Sometimes she was so intent on getting answers that she caused witnesses to clam up instead of opening up. She said, "It's not unusual for people to miss little details at a crime scene due to shock. Give it some time. Other details may come back to you later on."

Pebbles piped in, making sure to use her pet name for Anlon, "A.C., when you said 'it' may have been dark blue or black, did you mean the hood or the clothing, or are you saying he was wearing a hoodie?"

Anlon considered this for a moment and replied, "You know, now that I think of it, it did kind of look like one piece, so I would say a hoodie."

Pebbles followed up with, "Did he make any sounds when he ran away?"

"Hmmm...I don't think so. He struck me as stealthy, very quiet. What are you getting at?"

"I think," Jennifer interjected, "Eleanor is trying to ascertain what kind of shoes the thief was wearing. Good thinking. The officer on scene found fresh footprints of sneakers in mud in the woods behind the funeral home. It's not conclusive, but it's likely he wore sneakers. I'm going to guess black sneakers because white would most likely have caught your eye. And while we're on the subject, the sneaker prints could belong to a man or woman."

"So because Anlon didn't see the thief, you can't rule out that a woman might have been the culprit, correct?" Pebbles clarified, pleased that Jennifer had acknowledged her deduction about the shoes. Maybe she wasn't so bad after all, despite the tough bitch persona.

"Exactly," answered Jennifer. Okay, she's no bimbo. I'll have to look into her background later.

Anlon suddenly felt overwhelmed by the game of suspect profiling playing out between the two women. But at least he could see the level of tension was dropping, so he stayed quiet while they continued.

"It's weird the thief took the will and not the stone, isn't it? I mean, it sounds like the bad guy here came looking for A.C. specifically, so he must have known the attorney had the stone for safekeeping. And, Anlon, you told me in the car that the police officer said the car's lock showed no sign of forced entry which seems to suggest it was professionally picked. So whoever it was expected to find something in his car," Pebbles theorized.

"Stone? What stone? Anlon, you didn't mention any stone in our call. It's also not in the officer's report," Jennifer queried, leaning forward again on the sofa in an "I eat little children" posture. She then turned to Pebbles and agreed, "And yes, Eleanor, it does have the markings of an act targeted specifically at Dr. Cully."

Embarrassed, Anlon said, "Ah, sorry. I don't know why I didn't mention it. Well, okay, that's not really true. I guess I was a little worried it might be taken as evidence."

Jennifer was a little miffed by the intentional oversight and her face reddened enough that Pebbles noticed it out of the corner of her eye. Anlon was looking down at the table where the stones sat, afraid to look up at Jennifer. She said, "Come on, Doc, we agreed to be open with each other. That's a pretty big oversight. Geez, these stones come up with everyone I talk to about this case."

Suddenly Pebbles realized her slip of the tongue had put Anlon in an awkward situation. But, he never mentioned that he kept that part quiet, so how was she to know?

Lifting his eyes to gaze directly at the irked detective, Anlon apologized. "You're right, Jennifer. I should have told the officer, and you, about the stone earlier. It's the blackish one on the table right in front of you."

"Have you both handled it since the break-in?" Jennifer questioned.

Both of them nodded yes. She scratched her head and admonished, "Well, so much for possible forensic evidence."

There was a pause of silence for an uncomfortable moment as Anlon tried to think of a way to recover and Jennifer sought to calm her irritation. At last Pebbles spoke. "Um, going back to my question, why take the will, even if the stone hadn't been there?"

Shaken from her slow burning stew, Jennifer focused on Pebbles' question and said, "I don't know. Anlon, I'll need to see a copy of the will as soon as possible. Will you please contact Mr. Grant in the morning? It's likely the thief followed Anlon to and from the attorney's office and saw him walk out with the papers. Maybe you were right, Anlon. Maybe his death has nothing to do with the stones. Maybe it's simple greed. Someone wanting to speed along an inheritance?"

Anlon agreed to secure another copy first thing. He said, "I don't know, it's possible, but it doesn't…"

Their conversation broke off when the doorbell rang again. At last, the elusive Pacal Flores had arrived.

When Anlon opened the door, he was instantly mesmerized by the smallish man who stood before him. Pacal was stocky yet trim with darkish red skin, white hair and eyes that bore through Anlon. His weathered face seemed regal, reminding Anlon of an ancient Mayan king come to life. He was attired formally in dress slacks, white shirt, black tie and blazer. He bowed slightly and said in a deep, slow voice that cracked a tinge as he finished, "Dr. Cully, I received your note. I am Pacal Flores. I am heartbroken for your loss."

Anlon bowed graciously in return, and said, "Pacal, please call me Anlon, and thank you very much for your kind words. I am sorry for your loss, too. I can tell Devlin and Dobson were important to you. Won't you please come in. I have a couple of guests I'd like you to meet."

Anlon stepped aside and in strode the proud yet humble man. Anlon led him to the den where Jennifer and Pebbles rose to greet the new guest. He said, "Pacal, this is Detective Lieutenant Jennifer Stevens from the Massachusetts State Police. She's investigating Dobson's death. And this is Pebbles, er, Eleanor McCarver, a friend of mine who came to help out."

Pacal greeted each woman with an air of respect and sedate charm in his manners. He said to Jennifer, "Detective, may I assume, given that the police are involved, that Mr. Matthew's death is considered questionable?"

Jennifer nodded, but didn't elaborate much, saying, "Yes, Mr. Flores. We are conducting an investigation into the circumstances of Mr. Dobson's death. I know you came here to visit Dr. Cully, but I'd like to ask you some questions, if I may."

She was surprised Pacal brought up Dobson's death immediately. Not a shrewd move if he was the perpetrator. He also didn't seem fazed at all by her presence there. She motioned to the sofa and asked politely, "Won't you sit down?"

When Pebbles and Anlon moved aside to the sofa opposite where Jennifer and Pacal settled, they were no longer blocking Pacal's view of the table with the three stones.

Before his bottom touched the sofa, he spied the black stone and he vaulted up, excitedly proclaiming while clasping his hands together, "You found it! Thank the heavens, you found it!"

All three of the others were shocked by the sudden outburst. Anlon rose instantly and queried, "Found what? The black stone? You know about the black stone? About all these stones?"

Jennifer quickly stood between the two men and said, "Gentlemen, please sit down. We'll get to the stones eventually. I have some other questions first."

Pacal retrieved a handkerchief from inside his blazer pocket and wiped his brow and upper lip. Nodding in agreement, he quelled his excitement and sat down on the sofa. He slumped his shoulders in a manner that made Anlon think he was relieved.

Anlon desperately wanted to shunt aside Jennifer's questioning , but, he reminded himself, the most important thing right now was to catch Dobson's killer. He sat as well and tried his best to contain his ardor to discuss the stones and Devlin's research. He was more certain than ever that they were linked to both men's deaths.

Jennifer said, "Thank you. I know you both have a lot to discuss, but it can wait. First off, Mr. Flores, I understand you were a research assistant of Dr. Wilson's, is that correct?"

"Yes, that's correct," he replied, "I came to work for Dr. Devlin five years ago, but I knew him for much longer than that."

"So you knew and worked with Mr. Dobson, too?"

"That is also correct. Mr. Matthew was his closest associate and long-time friend. They were inseparable," answered Pacal as he placed the handkerchief back in his blazer pocket.

Pebbles sat in silence and observed. She paid close attention to Pacal as Jennifer proceeded to question him. Like Anlon, she felt his majestic presence. He did not look nervous, and his answers didn't strike her as evasive, but he also wasn't going out of his way to provide Jennifer with expansive answers, being sure to pause briefly before answering each question and choosing his words carefully.

Looking him over, she noticed that although he was dressed formally, his clothes were time worn in places. She could tell the soles of his wingtip shoes were thin from long wear. The right blazer sleeve had a button missing and the cuff of his shirt sticking out from the sleeve was frayed. She also noticed a flat-faced gold ring on his right index finger. The ring had markings on it, but from her vantage point she couldn't make out what they were. The only observation that stood as significant to Pebbles was where he directed his eyes during Jennifer's interrogation. They rested on two spots throughout the dialogue, Jennifer's face and the black stone.

Nonetheless, Pacal was incredibly patient, enduring the questioning without so much as a fidget or flinch. When she finished her barrage, Jennifer recapped his answers. "So, you last saw Mr. Dobson on Friday in the late afternoon. He mentioned to you that Dr. Cully would be traveling to Stockbridge on Saturday and asked you to meet with him and Dr. Cully here on Sunday at noon. After Mr. Dobson left on Friday afternoon, you locked up the barn office and left. You neither saw nor spoke with Mr. Dobson again and you did not visit his house at any time after you said goodnight to Mr. Dobson on Friday?"

Pacal nodded slowly in response before saying, "That is what I've told you."

An interesting turn of phrase, Jennifer thought, but she didn't fence with him on semantics. Instead she continued, "Thank you for your cooperation, Mr. Flores. I would appreciate it if you would stop by the Stockbridge Police Department to let them fingerprint you, take a hair sample and swab your mouth for a DNA sample. It's standard procedure in a case like this, nothing to be alarmed about. Dr. Cully provided us his samples on Sunday."

Pacal bowed slightly and said, "I will do as you ask, Detective."

That's one cool customer, Jennifer concluded. Either he's totally innocent or a gifted actor. She held off on asking him about Devlin's death and Dobson's suspicions. She planned to tackle that topic after they talked about the stones. Peering over at Anlon, she could see the impatience in his expression. She said, "All yours, Doc."

Pacal interjected, "Before we do, Detective, how did Mr. Matthew die?"

She hesitated and looked away to Anlon and Pebbles before replying. "Confidentially, he died of carbon monoxide poisoning. He was found locked in his car in his driveway. It appears to us as if someone knocked him unconscious and stuffed a rag in the tailpipe with the motor running."

Pacal considered this in silence for a long minute, but did not otherwise react. At last he said, "Thank you, Detective, I will not repeat what you just said to anyone. Now, Dr. Cully, the Life Stones."

VIII

THE STORY STONE

"Life Stones?" Anlon queried, "is that what they're called?"

Pebbles disappeared from the room and returned with two more wine glasses and a second bottle of Cabernet. She set one of the glasses in front of Jennifer and poured a generous amount from the already opened first bottle. The second bottle was purely for backup. Jennifer smiled a friendly thank you and reached for the glass. She was warming up to Pebbles.

Pacal responded, "We do not know what the makers called them. The language spoken on the Story Stones is unknown. Dr. Devlin called them the Life Stones and so that is the name I know them by."

Pebbles placed a wine glass before Pacal and he said, "No, thank you, Miss Eleanor. But if Dr. Devlin has any of his fine scotch left, I will be pleased to drink to his memory."

With lightning speed, Pebbles spied the scotch bottle among others in the wet bar between the study and kitchen and returned with the bottle and a heavy, square-cut crystal whisky glass. With Pacal holding the glass, she poured him three-fingers' worth and resumed her place on the sofa next to Anlon. While Pacal spoke, she turned her attention again to the stones and studied each closely.

"Story Stones? Those are the square ones on the table here, right? And the other is called what?" Anlon asked, sitting on the edge of the sofa.

"Thank you, Miss Eleanor," Pacal responded. He took a healthy swallow of the aged scotch and continued. "The other stone we call a Sound Stone."

"Okay, Story Stone and Sound Stone. Let's talk about the Story Stones first. How do they work? I know they are highly magnetic from what Dobson shared, but he didn't show me how they function before he died." Anlon inquired.

"The Story Stone requires a second stone to be used. A stone that Dr. Devlin called the Port Stone. It fits in the circle on the back of a Story Stone. It is circular, about the size of a small can of tuna. The Port Stone is very magnetic," answered Pacal.

"Is there a Port Stone here? There wasn't anything like you described in Devlin's safe where these were kept," asked Anlon.

"Yes, there is one in the barn," Pacal replied. "I am still amazed that your uncle discovered how to use the two together."

"What do you mean?" Anlon asked.

Pacal took another large gulp of the scotch and ruminated, "Ah, I will miss sitting here with Dr. Devlin talking of ancient legends. He was a master on the subject of legends. He studied any text, scroll, glyph, oral histories or drawings he could find. He stored it all away in his mind.

"Once we discovered the Story Stone was magnetic, your uncle sat in the barn for hours just thinking. Something caused him to recall an old Olmec legend.

"In that legend, as told by a scribe who recorded the oral history of an elder Olmec leader, the storyteller wrote that men dressed like fish came out of the water and visited the Olmecs. The 'fish men' touched two stones together and showed the Olmecs how to farm the land.

"Other archaeologists and anthropologists thought this legend was an allegory, as they judge many other legends. But your uncle wondered, what if it's a literal translation? That led him to search his archive of notes and texts from other East and West legends for similar tales...and he found them.

"Somehow from these stories, he reasoned the second stone must be a magnet since the Story Stone itself is magnetic. So we tried magnets with the Story Stone. In fact, we tried many different magnets of varying strength and size but none worked.

"We were disappointed, but your uncle would not let go of his hunch. He was convinced that magnetism was the key to unlocking the stone. So, he shut himself away in the barn to think. Again, he asked himself, 'Is this story a literal translation?' If it was, then there must be a second kind of magnetic stone.

"He asked Mr. Matthew and me to find out if there were other stones recovered at the sites where Story Stones were found that looked circular like a hockey puck, but were smaller and exhibited unusual magnetic properties.

"It took weeks of searching, but we finally located such a stone in an antiquities storeroom of a university museum. To the curators, it was a piece of little value and so they sold it to Dr. Devlin for a small amount.

"When he brought the Port Stone into the barn, the Story Stone was on a counter. It started to vibrate. The closer he brought the Port Stone, the more violent the Story Stone shook. At last, when he picked the Story Stone up and rotated it so that the circular depression lined up with the Port Stone, the two stones snapped together with a loud clap."

Anlon was speechless, rapt in fact. He sat with mouth open and hands grasping his knees firmly. "So," he implored, "what happened then, and what about the other two depressions on the backside edges of the stone?"

Pacal nodded appreciatively, "Very good, Dr. Anlon. Yes, the other contours are very important. At first when the two stones snapped together, nothing happened. It was very disappointing. Dr. Devlin was crushed, although he did not know what would happen when the two stones met. It wasn't until he was handling it, flipping it this way and that, trying to understand the purpose of the two magnetic stones locked to each other, that the Heavens acted.

"Dr. Devlin held the Story Stone in front of him and rotated it so that the orientation aligned with the etching on the front. This caused his fingers to grasp the stone on the sides, touching the inside of the depressions. When he did, he cried aloud and trembled. Mr. Matthew and I were afraid he was hurt somehow. He stood trembling for several seconds before he looked at us and called out, 'Unbelievable.' "

As Pacal reached that point in his recounting of events, Anlon leapt off the sofa and stabbed a finger in the air, "Electrical impulse. The fingers triggered the magnetic stones like a start button. Oh my God, that's astounding. How was such a feat possible?"

"Exactly! Well done, Dr. Anlon," Pacal applauded, "Your uncle chose wisely to pass his research on to you."

"So what actually happened, did a video project? Did audio sound out?" Anlon queried in almost a frantic manner.

"No. To Mr. Matthew and me, nothing happened. But your uncle, the holder of the Story Stone, received both video and audio images in his mind," Pacal remarked, draining the last of the glass.

Anlon's hands riffled through his hair. He peered over at Pebbles and Jennifer. Both were awestruck by the story, but neither understood the implications like Anlon did. An ancient civilization — these Stone Benders — more than 10,000 years ago, had transferred mental images, including video and audio, onto a stone and created a way to access those images with the simple use of another stone. The stones themselves must be very rare or the makers understood rock in a wholly different way than man today.

It would be among the greatest scientific discoveries ever made. Wow! It was too much to fathom. Anlon slumped back on the sofa and disappeared into thought.

Pebbles, who had never seen Anlon so agitated, decided it was best to let him come down on his own. While she'd been listening to Pacal, she studied the Story Stones. She asked, "Pacal, are these the only two Story Stones?"

"Why, no, Miss Eleanor. There are hundreds of them spread around the world in different museums. There are likely hundreds or thousands more that lay undiscovered or were destroyed or cast away as useless pieces. What museum needs another mosaic tile or dinner plate? That's what they think these stones are."

"And the markings on the stones, they are labels? They indicate what story is depicted on the Stone?" Pebbles continued, picking up where her earlier conversation with Anlon had been interrupted.

"Very impressive, Miss Eleanor. Yes, Dr. Devlin thought the same, but he only viewed a handful of the Story Stones so he was not absolutely sure. May I have some more scotch, please?" Pacal inquired after praising Pebbles' question.

"Of course," she answered while pouring another two fingers for him. "And why are these two stones of different colors? Is it also some way to code or categorize the stones and are there other colors besides these two?"

Pacal nodded up and down slowly and said, "Dr. Anlon, you have a valuable assistant. She is a quick study. There are three other colors Dr. Devlin found besides these two on the table. There are sets of green, grey and dark brown stones in addition to sets of red and black like these. The black are the rarest. I've never personally viewed one. In fact, I did not know Dr. Devlin still had one in his possession. Where did you find it?"

Before Anlon could answer, Jennifer jumped in. Now that Pacal was relaxed, spinning tales and enjoying his scotch, it was time to ask about Devlin's death. She said, "Mr. Flores, before we talk about the black stone, did Mr. Dobson discuss Devlin's death with you?"

Pacal edged forward, still holding the scotch glass in one hand, and said, "You mean to ask, Detective, if Mr. Matthew thought the Professor was pushed off the mountain."

"Yes, that's exactly what I mean to ask," she responded, purposely raising her glass to take a sip of red wine as if to say, "We're all good friends here, enjoying a drink together, we can share secrets."

Pacal, gritting his teeth in a flash of suppressed anger, uttered, "Mr. Matthew did not need to say it. I thought it myself!"

Jennifer pressed on. "Why, Mr. Flores? Why did you both think he was pushed? Was he in some kind of trouble? Had someone threatened him? Is it anything to do with these stones and his research?"

Pacal threw back the remaining scotch in his glass and lowered his head. It was the first time the entire evening he did not directly look at the person asking him questions. Interlocking his fingers in a prayerful manner, he murmured, "We are all now in danger."

It was not a direct answer to the questions Jennifer posed, but his macabre statement heightened her suspicions. Devlin Wilson and Matthew Dobson had been murdered by someone with a strong motive connected to the research surrounding the stones.

Earlier, when Jennifer returned to her barracks from the sojourn to Mt. Whiteface, she spoke with her Captain, Bruno Gambelli. She relayed her conversation with Officer Keller and noted the coroner's surprise at the extent of the injuries and Dobson's mention of stones. She also mentioned the break-in of Anlon's car and the theft of the will. She was still irked that Anlon hadn't filled her in on the black stone. It might have sealed Gambelli's concurrence, given what Jennifer found when she searched the Blueberry Ledge Trail herself.

With Pacal's sinister words hovering in the silence, Anlon re-engaged in the discussion. He had only half listened as Pebbles and Jennifer deliberated with Pacal, but this last comment shook him. He exclaimed, "In Danger? All of us? Why?"

Spreading his hands in front of the stones, Pacal said, "They will discover you know about the stones. They will assume you are following Dr. Devlin's trail. They will try to stop you. They will come looking for me. They will try to take the stones."

Chills ran up Pebbles' spine. Instinctively, she reached up and loosened the bun atop her head and allowed her silky hair to fall and cover her bare neck. Anlon noticed her motion from the corner of his eye and turned to look at her. Not only had Pebbles ditched her purple dye, the shaggy locks had been styled into a classic, albeit a little long, bob cut. If Anlon had passed her on the street in a rush, he might not have known who she was.

"Who is 'they,' Mr. Flores?" Jennifer cut in.

Shaking his head and raising his palms to face Jennifer, Pacal said, "That, I do not know. People who want the stones."

"But, Pacal," Anlon questioned, "if there are so many other Story Stones, why do they want these stones? Dobson said there were others on the trail of Devlin's work. If someone else has figured out what he knew, why not go public immediately? They'd be world famous for all-time."

Jennifer answered before Pacal could speak, "Anlon, I don't think this is about claiming scientific credit or fame."

"What then?" a frustrated Anlon challenged. Though he was a gifted scientist, the waters they were treading in — motives for murder — were uncharted for him.

"Money," Pebbles chimed in while warming her frigid arms with her hands. "This kind of discovery would be worth a lot, don't you think?"

"Bingo!" Jennifer declared. "Money or greed is a very powerful motive that is at the core of many murders. There are elements of these two murders that point to money."

"Such as?" Anlon innocently asked as he stood to light the fireplace having noticed Pebbles' discomfort.

"I don't want to discuss our working hypothesis right now," Jennifer quickly responded. Actually, she didn't want to discuss the hypothesis in front of Pacal, whom she still distrusted despite all the information he had provided. She was confident that he was hiding something and it was time to get it on the table. "There may be other motives and I don't want to limit the field. Besides, there is more that Mr. Flores hasn't shared with us yet that may shed more light on possible motives. Isn't that right?"

"What do you mean to ask, Detective?" Pacal asked, showing no reaction to her accusation.

Okay, she thought, let's dance.

"How long ago did Dr. Wilson acquire the red Story Stone?" she asked.

Pondering the question, Pacal rubbed at his chin before slowly answering, "Nearly three years ago."

"And you said earlier that it was weeks after that before he first knew for certain what was on the stone?" Jennifer continued.

"Yes, that is what I said."

"So the Story Stone's contents and how to use it were known nearly three years ago," Jennifer prodded further, stating her observation rather than asking Pacal to confirm.

Anlon was struggling to keep up with Jennifer. He was at a loss to understand why the timing of the discoveries was important. He was aware, however, that Pacal twitched for the first time during the visit. Anlon said, "Jennifer, I'm afraid I'm lost in the dig here. Why does it matter when the discoveries were made?"

Though Jennifer answered Anlon's question, she never took her eyes off Pacal as she spoke, "The urgency of the crimes doesn't make sense. These murders were very public, despite the fact there are no witnesses that we know of yet. That means the killer took a big risk to pull them off.

"Someone could have been on the trail near Dr. Wilson and seen him get pushed. Someone may have driven down the street when Dobson was knocked out in his driveway. There is recklessness in the crimes and that suggests there was a very recent catalyst that demanded quick action. I agree with you, Mr. Flores. We are all in danger now. Perhaps you would be so kind to enlighten us as to the precise nature of the danger?"

Tapping the crystal glass with the gold ring on his hand, Pacal sat silently mulling Jennifer's analysis. Pebbles noticed beadlets of perspiration dotting his forehead. He's trapped, Pebbles thought, and he's going to shut down.

It reminded Pebbles of a deposition she'd been present for during her brief stint as a first year associate. She was just a gofer in the matter, making copies, tracking down witnesses and grabbing coffee for the more senior attorneys working the case.

For most of the deposition, the critical witness had been affable, almost cocky. When the lead attorney sniffed a hole in his story, the counselor dove in hard with devastating effect. The change in the witness' body language overtly shifted to a defensive posture. The witness' lawyer asked for a break. The lead attorney, recognizing the tipping point, paused his questioning and turned off the recorder. He excused himself from the room and let the witness sit with his own thoughts and his lawyer. A junior attorney from Pebbles' firm offered the man a fresh bottle of water and stepped out of the room, too, motioning Pebbles to join her.

The three stood in the hallway together for about 15 minutes before the lead attorney sent the junior attorney back in the room. A moment later, the junior attorney texted the lead litigator to return, as the witness was ready to come clean.

Pebbles now watched Jennifer execute a similar strategy, though with her steely gaze riveted on him, she wasn't giving Pacal much space to reflect on his options. Pebbles tried to break the tension by retrieving the scotch bottle from the coffee table in front of Pacal. She smiled softly at him and poured a little more in his empty glass.

As Pacal raised his head to return the smile by way of thanks, Anlon thought again, "cleverly engaging," as he warmed himself at the fire. The fewer eyes trained on Pacal the better, understanding the purpose of Pebbles' gesture.

Pacal sipped the scotch and loosened the tie around his neck. Jennifer's glare continued unabated, but she did not speak.

At last, Pacal stammered, "If I, if I tell you, you will be in more danger than you are now."

Undaunted, Jennifer pronounced, "Let me help you start, Mr. Flores. The black stone is the catalyst, correct?"

Pacal nodded in assent.

"And the black stone, as you mentioned, is very different than the other Story Stone, correct?"

Again, he nodded but didn't speak.

"If I guess correctly why the black stone is the catalyst, will you at least acknowledge I'm on the right track?" Jennifer asked, relaxing her posture and pouring herself a splash of the scotch into her now empty wine glass.

Anlon darted a look of "what does she have up her sleeve" at Pebbles who shrugged in return, a sign of mutual ignorance.

Downing the scotch in a single swallow, Jennifer mused, "Dr. Cully told me yesterday that when Dr. Wilson died unexpectedly, he was in pursuit of four new avenues that were somehow connected to his research into these stones. I think Dr. Wilson discovered those four new avenues on the black stone."

Anlon wanted to knock his head against the wall for not seeing the connection earlier. Again he found himself impressed by Jennifer's memory.

She continued, "I think when he started digging in, or when all three of you started digging in, it caught someone else's attention. And that someone wanted Dr. Wilson stopped in his tracks immediately before he made any further progress.

"Of course, Dobson had to be dispatched quickly, too, for the same reason. Which means there is a target on your back as well, Mr. Flores.

"And now Dr. Cully is here and is poking around on his own, and the police are now involved, too, because our villain here was sloppy. Reckless.

"The killer wants the black stone, not because he or she needs it. My guess is the killer already knows what's on it. No, what our unknown perp wants is to prevent anyone else from finding what the killer found on the black stone.

"How'd I do, Mr. Flores?"

Pacal's nervous disposition ebbed and he slumped backward against the sofa. He remarked, "Kudos to you. You are close to the right path, Detective, but not on it."

Anlon couldn't stand it any longer. He returned to the sofa opposing the one Pacal and Jennifer shared and cried, "Whoa! Jennifer, explain to me how you sorted all that out? I barely got a chance to talk to you about the black stone."

Pebbles offered an explanation before Jennifer could speak. "There are six rays on the black stone carving that each point to different etched objects. Two types of stones have already been discovered, so the remaining four types must be described on the black stone."

"Way to go, Eleanor!" said Jennifer. "That's exactly what I thought when I looked at the stone and recalled my talk with Anlon last night."

Pebbles smiled broadly in response to Jennifer's praise and said, "You can call me Pebbles."

Anlon rolled his eyes at the lovefest between the two sleuths while inside he was still playing catch up. As he continued to consider Jennifer and Pebbles' deductions, he shared, "Devlin's attorney told me that Devlin brought the stone to his office four days before he died. Mr. Grant said Devlin was adamant that he wanted Grant to hold it in his office safe and that he was only to give it to me if something happened to him.

"That implies he was very uncomfortable keeping it here, which does seem to point to the black stone having more value than the other ones. But if you're right, Jennifer, why didn't the thief steal the stone when he had the chance this afternoon when he swiped the will from my car?"

Jennifer had to agree with Anlon. "It is a hole in my theory, no question."

Pebbles' eyes were glued on Pacal. While his edgy countenance had abated, she noticed him twitch during the last exchange between Anlon and Jennifer.

Turning towards Pacal, Anlon implored, "Won't you help us, Pacal? My uncle trusted you and now that he's dead I need your help. If we don't figure this out together, then Devlin and Dobson's killer gets away with murdering your friends. Is that what you want?"

Pacal was slow to respond. He absently twisted the gold ring on his finger before saying, "Dr. Anlon, I want justice for my friends, but I don't want it at the price of more deaths."

"That's noble of you, Pacal, but, as you can see, I am a grown man capable of defending myself. And with these two expert detectives at my side, one of them who wears a badge and a gun, I'm not stopping until I get to the root of the matter, whether you help me or not," Anlon countered with confident resolve.

Pacal shook his head and said, "You won't see them coming. You have no idea what they can do. The Detective's gun will do you no good. I see I'm going to have to show you what I mean."

IX

THE SOUND STONE

It was dark by now outside and despite the summer sounds of crickets chirping and frogs croaking, it was a rather cool evening.

The group stood in the driveway in the dim light cast by lantern-shaped fixtures aside the garage bays. The diminutive Pacal had removed his jacket and gallantly handed it to Pebbles, as she was underdressed for the evening compared to Anlon and Jennifer. She warmed her hands in the pockets while Pacal turned the Sound Stone over in his hands and asked Anlon, "Did Mr. Matthew talk to you about the Sound Stone?"

Pebbles and Jennifer paid close attention to Anlon's answer. Neither had heard him describe the stone in detail. He said, "Dobson said it was a projector of sorts. A stone that created sound waves that could move other objects. Very large objects. He spoke of Tiahuanaco and the Pyramids and said that men used the Sound Stones to lift, carry and place the massive blocks. But he didn't get a chance to demonstrate it before he died."

Pacal nodded in agreement with Anlon's description, but corrected him on a few points. "A good description but forgive me for pointing

95

out that the stone has more than one potential purpose. Yes, it was used for building and moving, but it was also used for destructive purposes. It can also heal wounds, according to the Master Stone."

"Master Stone?" Anlon intervened, "What is the Master Stone?"

"Oh, I am sorry, Dr. Anlon. I thought I mentioned it earlier. Devlin called the black Story Stone the Master Stone," Pacal answered.

"Why did he call it something different? What makes it so special?"

"I will tell you later. Let us first discuss the Sound Stone. The scientists who crafted it over 10,000 years ago understood that each object, living or inanimate, has a sound frequency that can be agitated. If one taps into an object's unique frequency and agitates the object with consistent force, it can create movement. Agitate softly and it can speed the healing of broken bones and other wounds through vibration. Agitate it with aggressive force, it can produce lethal effects."

Anlon was annoyed that Pacal skirted by the Master Stone, but he was fascinated enough by his description of the Sound Stone that he didn't challenge him.

The simple elegance of the Sound Stone intrigued Anlon. Small enough to be carried most places, it was a crane, weapon and first aid kit in one. Incredibly imaginative. He knew from his own scan of peer-reviewed journals that a range of researchers believed sound could be used to move objects. And with ultrasound, the medical profession had discovered the use of sound to detect biological anomalies and heal certain kinds of injuries, not to mention clean teeth. So the scientific basis of the Sound Stone was credible. It was mind-blowing that such a device had been around for so long and no one had any idea.

Pacal told them that, again, Devlin relied on literal translations from Egyptian and Incan oral histories — combined with some rudimentary drawings at several sites — to seek artifacts that fit the description.

Like the Story Stones, they also found numerous Sound Stones gathering dust in various museum artifact collections. Deemed unremarkable, the museums were more than happy to donate three of them to Devlin.

Then, with Dobson's and Pacal's help, Devlin had to figure out how to *use* the stone. After watching a demonstration of its use on the red Story Stone — where they learned of the existence of the Sound Stone in the first place — they each tried various experiments with their own Sound Stone to make it work.

"It turned out that I was the best at utilizing the device," Pacal proudly announced.

Turning to Pebbles, he asked, "Do you trust me, Miss Eleanor?"

"Um," she answered, "depends. Why?"

"Please stand still for a moment," Pacal requested. "Dr. Anlon and Detective, please take a few steps back."

"Anlon?" Pebbles cried, unsure and frightened about what was about to happen.

Pacal stood before Pebbles and placed his mouth to the back of the stone, pointing it at Pebbles and crouching his body so that his aim was focused on her center of gravity near her hips. Then he began to hum against the stone. At first, Pebbles felt nothing, but then she felt a tickling, vibrating sensation start to flow through her body. Again, she cried, "Anlon, what's happening?!"

Pacal stood erect, still maintaining his hum, and Pebbles' feet lifted about two feet off the ground. She screamed, waving her arms and legs wildly as if trying to balance as she floated, suspended in mid-air. Pacal held her aloft for a few more seconds before gently lowering her back to the ground. Pebbles stumbled when her feet touched the ground and she fell over onto the driveway's surface.

Anlon rushed to her aid, but she pushed him away as she regained her feet. Blowing strands of her disheveled bob from her face, she panted, "I'm okay. That was kind of cool, even though I freaked out a little. Do it again, Pacal! Sit me on top of the Land Rover."

There was the scrappy Pebbles McCarver he knew, Anlon thought.

Pacal lowered his torso again and raised Pebbles 10 feet in the air effortlessly. Turning with her held by the sound waves generated by the stone, he guided her through the air until he positioned her over the luggage rack of the Land Rover. Pebbles, more confident in his skill this time, raised her legs so that when she descended under his power she was in a sitting position. He ceased humming about an inch above the SUV and Pebbles plopped on top of the car with a small thud.

"Ouch," she yelped before laughing, "your landings need work, Pacal."

He laughed, too, a deep booming laugh that was disproportionate to his small body. In answer, he said, "I'm learning, I'm learning!"

She started to crawl down when Pacal shouted, "Stay there, Miss Eleanor. I have another demonstration for you all."

Pebbles nodded eagerly. This was fun! She awaited Pacal to resume humming, expecting him to lift her and return her to the driveway. She closed her eyes and held out her arms as if waiting to be carried. Her ears detected the sound of Pacal's hum but it was a different pitch this time. She felt vibration again but this time it wasn't in her body. All of a sudden she realized what was happening and flung her hands around the bars of the luggage rack just as Pacal lifted the Land Rover off the driveway surface. Up, up, up she and the vehicle went until she was treetop level. Petrified, Pebbles wanted to scream but no sound emitted from her mouth.

Anlon watched in stunned silence as Pacal lowered them both back to the driveway, this time placing the auto on the macadam surface as gently as a mother lying a baby in a manger.

Jennifer Stevens staggered backwards and blinked repeatedly, cursing the mix of wine and scotch coursing through her blood vessels and brain.

When the SUV landed, Pebbles jumped off and announced, "Okay, I'm done being the guinea pig here. I think I wet myself."

Anlon roared with laughter and said, "Now I believe the story about how you earned your nickname! Wow, that was amazing! What technology!"

Jennifer, still not trusting her eyes, asked of no one in particular, "Did I just see that? Did he pick Pebbles and the car up to the top of the house like they were a kite?"

All of them burst into laughter, and Jennifer ran to exchange high fives with Pebbles, bellowing, "You're fearless!"

Pebbles, in a giddy, wine-influenced mood herself, retorted, "Not me. I had zippo idea he was going to do that. Seriously, I wet myself a little!"

When their hooting subsided, they noticed Pacal standing solemn-faced looking at them. Anlon, standing apart from where Jennifer and Pebbles met to slap hands, inquired, "What's wrong, Pacal?"

"I'm terribly sorry, Dr. Anlon," the regal research assistant earnestly replied.

Quickly, he ducked, pointed the stone at Anlon, raised the stone to his lips and blasted a sharp toned hum against it.

Anlon had no warning, he never sensed it coming. The sound collided with him in a violent burst and he flew 10 feet past the driveway and tumbled several times on the grass before coming to a sudden, painful halt. Gasping for breath, his lungs devoid of air, Anlon could barely see through hazy eyes. His ears rang and his head throbbed where he struck the grass-covered ground.

Jennifer shouted at Pacal, "What in the hell was that for?! Anlon, are you okay?"

Jennifer and Pebbles both rushed to Anlon's side, gently lifting him into a sitting position while he moaned and tried to clear his head.

Pebbles, angry and shocked, spat at Pacal, "You could have killed him!"

Pacal absorbed the abuse as he walked towards Anlon. "Yes, I could have killed him. Easily. And he never would have seen it coming. As I said. The same way Dr. Devlin and Mr. Matthew never saw it coming."

"What do you mean?" a flustered Jennifer demanded. "Stop speaking in riddles!"

Pacal held the stone out in his hand and quietly said, "I mean, Detective, that you are most likely looking at the type of weapon used to kill Dr. Devlin."

Anlon laid on the sofa soaking in the bathing heat from the fireplace in Devlin's study while holding a freezer bag of ice cubes against his left shoulder. Pebbles sat on the coffee table next to him and ministered some liquid ibuprofen she had just purchased on a quick trip into town.

By now, it was after 10:00 p.m., and both Jennifer and Pacal were gone. Before they left, Pacal again apologized to Anlon and said, "The makers of the stones, Dr. Anlon, they bent their will into these special rocks by means we don't understand yet. But the people chasing their secrets are not like you and I or Dr. Devlin. They care not for the wonder of discovery and breakthrough technologies. From their actions, it is clear they are ruthless and single-minded. I fear they will find the other four objects and use them for evil purposes."

Anlon, wincing as he spoke, asked, "What are the other four stones, Pacal?"

Pacal waved him off and replied, "Not tonight, Dr. Anlon. It's been an eventful evening and I think we all would benefit from clear heads before discussing anymore."

"Careful," Anlon smirked in return, "the last guy to say those words to me was dead before sunrise!"

Pacal nodded understanding, shook Anlon's hand, bowed to the two women and stepped out the front door.

As he descended the stairs, Jennifer called after him, "Mr. Flores, please remember to stop by the Stockbridge Police Department tomorrow morning, and please don't leave the area without my permission until I say otherwise."

He waved his understanding and disappeared down the driveway. Until that moment, none of them realized Pacal did not arrive in a car.

Pebbles rubbed Anlon's forearm holding the ice bag and inquired, "For real, how bad is it, A.C.? Do we need to get you to a hospital?"

The tender look from her eyes was healing in its own way. Anlon said, "Nah, I'll be fine. I'm sure it's just a pulled muscle. Thank you for the medicine, it tasted nasty by the way."

She smiled and then stuck her tongue out at him. No tongue stud either, Anlon observed.

Now that they were alone, he asked the question he'd been dying to put to Pebbles all day. "Seriously, thank you. Not just for the pain reliever, for everything. I know it's been a very long day for you, with travel and all, but I gotta know, what's going on with you? Eleanor? The new look? Mind you, I'm not complaining, you look hotter than you did before, if that's possible."

Pebbles blushed and displayed an over-dramatic open-mouthed stare before answering, "Why, Dr. Cully, that's the first time you've ever said you think I'm hot. I was beginning to believe you didn't think about me in that way."

Anlon, sheepishly bit his lip and replied, "Oops, guess *my* secret is out now."

"Ha ha. I think the medicine, Cabernet and Sound Stone attack have loosened your tongue, Anlon. What else would you like to tell me?" She winked at him seductively.

"Pebbles, are you purposely avoiding answering my question?" he posited, winking in return.

Leaning forward, Pebbles hovered her sleek body inches above his outstretched figure on the sofa. She was a bit tipsy, too, and whispered, "I like it when you're loopy."

Anlon quivered from the vibration of her whisper in his ear. As she sat back on the table with an evil grin, Anlon remarked, "Yep, definitely avoiding the question."

"Okay, okay," she said with a feigned pout. "I suppose we're going to discuss this sooner or later, so we might as well do it now since you're drowsy and there's a strong possibility you won't remember my answer in the morning."

Pebbles lowered herself to kneel on the floor next to him so that her face was close to Anlon's. She looked down anxiously at her unpainted fingernails, her raven bob shrouding much of her face. She spoke in a soft, uncertain voice. "You've been so good to me, Anlon. When you asked me to come and help you, it made me feel so good. I don't want you to think of me as just a happy hour buddy. I want to make a difference for you. I didn't think you needed a freak show right now, a distraction. You need someone focused and, well, professional. So I thought I should put aside Pebbles and reconnect with Eleanor, because Eleanor kicks ass...demurely."

At this last statement, Anlon burst out laughing until his shoulder and ribs reminded him of his injuries. He peered up at the soft radiance of the fire shimmering on her face and raised his hand to stroke her cheek. Pebbles was truly a sweet soul, Anlon had always known it. That she cared so much about how he viewed her surprised him, and her words touched his heart. He said, "I don't care what you look like or what you call yourself so long as you stick around. You are a treasure."

Small tears welled in her eyes and she leaned forward to kiss him. Their first, real, this-is-more-than-friendship kiss.

When they separated, she wriggled her nose and said, "That was wonderful...and weird! Let's do it again!"

They kissed again, and again, and again. Coming up for air, Pebbles said with sudden surprise as she rose and ran back into the kitchen, "Oh, I forgot something important."

Anlon, his shoulder and rib pain now lower in the pecking order of physical sensations pulsing through his body, sat up a little and called, "Hey, come back here! I liked where that was going!"

He could hear her laugh echo from the kitchen. She returned dangling a white cloth by its corner with two fingers. She extended it for his observation and proudly said, "Look!"

Anlon, puzzled by the cloth and by her sudden shift from the spark of romance between them, questioned, "Um, okay. A white cloth. Are you surrendering?"

She placed both hands on her hips and said, "No, silly. If I were surrendering to you, I would be *waving* the cloth not holding it still... and I'd be naked. Duh."

"True," he chuckled, lying his head back on the sofa's throw pillow. "Tell me about the cloth."

"It's Pacal's handkerchief. I stole it from his jacket when he let me wear it," she beamed.

"Now why would you do that?"

"Because there's no way he's coming back, Anlon. And he's 100 percent not stopping by the Stockbridge Police Department to give samples tomorrow," she said with a mocking "how could you be so naïve" expression.

Anlon was confused. He did wonder if maybe he was suffering from a concussion and experiencing a hallucination. He questioned, "Oh really, and how, Sherlock, do you know that?"

"Jane Marple, not Sherlock, if you please," she teased. "Call it a woman's intuition. I have here his fingerprints and DNA from his sweat. Remember when he wiped his face with it? Oh, and what did you make of the etching on his ring?"

Anlon screwed up his face in a "what on God's green Earth are you talking about" look, and said, "Ring?"

"Yes, the one on his right index finger. You know, the one he was tapping on the whisky glass. I got a couple good looks at it when I poured his drinks," she prodded.

"Sad to say I didn't notice his ring. Did you steal that, too?" Anlon asked.

She uttered a playful laugh in response, shaking her bob cut in the negative, and sat back down on the coffee table facing Anlon, carefully placing the handkerchief next to the three stones. She gingerly picked up the black Master Stone and held the face so Anlon could view it. Pointing at one of the carved objects, she exclaimed, "His ring had an etching just like this one right here."

Anlon sat up to face her, his sore ribs resuming top sensation priority, and stared intently at the object, saying, "Really? Wow, good observation, Pebbles. I'm not sure what to make of it until we know what the object is."

"I know what to make of it, even though I don't know what the object is. It's confirmation that Pacal's going to disappear," Pebbles confidently stated.

Anlon stared at her with mouth agape. *Either I'm a total moron or she's a total savant. I'm not sure which is more frightening*, he thought.

Pebbles continued, "Don't you see? Pacal was purposely trying to scare us off. Why? Because he's after one of the objects himself and doesn't want us to find it before he does."

"How can you be so sure? It was incredibly stupid of him to wear the ring if that's the case."

"But he didn't know the Master Stone was here! Don't you remember how surprised he was when he saw it. Remember, too, that he said he hadn't viewed the black stone himself. So that means he knew about the other object from somewhere else. I'll bet he's been searching for it on his own."

"You're out pretty far on a limb, young lady," Anlon cautioned, "but...I have to admit, your theory sounds plausible to me. We won't have long to wait to find out, right? If he doesn't show up for fingerprints, you officially possess Spidey-senses."

"Oh, I'm right, you can count it, Doctor-Know-It-All," Pebbles zestfully needled as she stood and hopped up and down. "I'm not out on a limb, I'm dancing on it!"

"Is that a fact?" challenged Anlon, rising to face her, broad smile on his face. He dropped the ice bag on the floor and said, "How about a friendly wager?"

"Ooh, I like. And I know exactly what you're giving me when I'm right!"

Anlon arched an eyebrow and said, "Oh really, and what might that be?"

"The keys to a certain shiny, hot pink scooter that's gathering dust in your garage!" Pebbles stated, shaking an invisible set of keys before Anlon's face while continuing to hop up and down.

"Perfect!" Anlon rejoined. "And what do I get when the limb gives way and you and your ego come crashing down?"

Pebbles ceased hopping and withdrew her imaginary jingling fingers from Anlon's face. He really was fun to be around. She was glad he didn't get angry with her trash talk.

She stroked her chin and furrowed her brow as if deep in thought pondering her side of the wager. Then it came to her and she grew a devilish grin and suggested, "Okay, Anlon. In the remotest of scenarios where I might be slightly off base and he shows up for fingerprints tomorrow, then..."

"Yes, yes, get on with it."

"I'll waive that white flag and surrender to you," she seductively winked.

Anlon flushed a tad and his eyes fluttered a little as he visualized her naked surrender. He extended a hand and said, "You have a deal, demure Miss Eleanor."

"Uh, uh," she admonished, "this deal gets sealed with a kiss not a handshake."

She stepped forward and circled his waist, pulling Anlon against her warm, firm body. Their lips tenderly danced as they tightly held one another with eyes closed. Pebbles felt triumphant. She thought, I win either way!

Anlon, reveling in her embrace, prayed, "Holy Smokes, I hope I win!"

When the lights extinguished throughout Devlin's house, the burly hooded man crouching in the underbrush near the barn, exhaled a sigh of relief, "Whew, gone to sleep at last."

He waited another 20 minutes as a precaution before creeping quietly across the dewy grass to the low slung side of the building closest to the trees. He jumped and caught hold of the protruding awning with his gloved hands and hoisted himself atop the lower roof. Moving quickly and silently along the modestly sloped surface, he arrived at the backside of the barn.

Holding the edge of the steep-pitched upper roof with one hand, he extended his body to reach one of two small, square windows that provided light to the barn's loft. With gloved hand, he punched the glass above the inner latch, breaking a section of the upper pane's glass.

The muffled crack of the breaking window and the tinkle of shards falling on the loft floor were barely audible and, as he expected, no alarm sensors were on the upper floor windows. Even so, the hooded man rested in a prone position on the lower roof for several minutes, patiently watching and listening for signs of stirring from the main house.

When none followed, he flipped the latch open, raised the lower pane and grasped the window ledge. Letting go of the edge of the steep-sloped upper roof, he stepped off the lower roof and dangled by one hand on the window ledge until joined by the other hand. He powerfully raised his torso up and slithered through the open window.

Once inside, he knelt on the floor and carefully swept away the shards he could sense with his gloved hands. He unhooked the slimline pack strapped to his back and retrieved a lightweight pair of night vision goggles. Reaching in the bag again, he extracted and then slipped on fabric shoe covers over his boots.

He paused for another few moments to allow his eyes to adjust to the greenish light of the goggles before beginning his exploration. As much as he wanted to quickly grab what he had come for and flee, he knew it would take some time to find the articles among Devlin's artifacts.

He reminded himself to be patient. He would only get one crack at this. Once the break-in and missing pieces were discovered, Cully would install more elaborate security and the opportunity to handle matters stealthily would be history.

Slinking down the loft stairs, he first concentrated his search on the two tall storage racks where rows of shelves held trays with a variety of relics. With methodical purpose, the hooded man started along the top row of the first rack removing each tray and inspecting its contents, ever-vigilant to avoid making noise.

Thirty minutes into his search, he was frustrated. So far, no Stones, no statues and no map. He replaced the last tray on the lowest shelf of the second rack and turned his attention to the bank of wide cabinets in the main room. The locks were childishly easy to pick and soon he was sliding wide, thin shelves out to reveal smaller trinkets and documents. The documents would not be readable with the goggles, so he reached in his pocket for a thin flashlight with adjustable beam, and raised the goggles atop his head, pushing away the hood.

Another 30 minutes into the search and the burly man was outright livid. He searched every shelf, every cabinet and every drawer. No sign of any of the pieces. He knocked on walls and scanned the floorboards for signs of a hidden safe or storage.

The only things left to inspect were two laptops. The laptops would definitely have passwords and that meant it would take time to crack their codes. Looking at the glowing face of his watch, he realized he didn't have time to try now. But there was a dilemma.

He only had room in the slim backpack for one of the two laptops. At first he considered tossing the second one from the window but thought the fall would damage it and was concerned it might make noise hitting the gravel bed below the backside of the barn.

So he had to make a quick decision about which one to take. Scanning the desks for clues, he opted to take the computer on the desk that was piled with documents written to Devlin versus the one with papers addressed to Dobson.

The thief paced as he pondered what to do with the second laptop. He thought of smashing it, but again worried about the noise. It was possible they had glass break sensors on the first floor that might activate with an attempt to destroy the laptop. He didn't have anything magnetic that would wipe the hard drive with him, and he rightly assumed they probably had back up files anyway. He reasoned it was more important than any other consideration to know what was on Devlin's computer before Cully discovered the break-in.

So he stuffed Devlin's laptop in the backpack, scanned around the shop to make sure he hadn't left anything behind and scurried up the loft stairs to exit the loft window.

"The map better be on the computer," he angrily spat to himself as he disappeared into the woods, "or this is going to get uglier fast!"

X

CHASING SHADOWS

"No dice, Stevens," Gambelli barked, arms folded across his chest. "There is zero chance I'm walking into the Lieutenant Colonel's office or the DA's office upstairs with the story you just told me and request a search warrant. Not happening."

The following morning, Jennifer sat expressionless across from Gambelli's desk in the Pittsfield office of the Berkshire Detective Unit and absorbed the tirade. She was no fool; Jennifer knew before she told Gambelli about Pacal's demonstration it would be hard to believe, but she thought she could still finesse her way into a search warrant of Pacal Flores' home. In retrospect, she wished she'd had the presence of mind to video the demonstration on her cell phone.

"Pacal promised to come in today to give us fingerprints, hair and DNA samples. If I get a ping from any of those matching physical evidence we have from the crime scene, will you reconsider?" Jennifer inquired.

"If you have a witness or some sort of physical evidence directly linking Mr. Flores to the crime, I can go to bat for you. But right now, we have no witnesses for Matthew Dobson's death, very little physical evidence to pursue — none of which, by the way, points at Mr. Flores currently — and no credible motive for the crime, other than Dobson's inheritance from Devlin Wilson. Heck, even if the story you told me is true, Dobson didn't die of a knock on the head. He died from CO poisoning. We're speculating he was placed in the car unconscious, and we don't even know that for sure! I need more to go on besides stones that can make people fly by humming on them! Come on, Detective, you know better than that."

When he finished, Jennifer asked, "What about Devlin Wilson's death?"

"Again, you have no definitive connection between the two deaths, and it's not in our jurisdiction anyhow. Wilson's death was ruled by the coroner as an accidental fall and Meredith PD's report gives no reason to think otherwise," he railed, slapping the desk to emphasize his point, causing his Patriots bobble-head collection to start a chorus of head shaking.

Jennifer questioned, "And the GPS device I found in the rocks above where his body was found? I think we should send it to forensics for fingerprints."

"Nope," Gambelli admonished. "It was an excellent piece of detective work to find it, I give you that, Stevens, but it's not our death to investigate, and not in our jurisdiction, as you know very well. Send it to the Meredith PD and let them deal with it. If Wilson's prints are on it and it changes their view about his death, then it's up to them to pursue the lead. Look, I'm not trying to beat you down here, but you're grasping at straws, Stevens."

She was disappointed with his answer, but Jennifer had half expected the denial before she opened her mouth. Her face reddened with frustration and she looked away from her boss to the GPS in the evidence bag in her lap. Jennifer was confident it was a valuable clue and now she'd have to give it away before she knew if it held anything of importance.

Gambelli softened his tone and said, "I know this is a tough case, Stevens. There's very little to go on, but rather than get wrapped up in conspiracy theories and phantom weapons, you need to follow the leads you have. Find out if Dobson had a will, find out who benefits from his death. Search his house again for evidence. The first search focused solely on any physical signs of entry or theft that might connect to his death. I'd also take a look through Wilson's office to see if Dobson left something there we can chase down, or if there's anything connecting the two deaths. Those are your best bets and the trail is getting cold, Stevens. You need to pick up your game."

"Okay, Cap, I hear you loud and clear," Jennifer replied on her way out of Gambelli's office.

Returning to her cubicle, she took a moment to compose herself. Even though she couldn't argue the bases of Gambelli's rejections, Jennifer was convinced Devlin and Dobson's deaths were connected and that Pacal and the stones were mixed up in it somehow. She would follow the Captain's recommended course of action, but she wasn't giving up on pursuing her own line of investigation.

Flipping open her notepad, Jennifer found where she'd scribbled Officer Keller's cell number. After a few rings, he answered, "Keller."

"Hey there, Sam, it's Jennifer Stevens from the Mass State Police. We spoke yesterday," she said in a friendly voice.

"Oh, hello, Detective. What's up?"

"Well, I've got something that might interest you. I decided to go have a look at where Devlin Wilson's body was found and while I was hiking, I found a GPS tracking device," she casually mentioned, hoping her snooping around their crime scene didn't irritate him. She was sure she would need his help and didn't want to alienate him.

"Really? Close to where the body was found?" the surprised officer queried. "We were very thorough combing the area."

Quick to avoid the appearance that she was questioning their professional search skills, she added, "Actually, no. I found it about 300 feet higher than the spot on the trail where it appears he fell from."

"Hmmm…it's probably not his then. Lots of people drop things along the trail," a disinterested Keller reasoned.

"I hear you, and under other circumstances I'd agree, but this device has his name written on the back of it."

There was a silent pause on the other end of the line as Keller processed Jennifer's comment. Finally, he said, "You said about 300 feet above where we think he fell from? But the trail doesn't bend back around at that elevation."

Jennifer realized she was treading on delicate grounds by pressing the matter. "Yes, I know. I did a little rappelling down the rocks on the face of the cliff from higher up."

"That's pretty dangerous, Detective, even for an experienced climber," chastised Keller, his voice developing a hint of annoyance.

And what makes you think I'm not an experienced climber, she thought, but she let this comment go uncontested. Jennifer suspected that Keller considered Devlin's death a closed case and was starting to resent her poking around.

Nevertheless, she pressed on. "Well, when you told me the coroner thought he fell from a greater distance, I decided to check it out. I'm going to send it to you by overnight express. I bagged it so you can run forensics on it. It may end up being a waste of time. If he climbed up that sheer face, I can easily see how he could have slipped and fell. But, just to be sure, I think it's worth checking for prints."

Keller reluctantly agreed. "Okay, no harm in checking, but seems like a long shot. I'll let the coroner know. Even if there's someone else's prints on it though, I don't know if it proves anything. Some random hiker could have found it and tossed it there."

Jennifer didn't want to denigrate his speculation, but someone throwing a handheld device nearly straight up 300 feet was impossible, and why would any hiker toss away an expensive GPS device? She passed on the opportunity to correct him and pleasantly said, "Thanks, Sam. I'll send it tonight. Would you do me two favors after you receive it?"

"Depends. What's on your mind, Detective?" Keller warily asked.

"Could you let me know if you find any prints on it besides Devlin's so we can compare them with prints we have from the scene of Dobson's murder to see if there's a match? I know it's a longshot."

"Okay, that shouldn't be a problem. And the other favor?"

"I didn't handle the device before I bagged it and its battery was dead when I found it. After your forensic people get done with it, can you have someone power it up? It has a mini-USB port on the side for charging. I'd be interested to know if there's anything helpful on the device once its powered."

"Like what?" the Meredith PD officer suspiciously asked.

Obviously, Officer Keller was not a rappeller, hiker or mountain climber. The device might show multiple interesting things. It could show the path Devlin took, it might show his planned destination, it might show how long and how far he'd hiked or the last recorded point of his hike, and it might just show if he shared his intended route with anyone. Jennifer earlier wrote down the make and model number of the device to check out the possibilities later.

"I'm not sure," she falsely answered, "but if you get it powered up will you let me know if you found anything? It's also a longshot, but it might have a bearing on our investigation down here."

"Okay, will do. Thanks for the lead, Detective."

Munching on doughnuts for breakfast, Anlon and Pebbles went over their plans for the day at their table in Stockbridge's Main Street Diner.

"So I say let's divide up and get twice as much done today, agreed?" Anlon proposed, watching Pebbles devour her second chocolate-covered glazed doughnut. The bulge of food wedged in her cheek while she chewed looked like a wad of chaw in a baseball player's mouth.

She nodded in agreement, exhibiting the social grace not to speak with a mouthful of food, but her eyes were glued on the third chocolate-glazed doughnut on the plate between them and not on Anlon.

He said, "I called over to Devlin's attorney, George Grant, before we drove over here and let him know you might be stopping by his office to pick up another copy of Devlin's will instead of me. I gave him a description of you and your full name. He said you'll need to show him your driver's license to get the document.

"Grant also gave me Anabel Simpson's address again over the phone. I'll concentrate on her this morning. She lives up in Bennington, Vermont, so the drive to and from will eat up a good chunk of the day, assuming I can reach her by phone and arrange to meet her today."

Pebbles, after washing down the doughnut with a tall glass of skim milk, said, "Man those are good! Nothing like bakery-fresh doughnuts. Your plan sounds good to me. Is there anything else you want me to follow up on?"

"Yes, you might ask Grant if he was able to track down Dobson's will or attorney. And I could use your help finalizing a couple of things for tomorrow's funerals. I asked the funeral home director to arrange the reception afterward at the Two Lanterns Inn. It would be great if you could check with the inn manager, Mrs. Neally, to make sure everything's all set," Anlon requested.

"Okay. I can handle all that, but isn't there a pretty important task we should tackle first?" Pebbles tentatively questioned, finally breaking her concentration on the third doughnut to look up at Anlon.

Anlon saw the expectant expression burgeoning on Pebbles' face and searched his mind. What was she hinting at, he wondered? He ran through their conversation last night and realized he overlooked the handkerchief and the ring.

"Yeah, I guess we should let Jennifer know about Pacal's handkerchief and the ring, but can't we do that later today?"

"Oh, that? Sure, we can tell her about those whenever you want but I'm thinking about something else. I can't believe you aren't more anxious about it!" Pebbles answered, gazing at Anlon's eyes to judge whether his pupils were enlarged. "Maybe you do have a concussion. How's your shoulder feel, by the way?"

Anlon rubbed his shoulder and replied, "It's a little sore, but much better than last night. I took some more of the pain reliever this morning so it shouldn't bother me today. And my head's fine, Pebbles. What are you driving at anyway? You look like you're waiting for a light to go on in my head."

Pebbles tapped her index finger on her lips while studying Anlon's confused face. It really surprised her that he'd forgotten all about the Port Stone.

"Maybe it was the kissing!" she exclaimed with a siren's wink. "It probably muddled your brain A.C. I have that effect on guys, you know."

Anlon laughed in response, "Quit teasing, Pebbles...and I believe it!"

He was glad this morning wasn't more awkward after their spontaneous make-out session last night. Yes, their mutual attraction was now out in the open but it didn't feel like their relationship had morphed into something dramatically different overnight. It was just pointed in a bit different direction now.

"Your kissing was, without question, intoxicating, but quit toying with me, young lady, and come out with it!"

"Mmmm...intoxicating. I like your choice of words. And you know what it does to me when you call me young lady," Pebbles whispered as she leaned seductively over the table, the locks of her bob swaying like a hypnotist's watch.

Strike that, he thought, our relationship definitely is now heading in a much different direction!

Suddenly she laughed aloud, sensing the discomfort she caused Anlon with her sexy banter. "Okay, I'll stop. Sorry to make you uncomfortable, Doc. We never went over to the barn last night to get the Port Stone! Personally, I want to use it, like right now, but I know we have other things to do today. Don't you think we should find it and at least put it in Devlin's safe?"

Anlon smacked his forehead and said, "I can't believe I forgot that!"

Maybe I do have a concussion after all, he thought, unwilling to entertain the notion that Pebbles' kissing had scrambled his mind.

"The other stuff can wait. Let's head out now and deal with that first!"

Ruefully, Pebbles cast a last forlorn look at the lonely uneaten doughnut still staring up at her from the plate and followed Anlon to the cash register and then out the diner door.

When they arrived back at the house, Anlon dashed inside to retrieve the slip of paper on which Dobson wrote the alarm codes. Scurrying back outside to where Pebbles stood in the driveway, he race-walked to the barn door.

Pebbles, dressed today in black Capri pants, white button-down shirt, and the same red flats she wore the previous day, sauntered behind Anlon at a leisurely pace, breathing in the fresh country air scented with honeysuckle. It was her first chance to survey the breadth of Devlin's property in full sunlight and she savored the mix of classic New England architecture amid the bucolic rolling terrain.

"Come on, slow poke," Anlon encouraged after unlocking the front door and punching in the security code. "We've got lots to do today."

When they entered, Anlon was bowled over by the appearance of the spacious office. It looked more like a modern university laboratory to him than what he imagined when Dobson said Devlin had refurbished the barn.

Directly ahead, at the far end of the first level, there were three partitioned nooks that looked like mini-offices. Anlon guessed they were meant for Devlin, Dobson and Pacal.

To the right of the nooks was a long wall of professional-grade cabinets for storing small artifacts and documents, and a set of tall storage racks holding larger relics. To the left of the nooks ran a wall-length kitchen counter with cabinets above and below, two separately placed sinks and a small under-counter refrigerator. On the counter was an assortment of measuring scales, microscopes, cameras and other devices purportedly used to examine relics and documents.

In the center of the room were three sturdy rectangular tables with tall, retractable lamps clamped to an edge of each. Attached to the ceiling above each table were special, high-power illuminating light fixtures. The tables were clean and devoid of any items. In fact, the whole space was pristine, with the notable exception of each man's individual office nook where varying degrees of clutter was evident.

Near the front entrance where Anlon and Pebbles stood, there was a floating staircase leading to an open air loft above. The entire space was bright and airy due to the combination of light-colored woods, white painted walls and plenty of ambient light from the half dozen windows throughout the barn.

"So, if you were holding a priceless piece of ancient history, where would you keep it stored in here?" Anlon hopefully queried Pebbles.

"Beats me, Doc. You're the scientist here. We're looking for a stone that looks like a hockey puck or tuna can, right? Why don't you start with the cabinets and I'll start with the racks." Pebbles suggested.

Anlon agreed, and they initiated their respective searches. Pebbles mentioned immediately that all the shelves and trays on the racks were labeled with codes. Anlon noted the cabinets were labeled in a similar fashion.

After opening the first cabinet, he called to Pebbles, "Hey, I know it goes without saying, but I'm going to say it anyway. There are likely rare pieces and papers in here, so handle everything with care. Oh, and please make sure you put back everything where you found it so we don't mess with their filing system."

Pebbles strolled across the room to stand before him, arms crossed and foot tapping.

"Hello!?" she sarcastically intoned. "Law degree here, plenty of experience researching in law libraries. Bartender here, plenty of experience arranging bottle racks."

"Hey, I said I know it goes without saying!" he cowered playfully.

Sticking her tongue out, she returned to the racks. Ah, Anlon observed, the tongue stud is back today along with her wrist bangles. He shuddered to think what a hybrid Pebbles/Eleanor might accomplish!

An hour of searching yielded no Port Stone or anything remotely close to the description Pacal gave. They sat down on the loft stairs and Pebbles said, "Well, that sucks. I thought this was going to be easy. I'm thinking we should look in their desks and on their computers. If they've coded everything, there's got to be some kind of registry or index that points to where the stone should be."

"Good idea. Let's hope they identified it as 'Port Stone' in the index," Anlon prayed.

As they approached the desk nooks, Anlon stopped in his tracks. He said, "Pebbles, is it me or are two of the computers missing?"

Looking among the alcoves, Pebbles noted that the only desk with a laptop visible was the one on the far right. All three alcoves had oversized monitors standing on the desk surfaces along with wireless keyboards and mice, but two desks were without laptops.

"Hmmm, that's odd. Maybe Devlin kept his in the house? Maybe Pacal or Matthew took theirs home with them at night? Lots of people do," she mused.

"Let's figure out whose laptops are missing," Anlon suggested.

It didn't take but a minute to sort out which alcove belonged to each man. The one in the center was Devlin's as confirmed by pieces of mail on the desktop and assorted pictures adorning the walls of his alcove. The one on the right was Dobson's, given a similar array of letters and photos. This meant the sparse, unadorned workspace to the left was Pacal's.

"Well, that's that," Pebbles said. "I guess Devlin kept his in the house. Did you see it in the study?"

"No, but honestly I didn't look for one," Anlon replied, anxiously gazing at his watch. "But we've been here for over an hour and the day's getting away. At least Dobson's is still here."

"Hey, what about up top?" Pebbles voiced, pointing at the loft, "I'll go check it out."

Anlon sat down at Devlin's desk idly shuffling through the documents on it.

"Uh oh!" Pebbles cried from above. "Better come up, Anlon, looks like someone broke in."

Anlon sat motionless for a moment before heading for the stairs, sarcastically shouting back, "Peachy. Well, so much for a productive day!"

When Anlon arrived up top, Pebbles was motioning to glass on the floor beneath the window and the raised lower pane. Shaking his head in disbelief, Anlon said, "I'll call Jennifer."

While they waited for the police to arrive, Pebbles did a quick survey of the loft. There was a twin bed to the right of the window with a small reading table and lamp. On the other side was a medium-sized sofa and a floor lamp. Lifting the sofa cushion revealed it to be a sleeper sofa. She guessed that when Pacal or Matthew or both worked late, they sometimes slept in the barn office.

Anlon slumped down on the sofa and Pebbles joined him. He remarked, "You know Jennifer's going to give us the what-for when she gets here for touching everything."

Pebbles commiserated, "Yeah, I bet she will. But how were we to know the place had been broken into?"

"She'll still squawk at us," Anlon murmured as he closed his eyes to think.

The Port Stone is gone, he thought. "Damn, I should have looked for it last night."

Pebbles reassuringly commented, "It might still be here, we don't know yet. And you can't be sure the break-in happened last night."

Anlon perked up at that thought. Pebbles was right. No one had been in the office since Friday night, according to what Pacal told Jennifer last night. That meant the break-in could have occurred any one of the last four days.

But in his heart Anlon was sure the Port Stone was gone, and equally sure the two laptops were stolen. Though he considered it strange that Dobson's was left undisturbed. Maybe Pebbles was right, maybe Devlin's was inside the house and Pacal kept his at home, too. He thought of his own prior work habits and acknowledged he had always brought his work laptop home in case he had a late night inspiration. And on this trip, Anlon realized, he'd brought his own home laptop to Stockbridge even though he hadn't yet removed it from his travel backpack.

That gave Anlon an idea to at least make some progress today. He drew out his cell phone and dialed Mr. Grant. When connected he said, "Mr. Grant, I've run into a bit of snag and I don't think I'll make it out to your office today to get another copy of the will. Any chance you can scan it and email it to me?"

XI

ASSESSING DAMAGES

"How bad is the situation?" read the text from Quechua212.

A burly, hooded AucuChan1 sat in a white panel truck by the roadside and typed in his reply. "Very bad. Didn't find the map. Didn't find any Stones or sculptures. Did swipe DW's laptop."

In fact, AucuChan1 had already managed to by-pass Devlin's password screen and scan many emails and documents. There were hundreds left to check but thus far no map or mention of one. He added another text, "Just drove by DW's house. Cops all over. Break-in discovered."

The burly man winced when Quechua212 asked, "What about MD and PF computers?"

AucuChan1 explained in his reply that Pacal's laptop was absent and that he had no choice but to leave Dobson's behind. Quechua212 scolded him. AucuChan1 pushed back with the reasons he left the laptop. Quechua212 was unmoved. "HUGE mistake!!! You better hope they don't search that computer! You can't keep messing up like this!"

The burly man stewed. He didn't like being called out, especially by the already arrogant Quechua212. He half considered keeping the map if he did find it but then thought better of it. Quechua212 had a long reach and a deadly touch.

"Only other place to hide everything is in the house," messaged Quechua212.

"Yep. That's a problem. AC NOT staying there alone now. Last night a PYT stayed there, too. With 2 people & alarm & break-in, tough now to sneak in undetected," answered AucuChan1.

As the stout man pulled a cigarette pack from his jacket pocket, he further thought, even if I get in the house without getting caught, it's a big house to search and Devlin has a safe in the house.

A long pause ensued on their two phone screens, text app cursors blinking as they pondered next steps. AucuChan1 lit a cigarette and waited for instructions. After a couple minutes of quiet, he typed, "IMO, we should lay low for a bit. When things cool off, I can try the house."

Quechua212's answer followed., "Agreed. We have no choice if we want to do this quietly. Really wish you hadn't left MD's laptop..."

"What's done is done," responded the other, smoke swirling in wisps as he dangled the lit butt out the truck window.

"Not sure I like that answer."

AucuChan1 changed course, "Forgot to mention, PF was at the house last night. He showed AC how the Sound Stone works. It was damn impressive. He lifted the PYT atop DW's SUV above the house and put it down as nicely as you please."

"You're depressing me."

Dragging deeply on the cigarette filter, the burly man typed, "PF also rolled AC across the lawn with it. Looked like AC got hurt. They were angry with PF. Shouted at him pretty good."

"Hmmm...maybe you should concentrate on PF for now. You said his laptop wasn't in the barn? He might have copy of the map. Also keep looking on DW laptop for map and while at it search for the security system codes for the house and barn," suggested Quechua212.

"It's an idea," the burly man typed as he flicked the spent butt onto the roadway, "but cops will make them change codes now."

Jennifer stood by the broken window and stated, "Yep, that's not an accidently broken window. You can see where the glass was punched out on the top pane in order to unlock the latch and slide up the bottom pane. Must have been a very strong person to swing out like that from the roof."

"How do you know he came in from the roof?" Anlon asked.

"There's a gravel bed directly under the window. I checked it out when I walked around the building. It's undisturbed, so he didn't use a ladder. I also don't see how he could have carried a ladder through the woods from the road. It's more logical that he climbed on the low roof by the woods and made his way to the back of the barn," replied Jennifer.

"We've scoured the tree line behind the stone wall," she continued, "and the ground is heavily trampled. It looks like the thief has been casing the house for some time."

Pebbles looked out the barn window at the trees and said, "That's creepy. Can you tell how long ago the break-in happened, Jennifer?"

"You mean from the trampled underbrush? Good question, Pebbles. Yes, some of the damage is very fresh, so I would say it happened overnight. You guys didn't hear anything?"

"Afraid not," Anlon answered, "speaking for myself, that is. My room is on the front side of the house so it would have been hard to hear."

Pebbles chimed in, "I didn't hear anything either and the room I slept in is right over the garage, closer to the barn."

Separate bedrooms, Jennifer noted. Hmmm...maybe they are just close friends. Shunting aside that piece of irrelevant information, she said, "Well, it's possible it occurred on an earlier night. If the thief didn't find what he searched for he might have come back again looking for another opportunity to get in. But I noticed there are only a few bugs flying around in here and the bedcover isn't damp. If the window's been open like that for a few days, I would expect more bugs and traces of the morning dew on the furniture."

"I see. Yes, those signs do point at last night," Anlon nodded, impressed again by Jennifer's observational skills. Not just a good memory, he thought, she's got a keen eye as well.

"I know it's probably a stupid question given what you told me on the phone, but do you know for certain if anything is missing?" Jennifer inquired.

"No, sadly not. Devlin and Pacal's laptops are not on their desks and we didn't find the Port Stone that Pacal mentioned last night. If you remember, he said it was in the barn," Anlon answered.

"Yes, I remember. Too bad none of us thought to look last night. I know I was so freaked out from the Sound Stone demonstrations that I forgot completely about it," Jennifer confided.

Anlon shot a wink at Pebbles and teased, "Guess I'm not the only one who was distracted last night!"

"Ha ha," a blushing Pebbles responded.

Jennifer was curious about the inside joke, especially when Pebbles' face flushed red, but returned to the main topic of conversation, "Before I walked back to the barn to see you guys, I spoke with the officers searching the house. Unfortunately, they haven't found any laptops besides yours and Pebbles'. I think it's reasonable to assume Devlin's laptop was taken by the thief."

"What about the Port Stone?" Pebbles interjected.

"That, I don't know. It's possible, maybe even probable, but my gut tells me it wasn't in the barn to begin with," said Jennifer.

"Pacal?" Pebbles asked, nodding in understanding.

Jennifer nodded in return. She was really starting to like Pebbles. She didn't miss much and their brains worked at similar speeds. Having pried a little into Pebbles' background, she wasn't surprised.

Pebbles, aka Eleanor McCarver, graduated with honors from Vanderbilt University's Law School, a top 15 law program. Prior to that, she graduated Cum Laude from George Washington University with a bachelor's in political science. While at GW, she also played volleyball for the university's women's team for two years and crewed for another. Her police record was whistle clean, but Jennifer did discover "Eleanor" had been briefly detained and charged in conjunction with a serious scandal not long after she graduated from law school. Jennifer wondered how much Anlon knew about Pebbles. If he was aware of the controversy surrounding her, he seemed to not care. Pretty understanding, Jennifer thought, for a guy who developed a distaste for the limelight.

Anlon interrupted Jennifer's train of thought. "What about Pacal?"

"My hunch is he lied about the location of the Port Stone," she responded. "You think so, too, don't you, Pebbles?"

"Yes, I do. It makes no sense that he went through all the effort to describe how the Master Stone works, but then never demonstrated it. The more I've thought about his comment that he never viewed a Master Stone, the more unbelievable it sounds to me. Now that we know the Port Stone is not here, I've started to wonder if he used the Sound Stone demonstration to distract us from heading over to the barn to get the Port Stone," Pebbles blurted out while she paced around the loft.

"He'd already stolen it, I bet," Jennifer added.

"What?" an incredulous Anlon intoned. "Why would he do that?"

Jennifer and Pebbles ignored Anlon's question. Pebbles asked the detective, "Did you notice the ring he wore?"

"Yes, I remember it. It was hard not to notice with him banging it on the scotch glass," Jennifer replied. "Why, is it significant?"

"Uh huh. The design on the face of it matched one of the Master Stone designs...exactly!" Pebbles excitedly shared.

"Really? I missed that. Good catch. Which design was it?" Jennifer asked in return.

"Hello?! Still here," Anlon called, cupping his mouth with his hands to make a makeshift megaphone. "Why would Pacal steal the Port Stone and then lie about where Devlin kept it?"

"In a second, Anlon. Please, Pebbles, go on," Jennifer said, holding out her palm to quell Anlon's interruption.

"The one that looked like a leaf," Pebbles answered Jennifer, self-consciously gazing at a quickly angering Anlon. She moved to his side and said, "A.C., it's like I said last night. I think he's after one of the other stones himself."

"So what does stealing the Port Stone accomplish for him? He doesn't have Devlin's Story Stone or the Master Stone," Anlon challenged.

"It slows us down from finding out what's on the Story Stones. It buys him time. Think about it, A.C., he didn't need to attack you with the Sound Stone last night to get his point across. He could just have easily picked a lawn chair to send flying across the yard. It was important for him to scare you, scare all of us," Pebbles theorized.

"By the way," Pebbles asked, "did he show up for fingerprinting this morning?"

"Nope," Jennifer said. "There's still time left in the day, but I wouldn't hold my breath. I think he's taken off. If he did, I'll be some kind of angry. I asked my Captain for a search warrant this morning to go through Pacal's home, but I got shot down...not enough probable cause."

"Still not enough," Anlon challenged. "You and Miss Marple here are just guessing at all this. For all we know, Pacal didn't lie. For all we know, the thief found and took the Port Stone. For all we know, it may not have been stolen. It could still be hidden in here somewhere we overlooked."

Jennifer nodded and said, "You sound just like Captain Gambelli. Points taken. I'm probably getting ahead of myself, as he said when he chewed me out this morning."

Anlon didn't enjoy throwing water on Jennifer and Pebbles' flourishing speculation. He admired how observant they were and how quickly they could draw conclusions, but he was concerned they were moving too fast. He said, "You two are amazing. You notice everything and you link pieces together super quick, but I think this whole situation is more complicated than it seems on the surface. I feel like we have to be more methodical and not rush to judgment."

Jennifer blushed a little, not from anger but from embarrassment. Anlon was right. It was the same speech she heard earlier from Gambelli, which made Anlon's comments sting all the more.

Pebbles also felt embarrassed seeing the disappointment in Anlon's face. She came to help him, not frustrate him.

"Sorry, A.C., my bad," she offered in apology.

"Don't apologize," he replied. "It's all good. I'm thrilled you're here and so enthusiastic to pitch in."

"Look," Jennifer said, "my hands are somewhat tied. My mandate was made clear to me this morning. Focus on Dobson's death, not Devlin's. It irritates me because I feel it in my bones that the two are connected, but we don't have any hard evidence. This break-in is more connected to Devlin's death than Dobson's, so I'm not sure what else I can do.

"On the bright side, the thief left Dobson's computer and his desk full of papers and other stuff. I even found a couple of flash drives in one of the desk drawers. If it's okay with you, Anlon, I'd like to take the computer and the papers as evidence back to my office for a few days. I'll be looking for any clues about Dobson's death, but if I find anything of interest about Devlin's death or the stones, I will let you know. Fair deal?"

Anlon answered, "Of course, Jennifer. But why not come back to look at the computer and papers here, though? That way we can keep each other up to date without you getting flak for helping us out. I'll board up the broken window this afternoon and I'll get the alarm company out here to install sensors on both windows in the loft. We need to sort through Devlin's and Pacal's desks, too, and conduct a more methodical search now that we have a better sense of where things stand. We might find something that helps you, too."

"Let me think about it...and make sure you change the alarm codes, too," she answered.

Pebbles spoke to Anlon, "Um, in the spirit of collaboration, can I tell her about the handkerchief now?"

"Absolutely, Pebbles. Let's not go too far the other way. Be yourself, I'll raise my hand if I can't catch up," Anlon smiled.

Pebbles relayed her story about lifting Pacal's handkerchief before she and Jennifer walked over to the house to retrieve it. As they stepped out of the house and down the back porch, Jennifer held up the evidence bag with the white cloth and said, "This is awesome, thank you. You're sneaky. I like that!"

"You're welcome," Pebbles bowed. "I kinda feel bad for swiping it, but I don't know, I don't have the warm fuzzies for Pacal."

"Neither do I," Jennifer concurred. "Let's go find Anlon, I have something to share in return as part of our collaboration."

When they found Anlon, he was on the phone to the alarm company negotiating an immediate service call. "...Look, I need someone out here this afternoon...Yes, I understand I don't have an appointment... Tell me, how much does a service visit normally cost?...Uh huh, I see...$100...and do you have a rush charge on top of that...yes, yes... another $100. Okay, I have a deal for you. If you can motivate someone out here in the next 30 minutes, I'll pay you $1,000 instead...Good answer, see you soon."

Anlon hung up and turned his attention to Jennifer and Pebbles who stood patiently waiting for his call to finish, giggling quietly at his successful, albeit expensive, negotiation.

Jennifer said, "I want to give you two the heads up about something. When I went hiking up at Mt. Whiteface yesterday, I found Devlin's GPS tracking device. I wanted to run prints on it and power it up to see if there were any clues, but I was directed to send it to the Meredith Police Department in New Hampshire. They're the ones who filed the original police report. I asked the officer in charge of the case on their end to give me a heads up if he finds anything worth sharing, but I have my doubts he will. The point is, the device was laying on some rocks about 300 feet above where Devlin supposedly fell. That means he fell more like 500 feet. And I have to tell you, the rock face I rappelled to find the device was not realistically climbable from below."

Pebbles looked at Anlon and then at Jennifer, bursting to toss out a conclusion, but she bit her tongue. Anlon, noticing her gesture, dead-panned, "Go ahead, Miss Marple. Let's hear it or you might just spontaneously combust."

Pebbles punched Anlon's arm, forgetting about the sore shoulder, and said, "You're mean!"

Turning to Jennifer she said, "So Devlin probably was flown high in the air like Pacal did to me last night, only the killer didn't provide Devlin as soft a landing."

This time it was Anlon who connected the dots. "So that's what Dobson meant when he said 'yes and no' when I asked if he thought Devlin was pushed!"

XII

FUNERAL PROCESSION

The funeral services for both men were short but surprisingly well-attended in Anlon's opinion, given the scarcity of their direct living relations and the threat of May showers.

Matthew Dobson's service was held first. He was a parishioner and regular worshiper of the town's Catholic church where services were held, and many of the funeral attendees were local residents who knew him from church and social events. Several fellow archaeologists came for both funerals, as did a handful of academic colleagues from Stony Brook University on Long Island where Dobson had occasionally lectured. Most of the people who came to pay their respects were unknown to Anlon.

George Grant, Devlin's attorney, did his best at Anlon's request to contact and notify Dobson's relations, but only two distant cousins were located and neither came for the service.

Dobson's wife, Clara, Grant had learned, died a decade earlier and was interred in a small Catholic cemetery south of Stockbridge. After both services, Dobson would be laid to rest alongside her. They were childless. His only sibling, a sister, Elizabeth, whose married name was Corchran, was also deceased as was her husband. But Grant was able to find and contact two of their children, a son named Kyle and a daughter named Margaret. Neither was local and both declined to attend the funeral even though Anlon graciously offered to pay for their travel. Anlon was disappointed to learn this from Grant the day before. Grant had stated his belief they declined out of indifference rather than animosity.

Anlon skeptically wondered if they would have come had Grant shared the size of Dobson's inheritance from Devlin. But Grant didn't discuss the inheritance with them, given he was still in the process of determining whether Dobson left a will.

After Dobson's service, Jennifer Stevens, Pebbles and Anlon milled about outside with other guests staying for both funerals while the church prepared for Devlin's service. Jennifer was dressed in the same tasteful charcoal pantsuit she'd worn when she first met Anlon on Sunday while Pebbles donned a simple, black, knee-length dress and patent leather heels. Anlon wore a dark navy suit, white shirt and black tie.

They had just finished speaking with Mr. Grant about his fruitless search for Dobson's will. He asked if it would be possible to search Dobson's home and office for the document or clues to its location. Jennifer mentioned she planned to be at Dobson's home the following day and agreed to take a look around. After all, the will might shed light on the motive for his murder. Pebbles offered to help Jennifer and volunteered to do a similar search of Dobson's effects at Devlin's office. Jennifer accepted Pebbles' offer and Mr. Grant looked much relieved.

The discussion of Dobson's will reminded Anlon to thank Grant for emailing him another copy of Devlin's will. He asked if the other copies had been distributed by now. Grant indicated he'd sent a copy to Anabel Simpson, who also declined to attend the funerals, and expected to hand deliver copies to Pacal and Richard Ryan after Devlin's service.

As new arrivals walked up casting nervous looks at the darkening skies, Anlon spotted the funeral home director by the church entrance and was about to walk over to discuss last minute details when he heard his name called aloud. Turning around, he faced his younger cousin, Richard Ryan.

"Rich," Anlon said, offering a handshake, "it's good to see you. You're looking well."

The 35-year-old Richard Ryan did not, in fact, look well at all. He had gained at least 50 pounds since Anlon had last seen him five years ago at a party Anlon threw for friends and family when the Whave engine patent was sold. Richard was a train wreck that night. He'd gotten uncontrollably wasted and made a fool of himself hitting on several female guests in crude fashion, including Anlon's then-girlfriend. When Anlon firmly escorted Richard to a quiet spot to tell him to chill out, the younger cousin had beseeched Anlon for money and broke down sobbing about his many woes. Anlon hoped desperately that today would not be a repeat performance.

"Thanks, wish it were true. But sadly my life sucks as usual. How's the good life on 'Blue' Tahoe treating you?" asked Rich, bitterness layered upon his words.

"I can't complain," Anlon replied, careful to avoid opening a window for Richard to expand on his state of misery. "I'd like to introduce you to two friends of mine. This is Pebbles McCarver, a friend from Tahoe, and Jennifer Stevens, a new friend from this area. Ladies, this is my cousin Richard Ryan."

Richard's mouth fell open staring, well leering, at the two beautiful, sedately dressed women. Anlon cringed, expecting any moment Richard would offer to take one of them off his hands, but Richard wasn't drunk yet so his response only carried a pinch of bitterness. "Wow! You sure collect 'em, don't you, cousin? Just like your cut of Uncle Dev's will. The rich just get richer. Nice to meet you both."

Pebbles and Jennifer shrugged off Richard's implication and politely greeted him. They chatted briefly about the weather, Richard's trip in (Anlon had offered to pay for his travel, too, and Richard heartily accepted) and shared condolences for his loss.

Just then Anlon felt a tap on his shoulder and wheeled to find himself face to face with an elegantly mannered man dressed from head to toe in black. The man's face was deeply tanned and thin, almost too thin. His black hair was drawn into a ponytail longer than Pebbles could manage with her new hairstyle and his suit was custom tailored, judging by the trim fit. Behind him stood two hulking, stern-faced associates in similar suits, wearing sunglasses and chewing gum in their chiseled jaws. When he spoke, Anlon detected an odd accent amid his perfect English diction. "Please pardon me for interrupting. You are Dr. Anlon Cully?"

"Yes, hello," Anlon answered, trying to detect the origin of the accent. He was clearly of Latino origin yet some of his words had a guttural quality.

"Dr. Cully, it is a sincere pleasure to meet you. My name is Klaus Navarro. I am very sorry that we meet on such a sad occasion."

"Mr. Navarro, thank you for your condolences. Did you know my Uncle Devlin?"

"Oh yes," said Klaus with a slight chuckle, "For many years. We often competed for the same treasures."

"You are an archaeologist then?" asked Anlon.

"No, no. I am a collector of antiquities, mostly Mayan and Incan pieces," Klaus corrected with a failed attempt to portray modesty. "I traveled here from my home in Argentina to honor the life of your brilliant uncle."

"Wow, that's certainly above and beyond, Mr. Navarro. Thank you for coming," Anlon said, hoping to break away from the conversation. Behind him, he heard Richard ask Pebbles, "So where's Bam Bam?" and he knew a rescue was in order.

But Klaus did not take the hint. He raised his voice a touch to recapture Anlon's attention. "Dr. Cully? If I might have one more quick word with you. I realize you are very busy with Devlin's funeral and I appreciate this is not the best time to engage in an extended conversation. I learned earlier today you are handling his estate and I need to speak with you later today or tomorrow about some pieces your uncle possessed. I would like to discuss purchasing them from the estate."

Anlon was taken aback by the forward manner, subject matter and timing of Klaus' request to meet. Devlin, after all, was yet to be buried.

He answered with a polite smile, "Um, I don't mean to appear rude, Mr. Navarro, but I'm not sure I will have time today or tomorrow to meet with you. If you give me your card after the ceremony, I promise to contact you when I am at a point where I can focus on Devlin's estate matters. I hope you understand, it's a rather hectic time right now."

Anlon bowed respectfully and turned back towards Pebbles and Jennifer. The quick moving Klaus stepped back in front of Anlon and pleaded, "But I have traveled all this way to meet with you and, of course, send off Devlin. My flight home is the day after tomorrow. Can you not spare me 20 minutes of your time to at least hear my offer?"

Irritation waxed in Anlon but he kept it under control. Tossing a look to Pebbles, he was at least relieved that she'd deftly handled Richard, who now stood alone by the church entrance scanning his cell phone. He took a deep breath and cast his eye at Navarro's. They exuded, he noticed, a palpable urgency reinforced by a small quiver of the skin below one of Klaus' eyes. Anlon offered a compromise. "Had I known you planned to travel to meet with me, Mr. Navarro, I would have suggested a later date. But since you are here for a limited time, let's talk again at the reception after the service and we can discuss a time to meet tomorrow. Best I can do."

"Thank you, Dr. Cully. I will see you at the reception," Klaus said before motioning to his associates and moving towards the church.

Pebbles scooted up to Anlon and whispered in his ear, "No offense, but your cousin is gross."

Anlon laughed and agreed, "Oh, wait 'til he starts drinking. You'll need to gird yourself for further lewd behavior."

She kissed him on the cheek, her first ever display of public affection towards Anlon, and whispered in his ear, "He's watching us now. Maybe this will kill his mojo."

Anlon returned the kiss and whispered back, "It'll make him want you more!"

They both laughed. Pebbles tucked the long curling strands of her bob behind her ears and said, "Who was that guy? He seemed kinda pushy. You looked like you were about to punch him."

"You read body language well. Correct on both counts. He appears to be some hot shot 'antiquities' collector, or at least thinks he is. He's desperate to talk to me about some Mayan or Incan pieces of Devlin's," Anlon explained.

"What's his name? I'll do a quick web search on him before we get in the church," Pebbles asked, digging in her clutch purse for her phone.

"Klaus Navarro. He said he's from Argentina," Anlon absently said, looking over Pebbles' shoulder at the man approaching him waving energetically. "Oh my God, here comes another one."

Pebbles spun to look at the barrel-chested, obese African-American man in a heavily wrinkled seersucker suit wobble up to them. Long shoots of white hair shot out in all directions as if he'd been shocked. He approached Anlon as Pebbles stepped aside to research Klaus Navarro and greeted him warmly. "Dr. Cully, what a treat it is to meet you! Devlin crowed about you many times, bless his soul. I'm Dr. Thatcher Reynolds."

"You are too kind, Dr. Reynolds. I take it you were a professional colleague of Devlin's?"

"More like rival!" boomed the beefy man. "Do call me Thatcher. Oh, we went at it like cats and dogs many times. We believed in very different views of man's rise from cave dwellers."

"Knowing my uncle, Thatcher, I bet many of those debates occurred over scotch and cigars," Anlon smiled, warming to the boisterous personality of the archaeologist.

"Too much of both!" he roared. "Oh I will miss the old codger. No matter how much we yelled at each other, we always ended our talks on good terms. You don't find that as much these days. So many people take things personally. That doesn't move science forward, an open mind does!"

Anlon arched his eyebrow and kiddingly asked, "Did Devlin open your mind about anything?"

The man stroked his chin, adjusted his gold-rimmed glasses and said, "You know, we held such different beliefs. I am a gradualist; he was a catastrophist. It's hard to find middle ground between those two schools of thought, but I do have to say that he often challenged me with questions I couldn't answer."

Anlon smiled. He liked Thatcher's honesty and gusto and he understood why Devlin would have liked the man, even if they didn't agree. He was also tasteful. He could have derided Devlin's views, but instead his words, honestly spoken, were intended to lift the memory of Devlin Wilson not diminish it. He said, "He challenged us all that way, Thatcher. And I'm sure you challenged him in return. I see the priest waving to me. I think it's time we went inside, but let's chat again at the reception afterward."

After parting from Reynolds, Anlon moved to the church door where Pebbles and Jennifer awaited him. He was thankful Jennifer came to both services and that she came in support as a friend instead of as a police officer. It was a sweet gesture that reinforced in his mind that underneath the rough, go-getter exterior, she really possessed a kind spirit. I guess that's true of most law enforcement professionals, he thought. Though they sometimes wield a stick, most of their time is spent helping people in need.

He took a deep breath when he reached the door and held out an arm for each of the women. They both accepted his escort into the church, all tension between them gone. For the first time that day, Anlon felt relaxed and ready to celebrate the life of Devlin Allen Wilson. Yet, as he stepped inside the church he felt a twinge of disappointment that Pacal Flores had not come to honor Devlin.

Mrs. Neally was the first to greet Anlon when he, Pebbles and Jennifer arrived for the reception. She cooed, "Dear Dr. Cully, I'm so sorry for your loss. The reception is upstairs to your right. If there is anything amiss, Miss McCarver, please let me know immediately!"

Anlon peered at Pebbles, who blushed and said, "Thank you, Mrs. Neally. I know your staff will exceed Dr. Cully's expectations."

When they climbed the stairs and entered the reception room, Anlon turned to Pebbles and inquired, "What did you say to her? She damn near knelt before you."

"Nothing," Pebbles nonchalantly said, "I just did what you asked. I made sure everything was all set."

When Anlon disappeared into the room of people to mingle, Jennifer pulled Pebbles aside. "Okay, what gives? I met that woman on Sunday. She's not the kind of woman to eat out of your hand. She's more the type that bites it off."

Pebbles smiled and said, "I know, right?"

Jennifer waited for a further explanation. Pebbles offered none other than to playfully run her fingers across her lips to signify they were zipped shut.

"So much for collaboration," Jennifer laughed. "Well, I need to get back to work. Will you please say goodbye to Anlon for me? I don't want to distract him from his guests."

Pebbles said she would and they discussed a time to meet the following day at Dobson's house before Jennifer departed.

Anlon kept a nervous eye on Richard, who was holding a full wine glass in each hand. While he moved between guests extending thanks and exchanging vignettes about Devlin, Anlon paused to realize that he hadn't thought of ancient stones, thefts or murders all day. It was a stress-relieving respite. Instead, he spent most of his time sharing and listening to grand stories about Dobson and Devlin.

Pebbles brought Anlon a bottle of his favorite San Diego microbrewed IPA. With a shocked look on his face, he praised her and asked, "How did you manage that?"

Pebbles hid her face while developing an evil grin, saying, "Let's just say I bonded with Mrs. Neally."

"You really have been wonderful," Anlon said. "It's hard to tell you how much it means to me, you being here. I don't think I could do this without you."

She blushed and replied, "Aw...by the way, scooter's mine now!"

Anlon chortled and hugged her, "Yes, you won fair and square. To tell you the truth, I was rooting hard for you to lose for very selfish reasons."

Her mouth opened in faux shock and she pushed him back with a hand to his chest. "Oh, were you now? Well, I might just give you a second chance to win, but I warn you, Doc, I don't like losing."

Their banter was truncated as Thatcher Reynolds stepped towards Anlon and said as he bowed to Pebbles, "My apologies for interrupting. May I speak with Dr. Cully in private for a moment?"

Pebbles nodded politely and started to move away when Anlon called her back. "Hold on, Pebbles. I'd like you to meet Thatcher Reynolds, a friend and self-professed rival of Devlin's. Thatcher, this is my associate, Pebbles McCarver."

Thatcher gracefully extended a hand and greeted Pebbles, "A pleasure, I'm sure."

He turned back to Anlon in an awkwardly dismissive motion intended to exclude Pebbles from their conversation. Anlon reached for Pebbles' hand as she turned to leave and gripped it in an unspoken request for her to stay. Anlon clarified for Thatcher, "Pebbles is my closest confidante. Anything you'd like to discuss with me I'll discuss with her anyway, so please, what is it you'd like to say?"

Pebbles bit her lower lip, stifling a chuckle, and again appreciated Anlon's recognition of her as a peer. Each time he exhibited his respect for her in this way, the more she felt like his peer.

"Oh," Thatcher exclaimed, "I see. I'm sorry, I didn't intend to be disrespectful. I wanted to ask you some delicate questions and I wasn't sure whether it was advisable to discuss the questions in a public setting, Dr. Cully."

"First off, Thatcher, it's Anlon. You're a PhD, I'm a PhD, no need for formality. Second, there are no secrets between Pebbles and me, so fire away."

Thatcher boomed with laughter and said, "I like you, Anlon. You're more like your uncle than you think. Very well, very well. I wanted to ask you some questions about Devlin's death. I was very surprised to hear of his accident."

Anlon's face twitched and Pebbles halted in mid-sip of her wine. They cast knowing looks at each other and Thatcher continued, "I see from your reactions that I've stirred waters already fished."

"An interesting way to put it," Anlon conceded. "What are you hinting at, Thatcher?"

"It's just that his death seemed untimely and I thought it might be linked in some way with his research," Thatcher innocently shrugged.

"What do you know about Devlin's research?" Anlon queried. "I had the impression he kept his investigations close to the vest."

Thatcher laughed again and said, "If bulls wore vests careening through china shops that might be true! He didn't share details about his findings, but all one had to do to know the direction of his research was follow the broken pieces of china."

Thatcher continued, "It was well known in the archaeology and anthropology communities that Devlin believed civilized man significantly pre-dated acknowledged societal development. Most of my colleagues were not kind to Devlin, demanding he produce definitive proof to back up his theory. I know your uncle spent the last decade of his life relentlessly pursuing that proof and for that he was roundly, albeit quietly, mocked. In the end, though, I believe he might have found some proof. And may now be dead because of it."

Anlon listened with interest. In his opinion, Thatcher's coolly presented summary was close to the mark. Though Anlon largely stepped away from academia after the Whave patent was sold, he still had friends and associates in scientific circles and he still occasionally perused research journals. He knew how easy it was for a researcher to be maligned for a contrarian point of view. And Devlin was bombastic, feisty even, when it came to points of view he passionately held. So Thatcher's analysis was well-grounded, but Anlon was curious as to why Thatcher was convinced Devlin found proof and why he thought it might have contributed to his death. He also wondered how many other colleagues of Devlin's thought the same. He asked, "I can't argue your bull analogy or the way Devlin was viewed among his peers, but what makes you think he found proof backing his theory?"

"Simple, really," responded the eccentric looking archaeologist as he cleaned his glasses with his tie. "When bulls leave bits of broken china everywhere and then all of a sudden the bits stop, it gives the impression that the bull has found the piece of china he wants and has left the shop."

"Maybe he just gave up," Anlon weakly argued.

"Hmm...I thought you were more inquisitive than that, Anlon. Do you believe he just gave up?"

Anlon didn't answer the question. He was, in fact, starting to get a little irritated by Thatcher's probing. He looked at Pebbles and then back at Thatcher. "I'm sorry, why is it of your concern one way or the other?"

Thatcher replaced his glasses upon his face and put his cards on the table, saying, "If Devlin did find proof, then someone should pick up the hunt where he left off. With Matthew's unfortunate death so soon after Devlin, there's no academic left within his circle to further the work your uncle spent 10 hard years chasing. I'd like you to consider handing the mantle to me to continue his work and preserve his legacy. I've known Devlin's assistant Pacal for many years. Together we can make great strides."

Ah, so now we get down to the crux of the conversation, Anlon mused inside. How magnanimous of Thatcher.

"It's a generous offer, Thatcher, and I thank you for making it. But, handing his research over to someone else is not really something I've considered. Besides, you described yourself as holding starkly different views than Devlin. I wonder if that might make it difficult for you to pursue his research without tainting your own reputation," Anlon needled.

Thatcher expected this answer and replied, "Well, maybe I should have said it a different way. I have some backers who would be willing to buy Devlin's artifact collection and research papers, people who are keenly interested in furthering your uncle's legacy."

Pebbles finished her wine and handed the empty glass to a passing waiter. To her, the air between the two men was turning prickly fast.

Thatcher's initial innuendo had morphed into a lame attempt to steal, now buy, Devlin's collection. And Thatcher hadn't answered Anlon's question. This was about money not legacy, she concluded. Pebbles was amazed Anlon had maintained his composure thus far, but she wasn't sure how much longer his patience would last.

"Devlin's collection is not for sale," Anlon curtly answered.

Undaunted, Thatcher said, "But I understand you didn't receive any money from Devlin's estate, just his home and artifact collection. Won't it be a troublesome matter for you to dispose of his assets? Wouldn't you rather receive cash and be done with it? With some of the funds offered by my backers, you could establish a research grant under your uncle's name and support the next generation of budding archaeologists."

Anlon shook his head, glared at Thatcher and repeated, "The collection is *not* for sale. Good day, Dr. Reynolds."

Fuming, Anlon turned away. Thatcher reached out and gripped Anlon's arm to restrain his turn. He spat in a hushed voice, "I think you should reconsider, Dr. Cully. It would be unwise and potentially dangerous to continue the work yourself."

Pebbles shot Thatcher an incredulous look and interjected, "Are you threatening Anlon?"

Ignoring Pebbles' question, Thatcher stared coldly at Anlon and released his arm, warning, "It's dangerous for more than just you, Anlon. It's dangerous for anyone you care about."

XIII

LOST IN THE DIG

Yawning deeply, Anlon sat in the dark on the back steps of Devlin's house with beer in hand and listened to the sonorous harmony of crickets and frogs. While the nocturnal chorus soothed his troubled mind, it did little to alter Anlon's downcast mood.

It had been a very long and exhausting day, he thought. The funerals themselves were draining enough, but with the other dramas that unfolded piled on top, Anlon was spent.

Pondering the day's events, well, the last several days' events really, he did feel lost in the dig. He had come to Stockbridge primarily to attend Devlin's funeral and start the ball rolling on his duties as executor. Simple as that. Yes, he'd traveled earlier than he would have otherwise chosen in order to meet with Dobson, but Anlon hadn't expected that decision to lead to the mess he found himself mired in now.

As he contemplated these thoughts, Anlon heard the creak of the kitchen screen door behind him and the muffled steps of Pebbles' bare feet on the wooden porch leading to the stairs. She had been reunited with her everyday summer Tahoe wardrobe, daisy dukes and a black form-fitting tank top, thanks to a late afternoon shower that ushered in a warm front.

She descended the steps to where Anlon rested and slid down next to him, her own beer in hand. She nuzzled next to him and asked in a gentle voice, "How are you doing, A.C.? Want some company or should I leave you alone?"

He smiled and absorbed the heat of her skin against his, having adopted shorts and t-shirt himself. "You, young lady, are always welcome to join me, and I'm hanging in there I guess."

"Good answer," she replied, raising her lips to kiss his cheek, "So what's going on in that PhD brain of yours?"

Anlon said, "I don't feel like much of a PhD right now. I'm overwhelmed with all of this craziness to tell you the truth."

Pebbles slung her arm around his neck and patted his shoulder. "Aw, don't beat yourself up, A.C. I'm not sure anyone could make sense out of what's happened."

"Well, I know one thing for sure. I'm no detective!" he said.

"Oh, please," she answered, slapping his back, "you are too."

Anlon shook his head and patted Pebbles' knee. "You're being awfully kind, Pebbles, but I'm so lost right now I'm not sure I could find my way back in the house with a Sherpa and flashing signs."

Pebbles had not seen Anlon like this before. She couldn't remember a time she'd been around him when he wasn't relaxed and confident. He's human after all, she rejoiced!

He needs a pep talk and a good night's sleep, Pebbles reflected, though she wasn't sure which should come first. She reached for his hand as it sat atop her knee and intertwined her fingers with his. Silently they listened to the sounds of the night while she peered down at the trinity knot tattoo on the underside of her wrist. Gazing at the ink design, Pebbles took a swig of her beer to steel herself. Pep talk it is.

"Do you remember," she said, "when we were out on your boat the first time and you asked me about my tattoos?"

"Huh?" Anlon mumbled as he was drawn out of his thoughts by Pebbles' question. "Um, yeah, sure I do."

"You asked me if they had meanings, and I said no, not really. And you asked me if I had gotten them all at one time or at different times, and I said at different times. You then asked me a question that seemed odd to me. You asked me to point out the order in which I got them. Do you remember that?"

Anlon closed his eyes and recalled the shimmering lake waters, the golden sun, the warm breeze and the visage of Pebbles in white daisy dukes and a hot pink bikini top, her pink-streaked black hair wafting up in patches each time the breeze swirled. He remembered her guided tour of body art starting with her left ankle, moving up to her right front shoulder, then her left inner wrist, her right wrist and finishing with the right side of her neck.

"Yes, that was a tour I'll never forget," Anlon winked as he squeezed her hand lightly.

"And then later, around Christmas I think, when we drove over to Squaw Valley to ski, and in a weak moment I told you the hummingbird story about the tattoo on my neck while we rode up the T-bar. After I finished the story, you didn't probe, you just said it was a sweet story," Pebbles reminisced.

Anlon didn't comment, unsure where Pebbles was going with her trip down memory lane. She continued on, "And a couple of months ago while we were at your home in Los Cabos, sunbathing next to the infinity pool — love that pool, by the way — and we got a little drunk from tequila and the hot sun. We were kidding around and you blurted out that you'd finally figured out the meaning of my tattoos. I taunted you and said there was zero chance you knew. And you said you knew exactly what each one meant and in what order I got them, and that the order was different than what I told you on the lake."

Thinking back, he recalled her withering taunts and cringed, "Ah yes. I remember you were upset with me. I should have kept my mouth shut, I didn't mean to make you cry."

"I wasn't upset with you, Anlon, I was shocked you saw right through me. Even though I never gave you the chance to actually tell me your theory before I ran in the house crying, I knew the moment you mentioned my lie about the order that you were too close for comfort. I felt exposed, not angry. I didn't think you could look inside me like that," Pebbles said, wiping away a small tear from her cheek.

"I'm sorry, Pebbles, you're getting upset again. Let's talk about something else," Anlon answered, observing her weepy eyes.

She shook her head and said, "No, it's important. Tell me your theory, Anlon, I want to hear it."

"Oh, no way, Pebbles. I should never have gone there. I don't want to open up old wounds," Anlon answered, mortified by his choice of finishing words as they spilled from his mouth.

Pebbles squeezed his hand tightly and said, "Please, Anlon, I want to talk about it. It's time."

She nodded without further comment, encouraging him to begin. Anlon stared off into the mist forming over the grassy carpet surrounding the driveway and gathered his words carefully before softly speaking, "They tell a story. A love story...about devastating loss, despair, acceptance, new hope, renewed strength and fond remembrance. They serve as both reminders and sources of inspiration."

As he spoke, he touched each tattoo in order of the story. First, the huddled angel with folded wings and head bowed on her left wrist (despair/loss), the trinity knot on her right wrist (serenity/acceptance), the broken chain around her ankle (freedom/hope), the Chinese script symbol for strength on her shoulder (rebirth) and the hummingbird on her neck (loving reminder).

Drops trickled down her face and she sniffled, "You're incredible."

Anlon didn't mention the scars beneath the tattoos on her wrists, understanding the ink was intended to obscure the wounds.

He kept quiet about his observation that she always held her head a certain way when she looked at her hummingbird tattoo in a mirror and that when he positioned himself to look at her from the same angle, it appeared the hummingbird was kissing her ear lobe.

He left silent the fact that all the tattoos were on the front of her body in places she would naturally see over the course of the day, or the fact that she rubbed her wrists when nervous or unsure. Even when she wore bangles, she pushed them out of the way to massage the wrists.

Or when she teasingly flexed her bicep at him (which she did often when she playfully taunted him), it was always with her right arm. When she wore short sleeves, she always pulled it back to reveal the shoulder tattoo in conjunction with the mocking bicep curl.

Conscious and unconscious cues, some subtle, others overt, revealing the lineage of emotions caused by the traumatic event that led her to shed Eleanor and become Pebbles. A map of sorts, Anlon concluded.

Pebbles wiped away the tears, cleared her throat and asked, "Do you know the whole story? Did you look it up online?"

"No," Anlon said. "I thought about it, but I didn't want to pry."

"Well, you're a damn good detective, Anlon, don't ever believe anything different. You and I, our brains aren't built the same way. You don't always process things you see and hear as fast as I do, but you notice things I miss entirely and, man, can you string pieces together in a way that I can't. It's a gift I don't have or haven't developed yet.

"Don't you see, Anlon? You're feeling lost because the clues have been coming in rapid fire and you haven't had the space to sort them all out yet. But with the right amount of time to think, you will, I know it!" Pebbles stated, tussling his hair.

Anlon was dumbfounded by her message and the way she delivered it. He smiled back and said, "You're selling yourself short, Pebbles. You are very perceptive. Between the two of us, we make a pretty good team, don't you think?"

The next day Anlon awoke energized and determined to get to the bottom of things. Over doughnuts again, he and Pebbles agreed to split up their days in different directions to accomplish twice as much as they might together as they had tried to do before they discovered the break-in.

She would join Jennifer to go through Dobson's house and together they would return to go over the barn again in search of the Port Stone and anything helpful to Jennifer's investigation.

Anlon's plan for the day was centered on a lunchtime visit with Anabel Simpson, whom he'd spoken to in the morning to arrange a time to meet. First though, Anlon had another phone call to make. He needed to ramp up his education about Devlin's whole scope of research.

Unfortunately, Anlon didn't have the time to read every book in Devlin's study, every paper he published, every document in his files or every computer file on his still-missing laptop. So Anlon would need to be creative to accelerate his learning curve and he knew exactly where to start.

"Anlon!" shouted the voice on the end of the line, "how are you, my man?"

"Antonio, good to hear your voice, it's been a while," Anlon replied, "I know you are very busy. I appreciate you stepping out of your meeting to chat for a few minutes."

"Anything for you, what's up?" asked Antonio Wallace, the lead investigator on the Whave fuel and engine patent project. He had recruited Anlon to the team originally and had been the one who personally designed the combustion engine adaptation to store excess bursts of energy from the fuel additive. He was beyond brilliant, and now ran his own multi-billion-dollar technology firm, having quadrupled his share of the patent proceeds in the process. He had also recently purchased the controlling interest in the Bay Area's professional basketball team.

"I need a favor, and I kind of need it fast," Anlon said.

"Aim and fire! What do you need? Tickets for tonight's Warriors game?"

"Ha, I wish! They looked good in the first round of the playoffs. Everything you touch turns to gold! Anyway, you're still well connected in academia, right? I need an introduction to an archaeologist I don't know how to reach. And I need to meet him, like yesterday."

"Okay, what's the dude's name?"

"His name is Cesar Perez. He was a research colleague of my uncle, Devlin Wilson," Anlon responded.

Cesar Perez, PhD, had co-authored two books with Devlin and collaborated with him on a number of published research articles.

He also, according to the calendar on Devlin's desk, had three phone appointments over the past few months with Anlon's uncle. With Dobson dead and Pacal having vanished, Dr. Perez was Anlon's best bet to get a deeper understanding of Devlin's research in short order. At least, that's what he hoped.

"All right. I'll get on it and see what I can find. Call you back in an hour. Is that fast enough?"

"Better than I could have dreamed," praised a thankful Anlon.

"Everything okay, buddy? You sound stressed," Antonio asked in reply, concern in his voice.

"Yeah, I'm okay. I'm just in a little over my head at the moment and I need some expert advice. It's a time-sensitive issue," elaborated Anlon.

"Got it. Okay, I'll get back to you like I said. Anything else?" Antonio inquired.

Anlon paused, and then said, "Well, now that you mention it. Once you find him, any chance I can borrow your plane and pilot to go meet him? I'm not in Tahoe right now, I'm in Stockbridge, Massachusetts. I think there's an airfield in Pittsfield up the road. I'll reimburse you, of course."

A roaring laugh echoed over the line. Antonio bellowed, "My plane is your plane. I don't need your money, my man. Just bring the plane back in one piece with a full tank and rested pilot and we're good. Oh, and I'll want to know what this is all about when we both have more time. Deal?"

"Deal! I can't thank you enough, Skipper!" Anlon answered, invoking the Whave team's nickname for Antonio before ringing off.

As she parked her car in the empty driveway, Jennifer could see the police tape still layered across the entrance door of Matthew Dobson's split level home. While she waited for Pebbles to arrive, Jennifer killed time by flipping through the police report detailing the crime scene again, including transcribed interviews with Mrs. Minden, the woman who found Dobson, and other neighbors.

Jennifer planned to visit Mrs. Minden after they wrapped up their search and she brought along pictures of Devlin and Pacal for the follow-up interview. She was curious whether either man had visited Dobson in the weeks leading up to his death. The initial police report only mentioned that none of the neighbors, including Mrs. Minden, noticed any visitors (or anything else unusual) on the day Dobson was killed.

When Pebbles pulled up in Devlin's Land Rover, Jennifer grabbed her gear and exited her car. Smiling, she waved to Pebbles. "Hey there! Ready to dig in?"

"Ha ha," Pebbles retorted, "I was born ready, PoPo."

Jennifer extended a hand to greet Pebbles and then asked her to carry up a large, empty box for holding any evidence they removed from the home. Hanging around Jennifer's neck was a digital camera and she lugged an oversized case that looked like a fishing tackle box, otherwise known as an evidence collection kit.

When they arrived at the police tape, Jennifer placed down the evidence collection kit and opened it up. She removed latex gloves and foot covers for Pebbles and herself and handed them to Pebbles to hold until they entered. She retrieved a multi-tool from the kit and unfolded a knife to slice the police tape away at one end, asking Pebbles first to verify the tape was intact. Removing a notepad from her sweatshirt jacket pocket, Jennifer recorded the time and their names so that she could update the crime scene entry log when she returned to her headquarters later.

Jennifer replaced the pad in her jacket and deposited the multi-tool back into the top tray of the kit. She donned gloves and Pebbles followed suit. She retrieved a house key from an evidence bag she signed out back at headquarters and unlocked the door, causing the entry alarm to beep at a low pitch. Before they stepped into the house, Jennifer slid on foot covers over her running shoes and asked Pebbles to do the same.

"Okay, here we are. Let's do a quick walk through of the whole house and then we'll figure out how we want to attack it," Jennifer instructed after she entered the security code set by her Captain on the day Dobson was discovered.

On the main level was a living room, dining room, powder room, kitchen and laundry room. On the lower level was a family room, home office, a full bathroom and utility room. Upstairs, three bedrooms and two full bathrooms — one shared between two bedrooms — and the other within what appeared to be the master bedroom. Jennifer noted a framed panel in the ceiling above the main stairway, which she assumed was an attic entry. They returned back to the living room and Jennifer said, "Let's start on the upper level and work our way down. I'm looking for anything that might be connected with Matthew Dobson's death. Documents, pictures or other items that seem out of place or might even be remotely related to the crime."

"Got it," Pebbles answered, "and if we stumble across his will or anything related to Devlin's death?"

"We'll sort out what to do with anything like that when and if we find something," she replied. Jennifer was walking a bit of a fine line. It was unusual to allow a "citizen" entry into a crime scene but not out of the question. Detectives occasionally requested interested persons visit crime scenes to see if they noticed anything out of place or to assist them in locating potential pieces of evidence.

In this case, Pebbles wasn't as much a classical person of interest as she was another pair of sharp eyes who had a complementary motive for the search, albeit from a different perspective (Devlin's death versus Dobson's).

Jennifer started in the master bedroom while Pebbles checked the two guest bedrooms. They both observed that Matthew Dobson had been a man of simple but quality tastes. The rooms were uncluttered but tastefully appointed, though many of the furnishings were dated. Pebbles commented that Dobson must have preserved much of his wife's touches after she passed away. Jennifer agreed.

"Find anything?" Jennifer called.

"There are some old family pictures on both dressers but no documents in any of the drawers or in the closets. No unusual items that I can see," Pebbles answered.

"Alright, same here. Let's switch up. You go through the master bedroom and I'll go through the other ones," Jennifer suggested, knowing conducting completely split searches could lead to missing evidence.

"Hey, look at the family pictures on the dressers. Don't the kids in it look like the adults in the one on Dobson's bedside table?" Pebbles called down the short hallway.

Jennifer picked up one of the pictures delicately by its corners so as to preserve possible fingerprints and walked back to the master bedroom. Holding one picture up to the other, she remarked, "Yep, they do look similar."

"Didn't Mr. Grant mention yesterday that Dobson had a niece and a nephew who didn't come to the funeral yesterday?" Pebbles mentioned.

"You're right. He did, but I don't remember him giving us the names. Just said he found them and talked to them and they balked at attending. I'll follow up on that," Jennifer said, pulling out her pad and scribbling a quick note.

"Might be worth talking to them, you think?" Pebbles asked.

"Possibly," she replied. "Let's bag and record the picture of them as adults and move on."

Soon they had searched two of the three levels and now came to the lower level. They searched the den together, finding nothing more of interest other than a few more framed snapshots of Dobson with the same adults depicted in the picture in the master bedroom.

Their search heated up when they entered Dobson's office. They found statements from two different banks. They also discovered a cell phone statement, a powered-off laptop and briefcase which contained three spiral-bound notebooks. The notebooks caught Pebbles' attention in particular because they were labeled with Devlin Wilson's name. Each of these items they placed in evidence bags and recorded evidence tags. Jennifer took snapshots of each item where they originally found them and laid out together on the dining room table upstairs. But they didn't find a will, or any documents from an attorney.

"That's a bummer," Pebbles exclaimed once it was clear no will was present.

"Don't give up yet. We still need to check the utility room and attic. Sometimes people file away old documents in the strangest places. If you ask me though, I'll bet if he has a will it's in a safe deposit box at one of the two banks we found statements from," Jennifer replied.

"Oh, I didn't think of that. You're probably right! What about a safe? Do you think Dobson had one here in the house? I wasn't looking for one myself, but maybe he had a hidden one like Devlin?" Pebbles asked.

"It's a good thought. I've kept an eye out as we've gone through the rooms, but didn't notice any obvious areas where a safe might be hidden. Before we go, we should spin back through the whole house, but let's check the utility room and attic first," Jennifer suggested.

As they searched, Pebbles was conflicted. She really wanted Devlin's spiral notebooks, but Jennifer had already bagged and recorded them as evidence. She wasn't sure how to bring the subject up with Jennifer without causing friction.

The attic had been empty and the utility room held no file boxes or other clues. They were about to leave and re-seal the house when Pebbles remembered, "Hey, weren't we going to run through the house one more time looking for a safe?"

Jennifer peered down at her watch and said, "Ugh, I don't have much time, but you are right we should do it."

They retraced the rooms together but found nothing. Pebbles concluded, "I guess that's that!"

Jennifer nodded her head in agreement and they gathered up the box with evidence they'd bagged, as well as the collection kit. When they reached the front door, Jennifer halted and mumbled, "Rookie mistake!"

Pebbles turned and said, "What? What do you mean?"

"We never checked the kitchen! Or the laundry room," she exhaled as she placed the collection kit down on the foyer.

The laundry room held no surprises. Jennifer said, "Check everywhere in the kitchen. Cabinets, closets, refrigerator, canisters."

For the next 10 minutes the house reverberated with the sounds of banging drawers and cabinets mixed with the metallic shuffling of pots, pans and silverware. That is until Pebbles shouted, "Bingo!"

Stuffed behind a coffee maker on the bottom shelf of a cabinet by the refrigerator was a shelf-sized safe with an electronic combination lock.

Jennifer stared at the lock and said, "I'm so happy we didn't leave before checking the kitchen! Let's go back through his office and see if we can find the combination."

Another 30 minutes searching produced no combination. They powered up the laptop, but there was a password screen that would require the police IT guys to bypass. Frustrated, Jennifer said, "Damn! We'll have to note it and get our safe crackers to come back and take it away to open."

Pebbles fidgeted with her wrists and said, "Can we at least try to guess a few times before we leave?"

Jennifer shrugged and replied, "Can't hurt. This safe lock isn't sophisticated enough to cut off after a certain number of tries. It looks fairly old."

"Cool," Pebbles said, pulling out her cell phone.

"What are you doing?" Jennifer inquired.

"Research," smiled Pebbles.

After five minutes of tapping the cellphone's screen, Pebbles asked, "Do we think we need four numbers or three?"

"Um, I'd say most safes use at least four numbers to increase the number of possible combinations," Jennifer answered.

"Okay, let's first find out the maximum number of numbers we can try. Keep pressing the number one until the screen won't let you enter anymore."

Jennifer pressed the one key four times and the screen ceased showing additional digits. She said, "Clever for a novice."

"Can't take credit. Found that suggestion after doing a search on safe cracking. Okay, now try 1257," Pebbles stated.

"Nothing. That's the street address, right?"

"Yep," Pebbles answered. "What year was Dobson born?"

"Let me think...he was 74 when he died, so that means he was born in 1942."

"Okay, try that."

"Nothing again."

"Alright, reverse it, 2491."

The electronic keyboard pinged with each keystroke until at last the red LED light beside the keypad switched to green and they heard a click.

Jennifer stared at Pebbles in awe, "How did you do that?"

"Again, no credit. Safe cracking site said its common to use birthdays as codes. Also said to try it backwards," Pebbles answered, holding her hands up as if caught in the act of committing a crime.

Jennifer extended her hand and pulled the safe handle up. She opened the door and shouted, "Holy crap! Would you look at that!"

Pebbles knelt on the floor next to Jennifer and craned her neck to gape at the safe's contents...hundreds and hundreds of gold coins. She lifted one out and flipped it over and back atop her glove-covered palm.

Shivers ran down her spine as she randomly selected three others. She gasped, "Jennifer! Each of these coins have the imprint of one of the six objects on the Master Stone!"

XIV
ANABEL SIMPSON

The drive north to Bennington, Vermont, was cleansing for Anlon. He enjoyed passing through quaint New England towns, sweeping by fields filled with black and white Holstein cattle, spying the occasional forgotten syrup bucket plugged into maple trees by the road and the quintessential covered bridges along the way.

During the trip, Anlon spent most of the time developing an action plan. He firmly believed Devlin and Dobson's deaths were linked and that the common connection must be the stones. He reasoned that the killer must already possess knowledge about the stones, otherwise killing both Devlin and Dobson was a supremely idiotic move.

Pondering further, Anlon tried to construct reasons for the thefts of the will, Port Stone and Devlin's laptop. The Port Stone was easiest to understand. It was needed to access the Story Stones and Master Stones. Since the laptop appeared to be stolen at the same time as the Port Stone, Anlon conjectured that the laptop must contain relevant information about the stones, which on the face of it, seemed a logical conclusion.

The piece that didn't quite seem to fit in Anlon's mind was the theft of the will, especially given the fact that the case containing the Master Stone was untouched. What could be in the will that was so important? How did it fit in with the other events? What did it reveal? And why did Devlin leave such a large sum to Anabel Simpson? For that matter, who was Anabel Simpson and what was her connection with Devlin? All these questions circulated in Anlon's mind as he neared Bennington. At least, he thought, by the time he was on his way back to Stockbridge, he'd have some of those answers.

Anlon's train of thought was disrupted by the chime of his cell phone. As promised, Antonio Wallace called in less than an hour to report he'd found Cesar Perez. When Anlon asked his location, Antonio responded, "Not to worry, Anlon. He's on his way to you right now."

"What?" a stunned Anlon queried.

"You said it was urgent, I made it happen. It wasn't that hard. When I mentioned your uncle's name like you suggested, Dr. Perez became suddenly eager to see you," said Antonio.

"That's beyond believable, I don't know what to say, Skip," Anlon humbly remarked.

"Anlon, I've known you a long time. The last time you had the same kind of urgency in your voice as you had on the phone with me this morning, you made me a billionaire! I've always trusted my instincts. This meeting is important and time is of the essence. You said both yourself. He should be in Pittsfield by 9:00 a.m. tomorrow morning. You can pick him up at the airport or I can have a car bring him to you," Antonio said casually.

"I'll pick him up, Antonio. You are a true friend. Thank you," Anlon said in reply.

"No worries, Anlon, my man. Remember your promise though. I want to know what this is all about after you talk to him."

"You have my word," Anlon answered.

Antonio replied, "Good as gold to me."

Prior to hopping in the rental SUV for his drive to Bennington, Anlon did a little web browsing for background information on Anabel Simpson. He did not find much. When he spoke with her to arrange the meeting he could tell she was older than he, and Anlon was surprised to learn she knew some of Anlon's background from snippets Devlin shared with her over the years, or so she said. Anlon looked up her address online and was able to pinpoint its location and a street level view of the property. She lived relatively close to Bennington College, which made sense, as she appeared to have been a professor at the school for many years. Other than those pieces of information, Anlon was flying blind.

Anlon drove along the rutted, long driveway to the small, unassuming rambler surrounded by large, sloping lawn with an array of mid-sized trees enclosed by a white wooden fence.

Standing on the front porch, Anabel waved to Anlon. She was older as Anlon suspected, on the underside of 60, he surmised. Though her long, braided hair was mostly white, her skin was clear and barely marked by wrinkles. She had a lively smile and was dressed more like a college student than a grandmother in jeans, slip-on sneakers and an oversized bright red Bennington College hoodie sweatshirt.

"Welcome," she called cheerily as Anlon exited the SUV.

"Thank you, thank you, it's good to meet you. I'm Anlon Cully," he replied.

She motioned him to join her on the front steps. She greeted him with a polite hug and said, "You are much taller than Devlin! I'm surprised he never mentioned that."

"Well, he may not have remembered. We didn't see each other much the last 10 years or so," Anlon replied, "but I'm very pleased to meet you, Mrs. Simpson, though I'm sorry it's as a result of Devlin's passing."

"It was bitter news to hear," she acknowledged, bowing her head with a slight quiver in her voice. "Do come in and make yourself comfortable. We have a lot to discuss, and I'm no missus. Please, I'm Anabel."

Seated in her small living room, Anlon noticed at once the sampling of framed pictures on table tops and wall shelves showing Anabel and Devlin together over many years. Anlon was taken aback. He never really knew much of Devlin's personal life and even though he did occasionally discuss women in his life, he never mentioned the name Anabel to the best of his recollection.

"These are touching photographs," Anlon remarked, looking from one picture to the next of them smiling, hugging, holding hands, dancing and other happy shared moments. "I must confess, I had no idea Devlin shared a relationship with you but it's clear from your photo collection that you shared a warm and happy relationship for a very long time."

"That's sweet of you to say, Anlon. I cared deeply for Devlin and we shared many precious memories over the 35 years I knew him," Anabel said.

"Thirty-five years? Wow, I can't believe I didn't know. I'm sure he must have talked about you many times with me, but I must have tuned out," commented Anlon.

"No, Anlon, he probably didn't speak about me with you. Our relationship was very private. The world was very different when we first met. A 50-year-old professor in a public relationship with a 23-year-old student at the university where he taught would have been lethal for his career, and for the start of mine," Anabel explained.

Anlon understood her point, especially in light of the age gap between Pebbles and him. He supposed it was *a* reason but not the only reason why his relationship with Pebbles still was platonic, although it seemed to be accelerating towards a relationship of a more intimate nature the last few days.

"Looking at your photos, the age difference doesn't come across in my eyes. Like this one right here with the two of you, arm in arm, on one of his excavations," Anlon commented.

Anabel rose and retrieved the photo. She traced her fingers along the outlines of their smiling faces, and absently said, "What a magical time. This one was taken in Egypt in the mid-80s. I was a teacher and most of our time together was spent during school breaks in the early days. I never had so much fun and adventure as when I went off with Devlin to some exotic land."

Anlon felt her sense of loss through her sentimental memories. He said, "The Devlin I knew was such a charismatic man, I can see how being around him in his element was enchanting."

"Enchanting? What a lovely description," she beamed.

"So, if you don't mind me asking, why did you choose to keep the relationship private, even later in life?" Anlon uncomfortably ventured.

"I don't mind you asking. You know, it's very hard to explain. Since we spent so much time apart, we truly developed separate lives. He had other relationships with women, I had other relationships with men, but we always found some time to escape together for many years. I liked the escape, and he did, too. When we spent too much time with one another, our relationship was different...less exciting...more mundane. We just found a happy medium and left it that way. We eventually drifted apart and only recently reconnected. I have no complaints; it was as fulfilling a relationship as I could have imagined. I will miss him in my life," Anabel waxed, staring off in the distance, reliving precious memories.

Anlon admired the prism through which Anabel viewed her relationship with Devlin. She was at peace and had been so throughout her time with Devlin. He said, "Thank you for sharing, Anabel. It is heartwarming to know Devlin had a life full of love beyond his passion for archaeology."

"I'm pleased you noticed and asked, Anlon. It's nice to talk about Devlin with someone. Now, enough about me. You've come all the way up here to discuss other matters, I'm sure," she said, placing the photo frame back on a table and retraining her focus on Anlon.

"Not at all, Anabel. I appreciate you being so open. Learning more about your relationship with Devlin has already answered some of the questions I came to ask. But you are right, there are other matters I came to discuss. I guess we should first talk about Devlin's will. I presume by now that you've received a copy of his will from George Grant, Devlin's attorney?"

"Yes, I did. He had one delivered by courier yesterday. I told him I felt uncomfortable attending the funeral. I didn't tell him why, but between you and me, I didn't want to make a spectacle of myself. I will visit his grave to mourn when a little time has passed," Anabel clarified.

"Makes perfect sense now that I know more about your relationship with Devlin. When I first saw the will myself, I was puzzled about who you were. I was also told by Mr. Grant that Devlin requested I discuss the will with you in person, which seemed an odd request. Now I understand the reason for his request and why he provided for you in his will," Anlon said.

Given the nature of their relationship, Anlon was now surprised Devlin hadn't left her a more sizeable portion of the estate. Anabel must have read his mind because she interjected, "It was very thoughtful of Devlin to provide for me in his will, but he was so generous over the years it really wasn't necessary. He bought me this home, you know. He supplemented my income in the early years. And each year on our private 'anniversary', he gave or sent me a piece of his treasured collection, even after we drifted apart. He said they were gifts of his love, but also insurance policies. He told me if I ever found myself in need of funds, I should sell one or more of the pieces. I never have, mind you, they are too dear to me, but I had the pieces valued a few years back and was numb when the auction house appraiser told me combined they were worth over five million dollars! He said some pieces were rare enough that they might be worth much more if they were publicly auctioned versus sold privately."

Anlon perked up at the mention of Devlin's collection. He wondered if she possessed any of the Life Stones but it felt too awkward to pry. Instead, Anlon said, "Devlin was a good man. I'm happy he treated you so well."

"He did indeed," Anabel agreed.

"So, as executor of his estate, it's my responsibility to make sure his assets are distributed per the will. I'm not an expert at any of this, so I asked Mr. Grant to handle most of the formalities in terms of documentation and what not. He should be in touch very soon with some papers for you to sign and then I don't believe it will be very long after that before Devlin's bequest is transferred to you. If you have any questions or concerns, please feel free to contact me or Mr. Grant. I will do my best to limit the hassle factor for everyone concerned and expedite the distributions," said Anlon.

"Thank you, Anlon. I don't have any questions now and you've already provided me your number, and I have Mr. Grant's in the packet delivered yesterday. There are, however, two other matters I wanted to discuss with you. One on behalf of Devlin, and the other I thought you should know," Anabel said.

"Okay, which would you like to discuss first?"

"Do you know a man called Thatcher Reynolds?" she inquired casually.

Anlon's face flushed briefly in anger, "Yes, I met him yesterday at the funeral. It wasn't a pleasant conversation. Why do you ask?"

"He called me the day before the funeral to stir a hornet's nest. Said I was treated unfairly in Devlin's will. He offered to help contest the will and secure a larger portion of the estate. He said Devlin's nephew Richard had already agreed to accept his help. If I accepted his help, too, he said, it would give them a stronger case," she recalled.

Anlon buried his head between his hands and shook his head. "He's a troublemaker for sure. I can't tell you what to do, Anabel. If you feel you've been unfairly treated, it is within your power to challenge the will, but from what Mr. Grant shared, it would be a tough road."

"I told him to go to Hell!" Anabel said, pounding the armrest of the couch.

A relieved Anlon laughed aloud, "Did you? He tried to get me to sell him Devlin's artifact collection, and when I said it wasn't for sale, he threatened me. He's after something in Devlin's collection, he doesn't care about the money. I'm so glad you shut him down. What did he say when you told him?"

"The scoundrel hung up on me!" she laughed.

"If he contacts you again, would you please let me know? I'm going to have Mr. Grant get involved and stop this nonsense. I'm sorry he bothered you," Anlon responded.

"I'm fine, I just wanted you to be aware of his call," she explained. "Now, the other matter is a bit more delicate. Devlin gave me something to hold for you and only you. He told me it was by far the most valuable item in his collection and that he didn't trust anyone else with it."

Anlon's heartbeat galloped. She has the Port Stone! He nodded understanding, but remained silent. It was evident Anabel had more to say.

"You should know, Anlon, that Devlin came to see me the day before he died. In fact, he stayed overnight here on his way to Mt. Whiteface. He was very upset. I'd say he was scared. It stood out to me because he never before had been fearful around me. He rambled on a long time that night, telling me things he'd never shared before. Anlon, he told me he feared for his life!" Anabel exclaimed.

She trembled as she finished speaking. A tear appeared at the corner of her eye. Anabel continued, "The things he told me, he asked that I share with you along with the piece he left with me for safekeeping if something should happen to him. Some of what he told me I think you will find hard to believe."

Anlon chuckled and replied, "I've heard and seen a number of things the last few days that are hard to believe. I'm getting used to it."

She smiled in return and nodded her understanding. Anabel continued, "I didn't write any of it down so I hope I don't forget something important. I wanted to give Devlin my full attention.

"First off, Devlin suspected Matthew was stealing from his collection and selling what he took for his own benefit. There had been some rumors about black market transactions involving pieces Devlin knew to be in his collection. Devlin knew Matthew had also taken items from the office archive for unexplained and unauthorized reasons and then returned them later. One of the items he pilfered and then returned is the document he brought here for you."

Uh, oh, Anlon thought. She doesn't have the Port Stone. He uttered, "Document? Hmmm…I thought it might be a stone shaped like a hockey puck."

"No, I'm afraid he didn't give me anything like that, not even among the gifts he gave me from his collection. But I'll get to the document later. There are other pieces of our conversation you need to hear first.

"Devlin and Matthew had a terrible confrontation the day before he drove here. Devlin accused Matthew of purposely stealing to line his own pockets. Matthew denied it, but Devlin didn't need a confession. Several days beforehand, Pacal told Devlin he saw Matthew sneak in and return the document very early one morning. Pacal had slept in the office loft the preceding night and when Matthew entered, he wasn't aware Pacal was up in the loft. This added to Devlin's suspicions, and with Pacal's help they set a trap for Matthew a few days before the confrontation."

"Wow!" Anlon cried. "Did he tell you why he went to Mt. Whiteface? When I spoke with Dobson, he seemed perplexed as to why Devlin decided to hike there."

"Then Matthew lied to you. The same morning Matthew returned the document, Pacal noticed him remove an Incan sculpture and hide it in his desk drawer. Devlin said he had Pacal conceal GPS tracking devices inside their three artifact carrying cases. Devlin said Matthew took the bait, which I assume means he later placed the sculpture in a carry case and left with it. From the GPS tracker, Devlin knew where Matthew took the case for what he assumed was the handoff to the buyer.

"Devlin said the GPS tracker showed Matthew took the case home for the night and the next day drove straight to Mt. Whiteface. Devlin said the GPS tracker also showed Matthew hiked the trail to a point and then returned by the same route. Devlin assumed Matthew met someone on the trail for the handoff. The case came back to the office with Matthew, but the sculpture was gone. Devlin wanted to see the handoff site himself before he called the police on Matthew."

Anlon's head was spinning again. He asked, "Anabel, do you think Dobson killed Devlin? That seems where you're headed."

"When I first learned Devlin died on Mt. Whiteface, I did think Matthew was involved," she confirmed, "but less than a week later, Matthew was dead, too, and I then I wasn't so sure."

"Join the crowd!" Anlon dead-panned. But inside he paused to consider Anabel's story. It was conceivable Dobson killed Devlin given the confrontation about his thievery, but why then would Dobson have confided his suspicions about Devlin's 'accidental' death with the police and Anlon? That didn't make any sense.

Was it possible that Matthew told the buyer that Devlin was onto him? Did the buyer decide Devlin had to go? And then killed Matthew because he might, or did, put two and two together about Devlin's death? That scenario seemed very possible to Anlon. His mind immediately flashed to the pushy, arrogant Thatcher Reynolds and the smarmy Klaus Navarro.

"Anabel," Anlon asked, "did Devlin say what made him fear for his life? Something else must have happened to cause him to take precautions about the document he gave you and another artifact he left with his attorney, Mr. Grant. I can see why he might hide pieces from Matthew by removing from the office, but I don't see how his confrontation with Matthew would cause him fear — especially if Matthew denied stealing and selling pieces."

"Oh yes, I did forget to mention that, didn't I? When he asked me to hold the document for him is when he said he felt his life was in danger. I don't recall his precise words but they were along the lines of 'I'm afraid he'll go after the map. It's valuable enough to kill for' or something like that," Anabel said.

"Map? So the document he gave you is a map? What kind of map?" Anlon sharply inquired, shifting his body to the edge of the sofa.

"Yes, a map. It's a very special, rare map. A treasure map of sorts, according to Devlin. He told me to tell you the map shows where to find undiscovered Life Stones. He said that would make sense to you, but he didn't tell me anything more about it. Said it was too dangerous," Anabel shrugged.

Anlon shifted all the way back on the sofa and sighed in relief. Finally, he thought, Devlin left more than a piece of rock minus instructions or explanations. Even though Anabel's relay of Devlin's message wasn't much of an explanation, he wouldn't have to guess the purpose of the map.

Anlon disappeared into deeper thought while Anabel left the room to retrieve the map for him. So Devlin was searching for the other stones depicted on the Master Stone! And he either made a map of their locations or found a map showing the locations. Matthew had taken the map, but returned it. Did he make a copy, Anlon wondered? Maybe that's why Devlin was afraid. But his words to Anabel were very similar to the words Pacal used when trying to dissuade Anlon from pursuing Devlin's research — "too dangerous." Why?

He also struggled to understand why Dobson had insisted Anlon come early to talk about Devlin's research. At least Anlon now had a better idea why Dobson was so nervous when he met with him. But why not let sleeping dogs lie?

Maybe Dobson thought by helping me, Anlon considered, he could smooth over his past transgressions. Maybe that's why he was killed… once Devlin was dead, he realized his dealings were more dangerous than he originally thought and decided to cut off relations with the buyer and start fresh. That explanation fit a little better in Anlon's mind, but it still seemed not quite right.

Anlon would need to noodle it more later as Anabel emerged from the hallway with a silver metal attaché case. She placed the case flat on the coffee table and then Anlon realized it wasn't an attaché case, it was a portable safe, complete with both an electronic lock and key lock. Anabel punched in the combination and handed the key to Anlon to unlock the second level security.

Anabel motioned to Anlon to open the case. Inside was a heavy, black metal tube about a foot long with two metallic stoppers on each end sealing in the map. As Anlon lifted the tube from the case, Anabel said, "Devlin didn't show me the map. I'm curious to see what it looks like."

With one stopper out, Anlon carefully withdrew the map. He had expected it to be of ancient origin, but it was supple, unblemished, modern paper. He unfurled the scroll and anchored one end with the edge of the case and the other end he weighed down with the empty tube. Both Anlon and Anabel leaned forward over the map from opposite couches and scanned the map.

The map showed half a dozen large land masses separated by stretches of water, but the land masses were not labeled. There were longitude and latitude markings, so Anlon assumed he was looking at a map of the Earth. However, the large land masses looked nothing like today's global map in shape, size or position.

On the map were different color-coded markings at various points on the six large land masses, mostly near coastlines. However, no key accompanied the map, so the meaning of the markings was not evident.

Anlon gazed at the map with a puzzled expression. Anabel asked, "Does the map make sense to you?"

"No, not really. It looks like a world map given the longitude and latitude lines, but it doesn't look like any world map I've ever seen," Anlon replied, shaking his head.

"I think I can help you there," Anabel began. "I spent a lot of time with Devlin over the years and I know he was obsessed with a map found drawn on a wall inside the oldest known pyramid in Egypt. I never saw the map myself, but Devlin went there several times to study it in person.

"According to Devlin, the map was an enigma to Egyptologists and other archaeologists because it didn't comport with any known map of the Middle East region or the world.

"At some point, a scholar specializing in Dynastic Egyptian mythology put forth the theory that it was a map of the Egyptian underworld, a fanciful illustration to lend topography to the ethereal land of the afterlife. It seemed to satisfy most peers, but Devlin was not convinced. If I had to guess, I'd say this map is a reproduction of the pyramid afterlife map."

"What about the color-coded markings on the map? Do you know if they are on the pyramid map, too?" Anlon queried, hopeful that Anabel knew the answer.

She shook her head slightly and said, "No. As I said, I never saw the pyramid map. But remember I said that Devlin asked me to tell you that the map would tell you where to find the Life Stones, whatever they may be."

"Yes, I figured that was likely the case, but I'm at a loss to see how I'm going to find my way to the Egyptian underworld," mused Anlon.

It was late afternoon before Anlon finally started on his way back to Stockbridge. After he and Anabel examined the map, they returned it to its case and then munched on a light, late lunch that Anabel prepared.

Over lunch, Anabel regaled Anlon with several stories about her adventures with Devlin. Anlon watched her face light with joy recalling the exciting and romantic memories. As she described these experiences, he couldn't help but feel jealous of the close bond Devlin and Anabel enjoyed. It was remarkable, Anlon thought, that they sustained such an intense connection over decades, even though they maintained largely separate lives.

Anlon reflected on the last several years of his own life and how he purposely shut himself away after the deluge of public notoriety and scrutiny he experienced from the announcement of the Whave invention. He was burned on more than one occasion opening up to girlfriends and acquaintances who, in turn, went public with stories or pictures that embarrassed him. Anlon's solution had been simple, just don't open up. While it was a successful strategy in eliminating public invasion of his privacy, it did result unintentionally in a life without the kind of companionship Anabel and Devlin shared. That is, until Pebbles had stepped into his life, or he had stepped into hers.

Thinking of Pebbles, Anlon punched her cell number into the SUV's Bluetooth phone application and called to check in. The line rang three times and then Pebbles' excited voice blurted, "A.C.! Big news! When will you be here?"

Anlon laughed at her breathless volley, and replied, "Pebbles! Bigger news on my end! Should be there in about an hour."

"No way your day topped mine. I'm not sure I can wait to tell you! Didn't you get my texts?" she asked.

"No, I put my phone away when I met with Anabel. I didn't want to be disrespectful. Is everything okay?"

"Yes! Um, no. Well, no for a little while but all is good now," she said with a cheerful lilt.

"Hmmm…you're being very cryptic," Anlon answered.

Pebbles playfully admonished, "Well next time, Doc, read your damn texts! By the way, Jennifer is here. We were discussing ordering pizza but we'll wait 'til you get here. Hurry home but be safe!"

"Yes, Mother," Anlon teased as he rang off, suddenly desperate to read his text messages.

He drove another five miles before spying a gas station. He pulled into a spot in front of the station's mini mart and turned the engine off. Extracting his phone from the SUV's dashboard storage well, he touched the screen and saw Pebbles' name displayed on his notification screen with 10 messages waiting. Anlon couldn't remember the last time Pebbles texted him 10 times in a week. Opening his text app, Anlon read the messages from the bottom up in reverse order of when they were received:

3:37 p.m.	Please call with your ETA.
3:23 p.m.	Where are you?????????
2:56 p.m.	Jennifer here now. Everything okay. Swelling is down.
2:23 p.m.	OMG, I just found the PS!!!!
2:04 p.m.	Got a big lump on my forehead. Bastard.
2:02 p.m.	That Navarro freak showed up. He hit me! I kicked his butt!
1:35 p.m.	When do you think you'll be back, getting bored!
12:57 p.m.	Found nothing so far in DW office files.

12:10 p.m.   Back at office.

11:15 a.m.   Check out what we found at MD's!

Anlon sat in stunned silence looking at the phone screen. Attached to the 11:15 a.m. text was a picture of Pebbles' hand holding a gold coin. The design on the coin was familiar to Anlon, but he couldn't quite place it. Attached to the 2:23 p.m. was a shot of a tabletop with one item placed center-frame of the picture...the Port Stone.

XV

DAY OF DISCOVERY

Anlon slowed the SUV as he motored up Devlin's long, curving driveway. Parked outside the garage was Devlin's silver Land Rover and Jennifer's white, compact hybrid. Though sunset was still a good two hours away, the bright lights glowing from the house and barn created a warm and inviting aura. Anlon pulled alongside the two other vehicles and silenced the engine.

Stepping out of the car, he heard the back porch screen door slam and pounding steps down the staircase. Raising his eyes, he spied Pebbles running towards him at full tilt with a huge smile on her face and a rather noticeable bandaged lump on her forehead. She flung her arms around Anlon and crushed him against the SUV, kissing him square on the lips.

"Mmmm, I like that!" Anlon smiled and whispered as they separated. "What brought that on?"

"I don't know, I just felt like doing it," Pebbles cooed in return. "Well, maybe I'm a teeny bit medicated."

"Ooh, can I have some, too. Your poor forehead, it looks like it hurts," Anlon said, peering sympathetically at her wound.

"Nah, it's no worse than nicks I've gotten fighting my brothers! Besides, it's nothing compared to the hurting I put on that ponytailed scum bag!" she boasted.

"Come on," Anlon said, pressing his lips against hers again, "let's get inside. There is so much to talk about."

"Can't we stay here and kiss a little longer?" Pebbles winked.

From the porch, Jennifer watched their sweet embrace with envious but admiring eyes. So much for her long shot at Anlon, she thought, but maybe he has a cute friend! She cleared her throat and called down, "Okay you two, pizza's almost here. We've got work to do."

Pebbles leaned back while Anlon held her around the waist and turned her head to extend a mocking tongue towards Jennifer. "It's always work, work, work with you!"

They all laughed. Pebbles grabbed Anlon's hand to walk up the stairs, but Anlon said, "You go up, I've got to get something out of the car. I'll be up in a sec."

She nodded and raced back up the steps, stopping to smack Jennifer on the rear with the back of her hand before running into the house. Jennifer gasped at the unexpected blow and barked, "You're going to pay for that, Eleanor Marie!"

Pebbles halted suddenly inside the kitchen and spun around. With a quizzical look on her face, she called through the screen door, "How do you know my middle name?"

Oops, Jennifer thought. Out of view from Pebbles she blushed from her slip up, but decided to come clean, "I'm a copper. I did a little background check on you when you first got here."

Pebbles was a tad irked by the intrusion but she brushed it off. Jennifer had saved her bacon earlier, so she had plus side chits in her favor, even after the snooping admission. But Pebbles made a mental note to circle back and talk with Jennifer later about what she found. If she did a criminal search, it was likely she ran across some things about Pebbles that she didn't want Anlon to know yet. Or at least Pebbles wanted to be the one who talked to him about her past.

Soon the deliveryman arrived and they settled in the den to eat pizza and drink Cabernet while they talked. As usual, Pebbles ate with eyes glued to the remaining slices while devouring the one in front of her. Atop the square coffee table perched the pizza box, wine bottle, the gold coin and the portable safe. The Port Stone was in the freezer where Pebbles found it. She wanted Anlon to see for himself where she found it.

They were all famished so they ate in silence for several minutes, other than the muffled mouthful praise extolled by Anlon and Pebbles for Jennifer's choice of pizza parlor. After washing down their first slices with generous swallows of wine, they looked at each other expectantly. Finally, Anlon said, "Who wants to go first?"

Pebbles reached for another slice and motioned to Jennifer, "You first, copper."

Jennifer teased, "Okay, don't choke yourself while you speed eat!"

Their banter made Anlon smile. How their friendship evolved so rapidly was unclear to him but as far as he was concerned it was a welcome development. Together the three of them made a good team and that pleased Anlon. He did his best work as part of a team and knew that the only way they could solve the mysteries before them was to act as one.

"Let's start with the search of Matthew Dobson's house. We turned the place upside down for more than an hour. We didn't find the will but did find some possible clues to its location. This is all assuming he actually has a will.

"We found bank statements. I'm going to hit the banks tomorrow and see if he had a safe deposit box. We found some log books that look like they belonged to Devlin. Once our fingerprint guys get a chance to dust them, I will bring them by so we can take a look.

"Then, just as we were about to leave, I realized we hadn't checked the kitchen, so we went back and found a safe hidden behind an old coffee maker in a cabinet. As soon as Pebbles finishes chewing her cud, I'll let her pick it up from there since she deserves credit for cracking the safe," Jennifer sarcastically concluded.

Pebbles stopped mid-chew and shot Jennifer a nasty look. She held up her index finger and washed down the pizza wad with Cabernet. Exhaling, she said with feigned incredulity, "Chewing my cud? Are you calling me a cow?"

Turning to Anlon, she composed herself and with demure presence proudly announced, "Yep, it's true. I, Eleanor *Marie* McCarver, am now officially a safe cracker."

She expounded on the details of her web search and the various combinations they tried while Anlon and Jennifer withdrew another pizza slice each. With a flex of her bicep (pulling back the upper sleeve again, Anlon noticed), she crowed, "Nailed it on the third try!"

"That's where we found hundreds of these," Jennifer interrupted, rolling her eyes at Pebbles' dramatic tale. "All neatly stacked and all bearing the same symbol..."

Pebbles said over top Jennifer's comment, "It's one of the Master Stone symbols, A.C.!"

Anlon slapped his hands together. Of course, that's where he'd seen the symbol. He said with surprise, "Hundreds of them?"

He recalled back to his conversation with Anabel. She said Pacal observed Dobson returning the map. Now his actions made sense. Dobson took the map to pinpoint the location of the gold, returned the map, found the gold and kept it. He picked up the coin and turned it over in his palm. It possessed the same symbol on both sides, a drawing of a fish. Anlon wondered if the coins had some special property like the other Stones, but assumed they would find out for certain soon enough once they viewed the Master Stone.

He asked, "Where are the rest of the gold coins?"

"I had some officers come out to Dobson's house and haul the safe and gold to headquarters for forensics and safekeeping until we sort out where they came from and to whom they belong. My Captain was quite happy with himself for prodding me to search Dobson's home. I didn't tell him I almost forgot to check the kitchen! At least he and I agree the gold is the strongest of our possible motives right now," Jennifer answered.

"I think I know how Dobson acquired the gold, but I don't know where it came from yet," Anlon chimed in.

"Hold up, A.C., let us finish our side of the story. Do either of you want any more pizza?" Pebbles sheepishly asked.

"What do you think, Anlon?" Jennifer quipped. "Should we make her suffer?"

"Whoa, not me. I've seen her break up bar fights. I'm not picking one. I'm done eating, what's left is all yours," he chortled.

"I'm done, too. Happy now?" Jennifer asked.

Pebbles gave a thumbs up, her mouth already full with the first chomps of her next slice, and shot a closed mouth grin at Jennifer.

"Getting back on track, I waited for the evidence crew to show up to pick up the safe while Pebbles drove back to the barn to start the document search there without me. I planned to join her once I squared things away at Dobson's house," Jennifer added.

Pebbles swallowed and jumped back into the conversation. "My turn again. I came back here and searched through everything. The desktops, drawers, the file cabinets and I even checked the counters and cabinets along the kitchen wall. Nothing. I brought over my laptop and tried some of the flash drives I found in Dobson's desk but nothing again. I tried my safe-cracking skills on Dobson's laptop password screen but struck out."

"So then, how did you find the Port Stone and where did you find it?" Anlon breathlessly asked.

"I'm getting to that, chill out," Pebbles retorted. "Men, so impatient!"

After a dramatic head shake of shame directed at Anlon, she continued. "As I was saying before being rudely interrupted, I was trying to get into Dobson's laptop when I heard the door to the barn open.

"I turned and it was Klaus Navarro, all blacked-out again but without the two muscleheads who were at the funeral. I said, 'WTF, ever hear of knocking,' and the dude went off. He called me very nasty names and demanded to see you. I told him you weren't there and asked him to leave.

"He was very angry. Said you blew him off and now he had a plane to catch. He demanded to see the two statues he came to purchase. I told him that wasn't possible. He ignored me and walked towards the racks. I scooted in front of him and told him to leave again. Do you know what the SOB did?"

Anlon pointed to the swollen, bandaged red welt on her forehead without speaking. He was livid inside and almost didn't want to hear Pebbles' next words. Klaus Navarro would pay! Anlon would make sure of it.

"He grabbed me by my hair and slammed my head into the rack! I was so shocked that I didn't even feel pain at first. I wobbled a bit and had to steady myself on one of the examining tables. He turned his back on me and started rummaging the storage rack. I guess he thought I would tremble and let him just take what he wanted. Big f— ing mistake on his part!" Pebbles blurted, seething with anger as she relived the confrontation.

"I was woozy and my eyes were blurry. The shock began to wear off and my head throbbed. I could feel a trickle down my face and wiped it away and saw blood on my hand. I snapped. One of the clamped lights was right next to me. I loosened it and rushed at Navarro. The cocky bastard never even turned around. I swung the lamp like a baseball bat right at his shiny ponytail. Booh yah!

"He crumpled on the floor. I beat him over and over with the lamp until the lamp head snapped off. He was a bloody mess on the floor. Sorry about that. He kinda made a mess of some of the shelves, too, when he fell. I'll clean that all up tomorrow.

"Anyway, I ran over to the alarm and pressed every button I could. The claxon went off. Navarro was still on the floor trying to get his bearings. I ran back over and kicked him good a few times right in his manhood. I grabbed my cell phone and ran to the house and called Jennifer," Pebbles concluded while breathing heavily, having stood to re-enact Navarro's submission.

Anlon and Jennifer sat with wide eyes and open mouths. Pebbles reached up for her forehead, it was throbbing again now, and delicately resumed her place on the sofa.

"My God, Pebbles, I'm so sorry. You were very brave," Anlon said, reaching to soothe her shoulder.

She smiled and laughed, "I was scared out of my mind! It wasn't bravery, I just got super angry and stuff happened on its own."

"Don't buy it, Anlon. She was over-the-top brave. And lethal too. Even though Navarro escaped before anyone got here, the trail of blood is impressive. I don't think he'll be coming back anytime soon," praised Jennifer as she returned from the kitchen with an ice bag for Pebbles.

"He got away?" Anlon quizzed.

"Yes, he did. He's inflight on his way back to Argentina on his private plane. By the time we tracked down which airport he was flying out of, he was gone and out over the Atlantic Ocean. He went pretty far out of his flight plan's way to get out of United States' airspace as fast as possible from what Captain Gambelli told me after he talked with the air traffic control," Jennifer said.

"We'll file charges against him for unlawful entry, and aggravated assault, so if he ever tries to enter the U.S. again, he'll pop up on TSA's radar. Captain also suggested we file a complaint with the State Department and Argentinian Embassy, but I wouldn't hold my breath. Navarro, it turns out, is a wealthy and influential man in Argentina."

Anlon piped in, "Oh I plan to make his life uncomfortable with some calls to some influential friends of mine and a few lawsuits to boot. I'm going to see George Grant tomorrow!"

Pebbles teared up a bit. Between the two of them, they really did come to her rescue, even though they were late to the party.

There was a moment of silence while they all decompressed from Pebbles' tense recitation. Suddenly, Anlon said, "Hey, what about the Port Stone? How did that figure in? Where did you find it?"

Pebbles adjusted the ice bag on her head and said, "When I came back to the house, I was bleeding pretty good, so I ran in the kitchen and got a dish towel to hold against the gash. I opened the freezer for some ice, and…"

Anlon stood without warning and said, "It was in the freezer?"

Jennifer raised her hands to the ceiling with palms outstretched, "Always gotta check the kitchen."

Anlon flopped back down on the sofa and laughed, "I bet good ole Devlin put it there. I bet neither Pacal or Dobson knew where he hid it. Was it out in the open?"

Pebbles said, "Yes, it was! It was sitting on top of a pint of ice cream! Crazy, isn't it? I thought it was a can of tuna at first and I was like, 'who puts tuna in the freezer.' And then I picked it up and I almost wet myself again!"

Anlon and Jennifer roared with laughter.

"Wow, that's some story. You were not kidding, you had the bigger day! Both of you did! So how many stitches, Pebbles?"

"Five. It's okay, I can hide it with my bangs. Anyway, I put the Port Stone back in the freezer so you could see where I found it," she nonchalantly stated.

Jennifer jumped in, "That's it from our end. Now tell us about the visit with Anabel Simpson and tell us what's in the case. I've been dying to ask."

Anlon held up a finger and said, "We need more wine."

He disappeared into the kitchen and extracted another Cabernet from Devlin's wine rack. He returned, uncorked it and poured more all around. He took a long sip and let the oaky taste roll around his tongue. He hummed with satisfaction and said, "You know, it's hard to know where to begin. I learned so much. In some ways it cleared up a lot, but in other ways it made things murkier."

"Okay, let me play copper then," kidded Pebbles. "First question. Who is Anabel Simpson?"

"Great question, detective. Anabel Simpson was Devlin's lover for 35 years," Anlon said. He halted and let that soak in before adding, "She is in her late 50s now. She was a professor at Bennington College and actually was with Devlin the day before he died."

"Hold up," Pebbles said, "Devlin was in his 80s when he died, right? So he was like 30 years older than Anabel?"

"Yes, that's about right. You're off by a few years, but yes, Devlin was a 50-year-old professor and Anabel was a graduate student of his when they met. They fell in love and kept a private love affair alive for 35 years. She joined him on his excavations and other travels, and later in life they visited each other discreetly either here or in Bennington. She told me some fascinating stories about their adventures together," Anlon explained.

Jennifer said, "Now her bequest makes sense, but it seems meager by comparison to the others given what you just said. Was she mad about it?"

"Another great question. I worried about the same thing when she told me. But Devlin was very generous to her over the years, she said. Bought her the home she lives in, supplemented her income and gave her gifts from his artifact collection. She seemed very content with the will," Anlon answered.

"What a class act, both of them," Pebbles said.

"Yes, they definitely are. The more I learned about Devlin from Anabel, my view of him softened. To me he was a storyteller, an explorer, a bombastic man who liked scotch, cigars and ancient treasures. Who knew he was a thoughtful romantic at heart?"

"The case?" Jennifer impatiently inquired.

Anlon thought, see the hill, take the hill. Jennifer was on the hunt. He said, "Hey, you made me wait about the Port Stone! Exhibit some patience of your own."

Jennifer motioned a zipper across her lips. Anlon continued, "As I mentioned, Devlin came to stay with Anabel the night before he went to Mt. Whiteface. Now this gets important, so ears wide open.

"She said Devlin had a terrible fight with Dobson. He accused Dobson of stealing artifacts from Devlin's collection without permission to line his own pockets. It turned out Devlin and Pacal set a trap for Dobson by hiding a GPS tracking beacon in a case Dobson used to remove one of the artifacts. Dobson, for a still unknown reason, took the case into the White Mountains. That's why Devlin went hiking there, to find out where Dobson took the case," Anlon said.

"So, that's why he had the tracking device with him!" Jennifer exclaimed, vaulting out of her seat, "I knew it was important. I'm going to call Meredith PD first thing in the morning. I want to see what's on that tracker!"

"Settle down, Detective, it gets even more intriguing." Anlon assured, "Anabel told me Devlin said he feared for his life and left what's in this case with Anabel to give to me. I'm putting my own pieces together here, but I think Devlin was panicked. Something caused him to freak out, take the Master Stone to Mr. Grant, conceal the Port Stone in the freezer and hide the map with Anabel."

"Map?" Pebbles ears perked up. She removed the ice bag from her forehead and placed it on the floor. "What kind of map?"

"You know," Anlon observed, "I used nearly those exact words when I asked Anabel. She said Devlin told her to tell me that the map showed the locations of the Life Stones."

This time Pebbles vaulted up. "No way!"

"Yes way!" Anlon kiddingly replied. "I've looked at the map, and there are definitely markings on it that I assume pinpoint the Life Stone locations, but the map is unlike anything I've ever seen and the color codes used in the markings are undecipherable to me without further examination."

"What makes the map so unusual?" Jennifer asked.

"You ought to be a detective, do you know that?" Anlon teased. "Anabel thinks it's a map that Devlin was obsessed with — her words — taken from a wall drawing in an ancient Egyptian pyramid. She said most scholars consider the map a fanciful depiction of the Egyptian underworld. Clearly, Devlin thought otherwise."

"Can we see it?" Pebbles asked.

Anlon nodded and laid the case on the table, punched in the electronic combination and inserted the key into the physical lock. Jennifer and Pebbles made impressed faces to one another. Anlon flipped open the case, withdrew the heavy inner tube and again laid out the map, anchoring it the same way he had at Anabel's.

"Wow, I thought it was going to be some ancient parchment," Pebbles exclaimed, almost disappointed.

"So did I," Anlon agreed, "but it looks like Devlin traced the map from the wall drawing."

"It has longitude and latitude lines," Jennifer observed. "Can't we overlay it on a map of today's world and line it up?"

Anlon blinked several times absorbing Jennifer's suggestion. Of course, that's exactly what they should do! He shook his head in respectful wonder and said, "I retract my earlier tease, you're not only a Detective, you're a first rate scientist. I'll bet that's what Devlin did! He marked the Life Stone locations on the map of the wall drawing knowing unless someone overlaid it on a current map, they'd never figure it out."

"What do you think made Devlin so afraid, so quickly, that he hid these pieces?" Pebbles wondered.

"I've been thinking about that a lot actually," Anlon answered. "I mentioned earlier that I thought I knew how Dobson acquired the gold coins. I'm just guessing, but I think he may have taken the map to do a test run to see if he could find something at one of the marked spots. If it did in fact happen that way, maybe it spooked Devlin. It's even possible that Devlin challenged Dobson directly after discovering that he used the map. Whether he told the truth or not, my uncle might have felt compelled to take *some* kind of action. Unfortunately, I don't think we'll ever know for sure since no one else was present during their confrontation."

Pebbles scrunched up her nose as if deep in thought and then exhaled, "Maybe when we *finally* watch the Master Stone and Story Stone something will jump out."

Anlon said, "Good point. Gotta be honest with you both, I think we should wait until tomorrow to view the Stones. I'm wiped out and a little tipsy. I'd like to look at the Stones with fresh eyes."

"No argument here," Jennifer responded, yawning and peering at her watch. She redirected the conversation to her prime focus. "Not to be a buzzkill but can we go back and talk about Dobson?"

As she'd done before on a few previous occasions, she summarized what she pieced together from their joint discoveries. "Dobson was stealing from Devlin. Devlin set a trap for him. Dobson fell for it.

Devlin tracked him. Devlin died. It sure looks like Dobson killed him to cover his tracks. With the unexplained gold in Dobson's safe, it stands to reason that Dobson was afraid of being found out. But then who killed Dobson?"

They all sat in silence before Anlon spoke. "I went through the same thought process. I wonder if the buyer is the missing link here. Dobson meets the buyer, passes the artifact in the case and tells him he needs to cool it because Devlin is onto him. The buyer is not happy, doesn't want a good thing to end or doesn't want scandal traced back to him. Buyer kills Devlin and then offs Dobson to keep him quiet," Anlon proposed.

Jennifer nodded her head, "That's a good working theory. I like it."

"Oh my God! Is Navarro the buyer?" Pebbles cried out "Is that why he was so angry? Maybe he thought with Devlin and Dobson out of the way he'd convince you to sell him the collection to cherry pick the Stones."

Anlon replied, "It's a damn strong possibility, don't you think? Or maybe even Thatcher Reynolds? My money is aimed at Thatcher. Think about how he tried to get a plan B in place in case I balked at selling him Devlin's collection. Oh, by the way, Thatcher also tried to rile up Anabel the same way he apparently riled up Richard. Anabel told him to f— off."

"Good for her!" said Jennifer. "This is good. You guys are sharp. Tomorrow, I'll go to the banks and look at Dobson's records. Maybe there's a paper trail here that will point at one of these guys or someone else. Hopefully, Dobson had a safe deposit box at one of them."

"I'm also going to call Meredith PD like I said earlier and push my forensic guys to process the items from Dobson's house and Pacal's handkerchief," Jennifer said, disappearing suddenly into thought. Re-emerging, she said, "Pebbles, don't clean up Navarro's mess in the barn until I send over the forensic team. God, I can't believe I didn't think of that earlier. He probably left prints everywhere."

Anlon cautioned, "Yeah, but...remember he had the two burly goons with him at the funeral. I'll bet he doesn't do the dirty work, like breaking and entering and murder. But it can't hurt."

"Can't argue that, it's solid logic," Jennifer allowed. "Still, even if it eliminates him as a suspect, I have to run it down."

"What about phone records?" Pebbles interjected suddenly, "Has anyone looked at Devlin's or Dobson's calls leading up to their deaths? Their texts, too? I know we found a phone statement today at Dobson's."

"Yes, that's right!" Jennifer exclaimed. "It's gonna be hard for me to get Capt. Gambelli to authorize a search warrant for anything related to Devlin's death but Dobson I should have no problem. I'll get on that, too."

Anlon listened to the exchange and said, "I feel like we're finally getting somewhere! Oh, I forgot to mention something else. I am tired of chasing these Stones without understanding why they are such a big deal. I get the historical implication, but that in and of itself isn't a reason to murder people. Devlin, Dobson, Pacal and Thatcher all said pursuing the Stones was dangerous. I want to know why…explicitly. So I called in a favor to an old friend and tomorrow I'm meeting with an old associate of Devlin's, Cesar Perez, who is an expert in the mythology of the catastrophe Devlin believed happened."

Pebbles said, "Great idea! But we should look at the Story Stone and Master Stone before you meet him. That way, if we see things on the stones that we don't understand, we can ask him."

"Let's reconvene tomorrow at 7:00 a.m. if that's not too early for you two. I want to get in the office early to chase down these other leads."

"Seven it is," Anlon said. "Tomorrow is Friday, we can always catch up on sleep over the weekend."

With that, they rose and wished Jennifer a good night. Pebbles said, "I'll walk out with you, and then I'll come back and help clean up, A.C."

Pebbles and Jennifer walked down the back porch steps to the driveway by the garage. When they reached Jennifer's car, Pebbles said, "Thank you again for everything today, especially taking charge after the Navarro thing."

"No problem, it's actually my job," she winked, opening the car door.

Pebbles held the door open and said, "I like you, Jennifer. You're a good person. But I'm a little pissed off that you looked into my background."

Jennifer nodded. She expected Pebbles to raise the topic sooner or later. She replied, "Look, sorry it makes you angry, but it's my job. I'm not apologizing for doing my job. But I shouldn't have said anything in front of Anlon. For that, I apologize. It was a slip of the tongue after a long, eventful day. I didn't mean to out you."

Pebbles nodded. She believed Jennifer's explanation. She said, "Apology accepted, and thank you for being straight up about it."

"No problem, I like you, too. I don't want to hurt you," Jennifer answered, squeezing the hand Pebbles used to hold the door open.

"How much do you know?"

"Everything."

Tears formed in Pebbles eyes. She said, "Don't believe everything you read. Please, don't tell Anlon. I want to be the one that tells him when the time is right."

Jennifer's stomach twisted in sympathetic agony. Given what she'd observed in Pebbles over the past few days, she knew in her heart that Pebbles was not the woman described in the police records and news reports she reviewed. She said, "It won't be me that tells Anlon. And for what it's worth, I didn't believe a word of what I read."

Pebbles started to cry, cupping her mouth with her hand to stifle the sound as the tears rolled down her face. She couldn't mouth a thank you, she just nodded and walked into the darkness clutching at her abdomen.

Jennifer started after her and then thought better of it. She returned to her car and left. As she neared the main road, she mumbled under her breath, "Talk to him, he'll understand."

XVI
MOUNTING TENSIONS

Strutting through the crowded, palatial lobby of the Waldorf Astoria, Quechua212 did her best to appear calm and collected. Aviator sunglasses perched atop her long raven waves, she strode confidently to the registration desk clad in a short, body-hugging, white spaghetti strap dress and black cross-strap heels.

Behind her, the aging bellman toted her bags and ogled her deep tan, cut physique and almost certain absence of undergarments. When they reached the registration desk, she politely handed the man a $10 tip and indicated she could handle the bags from there. Dodging crisscrossing guests as he trundled away, the bellman turned a last time to take in the exotic young woman with a leering gaze and a soft whistle.

The crisply attired registration attendant, Claude, bowed slightly upon her approach and extended a formal greeting, "Welcome to the Waldorf Astoria. How may I assist you this evening?"

"Hello!" she perkily exclaimed. "I'm checking in."

"Certainly, miss. May I have your last name, please?"

Quechua212 was now used to invoking her alias, so the fictitious name rolled naturally off her tongue. "Moore, first name is Zoe."

Claude busily tapped the keyboard behind the counter, adjusted his glasses and said, "Yes. Welcome Miss Moore. I see you will be staying with us for three nights. A one-bedroom suite in the Towers."

"Yes, that's right," she replied. Zoe indulged herself with top-shelf accommodations when she traveled these days, a self-anointed perk of her questionably acquired wealth. She removed the sunglasses and tossed her head casually to adjust her bangs, the motion intended to settle her nerves as much as to depict an air of indifferent ease.

"Excellent. Your room is ready and we did honor your reservation request for a nice view of Manhattan. May I have your ID and credit card, please?" Claude inquired.

"Of course," Zoe answered, dipping her hand into the oversized black leather tote atop her rolling suitcase. After chastising AucuChan1 about his earlier mistake, Zoe was careful to extract the correct ID and credit card from her wallet.

A few minutes later, Zoe disappeared behind the private door leading to the Towers elevator bank and ascended in the lift to the 40th floor.

Settled now in the living area of her suite, Zoe peered out the window overlooking the sparkling skyline of nighttime Manhattan and unstrapped her heels. They plunked on the carpet in succession before she padded to the mini bar and opened a small whisky bottle. Zoe dashed its contents into a tumbler, swished the drink around a few times and took a steadying gulp.

Retracing her steps as the warmth of the whisky coated her throat, she curled in a corner of the sofa and glanced at her phone. She would have to call him in 15 minutes. To Zoe, that meant 15 more minutes to get herself together. It would undoubtedly be an ugly conversation. Klaus Navarro didn't take kindly to failure, and given the beating he'd endured at the hands of the waify PYT staying with Cully, Zoe was certain she would be on the receiving end of his wrath. But she was determined to not allow him to bully her.

Zoe was also worried about AucuChan1 and seriously considered whether she would have to step in to clean up the mess in which they found themselves. AucuChan1 still had not found the map and was unable to track down Pacal. And he had made mistakes. Too many. Zoe grew increasingly concerned that sooner or later one of those mistakes might very well reach back and ensnare them both.

Reaching into the tote again, Zoe extracted the disposable phone she'd purchased in Miami before her New York trip. Hooking a Bluetooth earpiece behind her lobe, she sighed and dialed Navarro.

On the third ring, the call was connected and Navarro's mixed accent chided, "Well, if it isn't the warrior princess. At least you are punctual, despite your incompetence."

His voice was muffled and more nasal than usual, the result of a swollen jaw and taped up nose. He barked, "Where is the Waterland Map? Is it in your possession? I hope so for both your sakes!"

Zoe gritted her teeth and absorbed his animosity. Clearing her throat, she replied, "We do not have it, yet."

"And the coins Dobson promised me?"

"We don't have those, either," she grudgingly admitted. "I know for certain Dobby found the gold coins. He showed them to us, but after his run in with Devlin, something changed. Suddenly he had a change of heart and was going to hand them over to Devlin instead of us. But, before we could persuade Dobby otherwise, he died, too."

"And the Master Stone?"

Cringing, Zoe lowered her head and massaged her temples, "No, we haven't found the Stone."

"The sculptures?"

Zoe's long, silent response was marked only by Navarro's labored mouth breathing. She reached for the whisky and swallowed another slug as Navarro sternly stated, "You have 24 hours to deliver all of it to me or our association is over! Do you understand me?"

Pacing to the window, Zoe pushed aside the sheers and longingly peered at all the cars and people below on their way to dinners, shows and other fun in the city. She had worked too hard to create her new life and worried she was on the precipice of seeing that life disappear if she did not succeed.

Steeling her resolve, Zoe reminded herself that she did retain some leverage in the relationship with Navarro. If he bailed she could always find another buyer, so when she answered, she did so with a firm tone. "Yes, I understand."

Navarro laughed, but the laugh quickly turned into painful huffs as his tender ribs reminded him of Pebbles' thrashing. When he could speak, he mockingly lectured, "No, I don't think you do! I paid you and your good-for-nothing associate $100,000 dollars in advance! And what do I have to show for it? Zero. The deal was clear. The map, sculptures, stone and gold in exchange for $500,000. You were given one month. You told me it would be no problem and now look at the dung heap you've created!

"First Devlin, then Dobson! Days apart?!? How stupid was that? Without even squeezing the gold coins or information out of him first! When I agreed to deal with you and your associate directly after Dobson decided to quit, I didn't expect you would cut out Dobson…literally! Then you draw more attention by breaking into Devlin's office! You represented yourselves as professionals! Professional morons?"

Anger seethed inside Zoe. Against her better judgment she shot back, "Who's the moron who forced his way into Devlin's office and attacked a woman? And was seen? How professional was that? No one would have suspected you being part of our little association, as you put it, but you stuck your own ponytailed mug right in the center crosshairs, genius, because you were too damned impatient!"

Navarro raged. Over the phone, Zoe heard heavy thuds from Navarro pounding on a table and deep wheezes as he fought for composure. "You slut! Don't ever, I mean *ever*, speak to *me* in that manner! Twenty-four hours. That's all you have left. If you fail me, I will make sure the severing of our business relationship is slow and painful for you and your half-wit associate. Are we clear?"

With incredulous outrage, Zoe spat, "Don't threaten me, you little bastard! You know what I am capable of and you aren't that hard to find. We have a deal and I expect you to honor your end. I will personally take over the recovery of the agreed items myself."

"Your insolence is…" Navarro began to shout before Zoe cut him off with vitriolic force.

"Listen, worm! For six months, even though Dobby was the middleman, we supplied you with every treasure you wanted from Devlin's collection without anyone the wiser. If you hadn't stupidly bungled your way into his office to sneak out one of your precious statues on your own, we'd have a lot easier time extracting the statues and the other pieces you want now! It's your fault, you hear me?!

"And who told you about the Stones in the first place? That's right, weasel, we did! We got old Dobby all liquored up, pressed his buttons about how Devlin wasn't sharing the wealth and he went ballistic. Told us where the 'real money' could be found in the collection. In fact, we've done all the work while you sat on your tail tanning yourself!

"I will get the pieces. You chill out and drop the threats or, so help me, I'll come down there with *my* Stone and cast your ass down your pretty mountain top home. Are *we* clear?"

Again, a long pause. When Navarro spoke again, his voice was nearly a whisper, an evil, animus-laden whisper, "And in 24 hours, if you don't get the pieces? What then, warrior princess?"

"Then I will have no choice but to pay a visit to Dr. Cully personally and motivate him to hand everything over by whatever means necessary," she answered.

"And if you are caught?"

"That won't happen. There may be bodies piled up when I leave, but mine won't be one of them."

"I sincerely hope you are correct. Twenty-four hours," Navarro's slithery whisper cautioned.

"Oh, two other minor points," Zoe rebutted. "Point A — you're not the only buyer interested. Don't do anything stupid. Don't do anything additionally stupid, I should say. Point B — I didn't kill Dobby."

Navarro roar-coughed again in laughter, "You have bigger balls than any *man* I know! And, please, don't be coy with me. Of course you killed Dobson."

With that, the connection terminated before Zoe could wedge in a last word. She grasped the Bluetooth earpiece and threw it across the room, her earlier nervousness now replaced by stone-cold malice.

After clearing their dinner dishes, Anlon returned to the study but found the room empty. Perplexed, he stepped out on the back porch in search of Pebbles. As his eyes adjusted to the dim light cast by the moon, he noticed her silhouette bent over in the middle of Devlin's back meadow. She seemed to be crying. Concerned, Anlon took a few steps down the back stairs but then halted.

If Pebbles wanted his company she would have come back inside, he thought. She went all the way out into the meadow for some privacy. So Anlon turned and tiptoed back up the stairs and went inside. He would check on her a little later, it was unlike Pebbles to get emotional. Perhaps, he thought, a result of her head injury?

Alone in the house, Anlon sat back down in front of the map. He grappled with the meaning of the codes. Though Anabel said the markings on the map represented locations where the Stones might be found, Anlon was puzzled why Devlin didn't use the Master Stone symbols as markings. Instead, he used simple colored dots (red, green, brown, grey and black).

It was quite possible the colored dots were meant to denote something else entirely. For example, he recalled Pacal telling Pebbles that the Story Stones came in multiple colors. Whatever the meaning, Anlon hoped the answer might be found on the Master Stone or the other Story Stone in Devlin's safe.

Even though they agreed to view the Stones the following morning, Anlon's curiosity led him to extract the Master Stone from the study safe and place it on the coffee table next to the open map. Then he walked to the kitchen and opened the freezer.

True to Pebbles' words, there sat the Port Stone perched atop a pint of ice cream. He smiled. It did look like a tuna can. He was surprised how light it was. It almost felt hollow.

Remembering Pacal's description of Devlin's first use of the Port Stone, Anlon carefully approached the table with the Port Stone held at a distance expecting the Master Stone to begin vibrating as it neared. But it remained inert.

This baffled Anlon. Was the Port Stone too cold to use? He placed it on the table a foot away from the Master Stone and still no reaction. He picked up the tuna can-shaped rock and hovered it above the Master Stone. Again, nothing. Then recalling that the Port Stone attached to the back of the Master Stone, Anlon flipped the square, black rock over, and voila, the Master Stone started to shimmy on the table. Turning the Port Stone back over again, the vibrations ceased.

"How interesting!" Anlon exclaimed aloud. If there had been any doubt before, the interplay between the two Stones on the table confirmed magnetism was at the heart of their operation. Well, it was better to say cooperation. One end of the Port Stone cylinder attracted the polarity of the Master Stone.

But unlike in a common magnet, when the other end, or pole, was exposed to the Master Stone, a repulsive action did not occur between the two magnetized objects.

In the distance, Anlon heard the back porch screen door open and shut. He called out, "I'm in the study."

Pebbles didn't answer at first, and didn't enter the study. Instead Anlon heard her start up the steps to the house's second floor. She called out, "I'm heading to bed. See you in the morning."

Anlon frowned. An odd reaction from a woman who a few hours earlier had nearly tackled him on the lawn. Something was definitely up. He quickly reflected in his mind, "Did I say something to upset her?"

He called back, "Okay, goodnight. Hope you sleep well."

She did not answer as she continued up the stairs. Anlon sat for a little while going through the three-way conversation over dinner. There was no point he remembered that seemed to upset Pebbles. In fact, she'd been jovial the whole time. Maybe, in a quiet moment, the shock of Navarro's attack finally sunk in?

Realizing there was nothing to be gained by imagining what was bouncing around inside Pebbles' mind, Anlon shifted his attention back to the Stones. He said aloud, "Now where was I? Ah yes, the Sound Stone."

His scientific curiosity awoken, Anlon went to the safe one more time and pulled out the Sound Stone. He had yet to seriously consider how the stone worked. Running his fingers over the smooth, grooved surface of the oval object, he recalled how effortlessly Pacal had lifted thousands of pounds high in the air by simply vibrating his lips on the back of the stone.

Anlon recollected that common speaker systems utilize magnets to transmit sound waves. He supposed the Sound Stone must also be a kind of magnet. A magnet that accepted sound waves from the user's humming against the surface and translated, no, *amplified* the smaller waves into powerful surges.

It was mind boggling to consider how the Stone Benders embedded that kind of power into a rock they shaped for this purpose. The imagination required to conceive the idea was gifted beyond comparison.

To satisfy his inquisitiveness, Anlon tried an experiment to test his theory. He held the Port Stone to the backside of the Sound Stone. No reaction. He turned the Port Stone onto its opposite side. Again, nothing.

"Hmmm," Anlon mused, "maybe I'm wrong."

Unwilling to give up on his theory, he rotated the Sound Stone to face the Port Stone. Before the rotation was complete, the Sound Stone shot out of his hand and crashed heavily against the wall.

"Whoa!" Anlon gaped, "now that's what I call reverse polarity!"

Anlon paced across the room and retrieved the Sound Stone. It wasn't damaged thankfully. He thought, "The magnetic properties of these stones are way more complex than I realized."

Closing the door to his office, Thatcher Reynolds quickly maneuvered around the tall, disorderly stacks of papers, artifacts and other materials that sat on the floor, desk and credenza. Life as a university professor at an institution that doesn't highly value archaeology as a field of study meant meager funding and office space allocations.

He tapped his foot restlessly on the floor as he awaited the call. Thatcher had a lot riding on this deal going through and his Hong Kong buyers were growing impatient. He needed more time!

Cully didn't cooperate as he hoped and Cully's legal team was now in full attack mode. It was probably a bad idea to threaten him, Thatcher admitted, and getting his cousin involved was inane.

But he was desperate. His confederate, Pacal, had proved just as inane in his decision to shoot Cully across the yard with Devlin's Sound Stone! Neither of their attempts to dissuade Cully from continuing Devlin's research had proved effective. In fact, the opposite was true.

By now, Thatcher was sure that Cully had viewed the Master Stone and it was quite possible he'd found the map. If he had, there was little chance Thatcher would find a Flash Stone for the buyer and Pacal could forget ever finding his precious Seed Stone.

The buzz from his cell phone startled Thatcher. He punched the green "accept call" icon and said, "Hello."

"Dr. Thatcher, it is I," the deep voice boomed.

Adopting a sugary tone, "Pacal, my friend, how are you?"

Silence echoed on the other end of the call. Even though Pacal had known Thatcher for many years, he did not consider him a friend. In this matter, he was purely a business partner. A distasteful but necessary one. At least, originally he had been necessary. Now Pacal wasn't as convinced. He finally answered, "I am weary, Dr. Thatcher. I have spent three days non-stop hunting for the map."

"And?"

"I am disappointed to tell you I do not have it. But I know who has it now and where it is," Pacal answered.

"You do? Is it Cully?"

"Yes. Dr. Anlon just received the map. I followed him to Vermont where he met with Miss Anabel, Dr. Devlin's woman friend. He entered the home with nothing in his hands and left with a briefcase. I am certain the map was in the case," Pacal explained.

Thatcher punched his thigh. Damn, he thought!

Pacal continued to speak, "Dr. Devlin took great pains to scatter the pieces necessary to find what we each seek before his unfortunate death. He must have suspected more was at work than just Mr. Matthew's thefts. I don't know how; I was very careful."

"Look, Pacal, I spoke with our buyers earlier today. They were very put out that we haven't delivered on our promise. They want the Flash Stone very badly. We are running out of time!" blustered a frustrated Thatcher.

His entreaties were meaningless to Pacal. To find the Seed Stone was all he cared about, and if he acquired the map on his own, Pacal didn't need Thatcher at all. As he gazed down at the Seed Stone ring on his finger, he thought, "With the map, I can also find the gold Trade Stone coins, and then I'll have all the gold I need to live a long and comfortable life...a very long life."

At first when Thatcher approached him a few months prior with his plan to "borrow" and copy Devlin's map, Pacal had rebuffed him. How Thatcher had learned about the map, Pacal didn't know. But when Pacal had challenged him, he was floored to discover Thatcher knew about the six Life Stones, too.

And he had made Pacal an offer that was hard to refuse. Bring him a readable copy of the map and his buyers would give Pacal a Seed Stone and Black Earth. How Thatcher knew of his lust for the Seed Stone was also a mystery. Though, the more Pacal had considered it, the more he realized he'd been indiscreet over the years as he sought the mythical life extender.

Pacal had pressed Thatcher about where he acquired his knowledge of the map and stones. The cagey professor said he had been following Devlin's progress from afar. Pacal did not believe him. More likely, he thought, the Hong Kong buyers manipulating Thatcher behind the scenes possessed the knowledge and fed Thatcher enough to make him sound credible.

In his heart, Pacal hadn't trusted Thatcher. He demanded proof. To his shock, Thatcher met him a week after his initial pitch carrying a tall, thin box. After awkward pleasantries, Thatcher presented the box to him without explanation. Pacal opened the box and inside was a flowering plant. An oleander potted in the darkest, most aromatic soil Pacal had ever seen or sniffed. Astonished, Pacal had looked at Thatcher and said, "Is this what I think it is?"

Though Thatcher had zero clue what he'd handed to Pacal, he nodded with surety. The Hong Kong buyer had instructed Thatcher to give Pacal the box as proof of their ability to deliver on their end of the bargain. And that sealed Pacal's commitment.

When Pacal reached home the evening he received the plant, he broke off a few of the fully blossomed flowers and crushed them into a tincture, mixed them in fruit juice and drank the concoction. It had been a huge risk.

Oleander is extremely poisonous to humans. If the buyer really had a Seed Stone and had been able to alter the molecular makeup of the plant's seeds, the fully mature flowers would lose their poisonous properties to humans. The flowers would instead contain enzymes that killed degenerative cells, turning a dangerous plant into a life-extending one.

And oleander was not the only plant the Seed Stone affected in this way. Several, common poisonous plants could be enhanced in the same way. Pacal didn't know how or why the Stone Benders had divined this methodology, he only knew he thirsted for a longer, healthier life.

Within four days, he'd consumed all the mature flowers of the oleander presented to him, unsure of how many to include in each tincture. He anxiously waited for new flowers to blossom and understood why the buyers had so readily provided the plant. The tincture's effects were noticeable within hours, but faded relatively quickly. In order to achieve the healing benefits, a more potent tincture was necessary. This meant a garden full of the flowers was required, not a single potted plant.

When Pacal was a boy, his grandmother told him fables about ancestors who lived unnaturally long lives, nearly double a human's current life span. She told him the "old peoples," as she referred to them, drank poisonous mixtures that renewed their bodies. She said the "old peoples" drew pictures of the poisonous plants on rocks in the Andes to remind them which ones to choose. She said they grew the plants in the valleys below the Andes using an inky soil that no longer existed. It was an extravagant story, one that stayed lodged in his memory.

As a young man, Pacal had shelved the memory. So full of life and vigor, the idea of death was inconceivable. Even as he aged, the memory served mostly as a good fireside tale to share when out on digs with visiting archaeologists. Until one day, almost a decade ago, when around a campfire he had told the story to Devlin Wilson.

Unlike the other archaeologists who listened to Pacal's fable, Devlin didn't laugh and mock him when he finished the tale. No, Devlin stared straight at him and asked him if his grandmother was still alive. He asked Pacal if he knew where the rock drawings were located. His interest shook Pacal up. Sadly, he'd shared, his grandmother was no longer alive and he'd never seen any drawings like the ones she described. It was just a myth as far as he was concerned.

Devlin had stared into the blazing campfire, watching the embers drift upward into the night sky and said, "I'm not so sure. I've seen the drawings. I just didn't know what they meant...until now."

From that moment, Pacal became obsessed with the fable and with building a relationship with Devlin Wilson. If there was any hope the story was true, Devlin was determined to find the answer and Pacal wanted to be there when he did.

It took several years to work his way into Devlin's service and he used those years to his advantage, seeking the answers on his own. Devlin, a gracious man, had even shared with Pacal the location of the drawings. He climbed to the spot, not far from the ancient Tiahuanaco complex, and copied the drawings. One in particular was repeated more frequently than others. It was the symbol that he had fashioned onto the gold ring holding his gaze.

Pacal had never been so close to achieving his goal as when Devlin discovered the Master Stone. For on the stone, the creators depicted each of the six stones and their purpose. They demonstrated how each was used and showed an image of a map that highlighted where to find caches of the Stones hidden around the world.

But to Pacal's frustration, Devlin became very protective of the Master Stone after discovering Pacal viewing it one evening without permission in the barn office. After that, Devlin took to hiding the Port Stone and that meant Pacal had no way to find the Seed Stones, or the rare Black Earth, on his own.

But while working at his desk in the barn office, he observed Devlin making a map. He didn't know how he'd been able to lift the image off the Stone; Devlin wouldn't discuss the matter. But when he saw Devlin inserting symbols on the map, he knew why. He was going after the Stones. And that would not do. No, it decidedly would not. Devlin would not rob him of his dream…Pacal would make certain of that.

XVII
THE MASTER STONE

Pebbles awoke early as the birds greeting dawn stirred her from a deep sleep. She extended a hand from beneath the covers to gingerly touch the sore knot hiding underneath her bangs. Her eyes fluttered open and closed again, her mind trying to recall coming to bed. Shifting under the blanket, Pebbles realized she was dressed in yesterday's clothes. Then she remembered sobbing and running off after her exchange with Jennifer. She mumbled, "Ugh, how mortifying."

Despite her embarrassment, however, Pebbles acknowledged the time alone in Devlin's dark meadow had helped her reach a decision. Jennifer was right, it was time to talk with Anlon. In fact, it would feel good to finally get it out in the open. Pebbles had not discussed that fateful night with anyone other than the psychiatrist since leaving the rehabilitation facility. Though her bones mended and bruises faded, the mental and emotional damage had lingered for too long.

Lifting her wrist to view the huddled angel and underlying scar, Pebbles rubbed along the raised line and shut her eyes again. She ached to shed the long shadow cast by the haunting memories.

Stretching her arms above her head while yawning broadly, Pebbles opened her eyes and peered around the room. She caught sight of a square pink box on the nightstand by her head. Curious, she propped herself up on her elbows and tried to focus her sleepy gaze on the box. There was a folded note atop the box. She reached for it and collapsed her head back on the pillow. Holding the note above her face, she flipped it open. It was from Anlon and read:

"Hey sleepy head. Hope you're feeling better this morning, didn't want to intrude last night. Thought you might be hungry when you wake up. I made sure to get you *three* chocolate-glazed ☺ It's a new day, young lady, see you when you're ready to get at it! xo A.C."

Pebbles' face bloomed with delight. She held the note against her chest and gave silent, reverent thanks for Anlon…and the doughnuts.

Jennifer lightly tapped on the screen door of the back porch. From inside, she heard a chair scrape on the stone kitchen floor. Anlon appeared at the door and whispered, "Come on in, Pebbles is still asleep."

The aroma of cinnamon and coffee filled the room. Jennifer inhaled deeply and said, "Mmmm…what are you having? It smells heavenly."

Anlon pointed to a plate with two huge cinnamon rolls and answered, "Went into town, got the first batch out this morning. Go for it!"

"God, I'd love to, but I just ran four miles. I'd put twice what I tried to burn back on," she bemoaned.

Anlon crooked a suspicious eye up and down Jennifer's sleek physique and said, "Having a hard time buying that. Besides, no one says you have to eat the *whole* thing. And I promise not to tell a soul."

Jennifer punched him in the arm while laughing, "You're evil!"

But she accepted the plate Anlon handed her, peeled away the outer curl of the bun and bit appreciatively into the warm, soft pastry, allowing the crusty sugar and cinnamon coating to melt on her tongue. Anlon poured her a cup of coffee and said, "I don't know why, but I'm really nervous."

Chewing slowly to extract all the flavor, Jennifer simply nodded in agreement. She had butterflies, too, but the nostalgic aromas and tastes were chasing them away.

She sipped the coffee and asked, "How is she?"

Anlon leaned forward, his elbows against the table surface, and said, "I think she'll be okay. She's tough as they come."

Jennifer peeled another strip of roll and looked quizzically at Anlon. She realized Anlon thought her question was in reference to Pebbles' head injury. Her inquiry was really meant to elicit whether Pebbles had talked with him about her past last night. Jennifer decided not to press the matter, as she had promised Pebbles not to reveal anything to Anlon.

Above, they heard floorboards creak. Pebbles was awake and moving about. Anlon said, "Come on, let's go get the stones out of the safe and set up in the den."

About 10 minutes later, Pebbles entered the den dressed in an oversized sweatshirt, sweatpants and socks. She smiled cautiously at the two of them as she slinked onto an armchair and curled up. She said, "Hey."

Anlon replied, "Hey, back atcha. Coffee?"

She nodded yes and Jennifer disappeared into the kitchen to pour her a cup. While she was away, Anlon asked, "Did you find the doughnuts?"

Pebbles smiled and whispered, "All gone!"

Jennifer returned and handed the cup to Pebbles, saying, "Here you go, it tastes wonderful. Apparently he makes coffee. Who knew?"

"No, that's not true," Anlon confessed. "The *bakery* makes good coffee. I just poured it in the urn when I got back."

Pebbles smiled softly. She felt awkward this morning, exposed, knowing Jennifer knew her secret now. And from his note, Anlon was surely aware something was wrong. He and Jennifer were trying a little too hard to exhibit an "all is well" vibe to lessen her uneasiness, but it just made her feel more out of place. She said, "You guys can stop with the velvet gloves. I'm okay. Last night was last night. Today is today. Now, let's finally watch these damn stones!"

Her exhortation broke the tension, although Anlon shot a puzzled look at Jennifer, who intentionally avoided his gaze. She cleared her throat and said, "Anlon, you should go first. Devlin left the Stones for you."

Anlon replied, "I won't fight you on that!"

He reached for the Master Stone, again observing the center, sun-like circle and the six evenly spaced rays that surrounded the circle. At the end of each ray was an etched design. Anlon focused on each design in clockwise order, starting with the fish symbol at the nine o'clock position in relation to the sun pictograph. This same design appeared on the gold coins Jennifer and Pebbles had discovered the day before.

The next symbol, at roughly the eleven o'clock position, resembled a plant sprig with a bud near the base and an open leaf or flower at its tip. He recalled Pebbles saying this symbol was etched on the face of Pacal's ring.

Moving his gaze to one o'clock on the Master Stone, the next design had the appearance of waves; three squiggly lines layered atop one another. This symbol was followed at the three o'clock orientation by a star-like image, and then at five o'clock by two open hands cupped together. The final remaining symbol, at a bearing of seven o'clock, was an offset square image that reminded Anlon of a rhombus.

Anlon flipped the Master Stone over so the back of the square black rock faced him. He motioned to Pebbles to hand him the Port Stone. As he maneuvered the Port Stone towards the center depression on the back of the Master Stone, both began to vibrate in Anlon's hands. When the two stones moved within six inches of each other, they suddenly snapped together with a loud clap, startling all three of them and nearly causing Anlon to drop the fused stones onto the floor.

Anlon darted a tense glance at Jennifer and Pebbles as he tried to calm himself. "Wasn't expecting that!"

He took a deep breath and flipped the Master Stone over to view its face again. Gingerly, Anlon inched his fingers down the stone to the arced depressions on the opposing back sides of the Master Stone, recalling Pacal's primer on how to activate the stone's contents. As soon as they slid into place, his fingers began to feel a buzz and, out of nowhere, video-like images leapt into Anlon's mind.

He stood and gasped, "Oh my God, can you two see this?"

Pebbles uncurled in the chair and perched on its edge, her face alight with curious wonder. "I don't see anything! What are you seeing."

"It's incredible!" he cried out. "It's almost like I'm not here but inside the video. It reminds me of a holograph or virtual reality."

Anlon stood in a sunlit, open air hall of white marble pillars. Between the pillars, tall sheer drapes fluttered in a light breeze. Anlon was astounded — he felt the breeze upon his face and the sound of the fabric flapping in his ears. How is this possible, he wondered?

He detected motion to the right of his view and rotated his eyes in that direction. Into the hall stepped four men and one woman, their sandal-covered feet tapping on the marble floor as they approached. Bronzed skin, golden haired and draped with sandy colored tunics edged in crimson, the five entrants walked towards Anlon with expressions of welcome upon their faces. A floral scent met Anlon's nose.

The woman spoke first. Anlon staggered backwards and unintentionally collapsed onto Devlin's couch. Her voice was crisp and inviting, though Anlon did not understand the language she spoke. Her eyes glinted with penetrating confidence, a look that struck Anlon as if she were saying, "trust me." She reached out and placed a hand on Anlon's...and he freaked.

Releasing the Master Stone onto the floor, the Port Stone separated and rolled away. Anlon closed his eyes, slumped over on the sofa and uttered a stupefied cry, "My God!"

Jennifer and Pebbles, chills running rampantly along their tensed necks and arms, watched with confusion and alarm at Anlon's writhing movements and facial expressions during his initial session with the stone. His eyes widened and shot from side to side, his brow perspired, he mumbled unintelligible words and his limbs twitched in spasms. When he dropped the stones, Pebbles vaulted out of the chair and screamed, "Anlon! What's happening? Are you okay?"

Jennifer rushed forward and grabbed Anlon's quivering hand in an instinctual gesture to reassure him. She softly spoke, "It's all right, Anlon. Take deep breaths. That's right, long and slow. Just relax."

She turned to Pebbles and said in a hushed tone, "He's in shock. Can you get some water for him?"

Anlon was dizzy, unable to concentrate his senses for nearly a minute. By the time Pebbles returned with a glass of water, the haze obscuring his vision and the muffled ringing in his ears were fading. When his eyes finally cleared, he realized he was lying on the sofa with two very concerned faces peering down upon him. He still could not speak, too overwhelmed to communicate.

Jennifer patted his shoulder. She'd seen this combination of symptoms many times in trauma victims. She said, "Deep breaths, Anlon. Follow my voice."

His head cocked slightly towards her. She said, "Good, that's good. Try to relax. Don't try to talk yet, all right? Just nod if you are okay."

Anlon's heart still pounded furiously inside as he tried to calm his respiration. He closed his eyes again and nodded yes. Tears formed in Pebbles' eyes and she angrily wiped them away. She felt utterly helpless as she stared down at Anlon's prone figure.

Jennifer's fingers pressed against his wrist as she timed his pulse on her running watch. Anlon's skin was afire. She again turned to Pebbles, who clearly was in shock, too, though far milder than Anlon's.

From her emergency responder training, Jennifer knew that giving people in mild shock simple tasks to perform helped to bring them back to a functioning state. She called to Pebbles, "Hey. Pebbles. Listen to me, he's burning up. Can you go wet a cloth with cold water for his forehead?"

Pebbles stared at her for a few seconds with a blank expression before rising from where she rested on the edge of the coffee table and scampering off to the kitchen.

Pebbles returned with the cold compress and layered it gently on Anlon's forehead and lightly stroked her fingers through his hair. Pebbles' soothing touch and Jennifer's tranquil voice combined to settle Anlon's anxiety. He mumbled, "I'm okay, thank you, both of you. Whew, that was really intense!"

A relieved yelp escaped from Pebbles' mouth before she could cup her hand to stifle it. Jennifer smiled and encouraged Anlon, "You look like you were tripping on some hallucinogenic drug. I thought I had crashed a rave."

He laughed and shook his head to clear further cobwebs. He slowly resumed a seated position before the two women and replied, "If that's what a hallucinogenic trip feels like...Wow!"

"It was so real. I wasn't here in this room; I was in some kind of marble building. Dobson told me I would see and hear things like a video. He didn't say I would feel and smell things, too," Anlon said.

"What do you mean, Anlon?" Pebbles asked, coming down from her own shock. "What did you feel?"

"A woman touched me with her hand. I felt it like it was one of you. I could smell her perfume; I could feel the breeze against my face. It was incredible, indescribable."

"No way!" Pebbles exclaimed, "What happened, why did she touch you?"

"I think she was trying to say trust me," Anlon answered. "She was with four men. They were dressed very similarly. Their faces and movements were inviting and gracious. They welcomed me... Extraordinary."

Jennifer asked, "Did they say anything to you?"

Anlon nodded, "Yes, the woman spoke, but in a language I couldn't understand. I remember Dobson or Pacal telling me that they didn't know how to decipher the language on the stones."

While Jennifer and Anlon conversed, Pebbles' curiosity trumped her fear. Before they could stop her, she snapped together the two stones and gripped the handle-notches.

She stood erect with tensed muscles and wild eyes for several seconds before there was a palpable shift in her posture and demeanor. The tension in her face waned while her eyelids slid closed. Pebbles' mouth parted and a protracted, throaty groan spilled out. She teetered briefly causing Jennifer to rush to catch her before she fell, but Pebbles steadied herself.

Jennifer turned to Anlon and said, "What should we do?"

Anlon shrugged and answered, "Hell if I know, but I'm thinking it's better to let her come out of it on her own instead of forcing her to let go."

"Yeah, I agree, but let's at least see if we can get her to sit down. I'm afraid she's going to do a header on the table or floor," Jennifer suggested.

They positioned themselves on either side of Pebbles and gently guided her down onto the sofa. In her trance, Pebbles didn't even seem to take notice. Unlike Anlon, her respiration was steady and her skin was not fiery. Already, she'd held the stone for twice as long as Anlon.

For another 15 minutes, they anxiously watched her gesture with her head and murmur incoherently as if speaking with someone unseen. To a random observer, it might have appeared as if Pebbles was having a nightmare. Without warning, her eyes shot open, she gasped and released the Master Stone. Again, the Port Stone separated and clunked onto the floor.

Anlon sat down next to her and reached for her hand. She asked, "Can I have some water, please?"

The glass Pebbles had retrieved for Anlon still sat half full on the coffee table. He snagged it and presented it to her. She tilted the glass back and gulped down the water in three deep pulls.

Anlon asked, "Doing okay?"

Pebbles nodded and said, "They talked to me, I understood them. Not the words, but their thoughts I think. I can't explain it."

"Really?" Anlon asked with surprise.

"Uh huh. When you said the woman approached and touched you, you said you thought she was saying, trust me," Pebbles explained. "So when she touched me, I said in my mind 'I trust you' and wham I could understand her thoughts!"

"You're creeping me out," Jennifer said, "the both of you!"

Anlon quipped, "I'm creeping myself out. Get in line!"

Turning back to Pebbles he asked, "You were under for a good 20 minutes. What else did you see? What else did they tell you?"

Pebbles gathered herself, clasping both hands over her mouth before slapping them on her thighs. "Do your fingers still tingle, A.C.?"

"No, but they did for a bit after I let go," he said.

"What a bizarre sensation, the whole thing," Pebbles mused, "but way cool!"

"Eleanor Marie!" barked Jennifer. "What did you see?!"

"Oh, right. You want to try it out for yourself? It will make more sense if you do," Pebbles asked Jennifer.

"Um, no thank you. I need to go soon, lots to chase down today and I don't need a LSD trip before I go. Just spit it out, girl. What happened?"

"I'll tell you what I remember, but so much flashed by it was hard to keep it all straight," Pebbles said. "I was in the same room Anlon experienced and he was right. I could see, hear, smell and sense touch.

"The five people sat down at a table in front of me. On the table was a diagram of the Master Stone symbols. The woman, she said her name to me, Anlon! Can you believe that! She placed her hand on her chest and said something that sounded like 'Mall-in-Yah.' She pointed to each of the men and they each spoke their name. Then she pointed at the diagram and touched each symbol and gave each a name. It was too much information to take in. I don't remember the names she gave the symbols or the men's names. We'll have to go back and watch it a bunch to learn more.

"Anyway, she reached for my hand and I took it. I honestly felt her hand close on mine, and she led me to a small waterfall that came out from the marble wall. I don't know how to explain it right but it reminded me of your infinity pool in Cabo, Anlon.

"Malinyah stirred her hand in the water and visions appeared. All the while, she spoke close to my ear while holding my hand as if to say 'don't be afraid.' I didn't understand all her words, but her voice was surreally comforting.

"I can only remember two of the visions. The first showed a planet, pretty sure it was the Earth. Another huge planet moved past the Earth, and not big like an asteroid, but huge, like a *planet*, and bigger than Earth. Massive bolts of lightning shot back and forth between the two.

"The other vision was of the greeters saying goodbye to another group of men. Malinyah and the greeters stayed behind while the men boarded ships with the other crew aboard. Their parting was very sad. She squeezed my hand."

Anlon listened to Pebbles' description while massaging his temples. He wondered if he was dreaming. How was such a feat possible 10,000 years ago? To not only devise a way to store information on rock, but to embed mental impressions that were interactive, almost living. Unfathomable. Preposterous. Insane. But absolutely, without question, real.

Devlin's decade-long search for an ancient civilization that pre-dated known societies led him to discover a people more advanced than modern man could dream. He imagined Devlin harassed by his colleagues — Where is the culture? Where is the art? Where is the language? All you have are rocks, Devlin, nothing more. When Devlin first viewed the Story Stone, let alone the Master Stone, the sense of vindication must have burst from within him.

He asked Pebbles, "You said they pointed at each symbol and gave each a name. Did they show visions of their purpose?"

She shook her head and said, "No, but I'm sure it's on there, Anlon. It's just gonna take us time to find the answers we want on the stone. My gut tells me the answers are on it."

Jennifer chimed in, "So I know you both have had religious experiences this morning, but can we bring it back to the here and now? I need to get going and follow up on the leads from yesterday. And, Anlon, if memory serves me, you have a guest arriving in about half an hour, right? Let's not do any more freaky-deaky trances today, okay? Let's keep our eye on the ball. The most important thing we can do right now is find out who killed Devlin and Dobson, how they did and why, and catch them if we can. After that, you'll have all the time in the world to explore the stones."

Anlon glanced at his watch. Jennifer was right, he had about 30 minutes before he needed to be at Pittsfield's airfield. He turned to Pebbles and asked, "Can you put this all away? Jen is right, I need to scoot to meet Cesar Perez. If I bring him back here, do you want to join us?"

Pebbles said, "Absolutely, but I need the combination for the safe. I'll take a quick shower and I'll be presentable by the time you get back."

Anlon answered, "Sounds good. We should set you up to open the safe as well. I'll show you the combination and we can scan your fingerprints for the safe."

"With any luck," Jennifer said, "one or more of our leads will give us a clearer view of the crimes and the killer."

XVIII

HISTORY DEMYSTIFIED

Anlon pulled into the parking lot at the Pittsfield Municipal Airfield just as his cell phone rang. Fishing the phone from his jeans, he answered the call, "Anlon Cully."

"Dr. Cully?" the caller asked, "this is Cesar Perez. I've just landed and Mr. Wallace's plane is taxiing to the terminal. Where should I meet you?"

"Good morning, Dr. Perez. I'm very grateful that you've come. I hope it wasn't too much of an inconvenience," Anlon replied. "I'll meet you by baggage claim in about five minutes. I'm parking now. I'm wearing a white dress shirt, blue jeans and brown boots. I've seen your picture on one of the books you wrote with Devlin, so I'll spot you."

Perez replied, "Very well, my friend. I am anxious to talk with you!"

True to form, Cesar Perez wasn't difficult to identify when he stepped into the terminal building near baggage claim. He was a man of medium height and build with a rugged, weather-beaten face baked reddish brown by years of exposure in the field, and close-cropped, black hair streaked with lines of grey. Yet, despite his aged appearance, Cesar moved with vigor and purpose. Anlon waved and Cesar strode towards him, his rolling suitcase trailing behind. He gripped Anlon's hand and said with a somber face, "Dr. Cully, I am so sorry about Devlin. I was so shocked when I heard the news."

"Anlon, please. Thank you for your kindness, and for coming all this way on such short notice. Where did Antonio find you, Dr. Perez?" Anlon asked in reply.

"Cesar, if you please," he answered. "I was in Peru, but when Mr. Wallace said it was urgent and mentioned Devlin's name, I of course came at once. I only regret I was unable to travel for his funeral, but I did toast to his memory many times the night I learned of his accident, and then again when I was told Matthew died."

"Completely understandable, Cesar. Peru? You must be exhausted from the overnight flight then."

"No, not at all. Mr. Wallace's jet was very comfortable, plus he has excellent taste in scotch! I slept very well," laughed Cesar. "I'm ready to help. Tell me everything!"

Anlon laughed and made a mental note to send Antonio one of his rare Macallan's when he returned to Tahoe by way of extra thanks. He said to Cesar, "Let's wait until we get back to Devlin's house. On the ride there, I'd love to hear about your current research project."

The drive back to Stockbridge went quickly as Cesar filled the journey with a rundown of his ongoing excavation near Lake Titicaca on the border of Peru and Bolivia, and a handful of stories about Devlin. Anlon laughed to himself, Devlin surely made an impression on everyone he met.

They were greeted at the back porch by Pebbles, who had transformed from her "rolled out of bed" look into "elegant research assistant." She was dressed in crisp tan Capri pants, freshly ironed baby blue button-down shirt with sleeves rolled up to the elbows and gold-tinge sandals. She managed to style her bob to cover most of the fresh bandage on her forehead. For added splash, Pebbles' diamond nose stud returned, along with two small loop rings along her right eyebrow.

Anlon started to introduce Pebbles, "Cesar, this is my associate..."

"Eleanor, Eleanor McCarver. It's a pleasure to meet you, Dr. Perez," she confidently stated, extending her hand in greeting.

"The pleasure is mine, Eleanor, and please, I am a simple man. I prefer that you address me as Cesar," he said, graciously bowing as he lightly squeezed her hand.

When they settled in the den, Cesar inquired, "Anlon, come now, please finally tell me why you asked to see me."

Anlon replied, "It's a long story, Cesar. I guess the best way to begin is to tell you we have strong suspicion that Devlin was murdered, that his death was no accident."

He paused to take in Cesar's reaction. Cesar nodded in understanding but didn't flinch in the least. Anlon interpreted the lack of reaction as an indication that Cesar suspected the same himself.

"We have been working with the state police here trying to find the killer, who we also suspect murdered Matthew Dobson," Anlon continued.

Again, Cesar showed no outward sign of surprise when Anlon tossed in Dobson's murder. His only reaction was to bow his head as if paying respect to the two fallen men.

"We believe both murders are linked with a research project of Devlin's. Specifically, his investigation of the Life Stones. I should mention that Devlin made me the executor of his estate and willed me his artifact collection and the entirety of his research work," Anlon added, throwing in the precise term "Life Stones" to judge if Devlin had discussed the objects with Cesar.

Cesar nodded silently when Anlon mentioned the Life Stones and subtly pursed his lips into a look that said, "I knew it."

Anlon said, "Good, I'm glad you have some knowledge of Devlin's research and the Life Stones themselves. I had counted on it when I sought you out. Over the last week, we've discovered or been told pieces of the Life Stones story, but we lack an overall, grand understanding of the story itself. With Dobson dead and Devlin's other research assistant, Pacal, missing, we need to quickly assimilate the full story in order to catch the killer. I hoped you might be able to aid us in stringing together some of the loose pieces."

Cesar did not take long to answer, "You shall have my help, my friends. I will tell you all that I know. In return, I would like to hear all that you know."

"Of course," Anlon answered. "May I start by asking about your connection with Devlin and his research? I've not read your jointly published books or articles, I only know that you collaborated with Devlin to write them."

"Ah, yes, that is a good place to begin," Cesar stated, shifting on the sofa and clearing his throat before continuing. "We complemented each other, Devlin and I.

"Your uncle sought answers about the rise of modern man, while I, on the other hand, specialize in the mythology of ancient cultures. More specifically, the focus of my research centers on discerning true mythology from overlooked or misunderstood history.

"Our lines of inquiry crossed when Devlin began to ask himself questions about a few ancient myths. Were they fables or an attempt to record history? He sought me out and our collaboration commenced."

Before Anlon could ask the next question, Pebbles queried, "What myths did Devlin discuss with you?"

Cesar turned to face Pebbles and answered her directly, "We discussed many myths, Eleanor, but he was most interested in the beginning about the great flood story. You may know it as the story of Noah's Ark.

"Christians like myself believe the Ark story to be a true telling of events, however altered by scribes over the centuries to fit Christian doctrine. Others believe it to be a myth, a story of convenience used by Church leaders to demonstrate the wrath of God upon those who lose their way and don't repent.

"What most people don't know, however, is that many ancient cultures have great flood myths. When read side-by-side, these myths have striking similarities. The world grew dark for days, a great flood washed over the Earth, lightning and huge chunks of rock crashed down from the sky as if thrown by God's hand and whole populations were wiped out, leaving a ragtag assortment of survivors to rebuild humanity.

"In well over 100 cultures, spread all over the globe, cut off from each other by geography and time, the same basic underlying story elements exist.

"Devlin, in the course of pondering his own questions about the rise of modern man, read the works of a range of authors spanning nearly the last 70 years of debate about the great flood myth. He found himself aligned with the view that the stories were not myths, but were, in fact, actual recordings of a real event that occurred thousands and thousands of years ago. In that, Devlin found an ally in me."

"So you believe there was a massive flood that nearly wiped out mankind?" Anlon asked.

"Yes, I do, Anlon. I can't say that my own work proves it one way or the other, but work done by others, in my opinion, offers compelling physical evidence. The muck beds along the Alaskan coastline, the erratic boulders of European farm lands and the mountain-top presence of sea fossils in the Andes and Himalayas are but a few physical examples of the aftermath," Cesar explained.

"In what way did believing in the great flood shape Devlin's work?" Pebbles asked.

"It's a good question, Eleanor. For me, connecting physical proof with ancient mythology helps build the case for claiming the myths are true stories. Confirmation or a refutation of mythology is where my research interest lies.

"For Devlin, the belief that the great flood story was a reporting of a historical event spurred him to 'dig deeper,' He wasn't satisfied knowing it was a true story. If it were true, he contemplated, then what was life like before the great flood? So he came to me to learn mythology about life preceding the great flood.

"There are many stories of course about life before the flood, but most are considered fairy tales by mainstream archaeologists and anthropologists," Cesar expounded.

"Why?" Pebbles asked.

Cesar rubbed the fingers of each hand with his thumbs and said, "Where's the proof?"

He chuckled to himself and added, "It makes one almost want to knock on their heads and shout, 'Hello, imbeciles, if a flood raced across the Earth and wiped out nearly everything, plant and animal, including man, isn't it likely that physical signs of the cultures described in the pre-flood myths were wiped out, too?' What did Sumatra look like after the 2004 tsunami?"

"So, Devlin, heretic that he was, decided to go find the proof, right?" Anlon posited.

"Exactly, my friend, exactly," exclaimed Cesar, clasping his hands before him in a "bravo" gesture.

Pebbles followed up quickly, asking, "So you said Devlin came to you for some of those pre-flood myths. Which ones did you share with him? Well, cutting to the quick, what myth led him to the Life Stones?"

Cesar said, "You two are nearly as excited as the old man himself! Actually, the stories that most interested Devlin turned out to be post-flood myths, not pre-flood myths. Stories about 'fish men' who came up out of the sea to help the survivors of the flood. As was the case about the great flood, the fish men stories could be found in multiple cultures' mythologies.

"In the stories, the fish men taught the survivors how to farm, raise livestock, build shelters, hunt, heal injuries, communicate, organize, trade, defend themselves and more. The myths were so similar. The fish men across the cultures were described in nearly identical language. Tall, golden-haired, bearded Caucasian men. They were viewed as gods and treated as such...for a time.

"In almost all of the fish men myths, the survivors eventually revolted against the fish men. They either killed them or banished them back to the sea."

"Wait. *Fish* men, like mermaids? And if they were so helpful, why kill them?" a fascinated Pebbles asked.

Cesar answered earnestly, "No. The description of their physical appearance varies, but they have always been described as humans dressed like fish. Most scholars ascribe the moniker to the fact they arrived by sea, but it has always puzzled me that many of the legends say when they arrived they *came up out of the sea.*

"As to the revolts, the legends say the survivors had learned all they could from the fish men. As they learned and gained confidence in their own abilities, leaders among the survivors emerged who challenged the authority of the god-like fish men. Some of the fish men laid down their scepters and departed. A few of them fought to retain power, unsuccessfully I might add.

"No one knows where the fish men came from, why they helped the survivors and where they went afterward. Without some physical evidence of their presence beyond the stories, the possibility of their actual existence was tossed into mythology. To everyone but Devlin. I wanted to believe it, but it was Devlin who opened his mind to seek the evidence."

Anlon considered Cesar's legends and realized Devlin went looking for the fish men. He thought of Pebbles' description of the greeters on the Master Stone extending farewells to men leaving in boats, and of the two planets in mortal conflict. Could the Stone Benders be the fish men...and women?

As a scientist, Anlon shuddered at the implications. History rewritten, a whole new realm of scientific inquiry to examine man pre-flood through an entirely different lens. Humans, not as crude cave-dwelling sketchers, but more technologically advanced in some ways than modern man.

He shook his head. Anlon still didn't understand why Devlin kept his discovery quiet. Going public with his proof would have made him the greatest archaeologist of all-time. He posed the question to Cesar. "There's something I'm struggling to reconcile. Why do you think Devlin didn't go public with his proof? For that matter, why didn't you?"

Cesar reclined back in a relaxed posture and waved his hand as if to swat away a fly, "I told you, I am content to know the myth is true. The real discovery was Devlin's, I just fed him the legends. He's the one who worked it out. As to why he didn't go public, I think he was more fascinated with the prospect of unraveling the full mystery than he was with the idea of being world famous."

Pebbles interjected, "I get that. I didn't know Devlin, well, I met him once. He seemed like a man who loves the race rather than the medal at the end."

"I guess I can see that being true, only the race in this case cost Devlin his life," cautioned Anlon.

Silence ensued as they each pondered the totality of their discussion. Pebbles, growing famished from the morning's events and conversations, suggested they order sandwiches from the deli that delivered their pizza the previous evening. There was agreement and Pebbles called in their orders while Anlon walked Cesar over to the barn to show him Devlin's office. To Anlon's surprise, Cesar had never visited Devlin in Stockbridge, so he'd not seen Devlin's artifact collection or his workshop.

When lunch arrived, Pebbles set it on the picnic table that resided in the corner of the covered back porch and jogged over to the barn to "ring the lunch bell" so to speak. They walked back together and gathered around the table to eat. Anlon laughed softly, Pebbles had two sandwiches set before her. Where does all that food go, he wondered, gazing admiringly at her slim, athletic physique.

Anlon said, "You know, I realize it's early, but I feel like a beer. Any takers?"

Pebbles, hunkered down over her sandwich, mouth stuffed already, raised her hand while staring protectively at her second sub. Cesar raised his hand aloft, too, and said, "That sounds refreshing. And when you return, it is my turn to ask questions of you two."

Anlon handed ice-cold bottled beers to Pebbles and Cesar and said, "Cesar, thank you again for agreeing to meet, and for allowing Antonio to whisk you up here."

"Not at all. Like I said, once I heard Devlin's name, I knew I would come. Of course, Mr. Wallace made it an easier decision by committing to pay for my summer season's field trip if I dropped everything right away." Cesar smiled, raising his bottle in a mock toast before drinking.

"Did he really do that? Looks like I'll have some serious debts to repay on our favor ledger," Anlon laughed. Maybe two bottles of the rare Macallan scotch...delivered in a new Rolls Royce!

"Jibes aside, I have questions. Such as, do you have the stones Devlin located, the Story Stones in particular?" Cesar asked.

Pebbles nodded, but let Anlon answer considering her mouth was full of the last bite of her first sandwich. He said, "Yes, we do. In fact, this morning we viewed one of the Stones, Pebbles and I, er, I mean Eleanor and I."

"I have not viewed a Story Stone myself. Would you object if I ask to view one?"

"No, I would not object. It's the very least we could do to thank you and to honor the help you provided Devlin," Anlon replied.

Pebbles gulped her beer and added, "It's very intense, but *so* worth it."

"So I've been told," Cesar said. "Then tell me, why do you think Devlin's and Dobson's deaths are linked to the Life Stones?"

Anlon described the finding of the gold coins at Dobson's house, Anabel's description of Devlin's temperament the day before he died, Pacal's demonstration of the Sound Stone and his ominous suggestion that it was the weapon responsible for Devlin's death. He also added in the intrusions of Thatcher Reynolds and Klaus Navarro.

Cesar attentively focused on each kernel laid out by Anlon. Behind his eyes, Anlon sensed Cesar absorbing and interpreting each piece. When Anlon finished, Cesar said, "Without a doubt, you are on the right track. It would not surprise me in the end if Thatcher or Klaus were mixed up in the crimes at some level. They are both notorious. Thatcher for his laziness and sleazy cunning; Klaus for his vapid manner and ruthless tactics. I'm sorry, Eleanor, that Navarro injured you. He is not revered for his treatment of women, I'm afraid."

Anlon was actually elated Cesar knew both men. He intended to put a hurting on both men, legally, and Cesar's insight would be valuable. He asked, "You know them both? Please, enlighten me on their backgrounds."

"Surely. I will start with Navarro. He is a very wealthy man. He made his money initially in copper mining, but eventually shifted into exports. Along the way, he developed a taste for antiquities.

"Some say his miners dug up the initial pieces that captured his love of ancient artifacts. Others say he became embroiled in the illegal smuggling of rare pieces as an exporter and came to appreciate the value of such artifacts among the rich and powerful.

"I, myself, believe a little of both occurred. Today, he is the most aggressive collector of ancient Mayan, Incan and Olmec artifacts in the world. I say aggressive because he pays astronomical prices for pieces sellers bring to market, and he steals others that are not for sale. Or so I'm told. He is not the kind of man that accepts defeat easily."

"Uh oh, guess I shouldn't have bashed his face in with the lamp," Pebbles sarcastically commented before rising from the table to fetch a new round of beers. Bartender habit, she acknowledged as she jogged inside...something about empty bottles and glasses made her nervous.

Anlon laughed, but then asked a serious question, "Cesar, are you aware of rumors in the community or in the markets, legal or otherwise, about Devlin's stones?"

"You ask a very interesting question, Anlon. The honest answer is no. That's what makes Klaus' presence at Devlin's funeral and his actions thereafter noteworthy. I am not an expert in these matters, but the fact he is involved feels to me like he is aligned with someone close to Devlin. That's the only way he'd know about the stones, as far as I can tell," Cesar revealed, accepting a fresh beer from Pebbles.

She heard Anlon's question and Cesar's answer from the kitchen. As she unwrapped her second sandwich, she mentioned, "To be fair to the SOB, he never said anything about the stones. He kept talking about sculptures. It might have been a ruse, but I didn't get the impression he was after the stones."

Anlon shrugged his shoulders. He had nothing in mind to refute Pebbles' honest appraisal. Damn, she sure is fair for someone who got her head smashed into a steel rack by the ponytailed menace!

Cesar pulled at his chin, deep in thought. Narrowing his eyes, he added, "I think it was a ruse. It's well known that Klaus covets Incan gold. Your mention of the gold coins interests me, but I am confused. There's no way he would have expected Devlin to keep gold in open storage boxes. And if Klaus knew about the stones, it's inconceivable he'd believe Devlin kept them out in the open. So his actions when he attacked Eleanor don't make sense if he had inside help."

Another fair-minded person, thought Anlon! Where are all the suspicious, devious minds when needed. He asked with an air of desperation, "What about Thatcher?"

"He's a slug," Cesar spat.

At last, Anlon thought, a scathing appraisal!

Cesar continued, "His whole career has been built on the backs of others. He changes his own views with the wind, a wind that seems curiously aligned with whomever funds his research. He has been caught in some rather compromising situations where his hand appeared to be inside the register at the expense of his sponsors. His threat about danger and reference to backers is entirely consistent with his reputation."

Anlon cheered inside…finally a villain!

And then Cesar dashed his glee in a simple statement, "But his tactics here don't mirror his past exploits, so I'm not sure he is at the root of this."

Pebbles noticed the deflated look in Anlon's eyes as she polished off the last bite of sandwich number two. She queried, "How are his tactics different?"

"Well, from what you described, it sounds as if he's resorted to legal maneuvers. You know, trying to get around the will, as you shared. That's far afield from his expertise and it seems a very tortuous and public way to achieve his outcome if his primary goal is to find the stones," Cesar said.

Pebbles sensed where Cesar was headed and pitched in, "So if Navarro is involved, gold is his target. If Thatcher is involved, I take it you think someone is playing him?"

Cesar nodded in agreement. Anlon shot a skeptical look at Pebbles and said, "I follow you about Navarro, but not Thatcher. What do you mean someone is playing him?"

"I mean someone is teasing him with a carrot so delicious, and he wants the carrot so bad, that he's doing goofy things to get the job done. Thatcher may be the front man, but not the brains pushing the buttons," Pebbles outlined.

Anlon leaned back against the porch railing and crossed his arms. An even more skeptical look washed across his face, but he trusted Pebbles' instincts enough to say, "Okay, I'll accept your premise. What's the connection with the stones then? You remember he was explicitly interested in taking over Devlin's research."

Pebbles turned to Cesar and asked, "In your opinion, is Thatcher the kind of person who can be deceitful in a subtle way?"

Cesar shook his head firmly from side to side.

"So, he more often ham-hands it. That's why he gets caught," Pebbles elaborated.

"You know him well," Cesar laughed.

"I got to watch him in action. In the span of three sentences he went from generously offering to take Devlin's research off Anlon's hands, to offering a king's ransom for it, to threatening Anlon and anyone he knows with imminent peril. Not exactly what I would call a practiced, smooth operator," she summarized.

Anlon, mouth agape, winked at Pebbles and said, "You're unbelievable, you know that? Where do you come up with this stuff? Don't get me wrong, it's amazing! What's your secret? Do I need to eat more? You know, two sandwiches instead of one kind of thing?"

Cesar roared with laughter and clapped his hands loudly. Pebbles giggled and stuck her tongue out at Anlon (noted: tongue stud there again). She said with an aristocratic flair, "A lady of exceptional talents never reveals her secrets."

Accompanying the bravado was a flexed bicep. She tried to lift the rolled up sleeve of the dress shirt to reveal her tattooed shoulder, but the shirt was too tight.

Adopting a more serious tone, Anlon said, "Fair enough. A gentleman does not ask a lady to reveal her secrets, exceptional talents included. I'm trying to follow you, *Eleanor*. So what you're saying is that someone is feeding Thatcher ideas on how to get access to the stones and Thatcher is essentially failing miserably at it. If that's true, why even use Thatcher?"

Pebbles swirled her half full beer bottle above the table, and teased, "You don't see it, A.C.?"

Anlon looked at Cesar who also had a Cheshire Cat grin on his face. He flushed with embarrassment and chided Pebbles, "See, I told you, I'm *not* a good detective! Help the man lost in the desert, will you, please?"

"You are a phenomenal detective, A.C. We've discussed that already. But to answer your question...if Thatcher is involved, the person behind Thatcher has already killed twice and still doesn't have the stones. He is using Thatcher as a distraction, a side show. Think about it — the barn break-in? The theft of the will? Acts of a desperate man, don't you think? Why not create diversion, too? Draw our attention elsewhere before he strikes again," Pebbles pronounced, pounding her beer bottle on the picnic table to emphasize her point.

Cesar added with a chortle, "Her skills, Anlon, are beyond mine as well. Yes, I see it in your eyes. She is on a different level than you and me. What she says about Thatcher? It fits perfectly with his character. He is more bluster than sting, but he might just be the perfect smoke screen for a deadly predator!"

XIX
DOBSON UNVEILED

The wait outside Detective Captain Gambelli's office was brief and Jennifer was thankful. There was a lot to chase down today and she was already behind her intended schedule. When his office door opened, two other detectives stepped out and Gambelli shouted for her to enter.

"Good morning, Cap," greeted Jennifer pleasantly.

"Morning, Stevens. I've only got about 15 minutes. What's up?"

"Appreciate you fitting me in, Cap. Just wanted to give you a quick update on the Dobson case."

"Okay, whatcha got?"

"It's looking more and more like there is a connection between the Wilson death and Dobson's. I learned last night that Dobson was allegedly stealing artifacts from Wilson and selling them. I think that's where the large cache of gold comes in. It either was given to Dobson in exchange for artifacts, or the gold coins are artifacts he intended to sell. I'm not sure which at the moment," Jennifer explained.

"Interesting. Who's the alleger?" Gambelli inquired.

"A woman named Anabel Simpson, lives in Bennington, Vermont. She learned about Dobson's supposed thefts from Devlin Wilson himself, the night before his alleged accident. She said Wilson told her he and Dobson had a big argument a few days before Wilson died," Jennifer replied.

Gambelli's face adopted a mildly annoyed pose. He said, "I thought I told you to stick with Dobson. The Wilson case is not our concern and there is no evidence that his death was anything other than a tragic accident."

"Yep, and I've followed your orders. I didn't speak with Anabel Simpson directly, Dr. Cully did, Wilson's nephew. He passed along his conversation with Miss Simpson last night. It seemed relevant to me, so I wanted you to know about it," Jennifer answered.

Even though Gambelli challenged Jennifer hard at times, he was, in fact, a big supporter of hers. She was thorough, diligent and resourceful at collecting evidence, in his eyes. She also had good instincts and possessed strong deductive reasoning. Her greatest weakness was exhibiting myopia when it came to suspects and motives. If she crafted a theory in her mind, it became hard to get her to consider other alternatives. He was worried it was happening with the Dobson case, despite his earlier cautions. Yet, he had to give her room to maneuver. She might be right after all. He said, "Okay, let's play it out. What's your theory?"

Jennifer had braced for a tirade when irritation flashed on Gambelli's face, so his question was somewhat unexpected. She replied, "Um, okay, let's start with motive. If Miss Simpson is telling the truth, I'd say money is the core of the crime."

"All right, seems reasonable. Now let's consider the murder itself. We agreed before that it was a reckless and risky killing, correct? Which implies it was not premeditated. So what are the possible reasons for a spur of the moment murder over money?"

"Double cross? Someone expected him to deliver and he didn't, possibly the gold in the safe," Jennifer speculated.

"That's one option. What other motive could there be besides money?"

"Um, let me think…okay, try this on…Dobson is called out by Wilson for stealing and selling artifacts. Dobson feels guilty, decides to stop. Possibly even tells his buyer or buyers that the gig is up. If he did, maybe one of the buyers gets scared the trail will lead back to him. Kills him to cover his tracks."

"Plausible. What about the will?"

"Haven't found it yet. As soon as we wrap up here, I'm on the way to his two banks. I'm praying he had a safe deposit box at one of them."

"What if there is a will? It still might mean money is at the heart of it, as you suspect, but the crime might have zero to do with Wilson's death or artifacts," Gambelli suggested. "Could be someone trying to move along an inheritance."

"That's fair," Jennifer allowed. "I agree it's a possibility. It's why I'm following up looking for the will. I also have the cell phone records, and we have Dobson's laptop. I'm hoping we'll get some more information from those that will push us in the right direction."

Gambelli said, "Good, just keep an open mind. My gut tells me your instincts are on the right track. The timing of Wilson and Dobson's deaths are too close to be coincidental, especially now that an artifact in Wilson's possession, the stone you mentioned, has an identical marking on it to Dobson's large stash of gold coins with the same marking. Add to that the confrontation Miss Simpson described and Wilson's allegations about Dobson's theft and you have ingredients that definitely are in murder recipes. But there are two big unanswered questions standing in your way."

"Okay, what questions?"

Gambelli explained, "If it was about the artifacts or gold or both, why didn't the killer break into Dobson's home to search or to steal? The house alarm never was turned off, there was no sign of entry, nothing appeared disturbed or missing. Why not wait for Dobson to get inside and then confront him? At least then the killer would have the opportunity to search or steal.

"If, instead, the murder was meant to silence Dobson from revealing the buyer, why kill Wilson in the first place? From what you've described thus far, Wilson suspected Dobson of theft. He laid a trap to prove it and then confronted Dobson once he knew for sure. But nothing you've found or been told would indicate Wilson had any idea who the buyer or buyers might be. So why kill him? It unnecessarily draws attention, and when combined with Dobson's murder so closely afterward, it sends up huge flashing signs that shout, 'look this way.' Not very smart for someone concerned about covering tracks."

Jennifer's vision was trained on Gambelli's Patriot bobble-head collection during his dissection. They actually moved at the tone of his booming voice. She had to admit, he poked some gaping holes in her theories. Gambelli watched her process the inconsistencies he pointed out and then said, "I'll tell you what. I can think of a motive you haven't considered yet."

Her eyes arched and her mind raced. What did I miss, she thought?

"Revenge."

"How so?"

Gambelli proposed, "What if there is only one murder here? Someone blamed Dobson for Wilson's accident, right or wrong, and killed him in revenge. It would explain why the killer didn't attempt to take anything from Dobson. It would explain why the killing was so reckless and risky — an emotional response, not a calculated one.

"I'll go you one more crazy idea…what if Wilson was murdered as you suspect, by Dobson himself or someone at Dobson's direction? Dobson then gets whacked in retaliation by someone convinced he was behind Wilson's death."

As she jotted his comments down in her notepad, she nodded in acceptance of the fact that she'd overlooked those two possibilities. On the surface, each sounded very possible. But there were two unexplained events Gambelli's revenge theory didn't satisfactorily address.

She rebutted, "I'm with you. Revenge could be a strong possible motive here. But what about the theft of Cully's copy of Wilson's will? And the later break-in of Wilson's home and the likely theft of his laptop during the break-in? Why would someone who had already satisfied his revenge do these things after the fact?"

"Good questions, Detective," Gambelli conceded, "I don't know the answers, other than to say they may be completely unrelated to Wilson's death or Dobson's murder. Might be vultures seeking to clean up leftovers. Or I could be wrong and they might be directly related to Dobson's murder and possibly support the contention Wilson was murdered. The point I'm trying to make here is the soup's thicker than you think right now. Examine each piece of evidence you find against all these theories, not just one."

When Jennifer presented her badge and business card to the lobby receptionist of the Great Barrington branch of Massachusetts First Trust Bank, the gum smacking, 20-something blonde lazily lifted her gaze from admiring her manicure and yawned.

Without saying a word, "Beckie" as her nametag read, slowly rose from behind the reception console and wiggled down the hem of her way-too-tight skirt. Shooting an annoyed look at Jennifer, she snatched the business card from the counter, twirled on her way-too-high heels and stalked away with a slight stagger. Jennifer quietly snickered as Beckie teetered towards the manager's office with her nose aloft.

A few moments later, a spindly but well-dressed Asian man emerged from an office and strode with purpose towards Jennifer, extending a friendly greeting along with his business card. "Good morning, Detective. My name is Min-Jun Cho; I am the manager for this branch. How may I be of service?"

"Good morning, Mr. Cho. Thank you for seeing me without an appointment. It's a confidential matter. Is it possible we might speak in private?" replied Jennifer, taking Mr. Cho's card and discreetly motioning towards Beckie, who hovered nearby smacking away on her gum. The assistant crossed her arms and rolled her eyes in a manner intended to communicate, "Whatever, bitch!"

"Of course, please follow me," answered the amiable Mr. Cho.

As they walked past Beckie, the assistant huffed, tossed her blonde locks absently and sashayed away. Jennifer wondered how long it would take Beckie to regain her post, given her skirt's tourniquet-like constriction.

When they arrived in his office, Mr. Cho offered Jennifer a seat and closed the door. With sincerity, the manager studied her business card and replied with a slight bow, "It is impressive to meet a Detective so young. You must be among the department's elite."

Jennifer smiled at his compliment and replied, "It's actually Detective Lieutenant, and I wouldn't consider myself among our elite, but I appreciate your kind words."

Given the tenor of Mr. Cho's ceremonial greeting, and aware of the importance in many Asian cultures of recognizing one another formally before conducting business, Jennifer inspected his card and said, "Your family must be proud of your accomplishments, Mr. Cho. Bank managers carry heavy responsibilities."

Mr. Cho lit up. He bowed and said, "Thank you, Detective Lieutenant. I have worked hard; I hope they are proud. Now, what can I help you with?"

"I am investigating a murder, Mr. Cho, and the victim was a customer of your bank, a Mr. Matthew Dobson. There are certain documents and possibly certain items relevant to the crime that we suspect may be stored in a safe deposit box. I am here to find out if Mr. Dobson maintained a safe deposit box at your bank. If he did, I need to access it to determine its contents. Here is the search warrant," Jennifer said, presenting the official document.

Bending over the document, Mr. Cho rapidly scanned the contents and turned to the computer on his desk. His fingers tickled the keys with lightning speed. He removed a pair of reading glasses from his suit pocket and tilted them on the tip of his nose. He nodded and said, "Yes, yes, Matthew Dobson. It appears he does, or I should say did, have a safe deposit box here. Do you have his key?"

Jennifer gave an embarrassed shrug and said, "No, I'm afraid we didn't find a key that looked like it might fit a safe deposit box."

It would have been closer to the truth if Jennifer had said she and Pebbles hadn't thought to look for the key. She internally admonished herself for the oversight and made a note to revisit Dobson's house to specifically search for keys. So much for ranking among the elite detectives, she frowned!

"Oh," he said, "Hmmm..."

"Is there a problem?"

"No, not really, but a safe deposit box requires two keys. We keep one for each box at the bank, but if you don't have Mr. Dobson's, we have to drill through the lock where his key would have been inserted. It just means there will be a small delay while I track down our security officer," responded the helpful Mr. Cho.

"Ah, I apologize for the inconvenience. I don't mind waiting. It's very important," Jennifer answered.

Mr. Cho left the office in search of his assistant and returned a few minutes later. Straightening his suit jacket and tie before lowering himself on the chair, Mr. Cho said, "He will be with us shortly."

The pause gave Jennifer the opportunity to sneak in her other purpose for visiting the branch. She queried, "Mr. Cho, while we are waiting, I have another question. We did find statements for Mr. Dobson's checking account, but they are incomplete and contain nothing significant as far as we could tell. I wondered if it would be possible to get a full set of his bank statements for the past year, and verify whether he had other accounts here?"

Mr. Cho nodded definitively, "No problem at all."

He flicked off a quick message to Beckie. From the slightly ajar office door, Jennifer heard a loud sigh echo from the hallway. Apparently, Beckie was put out by the request. Don't chip a nail, sweetie, Jennifer mused to herself!

Refocusing her attention on Mr. Cho, she asked, "Based on your experience, Mr. Cho, when you look at Mr. Dobson's account online, does anything jump out at you as unusual? Something that seems out of the ordinary from a banker's point of view?"

Without further discussion, he returned to his computer and examined the results of his keystroke flurry. Jennifer distinctly saw his eyebrows shift upwards. He muttered something unintelligible under his breath and engaged in several more bouts of rapid tapping, pausing every so often to adjust his glasses and review the oversized monitor.

Jennifer leaned forward, excitement building as she observed Mr. Cho's succession of puzzled facial expressions. There *was* something obviously unusual about Matthew Dobson's account. She queried, "Have you found something of interest?"

Mr. Cho slumped back against the chair and intertwined his fingers in his lap and said, "Your instincts, Detective Lieutenant, are rewarded. Yes, there are some unusual transactions in one of Mr. Dobson's accounts."

"Accounts? So he had more than one at your bank?"

"Yes, he had three accounts. The checking account you referenced earlier, a savings account and a money market account," Mr. Cho itemized before continuing. "As you have observed already, the checking account looks completely average. Nothing out of the ordinary. The savings account is small and there have been no transactions in the account over the past year."

Jennifer flipped open her notebook and scribbled away. Without lifting her head, she added, "But the other one is a different matter. Let me guess, there are some large transactions that moved in or out."

Mr. Cho cracked a wry smile and nodded his head, "Precisely."

"By any chance, did any of those transactions occur within the last month?"

His smile grew wider, "You are indeed among the elite of detectives."

Inside, Jennifer did a double fist pump. In response to Mr. Cho's compliment, she looked at him and blushed involuntarily. Edging further on the chair, Jennifer lowered her pad and pen and said, "I wish my Captain felt the same way! Before you elaborate on the transactions, may I guess?"

He said, "I have such a boss as well. Yes, I'm very interested to hear your point of view."

Thinking back to Anlon's description of his meeting with Anabel, she knew that if Matthew Dobson had been stealing and selling artifacts from Devlin's collection, there would be a payment trail somewhere.

Initially, Jennifer thought the trail might lead to the gold coins she and Pebbles found in Dobson's home.

But the more she considered the coins, the less they seemed viable sources of payment, given they were impressed with the Master Stone fish symbol. Rather, she reasoned, Dobson was more likely trying to sell them and stored them in his home for safe keeping.

So that left two options in Jennifer's mind. Either Dobson used his bank accounts for the payments or she would find cash in the safe deposit box. Given Mr. Cho's reactions, she surmised the bank accounts must have been used for payments.

"I'm going to guess large transfers were made into the money market," she confidently conjectured.

Wagging a finger back and forth, Mr. Cho said, "No, you are incorrect."

"So, the money flows the opposite way?"

"Yes and no. What's curious about Mr. Dobson's accounts is that he made three sizeable *deposits* over the past six months in the money market account, not transfers."

"Hmm, how large?"

"All three deposits were $250,000 dollars. One in December of last year, another in February, and the last, only three weeks ago," Mr. Cho catalogued.

Jennifer furrowed her brow, "You said the deposits weren't transfers. Are you saying he walked into your bank with checks or briefcases stuffed with cash?"

"Checks. But he didn't deposit them into this branch, I would have been notified of a deposit that size if he did. I never met Mr. Dobson, nor do I recall hearing his name before today. He deposited the checks into one of our Manhattan branches on Park Avenue near the Waldorf Astoria Hotel. All three checks were from the same company, Atlas Gem Traders. I have an electronic copy of one of the checks up on my screen. Have a look."

Jennifer leaned across his desk as he shifted the monitor for her to view one of the checks. Scratching her forehead, Jennifer slid back down onto her chair. She said, "Wouldn't checks of that size ring alarm bells? Aren't you required to report large deposits to the federal government?"

"Yes to both questions," Mr. Cho answered, "and I'm certain we did report the deposits. It's an automatic process that is centrally managed at our bank's headquarters. Why?"

Jennifer began to question her previous conclusion about the gold coins. Was Dobson *paid* with the rare coins and then did he periodically cash them in?

"It's possible the deposits are payments connected to illegal activity. Do gem traders deal in gold?" she asked.

"I don't know, it's possible. Our Park Avenue branch does a fair amount of business with the diamond and gem exchanges. Many of them are within a two block walk of the branch," Mr. Cho explained.

While Jennifer pondered the implications of the deposits, the security officer knocked on Mr. Cho's door. They rose and followed the security officer to the vault area.

Inside the gated area, the security officer punched in a code to retract the vault's interior glass door and the titanium grate beyond it. Mr. Cho extracted a key from his pocket and opened one of the first boxes inside the safe. Inside were the bank's keys for each of the deposit boxes. Finding the number for Matthew Dobson's box, he searched and pulled the box's key.

The security officer, drill in hand, followed Mr. Cho to the box. It was one of the larger boxes in the vault, about waist-high from the floor. The security officer drilled through the lock intended for Dobson's key. When finished, the bank manager inserted his own key, and the door shielding the box was opened.

The security officer slid the box out carefully and huffed when the full weight of the box rested in his hands. The box shifted slightly in his grip and a clatter of moving contents inside the box filled the air. Mr. Cho led Jennifer to a private room to examine the contents.

Alone in the private room, Jennifer slid open the box cover. A startled gasp fell from her parted lips. She blinked several times, her unbelieving mind refusing to accept what her eyes encountered. There were three main items layered on top, but what caught her initial attention were tall stacks of banded $100 dollar bills that filled the box's entire area beneath the items.

She donned latex gloves and removed her pad, pen and cell phone to snap pictures of each item she removed. On top were two stone sculptures approximately a foot tall each. One appeared to be oriental in origin. It looked to Jennifer like a dragon head attached to the body of a man holding a sword in a menacing manner. As she turned it over, Jennifer was taken aback to discover a carving on the back of the dragon's head that looked just like the fish symbol that was impressed on the gold coins found in Dobson's kitchen safe.

The other sculpture was less ornate and Jennifer couldn't hazard a guess as to its lineage. It was the stone figure of a crouching man, but there were no facial features or detail on his body. It kind of looked like an unfinished clay creation. However, in the figure's outstretched hands were two distinctly etched features. Both looked to her like rocks. One of the rocks was conical and its tip pointed forward towards Jennifer as she faced the sculpture. The other stone was tubular and the man seemed to be connecting them. It reminded Jennifer vaguely of how the Port Stone snapped into the back of the Master Stone.

Removing them carefully from the box, she photographed each one separately, making sure to snap pictures from multiple angles. When she was finished with the sculptures, she set them aside. Behind these two objects, pushed to the back of the safe deposit container, was a book-sized wooden box. As Jennifer removed the box from the larger container, she heard small objects roll inside. To her it called to mind the muffled sound of raw elbow macaroni colliding when poured out of the pasta box. The box itself was light and contained no lock.

Placing the closed box on the table, she took a couple of quick pictures before toggling the center snap to open the box. When she peered inside, she uttered, "Holy crap!"

Blue velvet padding lined the box to protect at least 100 loose, cut diamonds glittering inside. Jennifer shook her head to and fro in astonishment. She blurted, "Wow!"

Her fingers shook as she snapped pictures of the diamonds inside. When complete, she lifted a few of the diamonds from the box and laid them in her palm. She used a finger to maneuver the gems. They were large solitaires, she estimated approximately two carats each. Replacing the diamonds in the case, she sat back in the booth's chair and crossed her arms and legs and disappeared into deep concentration.

The diamonds must be how Dobson was paid for delivering the stolen artifacts, Jennifer surmised. She knew diamonds were often used as payment currency in organized crime smuggling transactions given the difficulty in tracing the origins of the gems.

When he desired to exchange the diamonds for cash, Dobson would take a portion of the diamonds to Atlas Gem Traders. He probably was unnerved by the idea of walking around with a large check in his possession for very long and scampered to the bank's Park Avenue branch to make a quick deposit. This, she realized, also conveyed the benefit of avoiding local attention to his large deposits.

The two sculptures were most likely objects he intended to sell before he was unexpectedly murdered. But why then did he keep the gold coins in his house? Could Dobson have been staging the coins in his home safe for imminent hand-off to the buyer?

Leaning forward, she snapped shut the diamond box and moved it aside with the sculptures. Next, she removed and tallied the cash stacked four levels high in the box. There were a total of 36 banded stacks of $100 dollar bills. Assuming no hundreds were missing from the banded stacks, that meant the cash totaled $360,000 dollars.

There was nothing underneath the cash stacks. No will, no other documents and no other artifacts. She snapped pictures of the cash, returned all the contents to the box and closed the lid.

Jennifer stepped out of the room and asked the security officer standing outside to retrieve Mr. Cho while she made a quick call. When he arrived, she said, "I'm going to need to take the box and its contents as evidence. First though, I've called to get an evidence collection team and armed escort for the contents. Then I'd like you to come in the booth, verify the contents and take an inventory. I'm sure you need that for your own purposes anyway. I'm guessing you'll need me to sign some forms and I'll need you to do the same."

"What did you find?" a shaken Mr. Cho inquired.

"You'll see for yourself. I have some other questions, though, while we wait for my team to arrive," Jennifer stated.

"I am at your disposal, Detective," he bowed.

"You have records showing when Mr. Dobson visited his safe deposit box, correct?"

"Yes, that's right."

"I'd like to get a listing of all his visits over the past six months."

"That should be no problem."

"Also, we only discussed deposits into his money market account. I know the account statements you're gathering for me will show all activity but I'm curious to know what kind of withdrawal activity you observed when you pulled up his account online?" Jennifer asked.

"That was curious also. There were no withdrawals, per se, but there were transfers. There were a total of six transfers to two parties who maintain accounts at our bank," he answered.

Possible conspirators, Jennifer thought! God, she hoped one of them was Pacal; she just had a bad feeling about him overall. She asked, "Do you have the two parties' names and their addresses?"

"Yes, I will get you their contact information, but I remember their names. Miss Zoe Moore and Mr. John Wood. This might interest you, also. I did a little research on both while you were examining the safe deposit box.

"Their accounts were opened at the Park Avenue branch about a year ago on the same day. The only deposits in their accounts are transfers from Mr. Dobson. Both Miss Moore and Mr. Wood routinely withdrew most of the deposits from Mr. Dobson within days, in cash, although they did not make the withdrawals at the Park Avenue branch. Miss Moore made her withdrawals at one of our Miami branches. Mr. Wood at a branch in Dallas," Mr. Cho explained.

"Wow, that's very kind of you, Mr. Cho. I appreciate your cooperation and insight. You're saving me a lot of leg work here," Jennifer smiled with a slight bow.

"I'm pleased to assist you, Detective Lieutenant. Plus, this saves me work later on when you would have invariably come back to ask more questions. I also should have mentioned earlier, but my brother is a police officer in Philadelphia. Helping you is to me like helping my brother," answered the humble Mr. Cho.

"Thank you, your help is of tremendous assistance. Your brother is very fortunate to have such a considerate sibling. Are you ready to start on the inventory?"

"Yes," Mr. Cho affirmed, "but I have one last piece of helpful news before we go. Miss Moore used a debit card linked to her account last night...at the Waldorf Astoria. The size of the debit card authorization leads me to believe she has more than a one night stay planned."

Another internal double fist pump. Jennifer grinned broadly, and said, "Min-Jun, you da man!"

XX
REVELATIONS

Anlon and Pebbles cautiously watched as Cesar released the Master Stone. He viewed the stone nearly as long as Pebbles had earlier in the morning, but his outward emotional reaction when he spoke was more composed than either of them expected after their own experiences with the Stone. He said, "Absolutely extraordinary. I am happy that Devlin found his proof before he died. If nothing else, he went to his Maker knowing he was right. How incredible to watch, listen and even feel messages from people 10,000 years ago..."

Cesar's voice trailed off as he retreated into thought. For a few minutes he sat in silence on the sofa in Devlin's study, rubbing his hands together and staring at the floor. Anlon imagined it must be a shock to find almost-living proof that a long-believed myth is actually true. The images on the stone, and the stone itself, challenged everything presumed about the history of man.

The more Anlon had reflected about the stones and the people who made them, his thoughts shifted from amazement to scientific curiosity. In particular, he marveled at this ancient race's ability to tap into a human's magnetic senses. That's really what was at the heart of the Stones, he speculated. Magnetism. Somehow the Stone Benders had discovered how to manipulate magnetism.

In his own study of biomechanics, Anlon knew that many insects, birds and animals have the ability to detect the magnetic field of the Earth. They use their magnetic senses to navigate, hunt, mate and sense danger the way humans use their senses of smell and sight. It made Anlon realize that, at one time, man must have had a prominent ability to detect Earth's magnetic field, but lost it over the ages.

Recalling his days as a student, Anlon knew the Earth's magnetic field was weaker now than it once had been. And even today the planet's magnetic field varied from place to place. He also remembered the magnetic poles of the Earth were not stationary. They had shifted numerous times in the planet's history and would shift again many more times going forward. A professor of his once described the magnetic field like currents in an ocean. They are dynamic.

They must have lived during a time when the Earth's magnetic field was very strong, or at least settled in an area where it was strong. It was strong enough that these people could sense it and, paraphrasing Pacal, *bend the stone to their will.*

At last, Cesar lifted his gaze and said, "Thank you, Anlon and Eleanor. It was surreal but undeniable proof of a fully formed, technologically superior society pre-flood. I was most overwhelmed by the sense of touch and smell when viewing the stone. It will sound childish, but I also thought emotion was communicated. No, that's the wrong way to say it. I felt Malinyah's emotions. Sadness, regret, determination and hope.

"It was almost as if the person who made the video, Malinyah, emblazoned a snapshot of her memories onto the stone. Didn't you think? In any event, the Stone brings into question a host of related myths."

Pebbles quickly agreed, "I hadn't thought of it that way, but yes! What do you mean, related myths?"

Cesar explained, "Yes, there are legends that some believe were aligned with the great flood. For instance, there are stories that suggest that when the cataclysmic event occurred — the passing asteroid/ planet — it caused the Earth to literally turn upside down. What was south became north and vice versa. Most often the way the myths talk about this phenomenon is that the stars rose in the opposite sky after a period of darkness following the flood."

As Anlon listened to Cesar, he thought to himself that the flipping of the planet definitely would have messed with Earth's magnetic field. Was it possible though? An entire planet rotating 180 degrees overnight?

"Are there legends about maps?" Pebbles asked.

"What do you mean?" Cesar inquired.

"Devlin had a map," Anlon explained. "He gave it to Anabel to pass onto me in case anything happened to him. She thought it was a sketch Devlin made of a map in an Egyptian pyramid. She said Devlin told her it was a map of their underworld."

Cesar rose suddenly, a mystified expression frozen on his face. He pounded a fist against his open hand, "Of course! The Waterland Map."

"Wait a minute," Anlon clarified, "I said underworld, not Waterland."

"No, no," Cesar rebutted, "I am not correcting you, Anlon. When you mentioned the map, it clicked a memory about another myth related to the great flood."

Cesar seemed lost in thought for a minute as he paced the room. At one point, he said out loud to no one in particular, "Yes, yes. That's what you were thinking old friend!"

A few minutes more of silent pacing and then he spoke again as if conversing with a ghost in the room, "Oh, Devlin, I didn't know you heard that legend. You brilliant man!"

Turning his attention to Anlon and Pebbles, he said, "I'm so sorry, my friends, please forgive my ravings. Let me explain.

"There is a legend told in multiple cultures that said when the great flood occurred, that which was underwater became land and vice versa. That when the great flood washed across the Earth, mountains thrust out of the ocean and land masses that previously existed were pulled to the ocean floor.

"You recall the story of the Lost City of Atlantis, for example. Legends say this advanced society sank in a single day. No trace of it has ever been found, though many have searched for it and some have laid claim to its whereabouts.

"There is one very obscure paper written by a controversial scholar that Devlin must have found on his own."

"Was the paper about Atlantis?" Anlon queried.

"No, it was not. I have read the research paper. The author challenged Egyptologists' interpretation of the Duat, the name ascribed by scholars to the Egyptian underworld. Extrapolating from hieroglyphs in various temples and tombs, anthropologists developed a view that dynastic Egyptians believed that when the sun sank below the horizon here on Earth, the sun rose in the underworld, or the Duat.

"One of the aspects of the Duat that has always puzzled Egyptologists is that the Duat is described in excruciating detail, meaning the glyphs contain robust discussion of its geographic features. It would be like the Bible describing and naming Heaven's mountains, rivers and forests.

"The controversial paper proposed that the underworld was an actual place. It was the Earth's land masses as they were known prior to the great flood. The reason, the scholar argued, that the Egyptians were so detailed in their depiction of the Duat is that they believed the sunken land masses of the world traded places with the new land masses, but they didn't disappear. They believed that when their people died, they returned to the previous world. This scholar referred to this land as the Waterland. He argued that the map found in the Giza pyramid was a depiction of the land mass of the Earth prior to the flood."

Cesar's description of the Waterland Map made sense to Anlon. The land masses were unrecognizable, yet Devlin had inserted longitude and latitude markers to provide context in relation to the world's topography today. Anlon said, "Cesar, on Devlin's map, we'll call it the Waterland Map, he inserted coded symbols at various locations on the sketched land masses. Through Anabel, Devlin said the codes indicate where other Life Stones can be found, but the codes are indecipherable without a key."

"May I see the map?" Cesar politely asked.

"Of course," replied Anlon as he rose to retrieve it.

When the map was laid out before them, Cesar leaned forward and touched the map as if handling a rare object. He shook his head in disbelief, "Extraordinary."

"We plan on getting a scaled version of a current world map to underlay the drawing to see if we can make more sense of the locations," interjected Pebbles.

Nodding, Cesar agreed, "Absolutely. I think I know what it will show."

"You do?" Anlon said with mild astonishment.

"Yes. I think you will see portions of current land masses within the boundaries of the land depicted on the Waterland Map. In the legend I mentioned earlier about the Earth flipping and land exchanging places with water, the survivors of the catastrophe didn't all take to water like Noah. Some scaled mountains, others hid in caves and there are even a few where intrepid souls climbed trees.

"Many of these supposed myths describe fire raining from the sky, terrible volcanic eruptions and debilitating darkness, the likes of which have never been described elsewhere in recorded histories. So, there were places on Earth that escaped the global tidal wave and other places where the wave washed over land, but then ebbed without changing the topography...or at least that's how I interpret the stories."

From a scientific viewpoint, Anlon thought, it was more plausible that portions of the Earth submerged or rose as a result of the gravitational forces exerted by a massive object passing close by the planet. The idea that there was a complete reversal of land and water seemed too extravagant. And if a full reversal had happened, it was hard to imagine how anyone could have survived.

What interested Anlon as he considered his earlier viewing of the Master Stone alongside Cesar's description was that the setting of Malinyah's presentation seemed untouched. And the waterfall visions Pebbles described detailed the catastrophe, so the recording was obviously made post-disaster, but wherever Malinyah and her compatriots resided escaped annihilation. Good fortune? Dumb luck? Or had they been able to protect themselves with the technology they developed?

Picking up on Cesar's commentary, Pebbles pointed to the map and asked, "What do you think the codes reference?"

"That, I do not know," Cesar replied.

"I've been thinking they mark where Story Stones were kept or taken instead of locations where other Life Stones can be found. Pacal told us there were five different Story Stone colors that he, Devlin and Dobson had seen in museums. The colors of the codes are the same as the Story Stone colors Pacal described," she threw out for consideration.

Anlon said, "I was leaning in that direction, too. But why do some groupings of codes on the map have more than others? Look here, at the tip of this land mass, all five are grouped together. But way over here, only two are shown. Each grouping is different."

"I see what you mean. Maybe there's more information on the Master Stone? Or the other Story Stone? We haven't even looked at that one yet," Pebbles suggested.

Cesar interjected, "Maybe Devlin didn't get a chance to finish coding the map before he died? But I think you're right, Eleanor, the answers to your questions are on the Stones you have here."

Cesar, Anlon and Pebbles talked for another hour about Devlin, myths and the Life Stones before the long overnight of travel finally caught up to Cesar. After the third extended yawn of the afternoon, Anlon suggested they wrap up. "Cesar, I think you might just rock over and fall asleep if we keep going! How about we drive you to the hotel I booked for you? You can get your things settled in the room, freshen up and we can grab a light dinner in the hotel pub when you're ready to come down."

Pebbles interposed, "Actually, A.C., I think I'll stick around here. My head's a little woozy still. I think I'll take a nap."

"Oh, right. Sorry, I forgot about your injury," Anlon apologized.

"I'm fine. Just a little tired," Pebbles casually replied.

In truth, the nap was a ruse. Pebbles intended to view the Master Stone again as soon as they left. There was so much more she wanted to know and...something had happened during her session with the Stone that she hadn't shared with Anlon or Jennifer.

She had hoped Cesar would experience the same phenomena when he viewed the Stone but he didn't mention it. If it had happened to him, Pebbles thought, it would have been easier to talk about. It wouldn't have sounded so weird.

As she had told Anlon and Jennifer, when Malinyah spoke, Pebbles began to understand what she was saying. Literally. Though the words sounded foreign as they rolled off Malinyah's tongue, Pebbles' brain interpreted them as if spoken in English.

But that wasn't all. Right before Pebbles released the Stone in shock — Malinyah had asked her two questions, "What is your name, little flower? And why are you so sad?"

Closing her eyes, Pebbles laid on the sofa and gripped the Master Stone. Her fingers began to tingle and the holographic visions commenced.

Again, Malinyah appeared. She smiled and walked towards Pebbles. In the background, Pebbles could hear birds tweeting, the sound of splashing and the laughter of small children.

Malinyah cupped Pebbles' hand in both of hers and said, "I'm so glad you've returned, little flower."

"Are you really talking to me?" Pebbles inquired.

The blonde goddess smiled warmly and answered, "In a way, yes."

"Oh my God! How?"

Malinyah placed her arm around Pebbles and led her outside the marble hall. She felt Malinyah's gentle fingers pat her shoulder and heard her sandaled feet tap on the floor as they walked. Arriving outside, Malinyah led Pebbles to a bench before the pool of frolicking children. They sat. Malinyah looked lovingly on the children and said, "Such untroubled souls. Such joy, don't you think?"

Pebbles smiled watching the boys and girls play tag in the water. The glow of the sun coated her face. She deeply inhaled the fresh scents around her and said, "In a place like this, I don't know how anyone could feel troubled."

Malinyah reached to caress Pebbles' inner wrist and whispered, "It is why I brought you here."

Startled, Pebbles released the Master Stone and leapt up off the couch. She grabbed at her wrist. It was still warm from Malinyah's touch.

"That did not just happen!" Pebbles tried to assure herself, "It was a dream. I fell asleep. A little too much beer, a little concussion, something!"

Stalking to the kitchen, Pebbles filled a glass with water from the tap and gulped it down. Through the back porch screen door, she caught the aroma of fresh-cut grass and noticed for the first time a landscaping crew was busy about the property. The whine of weed whackers and the drone of ride-on mowers were in sharp contrast to the light, gentle sounds Pebbles experienced on the Stone.

She turned her gaze back to the Master Stone lying on the leather sofa in Devlin's study. The logical part of her mind resisted the urge to reconnect with the Stone. Inexplicably, however, a deep yearning to be with Malinyah clawed in her stomach. It begged her to reconnect.

Pebbles ran outside onto the covered back porch and steadied herself on the wide wood railing. She closed her eyes and exhaled through pursed lips. Salsa music from the lawn crew's truck punctuated the gaps between the mechanical clamor of their equipment. It would have been an odd scene to a stranger. A shaken woman trying to calm herself while an unrelated torrent of activity and sound reverberated around her.

Then her eyes popped open, she pounded the railing with her fist and she sputtered, "Oh, F— it!"

Stalking back inside, she grabbed the Master Stone, snapped on the Port Stone and laid back on the couch. When her fingers found the side grips, she instantly returned to the bench with Malinyah. So weird.

Malinyah apologized, "I'm very sorry, dear. I didn't mean to upset you."

Pebbles found herself saying, "It's okay, Malinyah. You didn't upset me. I just don't understand. My name is Eleanor."

"Eleanor," mused Malinyah, "a very pretty name. A name very similar to one of our cherished flowers. It is a beautiful, deep shade of blue. We call it Alynioria. I will show you one before you leave."

Pebbles still struggled in her mind to believe the sensations occurring around her. A voice from her intellectual psyche demanded answers.

She said, "Malinyah, please explain. How are we communicating? How come I can understand you, feel you like I was sitting with you for real?"

"You *are* with me, Eleanor. Well, you are with my memories," Malinyah explained.

"Do you mean you were able to take the memories from your brain and put them on the stone?" Pebbles questioned with wonder.

Malinyah nodded and smiled, "More than just memories. Part of our consciousness, too. It's how I can sense your sadness, dear."

A long sigh escaped from Pebbles' mouth. She lowered her head and said, "I don't want to be sad."

Malinyah lifted Pebbles' wrist with the huddled angel tattoo and kissed the scar. She whispered, "No one knows why bad things happen to good hearts, Eleanor. But good hearts can heal, if you let them.

"My people, we called ourselves Munuorians, and our land we called Munuoria. We suffered greatly when the other world kissed Terra. I, myself, died not long after its passing, as did my children playing in the pool before you. Such terrible, unspeakable loss. I know the pain that pierces your heart.

"But my heart, Eleanor, it is light and filled with joy and warmth for the life and love I was blessed with. Even now."

Pebbles shook her head and asked, "I don't understand why we are talking about this, Malinyah. Why is it so important that I not be sad?"

"Because, Alynioria, sweet flower, we have much to discuss if you wish to learn the secrets of the Stones and how to use them. But your heart must be light and untroubled or you will not understand," she explained, as she stroked Pebbles' cheek. "If you heart is dark, you will be lured by the seductive power of the Stones to control and destroy rather than their grace to save, heal and grow."

Malinyah's floral scent wafted through Pebbles' nostrils and she deeply inhaled the soothing aroma. The Stone fell from her hands and she drifted off to sleep.

When Anlon returned to the house after dinner with Cesar at the Two Lanterns Inn, he spied Pebbles' slumped figure seated on the back steps and called, "Hey there! It's Friday. We should have some tequila!"

She didn't move and Anlon heard her sigh heavily. She called back, "Maybe later. We need to talk. Please come sit with me."

Anlon sensed she was upset, shaken even. He asked, "Are you all right? Is your head bothering you?"

Pebbles uttered a wry laugh and replied, "It hurts, but that's not what I need to talk to you about."

Part of her wanted to blurt out her visions with Malinyah, to tell Anlon what she'd learned. But somehow she didn't feel ready to talk about that yet. Instead, Malinyah's consoling words and touch filled her mind. Inside, she thought, "Okay, Malinyah, I'm trusting you here. Don't let me down!"

To Anlon, Pebbles said, "I want to talk about last night and about our earlier tattoo discussion."

Anlon lightly stepped up from the driveway to where Pebbles rested and planted himself next to her, leaning the weight of his body against her in an expression of affection. He didn't speak though. It was the kind of moment, he thought, where it's best to just be there.

He looked down at her face, faintly lit by the warm glow of sunset. She had been crying. His heart pounded in his chest. What was going on inside her, he mused with empathy.

She puffed out a long sigh, clenched her jaw and rubbed her wrists. She said, "I need to tell you some things about me. They are really, really hard to say. I'm so afraid you will hate me."

Tears dripped from her face onto the stairs below. Anlon wrapped his arm around her and whispered, "Not possible. We're a team."

Pebbles turned to face him, fully sobbing, and buried her head against his chest. He felt the shuddering contractions of her body as she let loose her anguish. She cried and moaned aloud. Other than the moonlight specter of her weeping in the meadow the night before, it was the first time Anlon ever witnessed her vulnerable. So much emotion burst from within her.

Anlon's resolve wavered, tears forming in his own eyes. Her agony was so deep it hurt him to imagine what she bottled up inside. From the scars on her wrists, he knew she had tried at least once to escape her pain.

Pebbles withdrew her face from Anlon's chest and stared down at the stairs, massaging her wrists. She said, "When I got out of law school, I met a guy named James Cunningham. We fell in love. I was engaged to him. He was a first year associate at an investment banking firm, came from a very wealthy, politically active family, just like my family. There was a lot of media buzz about us. Camelot kind of stuff.

"It was late summer and we went to the Hamptons for the weekend and stayed at his parent's beach house. We went out on a Saturday night to one of the clubs in town and met up with some of his friends. We all got wasted.

"One of his friends hit on me and I slapped him. The creep hit me back in the face and a full scale brawl erupted...but James stayed out of it. We all got tossed out of the club. I was so drunk I could barely walk. I was so angry at James for not coming to my defense, I said some awful things to him.

"I started to walk back to his parent's house. It was seriously five miles away. I wasn't thinking right. I had my shoes in my hands and he kept driving up next to me, begging me to get in the car. I ignored him."

Pebbles began to sob uncontrollably as the memories rushed forth. She managed disconnected words only. "There was a curve...didn't see it coming...James never saw it...the car hit James' car...he flew out...both cars hit me..."

She gripped Anlon's arm tightly, her fingernails digging into his skin. "He died! James died! I killed him, Anlon! That's what people said. The police arrested me! While I was in the hospital. My life...it was over."

Anlon laid a hand upon her soft hair and stroked while she bawled. He lowered his lips to kiss her brow, careful to avoid the knot left by Navarro. Anlon had imagined many scenarios once he pieced together her tattoo array but this was not one he contemplated.

He felt even worse now for cockily demonstrating his deductive prowess in Los Cabos. He cared more at the time about impressing Pebbles, but instead he danced match in hand, unconcerned about the consequences, upon the lid of a powder keg. How foolish! How selfish!

She didn't need to talk further. Anlon understood.

But Pebbles explained anyway. The charges against her were eventually dropped, but she was shamed beyond the ability to cope — by others, including her own family and by herself. She tried to kill herself, but fate intervened and she survived.

Eleanor McCarver tossed away her old life, unable to bear the stigma and the whispers. She assumed a new persona and escaped her misery in a different way.

As he listened to her, it amazed Anlon that the persona she escaped into was so positive, so hopeful. You can exchange stripes for spots, but underneath, it's hard to escape who you really are. And underneath, Pebbles and Eleanor were inherently kindhearted, loving, optimistic souls.

When Pebbles finished, she lowered her head and said, "So do you hate me now?"

Anlon kissed her again on the forehead and held her tight. He said, "Not a chance. In fact, I really don't think I could live without you."

As Anlon's words filled her ears, Pebbles burst into joyous weeping. Unable to speak, she raised her tear-soaked face to his cheek and kissed him. All the while, her mind sensed Malinyah's hand tenderly massaging her wrist. She offered grateful praise in mental reply.

XXI
THICK AS THIEVES

Once the evidence collection team arrived, Jennifer took leave of Mr. Cho and walked across the street and down two blocks to the second of Matthew Dobson's two banks. The visit was fruitless. There was no safe deposit box for Dobson and his account there was in every respect ordinary. At least she'd scored at one of the banks, Jennifer thought.

Arriving back at headquarters, Jennifer stepped in her cubicle to see a pile of envelopes and the message light on her office phone blinking. Setting down her tote bag, Jennifer decided to tackle the voice mail first. She punched in the code to access her voice mail. There were three messages waiting.

The first was from the forensic lab informing Jennifer that the test results for the evidence she collected at Dobson's house were completed.

The second message was from Officer Keller at the Meredith, New Hampshire Police Department. He didn't leave a detailed message, he simply asked Jennifer to ring him back.

The third and most recent message was from Mr. Cho. He called to let Jennifer know he'd emailed her copies of Zoe Moore's and

John Wood's driver's licenses. Mr. Cho explained in the message that customers seeking to open new accounts must present photo identification as part of the application process. The bank stored electronic copies of identifications for bank branches to access in case verifications of identity was needed.

Opening her email app, Jennifer cringed. Ninety-two messages were unread. She didn't have time to read them all now, so she searched for and found Mr. Cho's message. Without opening the attachments, Jennifer whisked off a quick note to Dan Nickerson, a detective trainee on the staff, to print out the attachments and do searches of the uniform crime registry and national driver's registry for Zoe Moore and John Wood. Before she asked Gambelli for permission to travel to Manhattan to speak with Ms. Moore, Jennifer wanted some background information on both people.

Setting aside the rest of her email for now, Jennifer sorted through the packages on her desk. There were five packages in total. On top was the couriered set of bank statements for Dobson's accounts at Massachusetts First Trust Bank. Jennifer wondered if poor Beckie had chipped a nail in the process of compiling the documents. She sincerely hoped so.

Next was the aforementioned forensic lab analysis of the items taken from Dobson's house, followed by a lab report on Pacal's handkerchief.

The fourth package on her desk was from the Meredith Police Department and it contained the copies she requested of Devlin Wilson's autopsy report and the police report detailing the finding of his body.

Last but not least was a package containing the cell phone calls placed and received by Matthew Dobson for the six months prior to his death. Nickerson had been assigned the task of identifying each number in the records, so when Jennifer opened the package, a summary he prepared was atop the listing of calls.

Jennifer rubbed her temples and sighed. Yesterday she had too few clues to pursue, now it felt like the opposite! Where to begin? As a professional courtesy, Jennifer opted to call Officer Keller first.

"Keller here," answered the voice through Jennifer's office phone.

"Sam, hi, it's Jennifer Stevens returning your call."

"Oh, hey there, Detective. Thanks for calling me back."

"No problem, Sam, what's up?"

"You asked me to call you once we processed the GPS device you found. Just wanted you to know the only prints we found on it were from Devlin Wilson. So the device was definitely his," Keller explained.

"Oh, okay, that's good information. Thanks," Jennifer replied. "Did you get a chance to power it up? Was there anything useful on the tracker?"

"That's really the reason I called you. We did charge the device after forensics was done with it and there were a couple of interesting pieces of data. When the tracker data is considered in context of where you found the device and the condition of Wilson's body, the coroner is now wavering in her opinion that his death was due to an accidental fall. In fact, I owe you an apology, Detective," said Keller.

Jennifer jotted down notes as she listened. When Keller extended an apology, her head shot up at full attention. "What did you find?"

A sheepish Keller continued, "Well, it seems Mr. Wilson had pinpointed a spot along the trail just as you thought. The tracker shows his progress towards the marked location on the day of the hike, so we assume he viewed the mark as a destination. I went up there myself yesterday with the tracker to find the marked spot. There was nothing unusual I could see. Just a bunch of rocks."

"But...?"

"But the marked location was still a good quarter mile from where he fell, or um, was deposited."

"I'm not following you Sam. Why is that significant? He could have fallen before he reached the destination," Jennifer challenged.

"Um, well...," Keller paused.

"Spit it out, Sam," she impatiently blurted.

There was a heavy sigh on the other end of the phone. It was a hard admission for Keller to make because he so easily accepted the accidental fall theory. But the evidence found on the tracker cast serious doubt on that theory, and the only reason they had evidence to the contrary now was due to Jennifer's initiative to search for other evidence and her foresight to have the tracker examined. Keller had thought she was howling at the moon and making a nuisance of herself. It turned out he was dead wrong.

Keller said, "The tracker shows Wilson was only 700 feet from the marked location when his progress halted, Detective."

While this information soaked in, Jennifer unconsciously rattled the pen in her hand against the edge of her workstation desk. When the implication clicked in her mind, the pen froze in mid-rattle. She said, "Sam, are you telling me that Wilson's body was found a good distance from where the tracker says he should have been?"

"Exactly, almost 600 feet back down the trail from the second-to-last ping recorded by the tracker," he said.

"Is it possible the ping interval on the tracker just didn't pick up Wilson backtracking on his own? Maybe he saw something that frightened him and he ran backwards?"

"Not likely. He had the ping interval set at one minute. Given the terrain, and his age, there's no way he could have descended the trail 600 feet in one minute on his own. Besides, the last recorded ping doesn't show he descended," Keller revealed.

And then Jennifer understood what he meant. The last recorded ping was where the device came to rest, some 300 feet above the trail. She knew at that moment what had happened. Someone with a Sound Stone, probably Pacal, had confronted Devlin Wilson on the trail as he neared the marked spot. The assailant lifted him off the ground, high into the air, the same way Pacal had lifted Pebbles and the Land Rover. Then the killer cast him arcing through the sky backwards down the trail. The tracker must have been yanked free and fallen as Wilson flew through the air. It was the only explanation for the combination of evidence and would also account for the coroner's observation that the damage done to Wilson's body exceeded the supposed distance of his fall. He just didn't fall, Jennifer realized, he was thrown down violently.

Keller interrupted her train of thought. "So you see the dilemma? How does a man fall 600 feet backwards and down another 500 feet on his own while his tracker shows a sudden rise of another 300 feet at a point in between? We can't explain what happened, but there's no way this was an accidental fall, unless the tracker is wildly inaccurate."

Nodding in agreement, Jennifer said, "I think I may be able to help you out with an explanation of what happened, but it will be hard to believe. I may even have a suspect to suggest."

Keller's voice perked up. He said, "I was hoping you might."

"Let me get through some stuff here in the office, Sam, and I'll call you back later. I want to run through some of this with my Captain before talking about the scenario I think happened," she replied, trying her best to honor Gambelli's "keep an open mind" caution before reaching a conclusion.

"Sounds good, Detective. One more item to mention about the tracker. I think it may link together our two deaths after all," he said.

For the third time in the same day, Jennifer extended a double fist pump, only this time she did so physically *and* mentally in the sanctity of her cubicle. She said, "Oh?"

"Yeah, the GPS device had previous trips recorded. The one that preceded Wilson's final use was recorded two days before his death. I followed the trail backwards yesterday using my car."

"Your car?" questioned a puzzled Jennifer.

"Yep, the tracked path begins at Devlin Wilson's home, heads to Matthew Dobson's home and then onto the Whiteface Mountains. The tracked path of that trip ends at the marker Wilson followed two days later and then the path loops back to Dobson's house and then Wilson's. There are a range of possible explanations, but given both Mr. Wilson's and Mr. Dobson's suspicious deaths, and the fact that the tracker shows a stop at Mr. Dobson's home on the way out and back, it sure does seem to me like there is reason to believe there is a connection between the two deaths," Keller added.

After finishing the call with Keller, an excited Jennifer craved to jump out of her cubicle, dash to Gambelli's office, push her way through the door and shout, "Aha, I told you so!"

But as satisfying as that might feel for the fleeting seconds after her pronouncement, she knew Keller's discoveries were not enough to sway

Gambelli. As Keller had said himself, there were a range of possible explanations. For sure, Jennifer planned on huddling with Gambelli to share the news before the day was out, but for now she directed her attention back to the pile of envelopes staring at her from the desk.

Arranging the envelopes into a row of five, one might have supposed Jennifer was about to play Solitaire. Stroking her chin, she sat back and wondered what each envelope might reveal. Before opening the first, she chastised herself, "Keep an open mind."

Reaching for the lab analysis of the items removed from Matthew Dobson's home, Jennifer flipped through the pages slowly. The notebooks that appeared to belong to Devlin contained three sets of fingerprints among the pages. Devlin Wilson, Matthew Dobson and Pacal Flores. The last bit of information confirmed for Jennifer that the lab analysis of the handkerchief did contain Pacal's fingerprints. Thank you, Pebbles!

Jennifer scrawled a quick note on her pad to read through the notebooks. She'd been careful to avoid contaminating the books before the lab analysis. Now that it was complete, she intended to read every page of the three journals.

The cell phone records and bank statements contained only Dobson's fingerprints, as did the picture frame she and Pebbles removed from Dobson's bedroom.

The last two pages of the report covered the gold coins. The analysis was intriguing. In total, there were 418 coins, not including the one Jennifer borrowed to show Anlon and Pebbles. Each of the coins weighed 2.5 ounces and their composition was pure, 24-karat gold. The analyst noted that at current gold prices, the coins' approximate value totaled almost $1.4 million.

Fingerprints were detected on many of the coins. Matthew Dobson's was among them. Devlin Wilson's and Pacal Flores' were not. The report indicated there were two sets of recent additional prints of persons unknown on a handful of the coins. Next to this observation, the forensic analyst had inserted a footnote asterisk. Shifting her focus to the bottom of the page, Jennifer read the footnote.

"On three coins there were partial older fingerprints. Their age is indeterminable but there was a dusty material mixed with the fingerprints and embedded in the etched grooves on the three coins. A microbial analysis of the dusty material shows its composition to be a mix of sea salt and soil. The soil contained low amounts of organic material, suggesting it was soil from an arid or mountainous location. The soil was definitively not sand as one might expect, given the presence of sea salt."

A slight shiver raced down Jennifer's spine. The forensic analyst didn't realize it, but he probably dusted fingerprints from a 10,000-year-old man or woman. Sea salt and arid soil. That is an odd combination, she thought. Closing her eyes, she imagined the scene Pebbles described on the Master Stone. Men leaving on ships…

Placing the report aside, Jennifer next picked up the same analyst's report on Pacal Flores' handkerchief. To her delight, Pacal's fingerprints and DNA were detectable on the fabric. To her dismay, neither were present in forensic evidence collected at the scene of Matthew Dobson's death. A second set of fingerprints and DNA were also on the cloth. A search of a national fingerprint registry positively identified the second set of prints as belonging to one Eleanor Marie McCarver. The additional DNA was listed of indeterminable origin, but Jennifer assumed it was from Pebbles.

Scrunching her nose, Jennifer pondered the reports. So far, nothing in them pointed to Matthew Dobson's killer. The only tangible discovery among the forensic evidence was that Devlin Wilson and Pacal Flores had not handled the coins. To Jennifer, this suggested that Matthew Dobson had procured the coins without their knowledge. She reasoned that if the coins had been in Devlin's possession at some point along the way, his and possibly Pacal's fingerprints would have been left on at least one coin.

Returning to the remaining three envelopes, Jennifer extracted the police report and autopsy report forwarded by Sam Keller. She scanned the autopsy report first. Indeed, Devlin Wilson's injuries had been substantial and the coroner's footnote illustrated her hesitation to totally buy into the accidental fall supposition.

The footnote read, "It should be noted that decedent's blunt force trauma exceeds that commonly associated with falls from relatively low altitude. The decedent's injuries are more consistent with tissue and bone damage found in trauma victims where terminal velocity is achieved prior to impact. Decedent's alleged fall as measured by the officer on scene was approximately 200 feet, far short of the distance required for humans to achieve terminal velocity (~1,900 ft.). However, since there was no topographical feature of that height within reasonable distance of the decedent's impact zone, there is insufficient evidence to suggest a competing cause of death other than accidental fall."

Jennifer understood better now why the tracking data caused the coroner to reevaluate the autopsy report's conclusion. While the distance discrepancies detailed by Keller on the phone were still well below that required to achieve terminal velocity, Jennifer rightly guessed that the coroner no longer suspected Devlin Wilson fell. Instead, he was thrown down with great force.

Indeed, while Jennifer sat in her cubicle fomenting this opinion, the coroner sat in her own cubicle calculating various iterations of the speed and time required to achieve terminal velocity by shooting a 180-pound object upward by at least 300 feet, across an arc extending 600 feet, and then down a total of 500 feet.

Normally, terminal velocity of a human body in a free fall is achieved in less than 15 seconds. The coroner's calculations demonstrated that it was possible to achieve a human's terminal velocity over the area of Devlin Wilson's arcing fall in less than 15 seconds. However, the calculations suggested that the force required to generate a speed in excess of 130 miles per hour in a 500 foot fall from peak to trough was not possible through any known natural means. To her, it was as if Devlin Wilson had been catapulted to the ground in a motion like the swing of a hammer...only at twice the force achieved by the strongest of men.

Placing aside the coroner's report, Jennifer picked up the police report and read through Officer Keller's summary.

Keller wrote that he arrived on scene at approximately 9:24 a.m. in response to a 911 call placed by a Mr. Kyle Corchran, who apparently discovered the body moments before two other hikers, a Mr. and Mrs. Charles Ludwig, passed by. The body had been found along the Blueberry Ledge Trail on Mt. Whitehead and bore obvious signs of blunt force trauma. Keller recorded the notes of his interviews with the three witnesses, drew a diagram of the crime scene, and detailed the search of the surrounding area for any clues. Keller also catalogued his search of Devlin's Land Rover in the parking lot and updated the report after the forensic team finished their analysis to detail the contents of Devlin's backpack and pockets. Jennifer frowned. She had hoped there would be something of additional value in the report.

Eyeing the two remaining packages on her desk, Jennifer set aside the bank statements. She learned enough already from Mr. Cho about Dobson's accounts to know there was monkey business in the details. She would get to that later. Right now, she was interested in scanning Dobson's phone records.

Nickerson, the meticulous trainee, had not only scoured Dobson's cell phone records, but his home's land line records as well. He attached a cover sheet with a summary of significant calls made and received and indicated that every call on the attached pages was sourced and annotated. Nickerson's analysis revealed that Dobson made or received a total of 86 calls over a six-month period. Three numbers made up more than half of the calls. One of the numbers was Devlin Wilson's cell phone. Another of the numbers was Wilson's office land line. The third was a blocked number. Three of the last four calls on Dobson's cell phone involved the blocked number. Two calls out and two calls in.

Jennifer rapidly flipped to the pages showing the most recent call activity. Consulting her phone's calendar app, Jennifer noted that Dobson made a 20-minute call to the blocked number at 7:00 p.m. two nights before Wilson died. The following morning, around 11:30 a.m., the blocked number called back. That conversation was short. Approximately five minutes. Two days after Devlin's death, Dobson received another call from the blocked number. That conversation was even shorter. One minute. Finally, the last call placed by Matthew Dobson occurred another two days later and was placed to Dr. Anlon Cully.

The blocked number stood out to Nickerson, who highlighted the calls in his compiled notes, as they did to Jennifer. Particularly given the timeline of the conversations, and her knowledge of the bank transactions. She was willing to wager the blocked number belonged to Zoe Moore, John Wood or Pacal Flores.

Glancing at the time, Jennifer realized it was nearly 4:00 p.m. and she'd yet to have lunch. Dipping into her tote, she hauled out her emergency snack stash — a chocolate peanut butter energy bar and a mini-bag of pretzels. Munching on her impromptu lunch, she reflected on all she learned over the day's course.

Focus on Dobson, first and foremost, she reminded herself as she flipped back to the notes she'd taken during the scenario discussion with Captain Gambelli.

Of the four they discussed, one held the most promise in her mind, given the day's learnings. Devlin Wilson challenged Dobson about the thefts. Dobson panicked and decided to shut down the operation. From the combination of cash, bank balances, diamonds and gold coins in Dobson's possession when he was killed, it would have been an easy decision to call it quits.

Dobson had accomplices...Zoe Moore and John Wood. From the bank account transfers, it appeared to Jennifer as if they received about 10 percent each of Dobson's deposits. She supposed they were not thrilled with Dobson's decision to shut down their scheme. They confronted Dobson. He resisted. In the heat of the moment, one or both of them lashed out and knocked him unconscious. Afraid Dobson might turn them in, they decided there was only one way to deal with him. Silence him.

That fit well, Jennifer thought. Now, what about Devlin Wilson? How did the dots connect? Was it possible Dobson killed Devlin to keep him quiet? Dobson knew how to use the Sound Stone, according to Pacal. In fact, Jennifer recalled, Pacal also said he, Devlin and Dobson each had their own Sound Stone.

"The Sound Stone!" she exclaimed. "What happened to Dobson's Sound Stone?"

It wasn't until that moment that she realized that the search of Dobson's home and Devlin's office had not uncovered any other Life Stones, including Dobson's Sound Stone.

"Ugh! I can't believe I didn't think of that earlier. It's a critical piece of evidence," Jennifer scolded herself. She made a note to go back through Dobson's house and search again for the Sound Stone.

If Devlin threatened to turn Dobson into the police, it might have spurred Dobson to act. With Devlin out of the way, Dobson wouldn't be discovered. Better yet, he could continue his plundering of Devlin's artifacts, including the Life Stones.

Ah, she thought! But there was a problem there. Anlon Cully. Dobson didn't know the contents of Devlin's will prior to his death and didn't anticipate his collection would pass to Anlon. He probably bet the artifacts would be donated to a museum or a university or be put up for auction. He thought he would have ample time while the estate was settled to remove pieces of value before any donation.

Crinkling up the consumed energy bar's wrapper, Jennifer tossed it in the wastebasket beneath her desk and sighed, "One big problem with that theory. Pacal Flores."

This reminded Jennifer that he was still missing. Though the word that Pacal was a "person of interest, wanted for questioning" had been circulated within the state's police network, so far no one had seen or heard from him since he walked into the black from Devlin's house.

Nickerson had been tasked with staking out his apartment and trying to reach him on his cell and home phones. But, as his note attached to the cell phone records shared, there had been no reply and no signs of Pacal at the apartment. In his note, Nickerson suggested a search warrant of the home, given that it had now been several days since Pacal was last seen. Jennifer chuckled. Been there, done that and summarily shot down!

But Nickerson was right. She had different grounds now for the search. He was wanted for questioning. He failed to appear to provide physical evidence. He was not responsive to repeated calls and visits to his home. As far as she knew from Anlon and Pebbles, he'd not shown up again for work at Devlin's office. Heck, it was possible that Pacal might be dead himself. Or he might have fled with no intention of returning.

The more Jennifer considered this scenario, Pacal wasn't the only piece that didn't fit. There was also the matter of the break-in of Devlin's office. And then it hit her.

Were Zoe and John still at it? Did they decide they'd had enough of table drippings? Oh my God! Did *they* have Dobson's Sound Stone? But if that were true, why didn't they wait to kill Dobson until after he handed over the gold coins? Why didn't they wait for him to steal the Stones? There must be a reason, Jennifer just couldn't see it.

Two pints in hand, John Wood made his way cautiously between people and tables in the tightly packed Rusty Musket Pub. The small basement bar of the Two Lanterns Inn was more cramped than usual this night as locals flooded in to catch the Red Sox take on the hated Yankees. That suited Zoe just fine; fewer eyes and ears to pry on their conversation. Originally dubious about meeting John in a public place, Zoe relented when he assured her the good people of Stockbridge cared more about their Red Sox than strangers sharing a pint.

To ingratiate themselves with the crowd and to further blend in, John had driven into Great Barrington earlier in the day and purchased two Red Sox caps, one for Zoe and one for himself. He also purchased an official game jersey for Zoe that was at least two sizes too big. He knew her sleek figure would catch attention otherwise, and right now the less attention the better. Zoe resisted wearing the jersey, but John's logic won her over. "Look, I've been in this pub on Red Sox game nights before, and the only two things that divert eyes from the game are empty pints and girls in tight clothes. I got you some awful-fitting sweatpants, too."

And so there they sat, at a small table tucked in a corner of the bar as far from the big screen television as possible. They toasted one another and took the first sips of their pints. Zoe, more relaxed than usual, piped up, "I can't believe you convinced me to wear this stuff!"

"Ha ha," he answered, "love the ponytail. Nice touch, you look just like the little girl I remember when we were kids."

The pub erupted when a towering shot by the Red Sox clean-up hitter soared over the Green Monster in left field. John joined in with hoots and high fives with giddy Sox fans around them. Zoe tugged the cap bill down lower over her eyes, took another sip and cringed. She desperately wanted to be in South Beach right now, lying by the Four Seasons pool with mojito in one hand and flirting with young, wealthy studs.

"Come on now. We need to focus," Zoe snapped at John, her relaxed mood dissipating the longer she visualized where she really wanted to be when the job was complete.

"All right, all right, simmer down," John replied. "Before we talk about tomorrow, I finished going through DW's laptop and struck big. I found a JPEG he made of the map, or at least I think it's the map. It's not super high quality, we'll need to enhance it. There are color codes on the map and there are grid lines, but I can't make any sense out of either the codes or the grid lines in the pic. It will take some time to figure out. I put it on two flash drives, one for you and one for me. Here's yours."

Zoe rose up, leaned across the table, and kissed him on the B of his baseball cap, "That's my baby brother! When did you find it? I can't believe you didn't tell me until now!"

Chuckling, John gulped his beer and said, "I found it this morning. I didn't tell you because I'm not sure it's 'the one.' "

"Anything else you found you want to share?"

"No, unfortunately that was it. There were some encrypted files. There are copies of those, too, on our drives. The file names were not descriptive, so they may not be anything of value," John said.

Another roar went up around them. The Sox catcher had just doubled down the right field line to extend the inning. This time Zoe put in a hoot of her own, her mood on the rebound with John's news.

"That's one less item we have to get tomorrow!" she said, lifting her pint to toast John.

With zeal, Zoe continued, "Tomorrow morning, we're heading over to DW's house, and we're not leaving until we get the stones, sculptures and the gold coins!"

"Amen to that," John answered, "and the best part is we get the main meal this time, not the leftovers!"

"Cheers!"

After a healthy swig, Zoe said, "When we get there, I will go to the front door and see if anyone is home. You said there were two people staying there, right? Dr. Cully and some girl. If they are there, I'll persuade them to let me in. If they aren't, I'll look for a way in that doesn't set off the alarm. You wait in the woods. I will text you when the coast is clear. We'll go through the whole house until we find what we came for."

"What about the code to the safe we were told about?"

"If we can't find the pieces elsewhere, we'll have to pry it out of them. If they aren't there, we'll have to wait until someone shows up and then pry it out of them," she answered.

"Could get nasty, especially if they don't cooperate," John stated. "Are you cool with that?"

"I've done it before, I'm not weak," Zoe condescendingly responded.

He laughed, "It's a little different, big sister, when you're standing right in front of them, not hiding in the shadows like you were before."

"Don't you worry about me. We're so close to cashing in, I won't let anything or anyone stand in my way!"

XXII
TIPPING POINT

A knock at the door interrupted Anabel Simpson as she cleared her breakfast plates from the kitchen table. Callers at this time of the morning were very unusual and she had half a mind to ignore the unexpected intrusion. When the doorbell impatiently chimed a moment later, Anabel deposited her dishes into the sink and cautiously approached the door.

Wiping her hands on a dishtowel, Anabel tiptoed from the kitchen to the living room and timidly peeked out through the gauzy sheers of the picture window to observe the caller.

Anabel recognized him immediately and relaxed. With a smile, she drew open the front door and exclaimed, "Pacal! How nice it is to see you."

A glum Pacal wiped underneath his nose and coldly replied, "I'm very sorry, Miss Anabel."

After Anlon and Cesar shared breakfast at the Two Lanterns Inn the following morning, they hopped in Anlon's rental and drove back to Pittsfield's airport. Antonio graciously had his plane and pilot stay overnight, so when he and Cesar arrived at the airport, their farewells were brief.

"Cesar, you've been an enormous help. I owe you a debt of gratitude. When you calculate out your summer dig expenses, please send the cost estimate to me and not Antonio. I insist," Anlon implored.

"That is very generous of you, Anlon, but I was only kidding about Antonio's offer. I came because of Devlin," the wiry archaeologist replied with a wide grin.

"As I said, I insist. I have a feeling before the hunt is over I will need your help again and I'd like to make it easy for you to say yes when I call," said Anlon with a dead serious look upon his face.

"I suspect I will hear from you again, and your call will be welcome at any hour on any day. I appreciate your generous offer, but my research is well-funded. Besides, Anlon, if you make enough progress in your hunt, there are some mysteries I would like solved for my own benefit. Mysteries that have troubled me for years," Cesar responded with equal solemnity.

Anlon's eyebrows rose at this last comment. "Such as?"

"We have not the time to discuss. If and when you find the other stones, then we shall talk. Until then, I am at your service," he answered with a formal bow.

And with that, Cesar boarded Antonio's jet and departed. Little did Anlon know as he watched the plane lift off that in less than a year he and Cesar would team up again in the darkest of moments.

On the drive back to Stockbridge, Anlon was deep in thought when he received a call from Jennifer.

"Good morning, Anlon."

"Hey, Jen, good morning."

"Sorry I didn't come by the house last night, was burning the late night oil at the office," Jennifer said.

Anlon replied, "No need to apologize to me. Any new developments?"

"Plenty. Will you be around this afternoon to talk?"

"Um, should be. What time?"

"I was thinking around four? I still have to plow through my email this morning and then I'm headed to Stockbridge around midday to follow up on a lead. I should be free by four," Jennifer explained.

"Oh, okay. Yeah, I'll make it work. We have some errands to run. I'll make sure we're both back by then. I really want to talk with you. I think I now know who killed Matthew Dobson and why, but I want to hear about your developments before I say anything."

"Really?" queried Jennifer. "Well, here's a quick rundown of what I found out yesterday. Matthew Dobson had some very questionable transactions in his bank account that seems to confirm the artifact smuggling theory. It also looks like he had two accomplices, a woman named Zoe Moore and a man named John Wood.

"He did have a safe deposit box, but no will in it. The box had diamonds and cash in it. Lots of both. And two statues. One looks oriental, the other one looks like it's somehow connected to the Stones. There's a lot more, but those are the highlights. Does any of that fit with your theory?"

"In a way, yes, but let's talk later," Anlon said.

After disconnecting, Anlon dialed Pebbles' cell number. On the second ring, she answered, sounding half asleep, "Hello?"

"Rise and shine," Anlon perkily admonished.

"It's early, A.C. Why, it's only 10:00 a.m. I usually don't get up until noon," Pebbles answered with a scratchy voice.

"Not today! Too much to do. You came to help, right?"

"Okay, okay. Keep your pants on..." Pebbles retorted, cringing as she realized the implication of her jest.

"My pants are fully on, young lady. Just spoke with Jennifer, she's coming by at four. Think you can take care of a couple things for me before then and get back in time to meet with us?" Anlon playfully answered.

"Um, yeah, absolutely. What do you need?"

"Something's been bugging me about the conversation with Thatcher Reynolds at the funeral reception, and about our meeting with Pacal. I'd like you to do a little snooping for me," Anlon said.

"Snooping?"

"Yes, and it will require you to impersonate a police officer, so I'm afraid the tongue stud will need to go," he teased.

"Seriously? I mean about the impersonation part, not the tongue stud," Pebbles clarified.

"It should be easy for you after what Ms. Neally shared with me this morning while I ate breakfast with Cesar," hinted Anlon.

Pebbles, still in bed, covered her eyes in embarrassment and said, "You weren't supposed to find out about that."

When Pebbles had gone to iron out the funeral reception details, Mrs. Neally had copped a major attitude. She stared disapprovingly at the tattoos on Pebbles' neck and wrists. At first Pebbles tried sugar. This fell on deaf ears. Mrs. Neally expected Pebbles, on behalf of Anlon, to bow before her. No prissy harpy would push the Two Lantern Inn's manager around. Big mistake. At least, that's how Pebbles saw it at that moment. She didn't care for bullies; she grew up with four of them. That's when she'd uncorked a torrid onslaught worthy of the most vapid starlet.

"Mrs. Neally!" she'd said, "I'm shocked! Don't you know who Dr. Cully is? Don't you realize how important it is that your inn show itself well for him? He's a billionaire, Mrs. Neally. That's billionaire with a capital 'B.' And not just any billionaire. His charitable works are world-renowned.

"Are you really telling me you aren't willing to go the extra mile for him? And to think, he told me just last night he intended to open a museum here in town to display Devlin Wilson's collection. Plans to donate the proceeds to the town's historical preservation efforts, including your inn, Mrs. Neally!

"Think of what that means for your establishment! The extra business the museum would bring. The costs of your restoration efforts lessened. It's insulting, given his generosity, that you won't lift a finger to ensure his wishes are honored. After all, Devlin Wilson and Matthew Dobson were pillars of your community. I'm speechless!"

The force with which Pebbles had delivered her tirade shook the ever-composed Mrs. Neally to the core. Her face turned beet red and her mouth widened with an emotion close to fear.

Pebbles had spun on her heels and stalked away, "I'm done with you and your inn. I will advise Dr. Cully to look elsewhere. I'm sure we'll find better and more hospitable accommodations."

At this, Mrs. Neally sprang into action. All pretense of superiority vanquished. Her voice had quivered as she chased after Pebbles. "Miss McCarver, please hold on. I'm so very sorry, I had no idea. Whatever Dr. Cully needs, we shall make it happen. You have my word."

Face hidden from Mrs. Neally's view, a devilish grin had unfurled on Pebbles' face. That was almost too easy, she thought. Now, what kind of IPA did Anlon drink at Sydney's?

Roaring with laughter, Anlon said, "I like your style, Miss McCarver. I guess I'm on the hook now to open a museum, but for the record, I'm not a billionaire, nowhere near it!"

"Ouch," Pebbles whispered, "sorry, A.C., she wasn't very nice to me and that made me angry. I guess I got carried away."

"All is forgiven, here's what I need you to do..."

Overnight, the list of unread emails in Jennifer's inbox had climbed past 120 messages. Groaning, she began scrolling through the message headers in hopes of trimming the task of reading each email. Her perusal was interrupted by the appearance of Dan Nickerson at the entrance of her cubicle.

Clearing his throat, the tall, stylish African-American detective trainee held out an envelope and said, "Good morning, Detective. Sorry to interrupt you, but I think you should see this."

Thankful for the escape from email hell, Jennifer responded cheerfully, "What's up, Dan?"

"Just take a look and see if you come to the same conclusion," he replied.

Jennifer received the envelope and opened it. Inside were photocopies of the driver's licenses of Zoe Moore and John Wood. She scanned the data listed on each identification and glanced at the pictures. She did notice something unusual. The licenses were granted in New York on the same date. She peeked up at Nickerson and questioned, "Fake?"

Nickerson nodded and then answered, "Ran the driver's license numbers and they don't exist. I'm not sure what the bank was thinking, but I ran both social security numbers that the bank manager provided. They are both valid, and are the socials for one Zoe Moore and one John Wood. But Moore died 36 years ago and John Wood passed away in the late 1990s."

"Good work, Dan," Jennifer said. "So our alleged accomplices have fake IDs."

Clearing his throat again, Nickerson said, "Um, Detective?"

"Yes, what is it, Dan? And stop with the Detective, it's Jen."

"Okay, Jen. Take a look at the pictures again," he suggested.

It was true, Jennifer had only barely glanced at the pictures. A hulking man with a crew cut and a nasty scowl. A dark-haired woman with an exotic look and elegant flair. The birth dates on the IDs couldn't be trusted but based on the pictures she guessed both were in their mid-to-late 30s. She shook her head and said, "You're going to have to help me, Dan. What should I notice that I'm not?"

Nickerson pointed at the envelope and said, "There's something else in the envelope. I might be off base. I don't know, maybe I'm seeing things, but the resemblance was strong to me."

Casting a suspicious look at Nickerson and then the envelope, Jennifer reached inside again and extracted an evidence bag with the photo she and Pebbles collected from Dobson's house. Holding the snapshot up to the two photocopied IDs, she lifted her head and stared at Nickerson, "Oh my God!"

A wide smile formed on Nickerson's face. He said, "Guess I might just be a detective after all."

Jumping up, Jennifer exchanged a hearty high five with Nickerson and replied, "Hell, Dan, they might just give you my job! Wow! Top notch, rookie."

"Thank you, Detective, er, Jen," beamed Nickerson, "but I only made the connection between the two sets of pictures. I don't know who they are."

Sliding back into her seat, Jennifer spun and scrolled through her email and exclaimed, "Gotcha covered. I don't know their names yet, but I do know who they are!"

She scanned the email headers until she saw the message from George Grant, titled *Follow Up*. Excitedly, she opened the email while Nickerson leaned over from behind her to view the screen. Grant's message read:

"Detective Lieutenant Stevens, in answer to your question, Matthew Dobson's niece and nephew's names are Margaret Corchran and Kyle Corchran. Miss Corchran lives in Miami, Florida, and Mr. Corchran lives in Dallas, Texas. The attached PDF provides their contact information. Please let me know if I may be of further assistance. Warm Regards, George Grant"

After reading the message, Nickerson announced, "I'm on it, just send me the email and I'll get working on their backgrounds and addresses."

Jennifer gave a thumbs up as she pressed send to forward him the message. Nickerson disappeared to trace the Corchrans while Jennifer sat back in her chair with a puzzled expression. She said aloud, "Why does that last name sound familiar?"

For nearly 10 minutes, she sat massaging her temples, trying to recall where she'd seen the name Corchran. It was recently, she knew that much. Jennifer stood and paced in an effort to jog loose her memory. And then a jolt of recognition caused her to lift her hand to her mouth and murmur, "No f—ing way!"

After Jennifer realized that Kyle Corchran had been at the scene of Devlin Wilson's death, she dashed into Gambelli's office and demanded an audience. She presented her findings from the visit to Dobson's bank, shared Dickerson's recognition of the photos, showed the Captain the Meredith PD police report and told him about the GPS tracker discovery.

Gambelli said, "Put it together for me, Stevens. What does it all mean?"

"I think it means Kyle killed Devlin Wilson, with or without Margaret's help. We have a witness, Anabel Simpson, who says Wilson caught Matthew Dobson stealing from his collection and confronted him. It's my guess Dobson panicked and told the Corchrans he was calling it quits. I think the bank records strongly suggest that the two of them were in on the thefts. I'm speculating, but I'd say they were the brokers between Dobson and the buyer… or buyers. Once we have their fingerprints to compare, I'll bet we even determine the two sets of unidentified prints on the gold coins belong to them!

"I think Dobson was seriously conflicted. On one hand, he had been a loyal friend to Devlin Wilson for a very long time. On the other hand, I think he looked at the lifestyle Devlin enjoyed and was jealous. He probably felt Wilson's wealth and notoriety were built upon *his* sweat and tears. But once he was caught, guilt ate away at him. I think he hoped to repair his relationship with Wilson. He could hand over the gold coins and return the statues and maybe that would placate Wilson enough to avoid charges.

"But Kyle and Margaret didn't want to stop; the money was too good. And so, without Dobson's knowledge or assent, I think they took his Sound Stone and killed Wilson to get him out of the way."

Gambelli interrupted her, "Hold up. Why do you think Dobson wasn't in on the killing?"

"After Wilson's death," Jennifer explained, "Dobson questioned whether his fall was accidental to both Cully and Officer Keller. Cully also said Dobson seemed scared when he shared his suspicion that Wilson was pushed. If he was involved, why would he raise the possibility the death wasn't accidental? And why would he hint at the use of a Sound Stone in the killing? Remember, he told Cully that Wilson wasn't pushed off in a traditional sense. Plus, I realized last night that Dobson's Sound Stone is missing."

"Okay, but Dobson could just have easily thrown the stone away after killing Wilson himself, couldn't he?" Gambelli countered.

"It's possible, but I think it's more likely that the Corchrans killed Wilson and then offed Dobson. Maybe he confronted them about Wilson's death. Maybe they were scared he would turn them in. Or maybe they were angry Dobson wouldn't cooperate on any more thefts. Hell, it may have been for all three reasons!"

"But wouldn't killing Dobson, too, cut off their access to more artifacts?" countered the skeptical Captain.

"Absolutely!" Jennifer agreed. "But remember, Cap, you said it yourself. These were reckless and risky murders. I'm guessing one or the both of them got super pissed at Dobson and acted without thinking. And it explains the break-in of Wilson's office and the theft of his laptop. They thought they could find what they wanted on their own.

"And, Cap, I'm getting concerned they offed Pacal Flores, too. No one has seen or heard from him in days," Jennifer imparted.

For a long minute, Gambelli sat with arms folded behind his desk, bobble heads frozen still. At last he nodded and said, "Okay, Detective. Your theory is compelling. It answers many of the open questions. Motive seems legit, evidence still is mostly circumstantial but like I said, compelling. What do you want to do with it?"

Without hesitation, Jennifer replied, "I want a search warrant for Pacal Flores' apartment. I want to put out a regional alert on Kyle and Margaret, including their aliases. I want to request NYPD go to the Waldorf Astoria and detain Zoe aka Margaret if they can locate her."

"Okay, get Nickerson and the two of you get the paperwork in motion. I'll walk up the search warrant request as soon as you put it in my hands. And then I need you to take care of an important missing piece to support your theory."

"Thank you, sir," answered Jennifer before asking, "and the missing piece; do you mean Dobson's Sound Stone?"

"No, though finding that could help. What you described seems like a slam dunk on the Wilson death. At least, strong enough to bring in the Corchrans for questioning, especially given Kyle's presence at Wilson's crime scene. We'll need to alert Meredith PD, by the way. It's still their case, even if it's linked to ours. But your theory on Dobson isn't quite as clear. We need to place one or the both of them at the scene of Dobson's death. Did you talk to his neighbors like we discussed earlier?"

Jennifer flinched. After searching Dobson's home, she had planned to interview the neighbors, particularly the observant Doris Minden. But once they found the gold coins, it had totally slipped her mind. She uttered, "Shoot! I forgot to tie that one down."

"Get it done, Detective. ASAP. If one or the both of them were seen with Dobson at his house on the day he was killed, or shortly before, then I think you have a stronger case. Especially if you are right about the unidentified fingerprints on the gold coins."

True to her word, Pebbles rousted herself and departed on Anlon's requested errands by the time he returned to Devlin's house.

He hoped Pebbles wouldn't lay it on quite so thick when she visited Pacal's apartment manager. The first errand he assigned Pebbles was to gain entry to Pacal's apartment and search for the copy of Devlin's will stolen from Anlon's rental and lift Pacal's laptop if it was present.

It confused Anlon how Thatcher knew the details of Devlin's will. At the time of the funerals, Grant said he had only provided copies to Anlon and Anabel. He remembered Grant mentioning he hoped to hand one to Richard Ryan and Pacal after the funerals. But Thatcher had spoken to both Anabel and Richard a couple days before the funeral to suggest they challenge their bequests. So how did Thatcher know that Richard and Anabel were beneficiaries before the funeral?

Unless Devlin shared the contents of his will directly with the self-professed rival, which seemed unlikely, the only way Thatcher could have known about the beneficiaries was if he'd seen the copy stolen from the rental car. No one else but Anlon had a copy at that point.

But Anlon was certain the fleet-footed thief was not the wobbly Thatcher Reynolds. So who was his accomplice? Anlon's money was on Pacal. Yes, the trusty assistant wasn't so trusty in Anlon's mind.

Casting his thoughts back to their meeting with Pacal, several bits of their discussion didn't square with pieces Anlon learned afterward. For example, he thought, why didn't Pacal mention Dobson's thefts during their discussion? It was a very odd omission. There was no downside for him in sharing the information with Jennifer.

And then there was the Waterland Map. From Anlon's conversation with Anabel, it was clear Pacal knew of the map. He saw Dobson putting it back. It's what led him and Devlin to lay the trap for Dobson! Why didn't he reveal this important detail?

Pacal had also been evasive about discussing the Master Stone and the Port Stone, and man did he get excited when he unexpectedly saw the Master Stone on the table.

But the two biggest thorns that stuck out to Anlon were not *omissions* on Pacal's part. They were two *revealing* things he said. The first was when Pacal told Jennifer she was close to the path in her theory of Dobson's murder but not on it. How would he have known? And why was he so curious to learn from Jennifer the manner in which Dobson was killed?

The second, and most damning to Anlon, was a slip of the tongue Pacal made after he used the Sound Stone on Anlon. Pacal had said, much like Anlon, that Devlin and Dobson never saw the Sound Stone attack coming. He had tried quickly afterward to correct his unintentional gaffe by suggesting the Sound Stone was responsible for Devlin's death...neglecting to add Dobson.

Arranging these unexplained puzzle pieces, Anlon was now pretty sure that Pacal was involved in Dobson's death, possibly in concert with Thatcher Reynolds. He remembered Thatcher suggesting that he and Pacal together could take up the baton from Devlin. And the motive? Was there something on the Master Stone and the Waterland Map that one or the both of them coveted?

Anlon guessed they both hoped to find the stone and map before anyone else. That's why Pacal assiduously avoided discussing the Master Stone and why he never mentioned the Waterland Map.

This speculation was also supported by the scary warnings both Thatcher and Pacal made. Both were adamant that Anlon not continue Devlin's research, and their choice of words when speaking of danger was eerily similar. Add to this the fact both Thatcher and Pacal had been MIA since the funeral and Anlon felt sure the two were working in concert.

Finding evidence to support his theory was the main purpose of the first errand he requested of Pebbles.

The second errand was unrelated. He asked her to track down a current world map that was as close as possible in dimensions to the Waterland Map. When he asked her to pursue the errand, he suggested Pebbles take the map from the safe and measure the distance between the longitude and latitude markers. If she was able to find a map with comparable scale between grid lines, it would be close enough for them to use for now.

Anlon was walking up the back porch steps when the cell phone in his jeans back pocket began to buzz. Tugging the phone out, he glanced at the lock screen. Anlon didn't recognize the number but the screen's caller ID indicated it was a Stockbridge-based caller.

"Anlon Cully," he said when he accepted the call.

"Doctor Anlon," said the deep voice on the other end of the line.

Halting abruptly on the porch in recognition of the voice, Anlon replied, "Pacal. I wasn't expecting to hear from you. Where have you been?"

Ignoring Anlon's question, Pacal said, "I have someone here who would like to say hello."

A quizzical expression crossed Anlon's face. What is that supposed to mean, he wondered?

Then a slight voice, a voice tinged with fear, quivered, "Anlon, it's Anabel. He's taken me!"

Lifting the phone from his ear, Anlon stared at it unbelievingly. He said, "Anabel? Are you all right? Who's taken you?"

Pacal returned to the line and coldly answered, "Doctor Anlon, I don't want to hurt Miss Anabel, but if you don't bring the map and the Master Stone to me right now, I will."

In the background, Anlon heard Anabel shout out, "Don't give him the map!"

Heartbeat racing, Anlon blurted, "Pacal? What are you talking about? This is nuts."

A heavy sigh filtered through the phone. Pacal said, "I tried my best to warn you, Dr. Anlon, but you did not listen. It is too late now. Bring the map, the Master Stone and the Port Stone to the abandoned Stillwater Quarry just outside of town. Come alone, do not call the police. When I have the Stones and the map, I will release Miss Anabel."

Running his hand manically through his hair, Anlon paced the porch in an effort to calm himself. He said, "Be reasonable, Pacal. This isn't necessary."

In a chilling voice, Pacal replied as he disconnected the call, "You have 20 minutes to get here, Dr. Anlon. At 21 minutes, I will kill Miss Anabel."

Finally! A break in their favor, thought Margaret Corchran. Crouched behind the stone wall near the barn, she and Kyle watched through separate binoculars as Anlon took a phone call on the back porch and then ran back in the house. Ten minutes later, Anlon rushed down the back steps, jumped in a SUV and sped off.

They had been watching from the cover of the woods for the past hour. When they first arrived, only the Land Rover was in the driveway. They debated whether to rush in and take whomever was home hostage. But then Pebbles skipped down the back porch and drove off in the Rover.

Figuring the coast was clear, Margaret tightened the straps of her backpack and started to creep across the meadow while Kyle positioned himself closer to the barn. And then to their surprise, another car started the long, winding path up the driveway.

After audible expletives, both Margaret and Kyle returned to the safety of the woods and recalibrated their plan. They had just resigned themselves to taking Anlon hostage when he abruptly left. Kyle, peering through the binoculars, noted that, in his haste, Anlon had left the back door open.

"Okay, show time!" Margaret whispered as they both stowed their binoculars. "No more pulling back. Let's go!"

Hopping the wall, they both sprinted to the house, bounded up the back steps and rushed into the house. Kyle, out of breath from the burst of physical exertion, puffed, "I'll take upstairs… you check down here."

Quickly applying gloves and shoe covers, the two ransacked Devlin's home. They removed and tossed drawers in every room. They cast down pictures and trinkets from every shelf. In every closet, they tore open boxes and cartons.

Early on they found the safe in the study, but neither had the combination and they realized it was not a simple safe to open or remove. So they concentrated their efforts elsewhere in the house to eliminate all other possibilities.

Kyle shouted out from the upper floor, "Nothing yet. You?"

Margaret kicked over a dining room chair and called back, "Not a damn thing!"

"Then they are either in the safe or in the barn," Kyle yelled back.

Margaret angrily paced the study as she considered their options. If they broke into the barn, she was certain the alarm would trigger and they'd have little time to search before the police arrived. So the better option appeared to be to lie in wait for Anlon to arrive back home. Given they were already in the house, they would have the element of surprise in their favor and could easily subdue him or the young woman staying with him. Uttering another expletive, Margaret collapsed on the study's leather sofa and shouted up to Kyle, "Go check the basement."

Heavy thuds sounded as Kyle descended the back staircase to the kitchen and hunted for the basement door. Finding it, he plodded down the second set of stairs.

A few minutes later, he popped back up and joined Margaret in the study, "No dice. What now?"

With an evil glare, Margaret hissed, "We wait."

XXIII

CRESCENDO

Pebbles was pleased the drive to Pacal's apartment complex in Great Barrington was quick. But when she arrived outside the building, she was crushed to find the place crawling with police.

Hunkered behind the wheel of the Land Rover across the main avenue from the converted low-rise office building, she scanned the gaggle of officers hoping to spot Jennifer, but Pebbles didn't see her. The man who seemed in charge, a young African-American in a tan suit, white shirt and cornflower blue tie, pointed at uniformed officers and barked orders.

"So much for errand number one!" a dejected Pebbles mumbled. She had really been looking forward to impersonating a detective. In fact, on the drive to Pacal's, she had practiced Jennifer's tough bitch face and honed her pitch to the landlord.

But Pebbles wasn't the kind of person to give up that easily, so she hopped out of the Rover and jogged across the street. She approached the man directing the officers and said, "Excuse me, are you with the Massachusetts State Police, by any chance?"

The man shot a sideways glance at Pebbles and replied, "Yes, I am. Kind of busy right now."

"Do you know Detective Lieutenant Jennifer Stevens?" Pebbles retorted as the man turned away from her.

He stopped and peered back around, saying, "I'm sorry, Miss...I didn't catch your name."

"Eleanor, Eleanor McCarver. Are you here to search Pacal's apartment?"

Dan Nickerson recalled her name immediately from the forensics report and also remembered Pebbles had been with Jennifer when they searched Matthew Dobson's house. He smiled and said, "Ah, the safe cracker!"

Pebbles blushed and laughed, "Guilty as charged! Look, I know you're busy. I'll get out of your way super-fast. Mind if join you for the search?"

"Excuse me?"

"My friend, Anlon Cully, you know of him, right?"

"Yes."

"His copy of the will was stolen a few days ago. He has a hunch that Pacal stole it. Pacal's laptop was also missing from Devlin Wilson's office. Anlon sent me over here to see if I could find them, but now that you're here, I thought maybe I could tag along."

"Um, no," Nickerson sternly answered. "I've got to run."

The young detective trainee hurried off to join the other officers while Pebbles stood unsatisfactorily glued to the sidewalk. Honesty, it appeared, was *not* the best policy in this case. She was tempted to chase after Nickerson to try another tack but decided not to get herself in trouble...yet.

Besides, she noted, the public library was only two blocks back. She could go deal with errand number two and look for a world map in the library. Then she could loop back and pop in on Nickerson a little later. That didn't seem quite as meddlesome in her mind. As she walked down the street, the cell phone in her back pocket buzzed.

Standing in the doorway of Mrs. Doris Minden's home, Jennifer held up the evidence bag with the snapshot of Kyle and Margaret Corchran huddled around Matthew Dobson.

"Oh yes," Mrs. Minden replied, "they visited Matthew often. Even came to a few neighborhood barbeques when they were younger. Kyle and Maggie, right?"

"Can you recall the last time you saw them visit Mr. Dobson?" Jennifer inquired, jotting down notes on her pad.

Mrs. Minden scratched at her head while shooing her inquisitive Labrador, Rufus, back into the house. She said, "Hmm, I seem to recall Kyle visiting recently. Yes, I'm sure of it. I was out walking Rufus after dinner one night and Kyle got out of his car in Matthew's driveway. I didn't say hello to him, I was too far away."

Jennifer's heartbeat picked up. As she replied, an incoming text message pinged on her cell phone. "It's very important, Mrs. Minden. Can you remember the date he visited?"

"You don't think Kyle and Maggie had anything to do with it, do you, dear? They were always very polite when I met them," the middle-aged housewife probed.

"I'm not pointing any fingers, Mrs. Minden, I'm just trying to clarify who visited Mr. Dobson before his death. It's routine, I assure you. Please don't read anything more into it."

And then Jennifer's phone rang with an incoming call. She reached inside her jacket pocket for the phone just as Rufus bounded out of the house and enthusiastically greeted Jennifer by burying his nose between her legs.

"Whoa! Easy there, Rufus," Jennifer called out as she pushed the dog's snout away. The phone continued to ring.

Mrs. Minden rushed forward and swatted at Rufus, "Bad dog!"

The relentless Rufus circled Jennifer, jumping up and barking playfully while Mrs. Minden followed behind, trying to grasp the dog's collar. Rufus darted off across the next door neighbor's lawn, barking lustily as he galloped away. All the while, Jennifer's phone rang.

"Mrs. Minden!" she called as the befuddled owner chased Rufus.

Jennifer shrugged. She didn't have time for this nonsense. She shouted to Mrs. Minden as she jogged to her police cruiser, "You have my card, Mrs. Minden. Call me if you remember when Kyle visited Mr. Dobson."

From the neighbor's yard, the frustrated Mrs. Minden called back, "I will think on it, dear."

Enough of the two of them! Jennifer thought. She got most of what she came for anyway...positive ID of Kyle and Margaret Corchran and confirmation that at least Kyle visited Dobson's home recently.

Back in the cruiser, Jennifer's phone began to ring again. Frustrated by the incessant ringing, she yanked out the phone and gruffly answered the call, "Stevens!"

"Detective Lieutenant? Am I calling at a bad time? This is Min-Jun Cho from Massachusetts First Trust."

"Oh, hi, Mr. Cho," Jennifer replied, adopting a gentler tone. "No, it's okay. What can I do for you?"

"I'm calling because I thought you might like to know...Zoe Moore used her debit card last night at a restaurant in Stockbridge, a place called the Rusty Musket," answered the pleasant Mr. Cho.

"Really?" a surprised Jennifer uttered in response. "Thank you for the information, Min-Jun. I'll check into it right away."

After exchanging pleasant goodbyes, Jennifer consulted her phone's contact list for the Stockbridge Police Department, ignoring the notifications on her phone highlighting the earlier text message and a waiting phone message. Finding the number, she called the department and reached Sergeant Jimmy Dixon, the duty officer.

"Good morning, Sergeant Dixon, this is Detective Lieutenant Jennifer Stevens from Mass State Police. I need your help, like pronto."

"Um, okay. What do you need?" answered the dubious local officer. Though interdepartmental cooperation was part of the job, Sergeant Dixon was leery of being used as an errand boy.

"You know a place in town called the Rusty Musket?"

"Yeah, of course. It's the pub at the Two Lanterns Inn. Why?"

"I need you to do me a favor. Did you guys get the photos we sent over this morning of Kyle and Margaret Corchran?" she said.

"I dunno. Let me ask around," Dixon said as he placed Jennifer on hold. A moment later, he returned to the phone and said, "Yeah, looks like two blow-ups of their driver's licenses?"

Jennifer excitedly responded, "Yes, that's right. I need one of your officers to go over to the Rusty Musket and show the pictures around to the staff there. It's almost noon, they're open for lunch, right? I just received a call from a reliable source that said one of them, the woman, used the debit card of her alias, Zoe Moore, there last night. I need to know if anyone saw her."

The Sergeant's skeptical tone was clear in his reply. "With all due respect, Detective, we're kind of busy here. A house alarm call just came in and my other two officers just left to check it out. I can't promise when we can get to it."

"Sergeant. Listen to me. They are wanted for questioning in the deaths of two people. In fact, I would consider them armed and dangerous. Do you want someone else to end up dead in your town, on your watch, because you couldn't 'get to it' in time?" Jennifer blared back as she pounded the steering wheel of the car. She didn't have time for this BS.

While awaiting the Sergeant's answer, Jennifer's phone rang again. Jesus, she thought, leave me alone!

Finally, the chagrined officer spoke, "Okay, okay. Don't get all worked up. I'll go over there myself."

"Thank you," she answered. "Oh, and while you're over there, can you check with Mrs. Neally, the manager of the Two Lanterns Inn to see if either of them stayed at the Inn, under their aliases or real names?"

"Roger that," the officer replied. "Anything else?"

"Yeah," Jennifer said, "if you find something out, call me back on this number immediately."

As soon as she disconnected the call, Jennifer darted a look at the latest caller. It was Captain Gambelli. As she clicked on the displayed number to call back, Rufus slammed against the car window. Startled, Jennifer gasped and dropped her phone.

While she fished for the phone on the car seat next to her, she heard Gambelli's deep voice echo in the car, "Stevens? Stevens? Are you there?"

Flustered, Jennifer snagged the phone and slapped it against her ear, saying, "Yes, Captain, I'm here."

"Are you still talking to Dobson's neighbors?"

"Yes, I was just leaving Mrs. Minden. Why?"

"We just received a call from the alarm company that monitors Devlin Wilson's house. The barn alarm just tripped. I have units on the way and Stockbridge PD is en route, but you're closer. Could be nothing, maybe Cully or the McCarver woman set it off accidentally."

"On my way, Cap," Jennifer said as she turned the ignition and sped off. "Sir, I don't think it's a false alarm. I just learned that Zoe Moore, aka Margaret Corchran, was in Stockbridge last night. I just got off the phone with Stockbridge PD. I requested they check into it."

"Is that so?" Gambelli mused. "All right then, wait for the back up to arrive before you go in. Looks like your instincts were right, Detective."

"Yes, sir," Jennifer firmly proclaimed as she flipped on the siren and flashing lights.

Kyle and Margaret Corchran sat idly amid the mess they created in Devlin's study. They'd been through everything a second time and still found no sign of the statues, gold coins or the Stones. Margaret was convinced they were in the study's safe. Kyle had his doubts.

Looking at his watch, he impatiently barked, "This is ridiculous. We can't sit here all day. We've looked everywhere. Let's go try the barn. If Cully left the house open, he may have done the same with the barn."

"And what if you're wrong, Einstein?"

"Then we bolt."

"And where does that leave us with Navarro, little brother?" Margaret sarcastically chided.

"I've been thinking about that while we've been sitting here on our duffs. We have a copy of the map. With that, we can find more gold coins and Stones. We just tell Navarro he'll have to wait a little longer," explained Kyle, proud of his theory.

"Ha!" Margaret sneered. "That won't fly with him. He wants Devlin's Master Stone. It's special, that's what Uncle Dobby said. Remember?"

"Then let's go check the barn!"

"No, we wait!"

"Screw you, Maggie. We run just as much chance of getting caught sitting here waiting for someone to show up. What if it's the little waif that shows up, not Cully? Do you think he gave her the alarm code for the barn? Or the safe? The safe has a fingerprint reader on it for Christ's sake," Kyle shouted in exasperation.

Margaret leapt off the sofa and stabbed a finger before Kyle's face, "We wait!"

Kyle jumped up and slapped away Margaret's hand. He growled, "Get your prissy little finger out of my face. You want to wait, be my guest. I'm going over to the barn."

He stomped away, crunching debris from their earlier pillaging beneath his steps. Margaret's face flashed with rage. She thrust her hand inside her backpack and hauled out the Sound Stone. She called after Kyle, "So help me God, if you take one step more, I will blast your ass out on the main road. You know how good I am with this!"

Laughing, Kyle kept walking. She might be good with stationary targets, he mused, but he knew she wasn't nearly as effective on moving objects.

When he reached the back porch door, he turned and yelled, "If you raise that rock to your mouth, you better hope your aim is true, big sister. I'm not an old man like Wilson. You won't get a second chance."

Margaret, full of fury, lunged over fallen furniture on her way to the kitchen. Kyle nonchalantly sauntered out on the back porch and yawned. He had reached his limit with her bossy attitude; it was high time he put her in her place.

One then might imagine Kyle's flabbergasted expression as, without warning, he soared off the back porch and crashed onto the driveway below. Groaning as he rolled on the macadam surface, Kyle grabbed at his arm and roared back at Margaret, "Bitch! You broke my arm."

"I warned you fair and square, bro! I said we wait! You're lucky I didn't f—ing kill you!"

Kyle staggered to his feet and stared viciously at Margaret. With bull-like force, he charged across the driveway towards her. He cleverly bobbed and weaved to avoid presenting her an easy target for the Sound Stone, but as he started up the stairs, he slowed just enough for her to focus another blast.

A mighty blast. One that released Margaret's full wrath.

Backwards, Kyle tumbled through the air. Over the driveway and up the hill. Horror filled his eyes. He was convinced his landing would be fatal.

Yet, as he impacted, it was Margaret who screamed. In her blind rage, she had inadvertently flown Kyle through the front door of the barn. The echo of her scream, however, was drowned by the loud claxon of the alarm sounding out.

Panic surged in her veins, and for the first time in a very long time, Margaret was afraid. And she ran, never looking back.

"Hey, A.C., what's shaking?" Pebbles said as she connected Anlon's call while approaching the Great Barrington Public Library.

Anlon's tense voice replied, "Pacal just called me. He's kidnapped Anabel Simpson. I don't have a lot of time to talk. I need your help."

Pebbles froze in mid-stride. A chattering group of seniors exiting the library almost plowed into her. She replied, "I'm sorry, what did you say?"

"Listen. I have to go meet him or he said he will kill her. He wants the map and the Master Stone. Says if I don't bring them to him at the Stillwater Quarry in the next 15 minutes, he's killing her. I've tried texting

Jen, tried calling her but I can't reach her. I need you to call her, call the Stockbridge PD, call everybody you can think of and get some help!"

"Okay, on it! But hold on. You can't really be thinking of going, Anlon!"

"I don't have a choice. I'm not going to let him kill Anabel," he firmly stated.

"But..."

"We're wasting time, Pebbles. Just do what I asked, please. I'll try to stall him until the police get there," Anlon barked back as he hung up.

Still stunned, Pebbles wavered for a moment, unsure what to do. She stood looking down at her phone, mouth open, trying to shake loose her mind and act. Then the anger started to build inside her. She spat, "Bastard! Pacal! I knew he was behind it!"

She took off down the street, searching her phone for Jennifer's number while she ran. The phone rang, no answer. Pebbles reached the Land Rover and tried Jen's number again. Straight to voice mail this time.

"Damn it!" she cried out. She glanced across the street. The police officers were still there. Without looking, Pebbles raced across the four lane main street of Great Barrington. Screeching cars caused Dan Nickerson to look up and spot Pebbles running towards him at full speed, arms flailing to get his attention.

"Help!" she cried.

Nickerson, taken aback by Pebbles' sudden charge, held his hands up and said, "Hold on. Slow down. What's the problem?"

Out of breath, Pebbles leaned on a nearby police car and sputtered, "Pacal...kidnapped Anabel...wants Anlon to meet him...says he's going to kill Anabel...Anlon can't reach Jen...please, help!"

"Okay, okay. Slow down. Take a deep breath," Nickerson said, trying to calm her down.

Pebbles was having none of it. She shouted back, "You take a deep breath! I need help! Anlon needs help! Now!"

"I'm trying to help you," Nickerson pleaded, "but you aren't coherent. You say Pacal Flores has kidnapped a woman, right? And your friend Anlon has gone to meet him? Where is this going down?"

"I...I...oh damn it! I don't remember. Some quarry," Pebbles blurted, tears starting to well in her eyes.

Nickerson's shoulders slumped. There were at least five quarries within an hour's drive of Great Barrington. He tried again to calm her. "Look, Eleanor, that's your name, right? Please try to calm down. We'll get help, okay, but I need you to focus for me. Can you do that?"

She angrily wiped tears from her face and kicked at the police car's tire. This was taking too long. Anlon was on his way already, and he was in danger. She knew it. She could feel it. Pebbles stared up at Nickerson, and shook her head back and forth. And then she bolted for the Land Rover.

Halfway across the road, the name of the quarry flashed into her mind. She spun, narrowly dodging a car turning from a side street, and screamed back at Nickerson, "Stillwater!"

When Jennifer arrived at Devlin Wilson's house, the Stockbridge Police were already there. She screeched to a standstill in the driveway and sprang out of the car. Her phone began to ring again.

Ignoring the call, she approached one of the officers and presented her badge. "Jennifer Stevens, Mass PD, what's the situation?"

The boyish looking patrolman answered, "We have a man down in the barn over there. He's alive. Barely. Ambulance is on its way.

"The house, well, the house is a wreck. Looks like someone tore it apart from rafter to foundation looking for something. By the looks of it, I don't think they found what they were searching for."

Jennifer started for the barn door, alarmed the fallen man might be Anlon. From the open cruiser door, Jennifer heard the dispatcher's voice announce her call number. Torn between which to pursue first, Jennifer cursed under her breath. Again the dispatcher called for her.

She sped back to the car, yanked the portable radio out and shouted as she ran towards the barn, "Dispatch, this is Echo Niner."

"Echo Niner, please stand by. Patching through Echo One Three."

A brief pause on the radio was followed by Dan Nickerson's voice amid a wail of sirens in the background.

As Jennifer reached the barn door and spied Kyle Corchran sprawled unconscious in the doorway, Nickerson shouted, "Jen, it's Dan. Just ran into your friend Eleanor. Said Pacal Flores is holding a woman named Anabel hostage at the Stillwater Quarry. Said Pacal lured Anlon Cully there. Said Cully tried to call you. We are en route with multiple units."

"Copy that, Echo One Three. On my way," Jennifer called into the radio. Turning to the Stockbridge officer, she said, "Gotta go. You got this?"

"Copy that," replied the freckled young man.

Peeling wheels across the lawn, Jennifer shot back onto the driveway just before she arrived at the main road. Picking up her phone, she now saw the notifications of the repeated phone calls from Anlon and Pebbles.

Jumping back on the radio, Jennifer called the Dispatcher and requested she patch a call through to Anlon's number. No answer. She then requested the dispatcher try Pebbles' number. On the second ring, a clearly distraught Pebbles angrily answered, "About f—ing time!"

"Sorry, no excuse. Where are you?"

"Where do you think? I'm going to the quarry!"

"Don't do that, Pebbles. We got this. Plenty of help on the way. I'm close, I'll be there in like five minutes," Jennifer reassured her.

"I'm closer. I'll be there in two minutes," Pebbles snapped back.

"Pebbles, seriously. This is the real deal. Wait for me, okay?"

"Hurry!" Pebbles implored, her voice cracking as she disconnected.

XXIV
BITTER JUSTICE

Anlon arrived at the abandoned quarry and noticed a solitary minivan in the makeshift gravel parking lot. While he sat in the Chevy working up the courage to step out of the SUV, he scanned the area but didn't see anyone about.

On the drive to the quarry, Anlon contemplated his strategy. First line of defense, he thought, stall until the police arrive. While Pacal had been clear not to call the police, Anlon had no intention of facing a killer all by himself.

As a second line of defense, Anlon left the map and Master Stone at the house. He had no intention of handing any of it over to Pacal. He even removed the map and Stones from the safe before he left the house and hid them all in the kitchen freezer under a few bags of frozen vegetables in case Pacal purposely lured him away from the house to have Thatcher swoop in and steal the relics.

Well, all but one Stone, the Port Stone. That was his last line of defense. It surely was a leap of faith, but Anlon believed it might protect him against the Sound Stone. Recalling his earlier experiment, Anlon thought it might be possible to disrupt the Sound Stone's waves by holding the Port Stone in front of him if and when Pacal tried to use it against him.

It was too much to hope that Pacal would get close enough for the Port Stone's repulsive face to tear the Sound Stone from his clutch but, at a distance, it might weaken or deflect an attack. Or so Anlon hoped. He marked a large X on the stone's repulsive side with a sharpie before shoving it in his jeans pocket on his way out of the house.

Realizing he was out of time, Anlon stepped out of the rental car and cautiously walked towards the other vehicle, his hand in his right front jeans pocket, gripping the Port Stone.

Reaching the minivan, Anlon peered inside. It was empty.

Further ahead, Anlon heard Pacal's voice call out, "Up here, Dr. Anlon."

Following the sound, Anlon spotted a trail leading up the terraced wall of the quarry. He hadn't seen it at first, as the trail was hidden by a stand of scrubby, gnarled trees. And though Pacal seemed to know he had arrived, Anlon couldn't see Pacal from where he stood.

Pacing slowly towards the trail, Anlon silently prayed that Pebbles had reached Jennifer. His footsteps crunched the rocky trail, the sound echoing against the quarry wall. A hundred yards up the path, Anlon arrived at a rock-enclosed clearing.

There stood Pacal Flores, a menacing sneer on his face and Sound Stone in one hand. Behind him, Anabel Simpson rested against the rock wall. Her arms were taped behind her back and her eyes were wild with terror.

"You are late, Dr. Anlon. Where are the map and Stones?" Pacal bitterly challenged.

Ignoring Pacal, Anlon focused his attention on Anabel. "Are you okay, Anabel?"

Her mouth quivered and she nodded. She was too scared to speak.

"Forget about the woman, Dr. Anlon. Where are my Stones and the map?!"

Anlon approached closer to Pacal. Though the proud Peruvian was deadly with a Sound Stone, he was smaller and much older than

Anlon. If he could stay close to Pacal, Anlon hoped he might tackle him before he could use the weapon.

Pacal shouted, "That's close enough. Answer my question!"

Lifting both hands in a gesture of compliance, Anlon answered with his own question, "What's this all about, Pacal?"

Raising the Sound Stone into position, Pacal screamed, "Answer me!"

"Whoa! Settle down, Pacal. You give me Anabel and then I'll tell you where to find the Stones and the map," Anlon calmly responded, though inside his body shivered with fear.

Furious, Pacal crouched into position with predator quickness and fired a volley from the Sound Stone at Anlon. The move caught Anlon off-guard, but he had just enough time before the waves hit to grasp the Port Stone from his pocket and pull it towards his chest. Unfortunately, the X on the stone was facing the wrong way and Anlon flew backwards and crashed against the jagged rock wall behind him.

Anlon felt and heard ribs crack and he released the Port Stone as he fell to the ground. With blurred vision and ringing ears, Anlon frantically searched the ground around him for the Port Stone while fighting to refill his lungs with oxygen. If Pacal had noticed the Port Stone tumble from Anlon's hand, he appeared unconcerned.

Anabel struggled to her feet and shouted at Pacal, "You animal!"

Pacal wheeled and glared at her. Defiantly, Anabel appealed to him, "Devlin trusted you, Pacal. Why are you doing this?"

Her entreaty diverted Pacal's attention long enough for Anlon to locate the Port Stone and regain his feet. Still gasping for breath, he said, "Why did you kill him? You and Thatcher have plans of your own?"

Pacal raised the Sound Stone and shot another blast at him. Anlon blindly lifted the Port Stone to his chest as the vibrations of the Sound Stone began to rumble in his abdomen. This time the odds were in his favor. The large X faced Pacal.

To Anlon's relief and Pacal's dismay, the sound waves bounced off the Port Stone. Anlon felt the stone tremble in his hand, and through bleary eyes, saw the Sound Stone wobble in Pacal's. He shouted, "Didn't count on that, did you, Pacal?"

Stepping back, an evil grin widened on Pacal's face, "Very clever, Dr. Anlon. But your Stone won't help Anabel, will it?"

Anlon stared in shock as Pacal spun around towards the frightened woman. Anlon called out, "Wait! Stop! Jesus, Pacal, why are the Stones so damn important to you?"

The older man suspended his movement towards Anabel and retrained his gaze on Anlon. He railed, "Life! Youth!"

Bending over, his left hand on his knee to steady himself as he winced with each labored breath, Anlon tightened his hold on the Port Stone with his right hand and pointed the hand at Pacal, "The symbol...on your ring...it's what you are after?"

"Clever again, Dr. Anlon. It's called the Seed Stone."

"Thatcher after that, too?"

"I don't know how you figured that out, but no. He wants the Flash Stone."

"Flash Stone?"

Pacal bellowed with maniacal laughter. He relaxed his pose and answered, "I guess you deserve to know why you're dying here today. Yes, the Flash Stone. It's a weapon. It makes this Sound Stone look like a twig."

"I see, that's why you two killed Devlin?" huffed Anlon, attempting to stand up straight.

"I did not kill Dr. Devlin!"

"Oh come on, Pacal."

"I did not! To get the Seed Stone, it was not necessary to kill the Professor. All I needed was to make a copy of his map, but I needed him to finish it first, so killing him was not advisable."

"Then who killed him? Thatcher?" Anlon queried, urging their conversation to continue in an effort to buy more time.

Pacal guffawed at Anlon's suggestion.

"Dobson?" Anlon probed.

Pacal shook his head back and forth and said, "No, but you're getting warmer."

"Ah, but you didn't know that for sure until right before you murdered Dobson, did you?" speculated Anlon. "You were convinced he was responsible for Devlin's death. Or were you just afraid he would get to the map before you?"

Pacal's thoughts flashed back to the confrontation with Dobson. He'd waited in the bushes while Anlon and Dobson said their farewells at Devlin's house. Angered by the possibility that his decade-long dream of acquiring the Seed Stone was slipping away, he had followed Dobson home. All the while, Pacal had gripped the Sound Stone in his hand. The more he thought of Devlin's unexpected death coming so soon after Dobson "borrowed" the map, the more livid he had become.

When Dobson pulled in his driveway and stepped out of the car, Pacal was already stealthily darting across a neighbor's yard. The motion caught Dobson's attention and he had turned to face Pacal, but before Dobson could speak, Pacal lifted the Sound Stone to his mouth and shot him through the air and against the car door.

The loud thud of the Mercedes door slamming closed stirred Rufus from a light sleep and the pesky Labrador had commenced barking. Pacal had dashed into the shadows by the driveway and fought to gather his emotions while waiting for the dog to settle down. Peering at Dobson lying next to the car some six feet away, Pacal had noticed he was still breathing.

Though still enraged, Pacal had been composed enough to realize that using the Sound Stone again might make too much noise. So while waiting for Rufus to finally stop barking, he had formulated a new plan. Reaching into his jacket pocket, he withdrew a handkerchief...

Roused back from his mental reenactment of Dobson's death, Pacal shouted, "Correct on both counts! Enough talk! The map? Where is it?"

Anlon's ears picked up the faint sound of sirens growing louder a moment before Pacal heard them. Straightening his stance, Anlon announced, "Game's over, Pacal. I'm not giving you the map or the Stones."

"Then you die!"

With astonishing speed, Pacal crouched and cast a sound wave at Anlon. Extending the Port Stone, Anlon only partially blocked the blow. The tuna can-shaped rock teetered in his hand. Before he could regain full control, Pacal blew two more quick bursts in his direction.

Anlon tumbled across the gravel floor, the Port Stone precariously gripped between his thumb and two fingers.

Anlon tried to swivel on the ground to point the X at Pacal but was too late to fend off the next attack. The sound wave vibrations were different this time. They rippled through Anlon's entire body. Before he knew what was happening, Pacal lifted him high above the tree line.

Hanging in midair, Anlon flailed in desperation. Pacal hummed steadily against the speaker-like rock, taunting Anlon by swaying him in the sky.

Anabel screamed for Pacal to stop. With gruesome force, Pacal jerked forward. The pull of the Sound Stone's waves whipped Anlon brutally downward.

All went dark for Anlon as he smashed into the ground, the Port Stone rolling loose from his spasming hand.

Careening down the two-lane road, Pebbles willed slower traffic to move out of her way and whipped into the oncoming traffic lane to pass when they didn't. Beads of sweat formed freely on her fiery face and arms despite the cool air flowing through the open vehicle windows. Her heart raced. She could not be late! If Jennifer didn't get there before she did, Pebbles was on her own to stop Pacal.

She hadn't had time to find a proper weapon before she sped off in the Rover, and during her drive the only weapon she could conjure up was a crowbar. She pleaded aloud her hope that Devlin had a crowbar stowed with the car jack. Tears clouded her vision briefly before she pushed them away. She could not lose Anlon, not now. Clenching her jaw, Pebbles crushed the accelerator to the floor and rocketed down an open, straight stretch.

Ahead she could see the makeshift parking area at the quarry entrance. Anlon's rental was there along with another vehicle but there were no police cars and no sign of Jennifer. It would be up to Pebbles alone.

Screeching to a sliding halt across the gravel of the parking area, she vaulted out of the Land Rover and ran to the rear lift gate, bouncing up and down on her sandaled feet while she impatiently waited for the electronic hatch to rise. Ducking under the half open hatch, Pebbles anxiously spied the cargo area and found the spare tire storage holds. Lifting the floor door up, she peered in and spotted the crowbar. In the distance, Pebbles heard the wail of police sirens. Recalling Jennifer's explicit instruction to wait for her to arrive, she blurted, "Come on! Come on! Hurry!"

Just then a scream echoed from above. A woman's voice. Pebbles' head snapped in the direction of the sound, and above the tree line she saw Anlon's flailing figure suspended in the air. For a second, Pebbles' face froze in a horrified grimace. When Anlon's body shot towards the ground, disappearing behind the trees, she screamed Anlon's name and took off in his direction.

Flying down the road leading to the quarry, Jennifer's white-knuckled fingers gripped the steering wheel of the unmarked police cruiser. As she zoomed closer to the parking area, she caught a glimpse of Pebbles racing past the open Land Rover with a stick in her hand. She hollered an expletive and floored the car. Into the police radio, she shouted, "Echo One Three, where are you?!"

In a sweeping arc, Jennifer braked the cruiser over the gravel, spewing dust high into the air. She leapt out of the car and swiftly attached a portable police radio to her belt while unsnapping the Glock holster beneath her arm. Dashing up the hill she called out to Pebbles, "Wait up, Pebbles! Wait!"

Another scream reverberated against the rocky hills bordering the trail. Jennifer's eyes shot wide open and she clicked into a full sprint. The trail was steep at the outset and curved sharply to the right. As she sped up the incline, legs and lungs burning, Jennifer detected motion above the trees ahead and beheld Anlon's twisted, motionless body wavering in the sky. A terrifying stab of anguish tore through her abdomen.

Panting heavily, she raced upward. As Jennifer rounded the bend, she heard more sirens below and the telltale sound of squealing tires behind her. At the same moment she caught sight of Pebbles about 50 yards ahead of her, barreling forward almost out of control as loose stones under her thin sandals caused her to slip and slide. Jennifer now recognized the stick aimlessly swinging in Pebbles' hand as a crowbar. All of a sudden, Pebbles pulled up, shouted ferociously and let loose the crowbar.

The next 40 seconds were a blur.

Jennifer yanked the Glock from her holster and chambered a round.

Pebbles, still leaning forward after heaving the crowbar, suddenly flew backwards and crashed against a rocky wall astride of Jennifer.

Slowing her sprint as she neared the opening in the trail, Jennifer crouched as she moved closer. She darted a fleeting look at Pebbles, who moaned and writhed on the ground, but already was scrambling to her feet.

With both hands, Jennifer raised the gun into aiming position.

Emerging into the clearing, Jennifer saw Pacal turn back towards Anlon, who lay bleeding and curled in a tortuous jumble on the ground. Pacal lifted the Sound Stone to his mouth again and for the third time violently lifted Anlon off the ground.

Anabel, hands restrained, cowered and cried against the rocky wall.

Jennifer raised the Glock and shouted, "Put him down, now! Easy!"

Pacal's concentration on Anlon was broken by Jennifer's command.

He pivoted, releasing Anlon from the clutch of sound waves, and again Anlon's limp body hit the ground.

Pacal hoisted the Sound Stone to his mouth, ready to blast back Jennifer as he had done to Pebbles. But he never got the chance.

She was not the best shot in the department nor the worst. She had fired her gun in action as a patrol officer, but never as a detective.

Maybe it was her long-idle Army combat training that took over, but from 12 feet away, Jennifer tapped out three quick shots as she slid down on her knees to avoid the sound waves from the stone pressed against Pacal's mouth.

The first shot missed and ricocheted off the rock behind Pacal's head. Tracking her aim lower as she slid, Jennifer's second shot ripped through Pacal's shoulder, causing his body to rotate away from her aim.

Before his body fully twisted away from her line of fire, Jennifer's third shot hit Pacal through the left side of his chest, sending him flying backwards against the wall. Pacal lost hold of the Sound Stone as he rocked backward and fell.

Pebbles, cheek bloodied from contact with the wall, raced past Jennifer towards Anlon, stumbling on hands and knees across the dusty trail.

As she neared Pacal, he slowly raised his hand to retrieve the Sound Stone. Pebbles noticed the movement from the corner of her eye.

Rage welled inside her and she rolled across the ground to where her errant throw of the crowbar landed. She snagged it and dove towards Pacal.

Before Pacal could reach the stone, Pebbles reared back and viciously whipped the iron rod at Pacal's lowered head. The crowbar shivered in her hand from the vibration of the cracking blow. Pacal dropped instantly.

Jennifer, gun still in hand, jumped up and darted towards Pacal and Pebbles, intent on disabling Pacal with another shot, but she couldn't fire with Pebbles in such close proximity. She cringed when the crowbar cleaved Pacal's skull, but watched with relief as his dead body slumped over on the ground.

Behind them, Nickerson and four uniformed officers came roaring up the hill with guns drawn, having heard the shots. Jennifer holstered her weapon and swiveled at the sound of their approach. She grasped the detective's badge swinging from the lanyard draped around her neck and displayed it for the arriving officers. She screamed at Nickerson, "Call for an ambulance!"

Anlon laid on the ground unconscious and convulsing. Blood trickled from his ears, nose and mouth. His left arm and right leg were bent in sickening, unnatural positions. Pebbles, tears streaming down her face, scurried across the ground towards him on her hands and knees. She clutched her arms across her abdomen when she reached him and screamed in agony up at the sky, "No! No! No!"

Directing her attention to Anabel, Jennifer called to one of the officers to unbind her and check to see if she was injured. Standing above Pacal's dead body, filled with anger and despair, Jennifer lifted the Sound Stone and threw it with all her might against the rocky wall, shattering it into a cascade of shards.

Looking down upon Anlon's expressionless face, Pebbles sobbed uncontrollably. Jennifer knelt down beside her and reached for Anlon's unbroken arm to feel for a pulse. It was faint, but still there. Through her own welling tears, she comforted Pebbles, "He's still alive! The ambulance will be here soon."

Pebbles moved to cradle Anlon in her arms, but Jennifer grabbed hold of her and yanked her back. She wrapped both arms around Pebbles and held her tightly.

"Don't…we can't move him…his neck…his spine," was all Jennifer could mouth as she fought to suppress her own feelings.

In a daze, Pebbles' mind flashed back to that awful night when James Cunningham lie lifeless on the Hamptons roadway, limbs similarly gnarled and bleeding profusely. Sprawled on the dune where she landed after bouncing off the colliding cars, Pebbles remembered reaching a hand in James' direction as she blacked out. He died alone. Above all the sad and guilt-ridden emotions that haunted Pebbles afterward, the image of James beyond her reach remained indelible.

Pebbles wrestled against Jennifer and cried out, "Let me hold his hand! Please! I need him to know I'm here!"

Releasing Pebbles, Jennifer stood and turned away to wipe tears from her eyes before her fellow officers noticed. She motioned to Nickerson that she wasn't hurt. Jennifer then turned to comfort Anabel and noticed her pick up something and put it in her sweatshirt pocket. Approaching Anabel, Jennifer asked to see what she picked up. Sheepishly Anabel reached into her pocket and presented the X-marked Port Stone to Jennifer.

Meanwhile, up the hill scampered three EMTs hauling a backboard stacked with medical gear and cases. The paramedics intensely labored over Anlon while Jennifer and the other officers secured the crime scene. Captain Gambelli arrived while Jennifer was detailing her version of events to Nickerson. He interrupted the interview and pulled Jennifer aside. He gazed at her with paternal concern and asked if she was okay. Jennifer made a brief effort to display stern-faced composure before bursting into tears. She buried her face against Gambelli's shoulder and wailed.

Police dramas all too often depict shootings as gratifying climaxes for the pursuing officers, Gambelli thought. In his experience, taking a human life in the heat of a violent confrontation is traumatic and shocking, no matter how tough the cop and no matter how vindicating it might feel the moment the bullet fells the villain. Add to that the emotions that rush forth for a fallen comrade and a shooting can be downright debilitating. Gambelli understood this all too well and corralled Jennifer in his arms while her pent-up emotion spilled out.

After triaging the scope of Anlon's injuries, the paramedics first focused their attention on stabilizing his vital signs. The EMT monitoring the vitals cautioned the other two that Anlon's blood pressure was dropping and his breathing pattern was becoming irregular, common symptoms of internal bleeding.

They administered oxygen and did what they could to quickly immobilize and secure his shattered limbs. As much as they desired to minimize further damage to Anlon, the paramedics knew if they didn't get him to an emergency room fast, his survival prospects were dim. They gingerly made a rapid assessment of potential injuries to his head, neck and spine, but they were running out of time. They implored the police officers present to help them lift Anlon gently so they could maneuver the board beneath him. They anchored his body against the board and briskly descended the trail to the waiting ambulance.

All the while Pebbles gripped Anlon's hand. One EMT tried to tend to her cuts and abrasions. She slapped his hands away and barked at him to work on Anlon instead. Another EMT motioned her to step away as they tried to secure him to the backboard. With a defiant thrust of her jaw, she refused. While the paramedics administered aid, she squeezed Anlon's hand tenderly every so often, quivering as she felt his skin turning cold to the touch.

Down the hill, into the ambulance and throughout the harried dash to the hospital, Pebbles never let go of Anlon's hand until they wheeled him into the emergency room. As the trauma unit's sliding doors closed, Pebbles heard a nurse yell, "We're losing him!"...

EPILOGUE

The bright blue waters of Lake Tahoe shimmered in the midday sun. Though it was the middle of July, nearly the peak of the summer season, Pebbles stood on the boat deck and gazed out from the secluded cove at a horizon devoid of companion vessels.

Closing her eyes, she embraced the solitude and relished a cool breeze that washed away the heat of the sun.

In honor of Anlon, she wore a hot pink bikini today, the closest shade she could find to match the color of the scooter he'd purchased for her last winter. Though she'd finally earned the moped, she couldn't bring herself to ride it. Not now.

Bowing her head, she sighed deeply and a tear dripped down onto the teak deck as she reminisced about past simple, relaxed moments with Anlon. Staring at the huddled angel on her left wrist, she could still feel the touch of his hand in hers...

And then from behind, Pebbles heard Anlon stir awake.

A cheerful smile bloomed on her face. Pebbles turned and studied him. Still encased in a full arm cast on his left arm, and a full leg cast on his right leg, Anlon squinted through sleepy, pain medicated eyes and eked out a small smile in return.

His jaw was wired shut and his abdomen was wrapped tightly to support several mending ribs. Remarkably, though doctors induced a week-long coma to quell swelling of his brain and surgery was required to remove his ruptured spleen, Anlon survived Pacal's brutal attack with the damage largely limited to broken bones. His recovery would persist for several more months, including rehabilitation of his surgically repaired leg and arm, but he was alive, and his doctors assured him his prognosis for a near-full recovery was high.

For this maiden voyage since returning to Tahoe, Anlon was dressed in a gaudy, floral Hawaiian shirt two sizes too big so as to fit over the arm cast and equally oversized navy blue board shorts for a similar reason. By his good arm sat a thermos filled with an ice-cold margarita. Extending from the thermos was an extra-long, bendable straw, a box of which Sydney Armstrong specially ordered for Anlon.

He reclined on a custom-constructed chair bolted to the boat deck. Antonio Wallace designed and then had his engineers build and install the chair so that Anlon could enjoy his treasured boat while he recuperated. Pebbles reminded herself to tell Anlon later that Antonio still wanted to hear the full story of their adventure when he was able to speak again.

Pebbles sidled up to Anlon underneath the retractable canopy shading most of the boat deck and kissed him on the cheek, her lip ring tickling his skin. She said, "Hey, sleepy head! How are you feeling?"

Anlon angled his head to gently touch hers and he offered a thumbs up sign, their communication limited for the time being to gestures and typed or written notes. He extended the fingers of his good hand and ran them affectionately through her soft, royal blue bob. She closed her eyes and welcomed his soothing touch.

Pebbles asked if he wanted a sip of his margarita, observing, "It's Friday after all!"

He nodded his acceptance and she guided the florescent green straw between his lips. After three long pulls, he gave another thumbs up and she extracted the straw. He motioned to the tablet on the cushion beside her. Pebbles handed it to him, he typed a question and displayed it to her. It read, "When will Jennifer arrive?"

Pebbles spoke in reply, "I pick her up from the airport next Tuesday. I'm excited to see her."

Anlon nodded in agreement. He had both Pebbles and Jennifer to thank for his narrow escape from Pacal's ruthless attempt to acquire the Waterland Map but he really hadn't been coherent enough while in the hospital to thank Jennifer appropriately. He typed, "How long is her suspension?"

Though Jennifer received multiple commendations for her actions that hot May afternoon (one for lacing together the clues that solved Devlin Wilson's murder, and the other for her heroism in preventing Pacal Flores from a second murder), she also was reprimanded for destroying valuable evidence, the Sound Stone.

It was an odd scene the day after the police chief and district attorney publicly awarded her the commendations. Gambelli called her into his office and reluctantly delivered the news. The district attorney was not happy she destroyed the weapon used by Pacal to incapacitate Dobson and inflict near-fatal injuries on Anlon.

Had Pacal not been killed in the incident and was instead brought to trial for murder and attempted murder, the lack of the Sound Stone as a piece of evidence would have been devastating to the state's case against Pacal. The DA demanded the police chief suspend Jennifer, without pay, for six months.

She appealed with the help of George Grant and won a reduction of the suspension to three months, with her pay reinstated.

Grant argued, rightly, that Dobson's death was due to carbon monoxide poisoning and no one could prove Pacal used the stone to knock him out, even if the police still had it in their possession.

Grant further contended that the scene at the deserted quarry was chaotic, and in the moment, Jennifer was overcome by the weight of the high-stress confrontation. In light of the outcomes, he claimed that the preponderance of her actions were of the highest caliber and far outweighed the theoretical damage envisioned by the district attorney.

The police union, Grant pointed out, supported Jennifer, as did her proud boss, Bruno Gambelli. Before concluding his arguments, Grant requested a private conference between only the DA, the mediating judge and himself.

Grant then peered skeptically at the stern-faced DA and inquired, "Do you really want me to go on television and online and tell the world my client was suspended because she broke a rock that can throw people through the sky? Are you sure you are prepared to answer reporters' questions about that, live on TV? Permanently circulating on the Internet with your face forever attached to it?"

The judge snickered and bit his tongue. He suggested that Grant and the DA work out a compromise.

Upon learning of Grant's victory, Pebbles suggested to Anlon they invite Jennifer to Lake Tahoe for the rest of the summer to "serve" her suspension.

Pebbles had already moved in with Anlon upon returning to Incline Village. When presenting the idea to Pebbles via a handwritten note on the ride back west in Antonio's plane, he said he needed someone around to help during his recovery.

Given Anlon's vast wealth, Pebbles ribbed him that he could buy all the home care he needed. Before he finished typing a protesting response, she accepted by declaring, "I kid. I kid. Of course I'll come take care of you!"

When Pebbles called Jennifer to extend the offer, the detective happily agreed to join them for three reasons. First, she needed the time and space to rejuvenate. It had been a harrowing and draining series of events and the unexpected fight afterward with the district attorney left her a bit disillusioned. She needed to sort her thoughts out and the idea of a getaway was welcome.

Second, she'd grown very fond of both Anlon and Pebbles and became unexpectedly blue when they left the Boston hospital where Anlon convalesced for the first month after the attack. It surprised Jennifer how close their friendship had evolved in such a short time, and she was elated by the prospect of a reunion.

Finally, Jennifer wanted to thank Anlon in person for stepping in to pay for her suspension appeal attorney fees and for offering her the chance to live rent free in his inherited Stockbridge home. She initially rejected his financial help, but Pebbles begged her to reconsider.

She told Jennifer that Anlon wanted someone he trusted to manage the restoration of the property after the destruction caused by the Corchrans. In his mind, Pebbles explained, Jennifer would be acting as caretaker and in exchange for managing the rehab of the property, he was offering a rent-free living arrangement and kicking in her attorney fees. Presented that way, Jennifer agreed.

"George Grant got it knocked down to three months," replied Pebbles in answer to Anlon's question. And then she winked and said, "Maybe once she's out here we can convince her to stay on like you did with me. But get her a blue scooter. Hot pink is *my* color."

Anlon's mumbled laugh was truncated when his sore ribs registered displeasure at his sudden expression of levity. He tapped out a response on the tablet, "Agreed, hot pink is all yours! Are you ever going to ride it?"

She cringed and said, "Oh, sorry! Didn't mean to make you 'hurt-laugh,' I'll get around to it when you can take a ride with me. For now, we'll just have to figure out how to entertain Jennifer for the rest of the summer."

Anlon typed, "I know exactly what we'll do."

Pebbles gazed at him with a mystified expression.

Anlon pecked out another response, "We have work to do. No way is Navarro getting away with Devlin's murder! Neither is Margaret Corchran! Plus, we need to find the Flash Stone before Thatcher gets his hands on it!"

They had not spoken about the Stones since Anlon awoke from his coma. During his initial recuperation, Pebbles deflected discussing the Stones anytime Anlon raised the subject.

However, not long after Anlon emerged from the coma, Jennifer had met with him to share the outcome of the investigations. Kyle and Margaret Corchran had followed Devlin Wilson to Bennington and then Mt. Whiteface to kill him before Devlin could cut off their black market artifact operation. Kyle had confessed to being an accessory to the murder in exchange for a lesser sentence and fingered his sister as Devlin's killer. As Jennifer suspected, Dobson's Sound Stone was the murder weapon used to throw Devlin from the trail — the same weapon Margaret used to incapacitate her brother.

But Kyle was adamant they did not kill Matthew Dobson. As Anlon painfully figured out, Pacal Flores did. During Anlon's coma, Jennifer learned the details of Anlon's confrontation with Pacal from Anabel. Jennifer had said to Anlon, "That was pretty stupid, you know. Taunting a man holding a lethal weapon isn't exactly PhD-smart, now is it?"

Anlon, through wired jaws, mumbled his agreement with her assessment before Jennifer continued on. She told Anlon they found a flash drive on Kyle Corchran that held a copy of the Waterland Map. Kyle told them Margaret escaped with an identical flash drive, and he also named Klaus Navarro as the man on the buying end of the artifacts. When questioned whether Navarro was involved in the plot to kill Devlin, Kyle vehemently denied Navarro's involvement. While Jennifer wasn't convinced, there was no proof otherwise.

"Thank you, by the way, for getting Pacal to admit to Dobson's murder and confirming Thatcher Reynolds' involvement. We haven't found him yet, but it's only a matter of time. The FBI is now involved."

Jennifer finished the case description by noting that Margaret Corchran's whereabouts were unknown, though she suspected that Margaret had escaped the country, likely with Navarro's assistance. Jennifer reached in her tote bag while seated next to Anlon's hospital bed and withdrew the X-marked Port Stone from inside. She placed it on Anlon's chest and teasingly said, "You should hold onto this, just in case Margaret shows up again."

"Oh, and nice move hiding the map and the other Stones in the freezer. When Pebbles and I opened the safe and they weren't there, we feared the worst," she finished.

With Devlin's house and barn in shambles, Pebbles sought out Antonio Wallace's assistance to securely store Devlin's artifact collection, including the Stones, in a location only known to the two of them. This hurt Pebbles to do, as she longed to chat with Malinyah again, but it was more important, for now, to keep them safe while Anlon healed. George Grant had secured the release of the two statues from Dobson's safe deposit box. They were able to confirm both were lifted from Devlin's collection. The gold coins, cash and diamonds remained in police custody as lawyers argued over what to do with them.

"A.C., you're in no condition to chase Navarro or Thatcher. We should just chill until you're all better," Pebbles implored.

He quickly shook his head no. His typed answer read, "Not a chance. Body's broken, not the mind. And I'm not giving up!!!"

She squeezed his hand and grew stern. "Okay, but you have to promise me one thing. And I'm totally serious about this."

His face screwed up in a questioning manner. She proclaimed, "No more running off to confront killers without me! I'm not kidding. Don't you laugh. If you even think about doing that again, I will kick your butt!"

The look etched upon her face carried the conviction of her words. She'd traveled too far down the road of emotional investment in her budding relationship with Anlon to allow a repeat of the horrific confrontation with Pacal to play out again. Anlon nodded understanding, and typed, "You have my word."

Pebbles extended a pinky for a soul-binding pinky swear and Anlon complied.

Pebbles didn't tell him but one of the activities she and Jennifer agreed to undertake during her Tahoe stay would be to teach Pebbles how to shoot. She'd already purchased her own Glock and had signed up for self-defense classes at the local community center. The next time she had to fend off a madman, Pebbles thought, she would do it with more at her disposal than a crowbar.

Pebbles relaxed her pose as she let go of the thought and sipped her own margarita through a hot pink straw from an identical-type thermos. With her free hand, she patted Anlon's knee and stared out at the lake.

Puffy white clouds drifted languidly overhead as the boat gently bobbed up and down. In the tranquil silence, Pebbles debated whether to broach the conversation she wished to have with Anlon or wait until he was fully healed. Though it probably wasn't fair to have the talk now because Anlon was loopy on pain meds and couldn't speak, somehow the peaceful moment felt right.

Breaking the silence, Pebbles softly said, "I've had something I've wanted to say to you, something I've wanted to talk to you about since Stockbridge."

She paused, unsure of how to continue. Inside, her heart thudded against her chest and her mouth ran dry. She lifted the thermos for another sip and returned her gaze to the vast blue carpet of water, afraid to look at him when she said the words. "You rescued me, Anlon. I was lost and wandering. And somehow you found me, gave me your hand and led me back. I am forever thankful."

Anlon stared at her and shook his head with wonder. He knew she owned her journey back, he was just around when it happened. But, if in Pebbles' eyes he rescued her, the reverse was equally true. Through the tablet he replied, "Rescue goes both ways. Figuratively...and in my case, you also *literally* saved my life!"

Pebbles shifted her gaze to the tablet and smiled at his response. "That settles it then, we're both fabulous!"

As they sat in silence and savored the bonding moment, Anlon wrestled whether to say what was on *his* mind. The phrase he wished to say was one better spoken, rather than typed or mumbled through wired bones. He also worried that she might discount the sincerity of his words given his current condition and chalk it up to an expression of survivor emotion. In the end, he decided to wait.

Instead, Anlon lightly rapped the Trinity Knot tattoo on Pebbles' wrist to draw her attention. When she turned, Anlon stared deeply into her eyes with penetrating effect.

Pebbles' face reddened and her eyes welled. She rose and embraced him as best she could without disturbing his wounds. Her warm tears trickled onto his chin as she leaned to kiss him.

Withdrawing, Pebbles stood and smiled broadly, "Okay, since I'm on a roll with confessions, I have two more for you."

Stepping out from beneath the shade of the canopy, her diamond nose stud twinkled in the full sunshine and she said, "First confession. I haven't told you yet, but I looked at the Master Stone a second time when I was alone. Well, maybe a third and fourth time, too."

A curious expression crossed Anlon's face, unsure of where she was going with this confession or how this was connected to their preceding embrace, but he nodded in recognition of what Pebbles described.

"You remember how I told you Malinyah spoke to me? That I could understand the meaning of her words."

Anlon nodded again.

"Well," Pebbles explained, "it turns out to be a lot freakier than that. I had a conversation with her, Anlon. Several. I know what her people call themselves, what happened to them, why they created the stones and went out to help survivors.

"And she was kind to me, A.C. She helped me confront my pain and to confide in you.

"She told me my name in their language is very close to the name of a flower they revere, Alynioria. The last time I visited her — I mean — viewed the Stone, she walked me into a field near a stream. It was so beautiful, Anlon! The field was filled with flowers a shade of blue I've never seen before.

"Malinyah picked one of the Alynioria and said the flower is used to heal. She said its name in their language means…salvation."

Reposed in awestruck silence, Anlon's mind grappled to comprehend Pebbles' tale, unsure whether the pain meds were playing tricks on him.

She returned his earlier penetrating gaze and said, "Salvation is what I feel when I'm around you. And so my final confession is I got a new tattoo while you were in the hospital in Boston to always remind me of you and what it feels like to be saved."

With that, Pebbles turned and faced away from Anlon. She reached behind her neck and untied her bikini top. It fluttered in her hand as a gentle breeze momentarily gusted. With the top perilously dangling in one hand, she hooked her thumbs under the thin waistband of the bikini bottom and guided the wispy fabric over her hips until it slinked down to her toes.

She seductively craned her head to spy his speechless reaction and leered at him deviously. Then she slowly twirled to face him. It took all of Anlon's limited resolve to concentrate his gaze on her intended target. On the lower right side of her abdomen, below the bikini line, she pointed to the new body art addition, a deep blue budding flower. Alynioria.

Anlon typed seven letters and raised the tablet for Pebbles to view, "Amazing."

She smiled. "The tattoo?"

His reply: "That, too!"

The Anlon Cully Chronicles series continues with *Race for the Flash Stone* and *Curse of the Painted Lady*. And the adventure doesn't stop there! The fourth installment in the series will be released in 2019 and will feature a new archaeological mystery for Anlon and friends to solve.

To receive updates regarding the series' fourth installment as they emerge, including the expected publish date, follow K. Patrick Donoghue - Novelist on Facebook, or join the author's email subscriber list by visiting kpatrickdonoghue.com and clicking on the registration link toward the bottom of the home page.

Also, look for *Skywave*, the first installment of a new science-fiction thriller series from K. Patrick Donoghue, in the fall of 2018.

ABOUT THE AUTHOR

Kevin Patrick Donoghue is the author of The Anlon Cully Chronicles series, including *Shadows of the Stone Benders*, *Race for the Flash Stone* and *Curse of the Painted Lady*. He lives in the northern Virginia suburbs of Washington, D.C., with his wife and two sons.

Ways to stay in touch with the author:

Follow K.Patrick Donoghue - Novelist on Facebook

Join the author's email subscriber list by visiting kpatrickdonoghue. com and clicking on the email registration link toward the bottom of the home page.

89734583R00195

Made in the USA
San Bernardino, CA
29 September 2018